THE WOLVES OF AMBITION

A NOVEL OF THE LATE ROMAN EMPIRE

EMBERS OF EMPIRE
VOL. IV

Q. V. HUNTER

Eyes and Ears Editions

130 E. 63rd St., Suite 6F
New York, New York,
USA 10065-7334

Copyright © 2015 Q. V. Hunter

*

All rights reserved.
No part of this publication may be reproduced, stored in a retrieval system, or transmitted in any form, or by any means, electronic, mechanical, photocopying, recording or otherwise, without the prior permission of the Publishers.

ISBN 978-2-9700889-6-7

This novel is entirely a work of fiction. The names, characters and incidents portrayed in it, while at times based on historical figures, are the work of the author's imagination.

Q. V. Hunter has asserted the right under the Copyright, Design and Patents Act, 1988, to be identified as the author of this work.

eyesandears.editions@gmail.com

1. Hunter Q. V. 2. Claudius Silvanus 4. Late Roman Empire 5. Historical Fiction 6. Rome 7. Fourth century 8. Constantius II 9. Espionage 10. Action & Adventure 11. Historical Thriller

TO P, 'OUR ROCK'

Also by Q. V. Hunter

The Veiled Assassin, Embers of Empire, Vol. I
Usurpers, Embers of Empire, Vol. II
A Back Gate to Hell, Embers of Empire, Vol. III
The Deadly Caesar, Embers of Empire, Vol. V
The Burning Stakes, Embers of Empire, Vol. VI

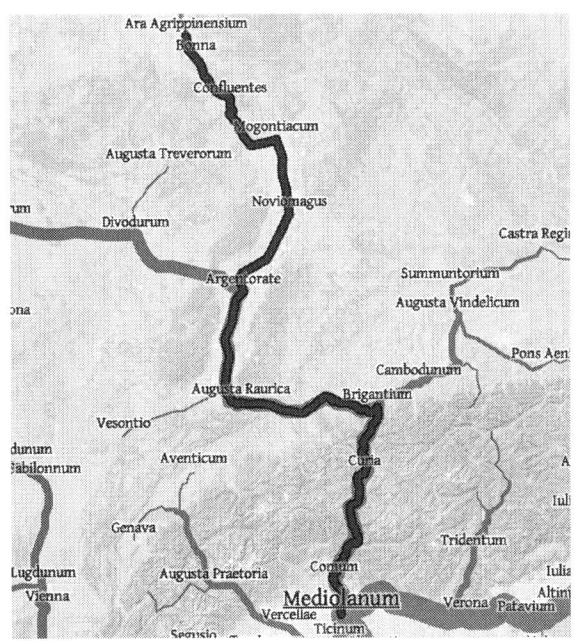

The ride up the Rhine Frontier

Table of Contents

Chapter 1, A Season of Treason 1
Chapter 2, An Empress Gambles 13
Chapter 3, The Count of Nightmares 25
Chapter 4, Two Traitor Fathers 43
Chapter 5, Bedroom Gossip 57
Chapter 6, An Emperor at Prayer 73
Chapter 7, The Broken Lands 91
Chapter 8, Roxana's Plea 107
Chapter 9, A Frankish Queen 121
Chapter 10, A Roman Payday 135
Chapter 11, Across the River 145
Chapter 12, The Only Course Left 163
Chapter 13, One General More or Less 175
Chapter 14, The Death of Hope 191
Chapter 15, The Wounded Must Die 203
Chapter 16, Friends True and False 219
Chapter 17, Two Generals Meet 233
Chapter 18, Trust Between Heroes 245
Chapter 19, Poison Can Be Good 259
Chapter 20, Two Men in a Tent 273
Chapter 21, A Barbarian at Prayer 285
Chapter 22, The Mastery of Dreams 301
Chapter 23, A Cleansing Fire 311
Chapter 24, What Leo Thought 323
Historical Notes 337
Places and Glossary 345
Acknowledgements 353
About the Author 357

Chapter 1, A Season of Treason

—MEDIOLANUM, JULY 355 AD—

The gruesome death of the Caesar of the East, Flavius Claudius Constantius Gallus, was not the end of the story.

Far from it.

This being the troubled reign of Emperor Constantius II, the Caesar's beheading in a squalid dungeon in Pola Istria triggered a torrent of more court intrigues. The chilly winter of 354 gave way to spring winds carrying fresh charges of corruption and insubordination, confessions and perjuries, alliances and betrayals, unexpected pardons—and to the unluckiest—torture and death.

Hardened courtiers muttered that it was just an ordinary season in the rivalrous Mediolanum court. Flavius Gallus was the fourth co-ruler to fall to Constantius' dominance of the civilized world—if you counted the usurper 'Emperor' Magnentius along with Emperor Constantius' two dead brothers.

'You testify today?' Cassius asked. The rider rattled the dicing cup under my nose to bring my thoughts back to our game.

'It's a mistake.' I shrugged. 'I've got nothing to tell them.'

'Indeed.' Cassius glanced at my fellow *agens* Rufus. 'Maybe they confused you with someone else?'

'The court isn't exactly teeming with Numidians, I admit.'

My concentration was shattered. My nerves were raw. I had been summoned from our *schola* as an 'impartial' witness, but my pretended nonchalance didn't fool my gambling mates.

Under Roman law, the *agentes in rebus* could not be convicted for acts committed on duty. It was common knowledge that I'd conducted an inquiry into the Antiochia administration of the failed Caesar of the East and his late *Augusta*, the Emperor's sister Constantia.

But the protection of old laws diminished by the week. I put little trust in Roman 'justice' during these hysterical times.

As a former slave, I knew what it was to be defenseless in the hands of the powerful. As a Numidian colonial, no matter how well read or loyal to the Empire, I was doubly an outsider.

As the three of us gambled away, the imperial jails below our boots groaned with state witnesses. Whenever a warder aired out the cells by opening a courtyard grate, the screams of Paulus Catena's 'customers' reached our dicing table.

Officially Catena was an ordinary imperial notary. Unofficially, the Dacian was Constantius' most trusted interrogator. His nickname, 'Paul the Chain,' referred not only to the shackles he clamped on his prisoners, but the cage of lies he forged around his victims. He'd give anything to get his iron prongs into me. While escaping his tortures in Sirmium, I'd left his voice box permanently wrecked by my bootlace garrote.

A pair of dice could keep my mind off Catena's recreations for only so many hours every day.

The 'Gallus trials' were being heard in the Emperor's inner council chamber—not as vast as the public reception halls of the Mediolanum palace, but more sinister. With its stiff, seating girded on three sides by clerks and secretaries, the *consistorium* always reminded me of a stage set from a Greek play.

Except that all these actors wore only one mask—Smiling Hypocrisy.

The hearings had dragged on for eighteen days. Time was running short. The Emperor needed to finish this spectacle of revenge before his convocation of Christian bishops starting later this week. As the protector of the Arian Christian Church and sitting as near to his god as a mortal could, Constantius looked forward to presiding over the final theological debate on the nature of Christ. Suspicion and cruelty must soon give way to public piety.

Rufus shattered my pessimistic reverie with a jerk of his head. 'Who's that kid across the courtyard?'

He took the cup from Cassius. The ivory dice tumbled onto the slate. The blue dots said I'd lost again.

—THE WOLVES OF AMBITION—

'He's staring at you, Marcus.' Rufus swept up my *nummi* with the smirk of an accomplished cheat. I wasn't falling for his ruse. I didn't know any kid. I kept my gaze fixed on his 'lucky' dice.

Why had the Court called me as witness, anyway? Constantius saw treason everywhere—behind the curtains, in his bath, and under his bed. Who conspired with Caesar Gallus against his throne? Who visited the young *Augustus*' court in Antiochia? Who inveigled the weaker Constantine to rise against, the Emperor?

I couldn't answer these questions.

But truth counted for nothing in today's political theater. Hundreds of years ago, a Cicero might have cleared the air before a Senate of honorable men holding independent power. Now the Roman Senate was a shell, lies were the preferred tools of statecraft, and I knew few honorable men. I was no longer a slave, but that childhood sense of being nothing more than a plaything of the Fates had crept back into my bones over the tormented days of waiting to be called.

A sudden scream broke through the barred window at our feet.

'Another round?' I sipped diluted wine and wiped the summer sweat off my brow. The gods knew I needed this game to distract me.

'Sorry. My shift is next.' Rufus reached for his shoulder padding. In the warm sun, he alone was wearing riding trousers and full courier gear. In five minutes he'd clap his *petanus* back on his head, collect the late morning imperial mail sack, and gallop due north out the Porta Comasina for Comum.

I'd stripped to the waist to keep my tunic fresh for court.

Cassius took pity on me. 'One more round, Rufus.'

Rufus fell back on his stool. Though my cash was nearly gone, it wasn't about the money. I had money enough, thanks to a legacy from the House of Manlius back in Roma. It was about losing to Rufus, a mere *equitor*, training class. He owed me a chance to make back my losses out of sheer respect for my rank of *biarchus*.

I made nothing. His dice looked all right to the naked eye, but no matter how I shifted my betting strategy, I lost. His two ivory *tesserae* were crooked.

'That boy has been staring at you for the last ten minutes, Numidianus. Go see what he wants,' Rufus said.

I wasn't in any mood for strange boys. These might be my final hours of freedom.

'I don't care if Empress Eusebia is hailing me stark naked from her private window. Keep playing, Rufus.'

'It would be a lonely empress who wasted time on a common *agens*, even as handsome as you, Numidianus,' Cassius said with a chuckle.

Only after Rufus had ridden off for the late Emperor Maximian's imposing city gates did I glance behind my stool.

The boy stood across the sun-bleached parade ground. He seemed rooted to the shadowy base of a marble column in the portico ringing the courtyard. He was that awkward age when each morning might mark the first clumsy shave. Was there something familiar about him?

He smiled at me just as a well-dressed woman of the court, so similar in feature and coloring she must be his mother, yanked him away. With angry whispers, she dragged him toward the imperial residential wing.

The *ducenarius* Gaudentius trotted down the palace steps to collect me. My stomach clenched at the grim look in his black eyes. I knew this *agens* only by sight and reputation. He was a humorless product of the Neapolis slums and had climbed up our ranks without the benefit of political pull or family favors—just relentless service. The instructors at the Castra Peregrina in Roma cited Gaudentius' surveillance and arrest techniques as models of ruthless efficiency.

He was a rare man in these cynical and corrupt times—but not popular. Even the good-natured Ahenobarbus, the officer to whom I reported in Roma, kept a safe distance from this particular *ducenarius*.

'My turn, Gaudentius?'

I rose from my stool and dressed. Gaudentius took in the white stripes that scarred my shoulder blades. I ignored his disapproving eyebrow. Those lash marks had been honorably earned working undercover on my first mission, the job that earned my manumission from slavery.

I straightened my tunic hem, finished fastening my sword belt and boots, and double-checked my *schola* insignia.

'You testify soon.'

'But about what? *Who* put me forward?'

Gaudentius glanced around for eavesdroppers. 'I don't know. They're still grilling the eunuch Gorgonius who attended the Caesar's baths.' He polished off my wine and wiped his lips. 'Remember him by any chance?'

'I never penetrated the Caesar's private suite. That had nothing to do with my investigation.'

'So you can't verify his testimony?'

'No. I avoid those types. Anyway,' I argued, 'Lord Chamberlain runs all the eunuchs in the Empire. Surely Eusebius can get one of his junior "brothers" off?'

I didn't have to add the joke that Emperor Constantius himself enjoyed only '*some*' influence' over Eusebius. The *praepositus sacri cubiculi* ruled the innermost imperial chambers. He was the greediest and most powerful eunuch in the entire Empire. Eunuchs had no other history or family, no other sponsors or protectors, than the devious *praepositus*—nor did they need one. Gorgonius needed Eusebius' corroboration, not mine.

Gaudentius shrugged. 'It's not clear the Lord Chamberlain views this Gorgonius as worth saving.'

I strode behind Gaudentius' muscle-bound figure toward the tall, carved doors of the main building.

'Who's doing the questioning?'

'*Magister Equitum in Praesenti* Flavius Arbetio took over from the Prefect Lampadius an hour ago.'

'Lampadius, the "austerity politician"? He called off all the games and races as Praetorian Prefect for Gallia.'

'Lampadius' questioning turned too insinuating. General Arbetio is sharper.'

'You mean *Consul* Arbetio, don't you?'

Gaudentius halted at the top of the steps.

'Only for a year. And he wants to make the most of it. Gorgonius is only an appetizer. The main dish on Arbetio's menu is his rival to succeed Constantius—General Ursicinus.'

'*Ursicinus* is here?'

I turned cold. General Ursicinus was the most powerful soldier in the Empire. I'd heard more than was safe about his ambitions from his military acolyte, the Master of the Guards in Antiochia, Barbatio. Would I be pressed to testify to those ambitions? Or lie?

I clenched Gaudentius' forearm. 'Is that why I'm here? My life depends on knowing.'

'What was your briefing from Apodemius in Roma?'

'The *Magister* told me to say nothing unless absolutely pinned to the floor.'

'Heed his advice. That's why he's our *Magister Agentium in Rebus* and you're still just *biarchus*, second-class. Play dumb.'

I stiffened but made no effort to defend my checkered reputation. Depending on my cooperation today, Gaudentius was capable of demoting me back to riding the northern circuit chasing the tail of that cheating dice rat Rufus—assuming I didn't end up in Catena's cells for further 'questioning.'

I followed the Neapolitan at a respectful clip through the echoing reception rooms toward the *consistorium*. We passed dozens of scurrying bureaucrats too busy to bother with us. Stony-faced sentries stared right through us.

Though one of the Empire's western capitols, the palace building looked more Eastern than ever to my eyes. If such unforgiving marble architecture could be feminized, the taste of our Macedonian empress had merged with the Emperor's fondness for purple, gilt, incense, and protocol. Mediolanum's court buildings had become an ornate and fuggy nest fit for the nervous, unblinking sovereign and his clever second wife.

Huge sprays of summer flowers wilted next to smoky braziers. Heavy draperies, embroidered with the gold letters *Chi* and *Rho*, the first two Greek letters of our emperor's 'savior' Christ, muffled the noise of the bustling city outside. Only the swishing robes and murmuring orders of thousands of secretaries, eunuchs, cooks, notaries, officials, and family attendants broke the reverential hush of the palace.

—THE WOLVES OF AMBITION—

My ears picked up the hum of the inquisition as we neared the bronze-covered doors to the *consistorium*. In my previous approaches to this sanctum, I'd never seen so many guards—fifteen on either side, each fully armed with *spatha*, *pugio*, and spear—and not parade weapons but battle-ready arms. The palatine *domestici* stood on high alert against any last-minute insurrections by the doomed.

I took a deep breath and thought of my grandfather, one of the Empire's last great senators and masters of public rhetoric. True, I was only the bastard child of the Manlius line by a Numidian seamstress slave, but my share of the Senator's aristocratic blood surged up to face the Emperor's hounds. Constantius himself knew me from services past, but many at his table of councilors didn't. They distrusted our *schola* of independent agents almost as much as they competed with each other for favor and appointment.

In short, I was about to enter an arena of political hyenas, each fighting for his own pack.

Gaudentius and I positioned ourselves behind a phalanx of clerks scribbling testimony in shorthand on wax tablets. I surveyed the crowded room from behind the *ducenarius'* thick shoulder. I had spotted that old enemy of our *schola*, the eunuch Lord Chamberlain. He presided like an insidious spider at the center of the long marble table.

The examiner Consul Arbetio had just laid his palms on that cool surface as he leaned forward to press home his point. He was of medium height with a long torso, thick waist, and thinning hair clipped short. Standing alone in the center of the room, without adviser or even a slave for support, Gorgonius trembled.

'Do you know this eunuch?' Gaudentius whispered.

'Only by sight.'

Gorgonius had the wide hips, soft face, and elongated limbs of a male castrated before puberty. I'd crossed his path once or twice during my investigation.

But I'd seen over a hundred eunuchs working in the Antiochia palace compound—chamber slaves from Armenia where castration was still legal, towering *domestici* on security duty, or small servant boys ill-favored by the Fates at birth—even a virile-looking Toxandrian prisoner of war. Despite his enslavement and mutilation, this Meroveus had proven himself still so much of a man that I'd rescued him for service with the *agentes in rebus*.

The northern Frank was still training at the Castra Peregrina in Roma. Our service had no prejudice against eunuchs. We even studied their ways under an 'expert' instructor. In our *schola*'s competition for information and control of communications across the Empire, it was good to have two actual eunuchs on staff.

'I recognize this Gorgonius from the mole on his cheek, but nothing more,' I whispered. 'He cannot be the reason for my summons.'

Gaudentius looked relieved. His object was to get me in and out of this hearing without drawing our *schola* into political controversy.

General Arbetio pounded the grand marble table with exasperation.

'Did you hear or see *any* soldiers of the *Legio X Fretensis, Legio XXX Ulpia Victrix,* or the *Legio II Flavia* in the Caesar's apartments?'

'Certainly not,' Gorgonius said. 'The Caesar did not entertain legionaries in his apartments for conference *of any kind.*'

'Don't parse my words while you still have a tongue!' Arbetio shouted. 'Did you ever witness the visit of any *officers* assigned to the *command* of *any* legions stationed in the East?'

'Yes,' Gorgonius relented. 'One, in the company of his senior tribunes.'

Arbetio struggled to hold his patience. The questioning was heating up as the morning wore on.

'At last. Would you kindly tell us who that "one" was?'

The eunuch muttered, 'The *Magister Equitum* of the East, General Ursicinus.'

Arbetio took a deep and satisfied breath. He cast a triumphant smile at his fellow *consistoriani*. 'Our Empire's valiant bear of a defender, Ursicinus,' he repeated directly to the Emperor.

Constantius' large cow eyes did not blink. That bulbous chin did not quiver. The nose that drooped at the end did not sniff.

—THE WOLVES OF AMBITION—

Everything that had been comely in his dissolute younger brother Constans was ponderous and excessive in Constantius.

'So Ursicinus was there. When, and why, Gorgonius?' Arbetio continued.

'In 351—no, no, 352. The general came to report his success in putting down the Jewish revolt.'

'Was the Caesar much pleased with his commander-in-chief?'

'Oh, yes, of course,' the foolish Gorgonius replied. 'I recall Caesar Gallus relishing all the details of the destruction of two cities, Tiberias and Diospolis. He told me as I scraped him clean that Ursicinus had razed Diocaesarea to the ground and killed several thousand rebels, some of them mere boys. The *Augustus* found the details of the massacre . . . um . . . exciting to repeat to me while he bathed. He enjoyed stories of valor.'

'He's an honest witness. Gallus loved bloodshed,' I whispered.

'Shut up,' Gaudentius hissed through frozen lips.

Arbetio smiled with even, white teeth. 'So the Caesar favored Ursicinus? The General's fame grew? Gallus promoted Ursicinus' victories to anyone who would listen? Even you—?'

'Yes,' Gorgonius said 'but—'

Too late he realized his mistake.

'When tradition holds that our Emperor should receive all credit for imperial success in the field?'

'The Caesar was only . . . grateful for the legions' protection.'

'How many times did the Caesar and the General meet?'

'I'm no eavesdropper,' the eunuch protested. 'I drew baths and cleaned his robes.'

Arbetio drew himself to his full height. He had dressed this morning to display both civil authority and military prowess to full effect. His bleached woolen tunic was hemmed in fine gold embroidery and his high rank was advertised by two huge embroidered *orbiculi* below his belt. His parade armor had been polished bright with fine sand and his boots of sturdy calfskin were spotless.

'But did you not stick to your master like a second skin? Surely you never left your post in his private chambers?'

'No, of course not.'

'Private dining room?'

'Sometimes.'

'Didn't the two men discuss things beside Jewish rebels? Didn't Gallus confide to Ursicinus his frustration? His hunger for more authority? Did the two men not discuss the civil administration of the Eastern Empire? Didn't the Caesar openly chafe under the seniority of more experienced administrators in Antiochia?'

'I ... have no idea.' Gorgonius searched dozens of impassive faces for rescue. 'I only know Flavius Gallus was grateful for Ursicinus' victories.'

'Oh, I'm sure he was. Wasn't Caesar Gallus so grateful that he entrusted investigations of treason in his own court to none other than General Ursicinus a year or so later?'

'I know nothing ... nothing more.' Gorgonius shot a plaintive look at the Lord Chamberlain, but Eusebius looked away from his appeal. 'Please let me go, Consul. Let me go.'

Arbetio had not finished using Gorgonius to trap Ursicinus. 'In fact, as we've heard in previous testimony, General Ursicinus' fame has been rising steadily throughout the entire East. The dioceses clamor for him. The rabble praises him. Leaders of good society admire him until they have almost forgotten the name of our beloved emperor.'

Arbetio glanced at his notes. 'Soon after his victories over the Jews, the General meddled in political affairs, didn't he, Gorgonius?'

The eunuch trembled. Arbetio crossed the room and slapped the eunuch's hairless cheek. Gorgonius' knees wobbled.

'Only at the Caesar's request, Consul.'

Arbetio lost his patience and kicked the miserable eunuch until he had him curling up in pain on the floor.

'You know far more, you specimen of bed lice. This tribunal is too lenient with you.'

Arbetio signaled to a sentry for Gorgonius to be hauled downstairs for Catena's version of further 'conversation.'

The eunuch lifted his sweating face off the polished *tesserae* and moaned, 'I know nothing more. I beg you.'

He inched forward on his stomach, one hand stretching to clutch the purple hem of the Emperor's stiff outer robe. 'Please,

—THE WOLVES OF AMBITION—

Imperator, please, by Christ's mercy. Do not send me down there. Christ, save your faithful servant, Christ!'

The Emperor's personal bodyguard, Teutomeres, kicked Gorgonius back from the dais. We listened to the eunuch's terrified sobs as a tablet from the Lord Chamberlain Eusebius now passed from hand to hand down the long table until it reached the dais and the bejeweled hand of the Emperor. Those unblinking Constantinian eyes read the message and tucked it beneath the carapace of heavy brocade engulfing his stolid figure.

'Release Gorgonius,' the Emperor said.

Arbetio's mask of consular impartiality dropped. His lips twisted up over his teeth like a hunting canine whose prey had just dodged into a thorny thicket.

'It wasn't Christ who just saved the little shit, I'll wager a year's pay,' Gaudentius mumbled.

'And you'd win, even against Rufus' loaded dice.'

I kept well behind Gaudentius. Eusebius hated our *Magister* Apodemius above all his opponents. I didn't want him to spot me. Meanwhile, the Emperor played his councilors against each other like no more than pieces on a *latrunculi* board. Arbetio had made his move and been countered by the Lord Chamberlain. Whose side did the others sit on?

'I know that fat councilor from my courier days in Treverorum,' I whispered.

Gaudentius followed my eyes to the bald man patting down his wet dome with a square of silk. 'You should. He was *comes rei privatae* to Constans in 342.'

'Mattyocopus, his money man? How has he survived? Constans was a gold-plated spendthrift who broke the imperial treasury.'

'And your "Sweets-gulper" still always takes more than his share. He's hung on to the edges of that council table since Constans' death by every dirty trick in the book. He'll do whatever Lampadius or Arbetio tells him.'

'Do I recognize the withered old man with the elegant profile?'

'You might. Quintus Flavius Maesius Egnatius Lollianus, the council's respected "pagan placeholder." Perhaps he knew the late Senator Manlius in the old days?'

'You mean Lollianus Mavortius who was Urban Prefect of Roma when I was a youngster?'

'The very one, recalled from retirement to play second consul—though he's only interested in astrology.'

'And the slim, sly one? Like a serpent standing on his tail?'

'C. Ceionious Rufius Volusianus Lam—'

'*That's* your insinuating Lampadius, the "austerity" politician?'

Gaudentius nodded. 'Yes, austere, frugal, vain, and arrogant—that's Lampadius. Next to him is Aedesius, the *magister memoriae*, in charge of sixty-two clerks and twelve *adiutores* and a right little toady. Aedesius is another pagan but Lampadius is a Christian. Yet those two are thick as thieves. Religious confession counts for nothing when it comes to complots here.'

I knew only one man besides the Emperor who put the unity of the Empire first—and that man, our *schola magister* Apodemius, would never warm a seat at this table. Through military uprising, civil corruption, and regional breakup, we *agentes* comprised the thousand-strong network that kept the imperial system running smooth—but we were hated all the more by everyone.

And why was I here? Why had Apodemius obeyed someone's order and dispatched me into this nest of vipers? To condemn Ursicinus on hearsay?

Scarcely turning his head, Constantius II prompted Arbetio to continue.

The consul recovered his poise and relished the single point he had scored. The witness Gorgonius had at least placed his hated rival Ursicinus in the court of the traitor Caesar Gallus.

Now he had the opening to strip that valorous giant of his medals and clear the way for his own ascension in Constantius' wake.

Arbetio gave the emphatic instruction to the guards at the chamber door.

'Summon General Ursicinus.'

Chapter 2, An Empress Gambles

—THE *CONSISTORIUM*—

The closed room grew only more suffocating. We heard heavy, brisk boot steps coming down the corridor before we saw the man himself framed by the great doors.

At last, the most senior soldier of the Empire marched into the chamber with a slight, if well disguised limp. Instead of coming straight up to prostrate himself and kiss the hem of Constantius' robe, the towering veteran turned his back on us and waited near the entrance. The guards had slammed the heavy doors shut, barring Ursicinus' escort party from accompanying him in force. We all waited through a confrontational silence. The towering soldier refused to acknowledge his affronted sovereign until the doors were re-opened.

Only then did Ursicinus lead forward his entire contingent—six *tribuni vacantes* under the banners of the *Legio X Fretensis* rounded up by the noble figure of his own son, Potentius, bearing the insignia of a tribune of the *promoti*. All wore full battle gear and looked formidably out of place in this ornate and cloistered assembly.

Where his *pugio* sheath should have hung, General Ursicinus carried a jeweled Persian dagger—certainly no gift from its rightful owner. His armor had been polished so often, it looked thin in places. He wore his gray hair close to the skull. One hand bore shiny scars of fire. The nape of his bull's neck was burnt mahogany by the Eastern sun.

The chamber shimmered with the newcomers' vitality. These men were fresh from a disputed front. Each of us knew that King Shapur II's armies would flood into any territorial vacuum weakened by a mistake made in Mediolanum today.

Constantius II lifted one eyebrow. He was no stranger to the uses of processional awe. These proceedings had at last reached the centerpiece of his campaign to root out the specter of any Eastern threat to his rule.

Returning the General's insult, he ordered his guards to push the enormous veteran onto his knees, forcing the military hero to hobble forward toward the dais to place his lips on the Emperor's hem.

Arbetio was impatient for these overtures to finish.

'General Ursicinus, you have been arraigned here on charges of high treason.'

'Innocent of all charges,' Ursicinus said in a gruff baritone as he rose stiffly to his feet. 'Jealousy, the foe of all good and loyal servants of the Empire, has grown more dangerous to me with each success.'

'Yes, yes, we know you for a brave man. Moreover, you are my own colleague-in-arms. I register these accusations against you with deep regret, General,' Arbetio said, bestowing the kind of smile I would hand over to a professional poison-taster before accepting.

Ursicinus stroked his helmet thoughtfully with that large, scarred hand. The little finger of his left hand was missing below the last knuckle. I recalled the far more grievous wounds my late father, Commander Atticus Manlius Gregorius, had sustained in an action defending an imperial border. My blood stirred with prejudice against these curled and scented councilors. And Arbetio himself had just faced battle as part of Constantius II's last autumn campaign against the Alemanni invading Brigantium. No matter how ferocious their rivalry for imperial favor, at least the consul had to show a fellow veteran respect.

Ursicinus gave a soft reply forcing even the Emperor to bend forward: 'I've submitted my explanations of all actions in the East in writing. This tribunal has all details on offers made to the Jewish rebel Patricius, the insurrections we suppressed, the defeats of the cities Tiberias and Diospolis to teach them a lesson and the complete destruction of Diocaesarea. I was called in to Antiochia for a time to investigate challenges to the Caesar's rule, but only as a military adviser, I assure you. I am no . . . *politician*.'

—THE WOLVES OF AMBITION—

Constantius cut off Arbetio's rebuttal with a raised palm. He kept his voice low as well. 'We have read your defense with interest.'

I could tell Constantius was full of rage, though his voice stayed even and soft: 'We have also heard that it was your cavalry squadron, lent to the rebellious Caesar, which stood by while the Antiochene Horse Guards dragged our personal representative, the Praetorian Prefect-elect Domitianus, to pieces through the streets. We heard rumors that you were in frequent conference with the court's Master of the Horse Guards—one Barbatio—who aspired to become *Magister Equitum* in the East once you replaced our cousin as Caesar.'

'Barbatio is as loyal to your rule as I. Why listen to slanderous conjecture based on disconnected events?' Ursicinus scoffed. 'To challenge the Caesar's treatment of Domitianus would be to challenge your own authority.'

'Was this not collusion? Was this not insurrection? Was this not treasonous contempt for our personal envoy and appointee?'

Ursicinus now proved himself a veteran politician as well as military man. 'I will not abase myself so far to satisfy envious tongues wagging hearsay. As for the Master of the Horse Guards' personal ambitions, where is Barbatio to answer these charges on his own behalf?'

'On border duty in chilly Mogontiacum,' Arbetio said. 'Perhaps he finds himself too frozen in place to lie for you on short notice.'

A nervous laugh ran through the chamber.

Ursicinus ignored Arbetio.

'*Imperator*, I serve at your command. I've maintained the Empire's Eastern defenses against the Sassanids in your absence, commanding the *Legiones X Fretensis, XXX Ulpia Victrix, III Scythica, II Flavia*—'

'Noble legions, all of them,' murmured the Emperor.

Ursicinus' tone hardened: 'Not all. You've also asked me to reform the rebel remnants of the dishonored legions, the *Magnentiaci* and *Decentiaci*, of your conquered enemies. Those men, *Imperator*, regard their transfer to the Eastern border as nothing less than a death sentence. To keep such hardened riffraff under command requires a strong hand like mine.'

The *consistorium* gasped at Ursicinus' lack of deference. The General had all but declared that only he could control the defeated troops of Constantius' late rival emperor.

Ursicinus gave a rueful laugh and stepped back from the dais.

'Shapur remains as insolent as ever. The border is unstable. Even answering this summons is dereliction of my duty to our troubled Eastern front.'

He strode right around the councilors' table; his right hand caressed his sword pommel and his helmet still nestled in the crook of his left elbow.

'Today I lament in my heart that uprightness is deserted by more powerful men and stands so insecure in this chamber. Anyone can see that loyalties in this room are handed around with no more thought than obedient *lictors* are transferred from magistrates to their successors.'

Constantius didn't deign to twist his head to watch Ursicinus' threatening prowl over the shoulders of his councilors. Instead he glared at Potentius who stared right back without fear. This steady, muscular young man was a reminder to everyone present of the Constantine heir our beautiful Empress Eusebia had not yet produced for her uxorious sovereign.

'We have evidence that you're ambitious not only for yourself but for this son of yours,' Constantius answered.

'What father isn't?' Ursicinus burst into laughter and cuffed the feeble Lollianus so hard, the drooling astrologer nearly fell off his seat.

Constantius persevered: 'We hold sworn testimony that our name is no longer mentioned throughout the Eastern provinces while your notoriety feeds on glory until you are touted and proclaimed as the only formidable foe the Persians face.'

Ursicinus had finished his tour of the council. 'There can be no evidence backing such rumors dreamt up by men in comfortable beds. For I have done nothing for the last five years but draw battle plans, lay siege, bully defectors back into soldiers, repel incursions, suppress rebellions, shed blood, and burn whole cities into the sand. And I've watched men, women, and children die under my sword—for your Empire.'

—THE WOLVES OF AMBITION—

Ursicinus fell on one knee, held out his battered sword at the Emperor's impeccable boots, and bowed his head.

It was a grand show. Although I still feared the unknown reason for which I'd been summoned, I was glad to witness this. How could Constantius fault his most loyal commander?

The Emperor sat immobilized by the General's bold speech. 'We'll consult among ourselves. Stay in Mediolanum, General.'

Ursicinus wasn't lingering for second thoughts. With a quick nod, he marched at a brisk pace out of the *consistorium*, followed by his confident son and loyal tribunes.

'It's over. They didn't call me,' I whispered to Gaudentius.

I dared not tell even Gaudentius—much less this council—that the ambitious and thick-skulled Barbatio *had* cherished hopes that Ursicinus would succeed a felled Gallus as Caesar. He'd told me so in Antiochia. General Ursicinus *had* encouraged the officer's fantasies.

In short, Ursicinus was probably guilty of the overweening ambition that Constantius II suspected.

The air was stifling. Anxiety over the day's events overwhelmed me. 'I cannot breath in this room for confusion, *Ducenarius*. Surely you know why I'm here? Spying on this court is your job.'

'They called you. I brought you in. It's not over.'

'If they didn't ask me to corroborate that rumor about Barbatio, what more can there be? Surely I'm safe from that bastard Catena's evil prongs.'

All heads but the Emperor's swiveled at bustling sounds and raised voices in the echoing corridor outside. For a moment I feared Ursicinus might burst back into the room to vent his temper and use his battered sword on all our heads.

Instead, a river of ladies swept in through the great doors, like a rustling, tinkling, swishing regiment of bright-colored silk flowers led by the Empress Eusebia. If it was not the entire *Domus Augustae*, these were surely the more eye-catching members of her private household. Here was another expert at the art of 'processional awe.'

Not one woman in her wake was vulgarly dressed, but the combination of saffrons, salmons, garnets, azures, ceruleans and spring greens dazzled the councilors into stunned silence. Wafting, transparent silk veils drew the eager male eye closer.

Well aware of her sensuous beauty, Eusebia granted an imperious smile to each of the councilors—save one.

It seemed our *Imperatrix* and I shared one thing. For by ignoring only the Lord Chamberlain, her loathing seemed all the more obvious than anything even my profound revulsion might have produced.

My attention was hooked away by the sight of the strange boy from the courtyard. He escorted his mother walking behind some half dozen women in Eusebia's train. My startled glance drew his eyes straight to me. I could not be mistaken because, once again, he smiled with relief at seeing I remained within reach.

'Who's that brat in the dark green tunic?'

'Junius.' Gaudentius shrugged. 'Shush.'

The Empress' ladies scurried and glided to position themselves behind her. For her part, Eusebia seemed to hold her breath until one of the *domestici* had fetched a gilded *cathedra* for her to settle into.

We were all astonished to see this select and secluded tribe of imperial ladies join the proceedings. Even Arbetio took a step back from the council table, as if to shield himself from unforeseen dangers. Some of the ladies had pinned their diaphanous *pallae* across their lower faces in the new Eastern fashion, while others modeled themselves on the confident Empress and bestowed open-faced greetings to privileged officers of the court.

'Your Council has one last witness for today, *Imperator*?' Eusebia asked Constantius.

Surely the Empress was not referring to me.

'I think we have done for the day,' Arbetio said, looking less sure of himself than earlier. The hated Ursicinus had slipped from his envious clutches.

'No, General, it seems our Lord Chamberlain has added a witness,' Constantius answered in his cryptic, flat tone. 'He submits further allegations regarding the Caesar Gallus' treason that require immediate examination.'

—THE WOLVES OF AMBITION—

'Please, we are ready,' Eusebia said, with a challenging glance at the Lord Chamberlain. Eusebius dodged her eye. Instead, the Empire's senior eunuch patted his fawn-colored hair, rearranged his voluminous damask maroon robes, and fiddled with a garnet ring adorning his pudgy left hand.

No one but Eusebia or the Lord Chamberlain, it seemed, could have predicted the Emperor's unexpected instruction to the *domestici* waiting near the doors.

'Please invite our cousin into this chamber.'

His cousin? Caesar Gallus was dead—as surely lifeless as the golden eagles fixed to the standards framing those doors! I myself had seen Barbatio mutilate the imperial corpse in that dank cell in Istria. If the headless Gallus had now returned across the River Styx to testify today, the court had crossed into a nightmare worthy of legend.

Confusion broke out among the Emperor's advisers. Murmurs swept the whole assembly, including the po-faced notaries and secretaries.

'I'm here already,' someone croaked. A short, bearded, almost goatish youth wearing a short tunic stepped into the center of the room from only the gods knew where.

'Welcome, Flavius Claudius Julianus.'

'I've waited many weeks without word, in the hope of merely seeing your August Presence,' the youth replied, sinking to his bare and hairy knees.

My mind raced. If the Lord Chamberlain Eusebius risked casting treason allegations at this last runt of the Constantine dynasty, it was only because he'd abandoned hope of dominating the poor benighted Julian as he had once ruled his half-brother Gallus and still controlled the Emperor himself.

Perhaps the great eunuch hoped to frighten Constantius a little and marginalize this harmless, round-shouldered youth for good. Eusebius could count on tacit support from his fellow councilors once they had observed for themselves Constantius' permanent ambivalence toward any family rival.

I still had no idea what part I played, but it was clear that this was the veritable season of treason—the most opportune moment for ambitious mongrels like Arbetio and Eusebius to sweep away any and every contender to succeed under the excuse of Gallus' downfall.

I pitied this awkward boy. The last two Constantine descendants to survive Constantius II's murderous purge had grown up together under house arrest in a fortress in Macellum with only eunuchs for company. Whereas Gallus had emerged blinking into the imperial sunlight to become a vicious, volatile caesar, his half-brother Julian had sheltered himself away behind Greek philosophy taught by kind eunuch named Mardonius.

Arbetio wavered. '*Imperator*, this Council has no questions for this witness. A member of the imperial house need hardly answer to us, your humble subjects.'

Constantius looked as troubled as any granite statue could. He sat still, a rock in which seething heat might be mounting over a dilemma the rest of us could not detect.

'The Lord Chamberlain must have a question, Consul Arbetio, or our beloved cousin would not be here today,' the Empress said in her bell-like voice.

The heavy figure of the Lord Chamberlain rose to his slippered feet with some assistance. 'Indeed, I have questions— only a few—and will not detain our imperial witness too long.'

Eusebius spoke in that silky manner I knew from previous encounters. 'Flavius Claudius Julianus, I'm sorry to have kept you waiting for so many weeks while we deliberated here in Mediolanum.'

'It is worth w . . . waiting these last six *months* to lay eyes on my beloved and esteemed cousin,' the boy answered.

'You received your education in Macellum?' Eusebius asked.

'During my eight years of incarceration in the fortress?'

'Yes, at the fortress.'

'Not exactly, Lord Chamberlain. At age seven, I was placed under the guardianship of the Arian Christian Bishop of Nicomedia, one Eusebius of Nicomedia. Mardonius, a eunuch of Goth origins, was my daily teacher. Only after Eusebius died in 342, did our *Imperator* send my brother and myself to Macellum, where the Christian bishop George of Cappadocia lent me books.'

Julian gave a sudden cough, spit onto the priceless mosaics under his boots and then righted himself. 'As you can imagine, I have had a lot of spare time on my hands.'

—THE WOLVES OF AMBITION—

'After leaving Macellum, did you not visit your half-brother, the Caesar Gallus, in Antiochia?'

'No, I did not. First, I became a lector in the Church. Then in 351, I took up studies in Asia Minor—of Neo-Platonism with the philosopher Aedesius and of theurgy with Aedesius' disciple, Maximus of Ephesus.'

'And did you not visit your step-brother Gallus as he passed through Constantinopolis?'

'No, Lord Chamberlain, I did not.'

Eusebius chortled. 'Certainly you did. Sheer fraternal loyalty would draw you to his side, I'm sure. You must have forgotten.'

'I do not forget things. I do not forget anything,' Julian said in a strange voice. There was a long and uncomfortable pause. 'I repeat, I did not visit him.'

His downturned eyes blinked hard. He pulled at his scraggly beard as he fought to disguise his confusion. The political waters of this room were over his bookish head and he knew it. The expressionless occupant of the dais listening to his testimony was the same ruler who had, as of the previous year, murdered every other male on their family tree.

'When your studies brought you so nearby? With a sibling ruling the entire Eastern Empire? Surely you met the Caesar—if not out of brotherly loyalty, then political opportunism—I dare not say. Who in your position would not? Do not dissemble out of fear of this council. We will understand.'

Eusebius used a fine linen handkerchief to pat the shine off his downy bulbous head as if treason was hardly his concern.

'I did *not* visit my brother in Constantinopolis,' Julian said in a clear voice to the audience on all sides.

'I am afraid we do not believe you.' Eusebius settled back down on his seat and shook his head.

'I tell the truth.' Julian turned away from Eusebius and looked his imperial cousin in the eyes. We waited.

So this hunched-over scholar had a trace of Constantine the Great's fiber left in him after all. His problem was that none of the other councilors who sat in judgment had visited Constantinopolis or Antiochia during Gallus' brief reign. Eusebius had. All the eunuch needed to do now was cast his sticky web of suspicion over Julian's homely head and the boy was as good as exiled from political safety.

'One can understand your right to familial privacy, but are you sure?' The unctuous eunuch gave the chamber an indulgent smile, as if he knew Julian was lying out of fear of the Emperor.

'Gaudentius,' I whispered, 'Julian never visited Gallus in Constantinopolis or Antiochia. I was there.'

'No one has called you. You're off the hook. No one asked you about Ursicinus and Barbatio.' Gaudentius bit his few words into pieces. 'Stay silent.'

'I can't let this pass. Eusebius is throwing an innocent to the dogs. He knows Constantius' fears. He's smearing suspicion that will stick to Julian until the boy finally falls.'

'Let him lie there. Look at him. He'll never amount to anything anyway.'

Ursicinus had fought for himself with the authority of the battlefield and Gorgonius had appealed to his powerful protector. The twenty-three-year-old Julian stood before us all—pimply, ungainly, and friendless—exposed to men who hated him only for his name.

In the long and awkward silence, Empress Eusebia took the measure of the assembly, her gaze roving until it reached our distant corner filled by a gaggle of clerks and guards. Her large brown eyes, circled with dark kohl, examined each face. My stomach sank to my knees when her scrutiny latched onto me, like Alexandria's famed lighthouse beaming straight into my eyes.

She smiled. Perhaps she remembered me from my foolhardy defense of Catena's victims during an imperial anniversary party for Constantius in Arelate years ago. Even so, events that night had nothing to do with Gallus in the East.

Yet now I read her mind. With a sinking heart, I finally guessed why I was summoned. It had nothing to do with Ursicinus and Barbatio.

The Empress Eusebia had taken a huge gamble by entering this cradle of conspiracies. Someone had told her of my investigations in Antiochia and my escorting Gallus through Constantinopolis to his execution in Pola. Someone knew I could defend Julian today from the charge of conspiracy. It was the Empress herself who now tossed the dice in my direction.

—THE WOLVES OF AMBITION—

Despite my common sense and in direct flaunting of Gaudentius' emphatic instructions, I gave a slight nod of assent to the waiting Empress.

She lifted her voice to the assembly, 'Is there no one to bear witness of our cherished cousin's innocence to this tribunal?'

Her dulcet invitation drew my boots forward, though the Lord Chamberlain recognized me with a deadly satisfaction and Gaudentius laid a warning hand on my arm. The *ducenarius* wouldn't let me pass without first condemning me with a vengeful scowl.

I prostrated myself at Constantius' feet and made a gesture of kissing the hem that I was too lowly to touch. Then I retreated to a respectful distance behind the imperial cousin Julian because, to tell the truth, the young scholar gave off a sour smell.

'I am the Marcus Gregorianus Numidianus, *Agens*, *biarchus* second class. I can testify.'

'This man is not on my witness list,' Arbetio countered, thumbing furiously through his vellum documents.

The Empress countered, 'Yet he volunteers his testimony.'

Arbetio glanced over at the Lord Chamberlain in confusion. The Consul had lost Gorgonius to Eusebius' intervention, seen Ursicinus slip through his grasp, and now saw the 'Gallus' proceedings torn right out of his control.

'What can you tell the court, *Agens*?' Constantius asked. 'We are eager to conclude this day's painful proceedings.'

'I spent some time in the Antiochia court on a special assignment for this court. I accompanied the Caesar during his stay in the Roma of the East. I also served as imperial escort on the journey to the fortress of Pola Istria. His mind was . . . unwell. There was always someone at his side. He was closely attended in Constantinopolis—night and day.'

'Get to the point, Numidianus.'

'At no time did Flavius Claudius Julianus visit the Caesar Flavius Claudius Constantius Gallus in Antiochia, Constantinopolis, or during his journey to the West. I stake my life on this.'

It was the simple truth. The Empress Eusebia's grateful smile enveloped me, but this hardly compensated for the Emperor's disbelieving expression, the Lord Chamberlain's red-faced fury and Gaudentius' angry eyes drilling into my back.

Julian adjusted his rough-spun Greek tunic, pulled at his wispy beard, and took a few steps toward the dais.

'*Imperator*, may I resume my studies in Greece?'

'You will go to Comum,' the Emperor said. 'We are happy to say that these trials are adjourned.'

He rose from his ornate, wide-armed chair. His poised and beautiful consort reached out and drew the awkward Julian to her side. The entire imperial household followed the three Constantines out of the overheated chamber in a stately but rapid march past the open mouths of the *consistoriani*.

That boy Junius threw me a pleading glance over his retreating shoulder.

The councilors rose and raced away on the heels of their infuriated senior consul. Livid with frustration, Arbetio even shoved a sentry aside in his flight to the imperial secretariat.

But the truth had not saved me altogether.

Gaudentius wheeled around and nearly spit in my face with indignation. 'There was no need to involve our *schola*. You disobeyed! I *saw* you nod. You *volunteered* yourself! I'm filing a report to headquarters in your disfavor.'

'But—!'

'It's no good, Numidianus. You were told to stay silent if at all possible, yet I *saw* you offer your testimony to the Empress.'

My superior marched out of the chamber, his boots sending dust motes into the sunrays streaking from high windows overhead.

I found myself alone in an empty marble vault still reeking of incense, perfumed oil, dying flowers, and nervous sweat.

I was a pawn on someone's *latrunculi* board, but who were the players? And was I standing with the ivory or ebony pieces?

CHAPTER 3, THE COUNT OF NIGHTMARES

—THE IMPERIAL FINANCE BUILDING, AT DUSK—

The mud of the civil war and nightmares of the massacre in Mursa in 351 soiled my spirit. In the back of men's minds—perhaps even Gaudentius'—the stigma of rebellion tainted my reputation. *Agentes* did not as a rule enter armed battle, but at the last minute, I had plunged into the fray on the side of General Magnentius and my father against Constantius II and his Eastern forces. I had only escaped bitter reprisals on the strength of my *insignia* and *Magister* Apodemius' protection.

The aftermath of the Empire's costly suicide in Mursa—Roman against Roman—still tumbled around us like a game of political knucklebones.

I, for one, could no longer follow the bets.

A year ago, I would never have predicted that the astute politician General Arbetio would ally himself with an intriguant like the chief eunuch Eusebius. Yet the Lord Chamberlain and the Consul were right now sharing a recent triumph in Aquileia. Conducting interrogations as a team, they had filled the prisons there to groaning point with officials, all accused of abetting the ugly death in Antiochia of the Emperor's disdainful envoy Domitianus and his ill-fated defender, a *quaestor* named Montius.

I had witnessed these two violent deaths at the whim of the Caesar Gallus. There had been no plotting beforehand. Yet Arbetio and Eusebius had returned to Mediolanum together with arms full of forced confessions. They regaled the nervous Constantius with boasts of having questioned, scourged, tortured, demoted, exiled, and executed dozens upon dozens of 'traitors'.

Constantius let them feed his fears. His appetite only grew with the eating.

I left the shadows of the palace and wandered the bustling streets of Mediolanum, eating my supper of meatballs in a rolled omelet from a streetside *taberna* where no one knew me. The city was not merely an imperial playground for the vast court of Constantius and Eusebia, but a vital hub linking the money of Italia to the produce of the north. The city usually offered enough to entertain an idle man, but this evening even the Circus, the *thermae*, the *tabernae*, and the imperial mausoleum couldn't distract me. Mediolanum's squat twenty-four-sided towers looming over the late Maximian's thirty-five-foot walls made me long for Roma's free and easy *fora*, hills and slums, even with their swill, stink, and society scandal. I longed to get back to the daily headaches of auditing the Manlius estates and tending desk assignments at the Castra.

I would leave for Roma tonight in the hope of forestalling Gaudentius' nasty report of my testimony by explaining myself in person.

I knew enough about the *ducenarius* to make me sweat, even in this evening's summer breeze. Not long ago, the Governor of Pannonia Secunda, one Africanus, had given a dinner party in Sirmium. His guests drank too much and let off steam about Constantius and his *consistoriani*. One blowhard, a tribune on furlough named Marinus, even claimed that an oracle promised 'a change in the wind.' Before the party was over, each of his companions had boasted that the omen surely meant his own advancement.

Stretched out among the guests, watching and listening was Gaudentius, sober as a Vestal. The Neapolitan repeated every treasonous jest to the chief steward of the praetorian prefect Rufinus—a nasty customer. Gaudentius would have said it was his duty, but I had two problems with what he did—first, his report damned the foolish banqueters without giving them a chance to clear their hangovers, and second, his observations should have gone first to our *magister*, Apodemius, not Rufinus, who had retired from our *schola* long before.

Gaudentius grabbed all the credit for himself. The Emperor's personal bodyguard, Teutomeres, had rounded up the revelers and hauled them all to Aquileia in chains. They were getting the prisoners ready for transfer to Mediolanum when they left Tribune Marinus in a tavern, within reach of a kitchen knife. The noble Marinus stabbed it into his side, forced it across himself, and spread his own innards out on the table where only moments before, Gaudentius had sat.

Constantius had been furious at the loss of a loyal tribune and ordered Rufinus' soldiers into exile for letting Marinus rob the *consistorium* of a hearing, but Rufinus himself was parading around the courtyards even now—thanks to a pardon wheedled from the Emperor by General Arbetio.

The rest of the diners had fallen to Catena's knives and irons until they confessed to their banter. Even now, what was left of them lay in the cells below, reduced to half-men facing a life of begging at best.

Nobody pointed a finger at Gaudentius, but I suspected he'd left the knife on the table within Marinus' reach. Only I wasn't sure why. Gaudentius was inscrutable, unsentimental, untouchable and ambitious. I did not need him as my enemy within the walls of our headquarters.

I had finished my meal and started a stroll through the crowds along the Via Moneta when I sensed someone was following me. I felt no alarm whatsoever. My tracker was clumsy—too slow in dodging out of sight as I turned a corner and too far away to do any harm.

After all, after giving such testimony in that infested chamber today, it was the invisible professional, the trained assassin whom I feared, not an amateur. Who was silly enough to trail an armed *agens*? A desperate footpad eager to grab my sagging purse emptied by Rufus and Cassius? A flirtatious lady of the streets who fancied an olive-skinned Numidian with a European's height and war-weary features?

I unfastened the strap over my *pugio* and kept walking, past moneylenders' stalls and toward the anonymity of the *horreum*, the shabby warehouse district. The daylight curfew banning wheeled traffic would soon lift. Heavy wagons full of wool, pigs, and produce would be trundling through the city gates and down these alleys. If any skullduggery were afoot, my 'friend' would try to tackle me in the confusion of butchers and wholesalers.

I was more than ready. I even lay in wait in a convenient alcove or two, downright eager to duel it out. Finally, I emerged untouched and more mystified than ever at the far end of the district. Returning to the main north-south boulevard, I reached the long rectangular forum just as the *aediles* were supervising the lamp lighting.

Had I imagined my shadow?

No, a slim, cloaked figure slipped along the edge of the public space, protected from exposure by customers around the stalls.

I picked up my pace and returned through the palace gates to the outer courtyard of the imperial domain and quickly made my way back to my shabby room. I needed rest before riding out the Porta Romana for the south and safety. I'd been assigned a small cell at the farthest end of the imperial headquarters—not even in the main palace, but on the Finance Building's ground floor, where visiting lowbodies were housed off a covered walkway in drafty cells with straw mattresses. I bolted the door against possible intrusion from Gaudentius, housed far more comfortably in a proper room nearby.

An hour later, I started packing up my shaving things, *petanus*, spare tunic and underlinen, *agens* papers and *Cursus* license.

Footsteps were coming down the stone passage to my door.

It was after working hours so I blew out my oil lamp and waited in pitch darkness for the stranger to pass my door. I was receiving no one that night—not even my superior officer if possible.

The polite tap of a toe on my door was too well mannered for Gaudentius and too abrupt for a lady.

I waited in silence.

So did the intruder.

After a quarter of an hour or so, I heard the bells of a distant church chime the evening prayers. I sat motionless until they'd finished.

So did my visitor. I heard a sniffle. Now I was sure who it was.

I threw my door open and stared into his hooded face. 'What do you want, Junius?'

—THE WOLVES OF AMBITION—

He jumped back from the doorway and trembled. He was a vulnerable figure, nearly as tall as myself but skinny as an *angon*. His expensive green wool processional cloak, hemmed with silver embroidered stags, was slipping off his narrow shoulders.

I jerked him inside my room, slammed and re-bolted the door, and threw him down on the narrow mattress some toady in Imperial Requisitioning called a 'bed'.

I relit the lamp, poured myself a bit of wine, and sat opposite him on the stool. He gave off a slight whiff of the aromatic wing reserved for women and children.

He hung his head. 'You must know why I'm here. They say you *curiosi* know everything about everyone.'

'You want to join up?'

'No, no,' he protested. 'I need help.'

'Ask your teacher.'

'No, I need *your* help. I have important information. I'm here to . . . trade information.'

'Trade? I can beat it out of you in less than a minute.'

'Beat me?' He looked astonished. 'You *don't* know who I am, do you?'

'Your name is Junius. Beyond that—'

'She promised you would.'

'Your mother?'

'No, my mother says if I meddle in court affairs, I'll end up below the pavement. Talk is deadly. Even dreams are dangerous around here.'

I handed him my half-finished cup. 'Why dreams?'

'Because even if you do nothing more than say over your breakfast that you dreamed of the color purple, the Palace Steward Mercurius betrays you to the Emperor. The ladies of the court curse him as The Count of Dreams.'

I thought of Justus Picenus, the father of the beautiful noblewoman Justina, given to Magnentius as a child bride. Unsullied by rebellion or marriage, the virgin was now safely back in Roma. But her unlucky father had been forced to kill himself for the crime of dreaming that he drew a purple robe from his side.

The boy scrutinized my thoughtful face. 'The Deputy *Magister Officiorum* Florentius says . . . do you . . . know Florentius, son of Nigrinianus?'

'My *magister* reports to his superior.'

'—Florentius is a good man, but even he says there are few men brave enough these days to admit they sleep at all, much less dream.'

'I'll remember not to doze off. Is that your big secret?'

The boy had lost confidence in me, the worldly agent. I recalled his mother's harried expression. By the flickering flame at our elbows, I detected disappointment cloud his brown eyes.

I pulled the hood off his chestnut curls and stared at his features. Their haunting familiarity both fascinated and flummoxed me. I recalled a similar face—confident, laughing, brave, and untrustworthy.

'No, you can't be . . .'

'I'm the only son of General Claudius Silvanus. I am a hostage here—a "good-will" prisoner to assure the Emperor of my father's eternal loyalty.'

I leapt off the rickety stool and took in his entire figure—the lanky limbs, the cast of the jaw, and the even, intelligent eyes.

'You were right to doubt me, Junius. All my training in observation—I should have seen it right away. What is this exchange?'

'I propose to help you save General Ursicinus and let you take the credit. In return, you save my father from conspiracy.'

'That's quite a bit of business,' I said, watering his wine. He gulped it down too fast, like a child. I pulled the cup out of his hand. I needed this child sober.

'Exactly what have you learned about General Ursicinus?'

'When the hearing ended, I followed the *consistorium* on the walk back to the imperial offices. I heard Lampadius name Ursicinus and then add "*corbulo*"—like some code word. And Consul Arbetio nodded.'

'*Corbulo?*'

'Just *corbulo*. What did they mean? Is *corbulo* dangerous?'

I'd spent my childhood as a slave reading history books to a blind Roman senator.

—THE WOLVES OF AMBITION—

'It could be lethal. You've neglected your schoolbooks, Junius. Gnaeus Domitius Corbulo was a Roman general, a consul, brother-in-law of Emperor Caligula, and father-in-law of Domitian. After Caligula, he served Emperor Claudius in Germania from the base camp Colonia Claudia Ara Agrippinensium.'

Junius started. 'That's where my father is stationed now. Then they were talking about him?'

'I don't think so, Junius. Corbulo built success on success, eventually fighting the Armenians and Parthians in the East. He was in command of the old legions *VI Ferrata, III Gallica* and the *X Fretensis*—the same legion as Ursicinus now. When Emperor Nero came to power, he grew so envious of Corbulo's popularity with the Roman people that he ordered Corbulo to commit suicide.'

Silvanus' large brown eyes blinked in shock. 'Did he do it?'

'Yes. To prove his loyalty, the noble commander fell on his sword. His last word was *Axios!*'

'*Axios!*' Junius whispered. '*He is worthy!*'

'My compliments to your Greek tutor. Corbulo was indeed worthy.'

I shivered for the implications for our imperial hero Ursicinus.

'But *Agens*, that was... three hundred years ago. We live in modern times.'

'Indeed we do. The proud Ursicinus isn't going to plunge that garish Persian trophy dagger into his own belly.'

'Still... they're going to arrest him tonight.'

'What?' I was no longer giving a history lesson. 'Constantius gave an order?'

'No, no, the Emperor didn't say anything,' Junius said with a sneeze. 'Lampadius said "Corbulo," Arbetio nodded to him, and Constantius just stared, like a statue with marble ears and went down the corridor to the imperial private suites. Lampadius and Arbetio rushed off together toward the Secretariat.'

'They let you eavesdrop on all this?'

'Oh, I'm nobody.'

Junius huddled down in his oversized cloak. 'I've been here for eight years now. I listen to women's gossip and spy on the courtiers. Even when they're taking a shit together or chatting in the *tepidarium*, nobody notices the Frankish puppy Junius.'

I recalled my adolescent slave days in a bustling noble Roman household—always invisible, always listening and learning.

'Who told you I would help? Who is *she*?'

'Roxana, of course.'

Of course. My old spying colleague Roxana was now General Claudius Silvanus' mistress. The *Magister* Apodemius always said Roxana was his single failure, but whether his error was recruiting his first female or letting such a talented agent resign from the *schola* wasn't clear.

'Roxana says if Father's in danger, you can protect him. But she warned me you won't want to, not unless I brought something to trade. I'm offering you a chance to save Ursicinus.'

'That's no offer. Going against the Emperor's suspicions of Ursicinus doesn't help me.'

'But you know the Emperor changes his mind all the time—if he knows his mind at all! Arbetio and Lampadius might have arrested Ursicinus already. After a so-called "hearing," they'll bring Constantius a bloody head. Then will be too late for the Emperor to realize his mistake.'

'It would be a fatal misstep. Without Ursicinus, the Eastern Empire is lost to the Persians. And this corrupt *consistorium* grows only more powerful over the imperial army.'

'So you'll report them? It might already be too late.'

'Report them . . . to whom?'

Like Gaudentius listening to the banquet of Governor Africanus, I should relay Junius' intelligence back to Roma. But if Ursicinus was about to be 'tried' and executed tonight, I had no time. I could think of only one person powerful enough to stop Constantius II from weakening his own empire.

I hesitated.

'But Junius, what endangers your father? Constantius owes General Silvanus his entire victory at Mursa, not to mention what order there is up in Gallia.'

For my part, there were good reasons for me to hate General Silvanus but I kept these resentments to myself.

The boy hesitated.

'Junius, who or what puts your father in such peril up in Agrippina?'

'These very men—Lampadius, Arbetio, Mattyocopus—and many others.'

'But why Silvanus?'

'Why? You just said it. He's suppressing the barbarians overrunning the wasted battlefields of Gallia. His success in the north draws their envy here at court.'

'I see.'

'Do you? You heard them today make wild accusations against General Ursicinus and Flavius Julianus. If the Empress remains childless, a good man—heir or hero—bars their way to the throne. Today you saved Julianus from suspicion. You must save Ursicinus and my father. You will be rewarded.'

'Go straight to bed now and tell no one—not even your mother.'

Before I closed the door on his cloaked figure, I added, 'And for gods' sake, don't talk in your sleep.'

※※※

I informed the deputy *Magister Officiorum* Florentius Nigrinianus that I needed to see the Empress on sensitive business. Florentius wasn't impressed. He had Gaudentius reporting to him all the time, inflating minor business into emergencies.

'Where is your superior?'

'I could not locate the *Ducenarius*,' I lied. 'General Ursicinus' life is at risk.'

'Yes, I wouldn't be surprised from what we witnessed in the *consistorium* today,' the slim and obscure-looking official muttered.

Florentius looked exhausted from running the business of the court. His ivory wool tunic was creased. He needed to shave. He had to manage the supplies and palace staff and the logistics of the ongoing 'Gallus Trials.' Preparations for the coming bishops' conference fell on his shoulders as well.

His main headache was the flow of bishops arriving from all corners of the Roman world. They were clogging the *Cursus Publicus*, flourishing their travel warrants as freely as lottery tickets, and impeding the flow of regular state traffic.

I was lucky he gave me even a minute of his time.

'Will you get me an audience? Now?'

'Can't you trust me with the matter, *Agens* Numidianus?'

'No, but you're welcome to listen in.'

'Thank you, no,' he said with a rueful grimace. 'If it's that delicate, knowing less around this court is *more*, if you follow me.'

'I'll follow you now, *Magister*, if you lead me to the *Augusta*'s chambers.'

We went quietly toward the narrowing corridors connecting the vast marble reception halls, empty and echoing, into narrowing and more aromatic passages where the warm, glowing braziers spewed incense plumes into the evening air.

'I have Gaudentius' report to *Magister* Apodemius about your evidence today, waiting for my signature,' Florentius said.

'I spoke only the truth.'

'You made new friends and enemies today with a single sentence or two. I hope you're prepared to deal with the consequences.'

'I hope I'm going to see a friend now.'

'Oh, indeed, indeed. But I would watch my back returning to your room.'

He preferred to speak of the coming religious synod as we made our way to Eusebia. He abandoned me for his duties at a point some fifty feet from the heavy draperies that set apart the *Imperatrix* and her household from the rest of the palace.

I had never seen the Empress Eusebia's private quarters. I suppose I expected them to resemble those of the *Augusta* Constantia, the late sister of the Emperor. Constantia had enjoyed a taste in extreme decor—furs, heavy hangings, and suffocating incense, 'lightened' in tone by ivory-handled whips, golden handcuffs, and gilt harnesses for 'recreational' purposes.

So I wasn't prepared for the simple elegance of Eusebia's taste. Being a noble Macedonian, she preferred color and harmony to granite and drama. The stony Mediolanum palace offered little comfort to a woman used to warmer climes. Her murals of ancient Greek scenes featured white classical buildings of pure line overlooking painted views of a pastel sea. Her upright chairs carved of precious ivory and cedar were softened with blue silk cushions. Silver lamps and braziers shimmered in the soft lighting. Her incense was jasmine but not overpowering. She had installed a small fountain that washed the air clean of corruption and intrigue.

Yet I wasn't fooled. The Empress Eusebia had survived. She could be both sympathetic and cool-headed. This afternoon she'd used me to thwart the Lord Chamberlain and *consistorium*'s exploitation of her panicked husband to eliminate the last Constantine. That anyone might view that unbathed bookworm as a contender for imperial power only underscored the depth of fear and ambition in every corner of this court.

Tonight I hoped to appeal to Eusebia's sense of fair play and political survival. If she knew Constantius could not afford to be seen murdering off his last male relative, the same went for his military right arm.

'You're the *agens*, Numidianus, come to collect your reward,' she said, entering the room with a confident swirl of lilac robes. She still wore a circular headdress set with garnets but had removed the veil that had hung down her back. The kohl around her dark eyes had worn off. Her rouge had smudged in the day's heat.

'I'm paid by my *schola*, *Imperatrix*. I have come to report to a *domina* who loves truth and justice.'

'Sweet flattery,' she said. 'So we owe you nothing for the life of Julian, our cousin?'

'Only your gracious ear and a moment of your valuable time.'

'More sweet words. You might almost be an Eastern courtier instead of a glorified mailman.'

'Hardly that,' I said, leaving her to parse my ambiguity.

She sat down and, after spreading her robe in a pool around her feet, settled her two golden hands on the arms of her chair.

'What is your report?'

'Lampadius and Arbetio are arresting Ursicinus as we speak. I am in no doubt that tomorrow the *Imperator* will awake to find his most effective and loyal general is no more than a severed head on his breakfast platter.'

'That's absurd.'

Her eyes flickered at the door connecting her chambers to those of her husband. Had she been a mere housemaid, she would have been dashing already to his warn him in his private bath.

'You are aware of the case of one Gnaeus Domitius Corbulo?'

She frowned.

I went on, 'Murdered in all but name by an envious Nero for his military success in the East?'

One eyebrow moved. Now she got it.

'You could have warned Ursicinus himself.'

'As the sad case of Corbulo reminds us, any general surrounded by praetorian guards would be hard put to resist the *consistorium*'s will tonight. Only the Emperor can act in time, on the advice of someone who has only *his* interests at heart—and no one else's.'

Eusebia knew I was right. She wasn't wasting more time with me. Loss of General Ursicinus meant more power for the *consistorium* pack of devouring hounds. It also meant losing her husband back to defend the Eastern front in person and possibly losing both her husband and the Eastern Empire to the Persian King Shapur.

'You talk nonsense, Numidianus.'

She rose slowly, trained from birth to move with a dancer's grace, but I noticed the fingers of her right hand tapping her thigh. She was measuring off seconds.

'Leave us now. We're sure General Ursicinus is safe in his quarters as our guest. But certainly we've taken note of you, Numidianus, and we appreciate your own love of truth and justice.'

⚜⚜⚜

I would leave in the morning after all. I'm not sure how long I slept, but distant chimes sounded once or twice through my dreams.

—THE WOLVES OF AMBITION—

Someone kicked on my door. This time, I could be sure it was a man, probably armed, on business.

'Who is it?'

The door burst its bolt and flew wide open before I could reach my lamp.

Paulus Catena entered the room, carrying a small torch. He looked around and gave a hoarse laugh. I leapt from my bed and stepped backwards, pulling on my riding trousers. I was more than ready to take him on, but only if I had to. Tall as I am, Catena's bulk outweighed mine by twenty pounds of sadistic brawn. If Mercurius was nicknamed The Count of Dreams, Catena was my own personal Count of Nightmares.

A set of perfectly decent features, taken singly, could turn repulsive when carelessly assembled. His eyes weren't the same size nor evenly placed. One sat closer and lower than the other to his pointed, pinched nose. His mouth was far too small for his black-stubbled jaw. This jumble of swarthy elements was bad enough, but thanks to me, his voice would never be what it once was. He wore a gaudy cotton scarf over the deep scars where my garrote had damaged his voice. The scarf was not printed with red. It was badly bloodstained.

'Take a good look around, because where you're going next will make this dump look like the Baths of Hercules.'

'You can't arrest me, Catena. You can't charge an *agens* for anything done in the course of service.' I reached for my insignia in case the two *domestici* standing in the corridor outside had forgotten their Roman law.

'We're not laying charges—not yet. But you're gone too far now, Numidianus. We're questioning you about slanders you've spread about the Consul, General Arbetio.'

'Where's General Ursicinus?'

'Sound asleep in his quarters. Where else?'

'Didn't the praetorian guards arrest him?'

'No. Which makes you a liar. Certain people want to know the source of such wild accusations. We're going to discuss that in my "office" below the palace.'

'They weren't rumors. Certain policies must have changed while I slept, that's all.'

'That's not what we hear.'

I was putting on my tunic shirt, playing for time, when one of the *domestici* came through the doorway. At Catena's nod, he punched me, hard. My weapons were on the far side of the bed. Knowing I kept a folded swivel knife tucked into the rolled cuff of my boot, Catena kicked both my high-cuffed *calcei* into the corner of the room.

'You won't need those while you're my guest,' he chuckled.

'Gaudentius, HELP!' I bellowed just before they gagged me with a filthy rag.

'*Ducenarius* Gaudentius was called away,' Catena said. 'Keep the bastard quiet,' he added. A second fist slammed into my jaw. I didn't see the third punch coming and lost count after the fourth.

Catena's two thugs lifted me half off my feet and threw my short riding cloak over my head. It must be after midnight, but they wanted to do as much damage as possible to me before daylight brought any reckoning for my injuries.

That is, if I survived at all.

They would have to drag me out of the room. I tried to kick the legs out from under one man but he dodged my foot. I managed to hook my other foot around the doorjamb for a minute before they almost broke my knee.

'Think ahead,' Catena whispered to me, as they struggled to get me out of the room. 'You might have to make some tough choices tonight . . . an eye? Or a couple of fingers? We're old friends. I'll let you choose.'

My vision was blurring. One of them went first into the darkness of the covered passageway lining the building. My feet dragged through a puddle of something foul. The silence was horrific. My head pounded. Their boot steps echoed and multiplied in that narrow passage.

Then I was sure there were more steps. Someone else had stumbled on Catena and his henchmen in the night's shadows.

His stammering query interrupted Catena's kidnapping. 'I'm . . . I'm . . . I'm looking for the *agens* Marcus Gregorianus Numidianus.'

The two henchmen straightened me up and adjusted my hood.

'The fool is sick with drink. We're taking him to the baths for a wash-down, *Domine*,' Catena rasped.

—THE WOLVES OF AMBITION—

My eyesight had clouded over from their beating, but my nose was still fine. I sniffed the acrid imperial goatling, Julian.

'I couldn't find the *Ducenarius* Gaudentius anywhere. I need an *agens* to issue the *diploma* for use of the *Cursus Publicus.*'

'In the morning, Flavius Julianus.'

'No, Notary Catena. Now. I want to leave now.'

'Sure,' I mumbled through the gag. Catena's thug snatched it off my mouth. 'I've got a seal. Let's go to the couriers' gatehouse.'

The Constantine youth wavered. 'He doesn't sound very good.'

This Julian was a fool. He believed Catena's drinking story. The Dacian monster was going to get away with it.

'He'll be sober in the morning,' Catena said.

'No, I want my certificate now. I'm sick of escorts carrying my bags and clearance papers. I'm going to Comum without delay.'

'Have you ever traveled alone before?' Catena blocked Julian's view of me with this barrel chest.

'That's none of your business, Notary Catena. Leave this *agens* with me. I'll make sure he gets back to bed.'

Somehow some blessed Constantine fiber hidden inside this unprepossessing philosophy student held taut against the foul Catena.

Paul 'the Chain' had no choice. He cursed under his breath. If he hadn't decoyed Gaudentius on some false errand, Julian wouldn't have resorted to looking for me.

The two thugs' grip on me loosened. The trio disappeared into the night. I slithered down a stone wall into a heap at the imperial boy's sandals.

My lip was swelling. I wanted him to know the truth as long as I could talk. 'Please, *Domine*, help me back to my quarters first. I'm not drunk. They beat me up.'

'I'm glad to hear it. Drunkenness disgusts me.' He gave me his arm.

I fell back onto the lumpy sack that served as my pillow. My temples thundered with a deafening *barritus* of pain.

Julian's body odor filled the little cell, yet I was grateful he was there. He lit the oil lamp in a matter-of-fact way. I worked open a single eye just in time to see him deposit a heavy bag and take my stool. He looked more beggarly than ever.

'Forgive me for asking you into such a wretched room.'

'Look at my short tunic. My thin sandals. My travel cloak of scratchy hemp. I prefer the ascetic to the decorative,' Julian said. 'Plato teaches us, "Beauty of style and harmony depends on simplicity".'

I allowed myself a bitter laugh. 'Well, simplicity doesn't give this room any harmony or style. I am normally stationed in Roma.'

He frowned. I'd insulted his beloved Plato. 'Can you issue me a *diploma* for the road?'

'It would be my privilege, if you would give me a moment or two more to focus my sight. But you should not travel alone, *Domine*.'

'I've n . . . n . . . never been permitted to travel unescorted anywhere. I'm eager to try.'

'You saved my life just now, Flavius Julianus. It's my *obligation* to advise you not to risk your life without protection.'

'I'm glad I came in time. I hate men like Paulus Catena.'

I felt my way to my basin and rinsed off my face.

He gave a nervous cough. 'I hate them all—the bodyguards, the scribes, Eusebius and his school of chamberlains, swimming and swarming over all our courts like hairless, cold-eyed fish.'

He straightened his round shoulders and looked me in the face. 'I also hate the *agentes*, spying on us all.'

I squinted at him. 'I'm an *agens*.'

'Maybe you're different. You told the truth as you knew it.'

'It was the Empress who requested my summons, wasn't it?'

'Perhaps. Every time someone pours poison into Constantius' ear, she drains it off as quickly as she can. I should hate her, of course.'

'Why?'

'Because she took my sister's place. Didn't you know the Emperor's first wife was my sister?'

'I heard a wife died three years ago. She was your sister?'

'I'm not surprised she is forgotten. She failed to have a child and so,' he waved a hand, 'her name is erased from Time itself. Eusebia must be careful. No one is safe, no matter how stunning.'

—THE WOLVES OF AMBITION—

He scratched his scraggly beard. 'She makes it hard to hate her. She is not only beautiful—she's generous. These are books she gave me for my studies in Athens.' He patted the loaded satchel at his feet. 'Are you a Christian?'

'No, *Domine*. I grew up in a Roman household of senatorial class, a respected house of pagans. The scion of the house is being raised as a pagan now, although his mother was born into a Christian family. Her late predecessor as *matrona* of the house was a Christian convert.'

'The usual modern mix,' Julian said with a sniff. 'Religion by convenience. My cousin is an Arian Christian, so I must be one too.'

'That doesn't sound like the highest measure of devotion.'

'I know what I have to be.' He leaned forward and whispered, 'Our Empress took a chance on you.'

'As you say, I told the truth.'

He fiddled with a wispy chin bristle. 'You could have played for the other side. I wrote letters to Gallus, you know, even if I didn't meet him in Constantinopolis. Surely you *agentes* registered all my correspondence, along with all the other court mail arriving in Antiochia?'

'I suppose so.'

'You could have testified that Gallus and I were a two-man conspiracy, exchanging plots by post. We didn't, but there's evidence that I wrote to him, if you seek it. No one would have doubted you.'

'But I wasn't on postal duty in Antiochia or Constantinopolis. I was on a special mission for Constantius himself. I told the truth. You never came to visit Gallus. Your absence was general knowledge in the court.'

'Still, you saved my life, so don't thank me for tonight. Now we're even, *Agens*.'

I fetched my stamp and took him to the gatehouse. We got a road license made out and authorized. I sketched out his route through Mediolanum and out the Porta Comasina heading north. I listed the state *mansiones* and *mutationes* where he should eat, rest, and or just swap horses.

He took notes on a small tablet, like an unusually hairy schoolboy, but his resolve was grown-up enough. Julian was determined to reach Comum before 'policy' changed yet again in the private wings of the palace.

So was I. It would be foolhardy to linger here after dawn in the vain hope of securing General Ursicinus' drowsy 'thank you' for a good night's sleep.

I was going to head off in the opposite direction, but I had no intention of riding back to Roma alone. After Catena's nocturnal prowl for the source of Arbetio's *corbulo* conspiracy, I realized I had to save that talkative Junius from himself—if I could.

Chapter 4, Two Traitor Fathers

—THE ROAD TO PLACENTIA—

The working day of a Mediolanum courtier started hours before dawn, but we *agentes*, especially Gaudentius, were up and working even earlier. He was now at my door just as I was pulling on my boots. Dressing myself went slowly. Catena's men had left green and purple bruises all over my body.

'Come in. The bolt is broken.'

He stared down at me with undisguised animosity. He had bathed and no doubt rigorously exercised. Both his chin and scalp were freshly shaved.

I felt like Cerberus' day-old leftovers. I shifted my scarred back and my battered face out of the circle of lamp glow.

'Numidianus, did you issue a *Cursus diploma* for the Emperor's cousin?'

'Good morning *Ducenarius*. I'll be out of your way and back on the road for Roma in a few minutes.'

'Answer me. Where is Flavius Julianus?'

'What's the time?'

'The beginning of the fourth watch.'

'Then I'd say he might have reached the first *mansio* to Comum by now. Why?'

'Gods' entrails.' Gaudentius fell back on the doorframe and shook his head.

'Have I done something else wrong? He demanded his paperwork on the spot. Was I to deny him? After all, he is a Constantine, of sorts.'

'Overnight, the Emperor reviewed the testimony from the Gallus hearings of last week. He is convinced there is more disloyalty to be dug up. He wants to recall Julian for a private "audience." He is not convinced the young man loves him enough.'

'Why should he love the Emperor at all? Constantius murdered his entire family. The young man was certainly keen to return to his Plato. Can you blame him?'

Gaudentius glanced over his shoulder and shook his head. 'I don't understand it. Why did Lampadius send me on a dog's chase after a chewed out bone last night? So that Julian could slip away? That makes no sense. I would have issued him a *Cursus* license.'

I tested the bruising to my ribs before I stood up.

'Your meaningless errand had nothing to do with Julian. The idea was that you wouldn't be anywhere within earshot of my screams for help. Catena and two of his friends from the lower floors came to "question me" about slurs I cast on Lampadius and Arbetio's plans for General Ursicinus.'

I filled Gaudentius in on my urgent meeting with the Empress facilitated by the deputy *Magister Officiorum*.

'Who was the source for this *corbulo* nonsense?'

'My informant insists on remaining anonymous. Luckily for Ursicinus this man knows his ancient history.'

Gaudentius' lack of education was a sore spot.

'If you can't name your source, what proves there was any threat to Ursicinus?'

'Only my injuries. Obviously the information that people were laying the ground for Ursicinus' "suicide" like the great Corbulo's brought Paulus Catena down on my head within hours.'

Gaudentius rubbed his shining chin as he reflected on my story. He was angry I'd passed over his authority, but he knew better than to pry too much. My source might be a senior official of great learning and influence, perhaps even a *consistorianus*. Even if I hadn't gone through the normal channels, at least General Ursicinus was breakfasting right now in the safe company of his son Potentius and trusted tribunes.

'The Mediolanum Court is your assignment, Gaudentius. Feel free to add all my fresh insubordination to your report,' I said. 'I didn't set out to circumvent your approval but if it pleases you, when General Ursicinus is briefed on last night's events, tell him he owes our *schola*'s protection to your quick actions rather than mine.'

—THE WOLVES OF AMBITION—

'Let me see your face.'

My lamp oil had burned out. Gaudentius threw the door wider to let in a streak of gray dawn. When he saw my swollen, split lips and bruised temples, he cursed under his breath and believed me at last.

'You can't travel in that condition.'

'Let me catch the first courier shift of the morning heading south so I won't travel alone. I'll even hand deliver your recommendation for my demotion straight to Apodemius myself.'

Gaudentius took another look at me and shrugged, 'I'll tell Florentius to forget my report. Just return to headquarters and leave this court's affairs to me.'

The *ducenarius* was at the top of the *schola*'s pay scale for his thoroughness, not his wits. He seemed placated for the moment, but I still hastened my departure plans as quickly as my broken body permitted. If I had mentioned the Frankish boy, Gaudentius might have started making dangerous connections. Later in the day, he was sure to be infuriated all over again, rightly suspecting that the Emperor's Frankish hostage had escaped detention in Mediolanum under my wings all the way to Roma.

As soon as Gaudentius left for his usual business in the main palace building, I headed straight to a side door of the imperial residential wing and sent a slave girl scurrying off with a message for Junius Silvanus to meet me in the anonymity of the busy imperial wagon yard. We would be free to talk there, hidden among gilt harnesses, embossed leather saddles, and parade vehicles of all descriptions.

Now that I knew Junius' identity, I recognized the Frankish sire hidden within those boyish lines. Yes, who would not recognize Commander Silvanus' confident strides in those spindly legs? Or the winning cast of the veteran's humorous glance in the boy's long-lashed reactions to my guidance? Perhaps there was also a trace of his courageous grandfather, the famous Frankish barbarian-turned-confederate, Bonitus.

A Salian Frank of Laetic origin, Bonitus was the first ever Frank to be made *magister militum*, in 324. He fought beside the great Constantine against his rival Licinius.

Even then, the Silvanus clan knew how to side with winners. Junius' secret 'deal' to a strange *agens* twice his age showed this same canny pragmatism.

'What happened to you, *Agens*?'

'A visit from Paul the Chain. It seems that Lampadius and Arbetio didn't like me spreading lies about them.'

'It was *not* a lie! Lampadius said *corbulo*. I heard him!'

'Calm down. I believe you. Powerful people are searching the palace for the eavesdropper with such big ears.'

That unnerved the boy for a moment. 'Did it work?'

'Yes, it worked. The dogs were called off. Ursicinus slept soundly. But he doesn't know why.'

'But you must inform him! Warn him they'll try again! I promised you the credit for saving him!'

'*Debitum in praesenti, solvendum in futuro*,' I quipped—*a present debt to be collected down the road.*

'You're not taking the credit? So you and I don't have a deal?'

'We can still do business, on one condition. You leave the city with me now, without telling anyone where you're going or with whom—,' I grabbed the collar of his expensive green tunic and felt his stringy neck muscle stiffen, '—not even your dear *mater*. I'm not safe here until those councilors calm down and neither are you.'

His worried face brightened up with confused surprise. The obedient child-hostage in him lost within seconds to the adolescent man-to-be.

'Leave the city?' Where are we going?'

'To the Castra Peregrina on the Caelian Hill. You have to repeat your story there.'

'I knew you were going to help me. Roxana promised I could trust you.'

'You can trust me, but I can't help you. I'm taking you to someone who might know what to do. And we need to get to him as fast as possible.'

I did not trust the palace grooms not to report our use of imperial horses. Twenty minutes later we two exited Mediolanum on post horses from the *agentes*' station at the Porta Romana. At full gallop, we followed the Via Porticata southeasterly through suburbs dotted with rich villas and lush gardens.

—THE WOLVES OF AMBITION—

When we passed the Basilica Apostolorum unimpeded, I breathed free. We'd eluded pursuit. Junius was right. For eight peaceful years, the boy had been such a good-natured fixture around the palace, no one in authority would suspect him of absconding for at least another day. Only his mother might realize within hours, but she'd be too terrified to confess his absence until he was long gone.

I was also relieved to notice that Junius was a decent horseman, because we would be traveling *agens*-speed by state-horse relay. His pampered bottom was bound to be raw by the time we reached the *mansio* outside Placentia.

If he didn't whine or fall by the wayside before nightfall, I'd permit him send a message back to his mother via a courier heading northwest.

After all, I might be the illegitimate son of Commander Atticus Manlius Gregorius, but I wasn't a heartless bastard.

҈҈҈

It was just as well that we set off as early as we could, for our progress was soon slowed and sometimes even halted, by clusters of travelers moving in high state toward Mediolanum. We trotted past expensively lacquered carriages full of bishops and their staff. Priests on horseback or whole clerical parties on foot stopped us to ask for directions to inns or public fountains en route.

I should have anticipated these delays. On our walk to my interview with the Empress the previous night, Florentius had talked to me of the synod to be held in Constantius' architectural showpiece, the Basilica Maior, ordered by Emperor Constans in 345 and only finished by his brother five years ago.

As we two hurried to Eusebia's suite, minions from other departments of the palace pestered Florentius for decisions about accommodation, wines, menus, or weird logistical complaints.

Constantius' reign had reached a turning point. The Christian Church was growing ever more powerful across the Empire and the Emperor wanted the imminent debate to be his final confrontation with sanctimonious recalcitrants who insisted that the theologian Arius was wrong about the nature of Christ.

Bishop Liberius in Roma—the most powerful Christian after the Emperor himself, had said 'no' to Arianism. In his corner, he had the support of the stubborn Bishop Athanasius of the See of Alexandria—who also insisted that Christ was of the same substance as God and not merely a son whose birth followed.

Our Arian emperor had failed to persuade all the Christian bishops from Gallia and the East at his council in Arelate two years before. Bishop Athanasius remained influential, if under a political cloud. Bishop Liberius had demanded a new hearing and Constantius would use it to squash these troublesome heretics for good. He would condemn all dissenting non-Arians and see them excommunicated from the Christian sacraments.

Florentius felt harried by all of this, to say the least.

'The Lord Chamberlain Eusebius even had me summon that troublemaking Bishop of Roma here for a private consultation last week in a dress rehearsal for the coming debate.'

'Did Liberius buckle?'

'Liberius came, but refused to bend. And now he has declined to attend the Council itself.'

'He returned to Roma to rally his priests and deacons?'

'Constantius will never give up. He sent the eunuch Eusebius carrying five hundred *solidi* to Liberius but the bishop refused the bribe. Eusebia sent it back and Liberius told her to give it to Constantius' soldiers.' Florentius stopped for a moment and whispered, 'The Emperor threatens to *exile* Bishop Liberius.'

These hordes of bishops trundling along the *Cursus Publicus* from all parts of the Empire were gearing up for the argument. Perhaps they obstructed our path, but I knew these men held powerful constituencies in their hands, not least the renowned Goth missionary Ulfilas, who had translated the Bible from Latin to Gothic for his converts. He was coming to Mediolanum all the way from Moesia Inferior by an eastern route.

Some powerful prelates were already in Constantius' corner, including Valens—that bishop who had prayed at the Emperor's side in a chapel, while less than a mile away, fifty-four thousand Romans had slaughtered each other in the fields of Mursa.

But not a few Catholic dogmatists openly called Constantius II 'the Anti-Christ.'

—THE WOLVES OF AMBITION—

Lucifer of Caligari, Eusebius of Vercelli, as well as Bishop Liberius remained diehard supporters of the Egyptian prelate's Nicene Creed.

'What difference does it make whether this Christ is the one true God or the Son of God or merely god-like?' I had asked Florentius with a shrug.

The harried bureaucrat had given me a knowing smile as we crossed the final public dining room leading to the imperial wing.

'To the bishops, it means the future of their souls. To our sovereign, it is a challenge to his imperial authority. While the Emperor and his commanders are defending distant borders, these churchmen grow stronger and stronger. They preach poverty, but grow rich from donations of estates and the legacies of pious widows or contrite politicians. They mingle slaves, freedmen, and citizens all together in the basilicas, saying that all souls are equal, but in so doing, they rend the fabric of our social order into confusion and discontent.'

'Are you a Christian, Florentius?'

'I attend all Christian ceremonies in the company of the imperial family,' he said, 'with the entire *consistoriani*.'

'Surely not including world's most worldly eunuch?'

'Even Eusebius. Especially Eusebius.'

※※※

Yes, of course, I thought this morning as I threaded my horse's path ahead of Junius between dozens of jouncing carriages overflowing with priests.

Of course the greedy Eusebius had realized the political possibilities of the new faith. The Christian Church could provide that spidery man with a vast new source of informants, property, and political resources to strengthen his sticky web. The Church of the humble carpenter had become a powerful community that our *Magister Agentium* Apodemius had neglected, though the good old man was tireless at gathering information and keeping alliances to strengthen the Empire's cohesion.

I chuckled to imagine the coming assembly. Eusebius would be in his element tending to their every comfort as they argued over Greek etymology in the Baths of Hercules, their black robes discarded for the towels of the massage hall and glistening swimming pool. At least old Bishop Liberius from Roma had kept his theological integrity intact.

It was one of the few times I felt a glint of admiration for any man of the new state cult. Once in North Africa I'd been jailed with a truly holy saint. Perhaps given time, he would have converted me by his selfless Christian example. But that man was long dead, tossed over a cliff to his death on the rocks below because he was too generous for his own good.

The first day's ride had started fine, but by noon thick rain clouds scudded overhead. My short *sagum* and the hide covering my *thoracomacus* underneath had been waterproofed with tallow. But by midafternoon, Junius' elegant court cloak had soaked up buckets of water. That sodden tent of a garment kept slipping off his narrow shoulders. By nightfall, mud spatters had ruined the intricate silver stag embroidery around hem and hood. His white leg bindings slopped around his ankles.

I was grateful he didn't complain. He was a likeable boy. But then again, I'd found his father charming—at first.

We rested for the night at the usual *mansio*. I lend him some salve from my medical box. Adding the difficulties of riding through such heavy traffic to his painful saddle sores and my own bruised condition, I resigned myself to the reality of babysitting a Frankish noble boy. What was nothing more than a three-day ride for a hardy *agens* courier promised to stretch out to five painful and miserable days.

And would the boy's tale of conspiracy be worth the crime of helping him escape?

☥☥☥

I may have overestimated Julian's endurance but not his humor. We'd had to overnight twice. But he told me much about his years in court that I filed away for good purpose later. The boy was more than observant—he sifted out important details from the hundreds of things that went on every day.

He would have made a good *agens* trainee, were his political status not so sensitive.

After I'd registered my presence in Roma according to laws governing all *agentes in rebus*, I led Junius through the boisterous crowd overflowing the Tavern of the Seven Sages. At this hour, the familiar drinking hole burst at the seams with last-minute customers slipping through the Porta Aurelia before the great city gates closed to foot traffic for the night. Soon only commercial wagons and other heavy vehicles could claim the city streets.

The roasting ovens bellowed their smoke into the fug of unwashed travelers and overused whores. Through the fumes, one of the *taberna*'s heartiest girls, Delicia, spotted our bedraggled arrival.

'Verus, he's here! Marcus Numidianus is here!' she shouted over a dozen customers' heads.

The noise was deafening. The Manlius townhouse's aged *dispensator* didn't hear her. By the time Junius and I had elbowed our way into a far corner of the tavern, we found a much-reduced Verus crumpled over an empty beaker of wine. He looked like he'd kept a vigil for me there for days. His rheumy eyes searched through the gloom of the lamplight until we appeared a foot away, squeezing ourselves between two hefty *circitores* off inspection duty.

I leaned over the battered wooden table and shouted over the hubbub, 'How fat is the bar tab this time?' He lifted up his creaking bones and thudded with relief into my embrace.

'Junius, tell the scowling barman over there that we need some pickled turnips and smoked cheese to fill up this drunkard's stomach,' I joked. 'And a fresh pitcher of *conditum*, honeyed and peppered.' I handed the boy some coins.

Verus watched Junius limp away through the throng to place our orders with a man in a greasy apron standing behind an L-shaped granite counter.

'Who's the little prince?' Verus asked. 'He's wearing enough silvery buckle and pin to pay for a week's worth of that menu board.'

'Just a traveling companion who didn't know the road, that's all.'

'What happened to your face?'

'The questioning turned a little rough up there. I'm lucky to come home with both eyes and all my fingers.'

'The gods help us. Didn't you tell them what you was supposed to?'

'That's the problem. My *ducenarius* didn't want me to say anything. Instead, I told the truth. How's *our* little prince?' I asked. 'And how's your mistress?'

Weeks before, I'd hugged farewell to the seven-year-old heir of the Manlius line playing in the atrium. I carefully explained my departure to his young, widowed mother—ever silent and melancholy—presiding over her vast and lonely bedchamber.

'Same, same,' Verus said. 'Her wounds have healed and her ankles don't give out much. But her mind, Marcus, her mind. She lays the first log on the morning fire, as duty dictates, but then she just sits or mends for the rest of the day. Only, she went for a walk down the market the other day with a lady friend. Shopping for some new dresses, the friend said.'

'But that's good news! She's starting to go back into society.'

The civil war that had cost Kahina so much had ended three years ago. The interior of Gallia still suffered devastation, but Junius' father was re-stabilizing Roman control and pushing barbarian raiders by the thousands back across the Rhenus. At home, Roman citizens had started to forget 'Emperor' Magnentius and the political destruction he and his rebels left in their wake. All around the Manlius townhouse on the Esquiline Hill, shattered lives were returning to normal. The dead were honored, but the ordinary pleasures of life had returned.

Only I couldn't forget the toll of the civil war, because in Kahina's docile, vacant smile, I lived with the consequences of her years as a prisoner-of-war every day.

The young Numidian widow of the aristocrat Commander Gregorius, *magister militum* to the Usurper Tyrant, had not been lucky. Her return home from exile had taken years to bring about. She'd escaped a long and humiliating enslavement, but only with her wits impaired, her body flayed and scarred, and her spirit utterly broken.

Verus and I were desperate to see Kahina revive and take an interest in life around her. I'd long ago abandoned my fantasies of ever being more to her now than a loving caretaker. Her recovery was so slow, I feared that Leo's mother would remain forever a strange, inexpressive shadow of the passionate, lively, beautiful North African girl I had secretly loved. Even carrying our child, she had obeyed me and married the Commander to honor her family's promise of betrothal and give Leo a brilliant future rather than a wretched one.

I now owed both child and mother my eternal loyalty and protection.

It was a lonely existence for me, lightened a bit by Verus' understanding of the family's hallowed history in Roman society. We had not only the noble Manlius bloodline to protect but also a rich estate in young Leo's name. The late Senator's will named me as the boy's *tutor legitimus*, the legal custodian of his future. It was scant compensation for never being able to declare myself his true father but it kept me in the family fold as more than a freedman.

'What did she buy? Something beautiful for her hair or a new robe? Some scented oils?'

'Nope. They comes back hours too early with empty shopping sacks. Lady Kahina lays down on her couch and sends that poor lady friend and her slave off without so much as an anchovy pastry for her trouble.'

Junius returned with our food. Verus ate greedily. Despite the Manlius wealth, I guessed that his mistress was neglecting her supervision of the kitchens and that the cook was profiting a little on the side.

'And Leo? His studies?'

'He needs a steadier hand when it comes to his book-learning,' Verus said. 'Nobody's asking old Verus, but I'd say the boy needs a private teacher.'

'What's wrong with his school? It costs enough!'

'He ain't been to school now for more than two weeks, not since you rode north,' Verus said.

'Why?'

'The same old story, some bullies calling him "Traitor Boy," and "Rebel Scum." I wouldn't want to sit in an open classroom with every Janus and Julius in the street hearing those slanders as they strolled by, would you? I don't blame Leo if he don't want to go back just to be insulted.'

'How old is he?' Junius asked. He'd just stopped himself from finishing all the snacks Delicia lay before us.

'Seven and bright.' I gave Junius another coin and sent him off to fetch roast ham, fish balls, and marinated eggplant.

'You're right, Verus. We need to get someone in the house to monitor his progress and keep him at his homework. I thought by now his mother would be . . .'

Verus wrinkled up his nearly toothless mouth. 'She never was much for the books, you know that, Marcus. Although the Senator encouraged her read to him in the old days. She was making good progress 'til he was murdered.'

'As soon as I finish my business at the Castra, I'll come home for a few days and we'll get someone lined up. In the meantime, ask the families around the Hill for a few names. Get some back-alley feedback on which ones are honest and smart and not just lazy rich boys who can't hold down a real job.'

'Oh, thank you, Marcus, We knew you'd see it that way,' Verus said. He filled our cups from the steaming pitcher and polished off his drink just as Junius settled his blisters back down with a groan to get started on the eggplant.

⚜⚜⚜

'Why are we stopping in here?'

'I forgot you're a Christian.'

'Of course I am.'

I turned my back on Junius and resumed my chores. 'Then you wouldn't understand.'

I'd bought incense from a stall on our climb up the Caelian Hill toward the headquarters of the *agentes in rebus*.

We'd identified ourselves at the gates of the three-century-old collection of low buildings that had once been the barracks for Roman *peregrini*, provincial soldiers called to Roma for special duty. In those days the Castra housed the *frumentarii*, the supply network-turned-intelligence service that became so corrupt, the Emperor Diocletian had no choice but to disband them.

Now it was the *agentes in rebus* who kept the state roads regulated, the accounts clean, and the intelligence flying from all points of our the Empire into a small, cluttered study occupied by one arthritic graying old man.

But before leading Junius across the parade ground for the main building, I had opened the heavy creaking oak doors of the

—THE WOLVES OF AMBITION—

Temple of Jupiter Redux, the Castra's pagan shrine, to give thanks for a safe return.

Junius hung back in the doorway and muttered, 'Looks like a tomb.'

I lit an oil lamp and stood for a moment of prayer in honor of many noble men—not only *agentes*, but also simple soldiers and brave commanders who'd died.

I could tell no one had visited for months. He watched me polish the bronze and stone plagues embedded in the walls. I lit my incense in a brazier to dry out the humid air and wiped down the neglected stone altar. Hundreds of years ago, this temple had stood in the bright sun and enjoyed constant use and offerings from grateful battle-weary men. Now a modern building cramped the temple's entranceway and blocked out the sunlight.

'What are you thinking?' Junius asked, impatient to warm his feet in the main building.

'I'm thinking of Commander Atticus Manlius Gregorius who died in the Battle of Mursa. He was my father, unacknowledged under the law, but known to me.'

'I never heard of him. I suppose he fought on the wrong side,' the youth said.

'So did your father, Commander Silvanus.'

'He fought for Constantius, our Emperor! And they won!' He pounded his fist on a basin of bloodstained marble.

'Your father was the *magister equitum* serving Magnentius until the morning of the final battle. The Western Army faced the Eastern Army in a stalemate, their troop numbers equal. Constantius knew it. He was offering Magnentius a political compromise, a share of power. Constantius didn't dare fight, not until your father's desertion brought him critical cavalry forces stolen from Magnentius' camp.

'My father wanted to save his troops from slaughter.'

'Is that what he says? If your father's betrayal hadn't tipped the scales, there would have been no battle at all. Over fifty thousand valiant imperial soldiers would be alive today.'

'How dare—?'

I slapped him across his downy face.

'Don't feed me your father's lies, brat. *I was there.*'

The boy set his two muddied boots apart, ready to fight me. We both knew he would lose.

'Your Commander Gregorius was a traitor to the Constantine throne.'

'Silvanus also swore his allegiance to the Emperor Magnentius. He turned traitor to his colleagues in uniform and to all the men who lost their lives in Mursa that night. He saved no one but himself. Tell me which traitor was worse.'

Junius' knobby adolescent throat bobbed up and down. His right hand slipped down to grip his jeweled sword, the undented showpiece of a court hostage. I doubted the blade was even sharpened, but it was a fine piece of workmanship. It might have been a gift from his northern clansmen or from one of the Franco-Roman officers serving Constantius in Mediolanum.

But here in a silent and decrepit temple, Junius stood unprotected and friendless. I'd just named his father as my father's murderer.

And I'd just taught him the dangers of trusting anyone in Roma, especially when trapped within the walls of the most powerful secret service in history.

'Are you saying you're my enemy, Numidianus? You lured me all the way down here to get me away from my Frankish guardians in Mediolanum? To revenge my father's decision in Mursa?'

'No, I dragged you down here out of simple professional duty—because your father holds the lower stretch of the Rhenus secure against the barbarians Franks just across the river. Because he's working hard to stabilize the rest of Gallia against the Alemanni. And because you claim to have information my chief needs.'

I grabbed him by the neck of his soggy cloak. 'You'd better deliver.'

'Won't *you* help me?'

'I've helped you enough. I'm taking you to someone too wise to hold a grudge. Make sure you don't waste his time—or I promise, you'll regret it.'

Chapter 5, Bedroom Gossip

—HEADQUARTERS, THE CASTRA PEREGRINA—

Junius and I had to wait for our meeting until well after dusk, when Apodemius started his working day. I used the time to wash, shave, and change into a clean tunic shirt and trousers. I ordered Junius to submit his wispy chin to the Castra's barber as well. To my amusement, he returned with the faintest traces of a Frankish moustache outlined on his upper lip.

A laundry slave swabbed the mud off his expensive green garments. The silver hem almost shone again and the twin *fibulae*, brooches of garnets pinning the cloak to his shoulders, gleamed like new.

I led him into the main building, climbing the stairs ahead of him to the *Magister Agentium*'s outer office. We watched Apodemius' deaf masseur pack up his liniments and towels. A balding secretary kept his eyes on his deskwork, registering the day's reports according to urgency and region. He presided over a mess of vellum, scrap papyrus, and gods-only-know what else from all corners of the Empire.

We had another five minutes to go when my Frankish recruit, Meroveus, entered the room.

'Well met, old friend,' I stood up to some hearty backslapping. 'How's the training been going? Is your department chosen yet?'

'Not yet, but I am happy, Numidianus. I owe you everything—for bringing me from Antiochia, for the recommendation to Apodemius and for—'

He broke off. He was going to say, 'An entirely new life,' but we both knew that there were some things a new job could never restore. He'd been captured and sold into slavery along the northeastern border, lost his testicles to a slave driver's expert knife, and been transferred to the East. I'd discovered him serving as a sullen doorman to the late Caesar's wife, the vicious sister of the Emperor.

The *Augusta* Constantia's sudden death had been Meroveus' salvation from servitude and his return to life as a free citizen—but never again as a whole man.

The inner door opened and Apodemius' secretary gave us a curt nod to enter the cluttered inner sanctum of Roman espionage.

'*Magister*, it is my duty to introduce you to—'

'Junius Silvanus, how do you do? You resemble your grandfather but I see a touch of your grandmother, Evochildis, as well. She was a formidable beauty in her day.'

'She's still well, *Magister* Apodemius.'

Apodemius had cut me off. No doubt Gaudentius had got speedy word to Roma of Junius' disappearance by horse relay while I was stuck watching the boy bandage his butt between Placentia and Pisae.

'*Magister* Apodemius, I've heard many things about you.'

'Oh, I'm unpopular with everyone who fears the truth. So I can imagine what you learn of me from the court of Constantius,' the old man said. He gestured us to two stools opposite his long desk.

Junius was smart enough not to respond.

The old man lowered his pained hip joints into the creaking leather chair behind his long desk. A cage of white mice scurried and squeaked behind him, finishing off their crumbled lentil crackers. A *latrunculi* game board stood on a side table and a long couch under the window, springing its stuffing, stood waiting for the massage sessions that kept the old man mobile.

Most important, a sprawling illustration of the Empire framed over cork hung on the wall behind the untidy white hair that floated over Apodemius' skull. Hundreds of pins, flags, and bits of painted paper—third quality *taeneotic*—studded the hand-drawn portrait of the political world on which we spied.

'Brief me, Numidianus.'

'It's for Junius Silvanus to explain,' I said. 'I'm only his escort.'

—THE WOLVES OF AMBITION—

'Drink up, boy.' Apodemius pointed to a beaker of watered wine. 'You look parched by your journey.'

'No, thank you, *Magister*.'

Apodemius waited for me to begin.

'I had my hands more than full in Mediolanum, thanks to our friend here, *Magister*. Junius Silvanus warned me of a move to arrest General Ursicinus the night I was due to leave. The Empress' intervention restored the Emperor to his senses and thwarted Prefect Lampadius and Consul Arbetio in their tracks. They planned on using the Corbulo precedent as an excuse.'

'Judging from your green and purple eyelid, you paid some dues for that. Was it Catena or Eusebius?'

'Catena.'

I filled a large bronze cup from the beaker for myself.

'The Lord Chamberlain Eusebius seems to have gone all religious on us for the moment.'

'So we hear. Religion is where the best property holdings are to be found and property is his weakness, as we well know.'

'But Eusebius didn't care for my testimony that Flavius Claudius Julianus wasn't in cahoots with his cousin Caesar Gallus.'

'I see. What was your impression of this Julianus?'

Apodemius was playing that trick of his—idly feeding flatbread crumbs to his pet mice as if he weren't hooked on every scrap of information I fed him.

'He's gauche and clumsy-looking but might be playing that hard to disarm his enemies. The *consistoriani* would like to see him marginalized for good. He knows it and plays dumb. He practices Christianity like his cousin. In fact, he was a lector in the Church. But he's on his way to Athens now to study theurgy.'

'What's theurgy?' Junius piped up.

'The magical and ritualistic side of paganism, uniting with the gods, calling on them to act,' I said.

'One can't see how theurgy can be so threatening, but one never knows.' Apodemius said. He turned to Junius. 'Now it's your turn. Follow Numidianus' example. Give me a concise summary. Don't worry about the details for now.'

'My father's life is in danger from a conspiracy, *Magister*. He has a... friend who said Marcus Numidianus could help me—

but to trust no one else. My mother forbade me to write Numidianus. When I heard that he was summoned to testify in Mediolanum, I knew it was God's will. I sought him out right away.'

'You look disappointed, Junius.'

'Instead he just brought me here. Who knows what might happen at court while I'm gone?'

'What is this conspiracy?'

Junius pulled his stool forward. 'Some weeks ago, an *actuarius* named Dynamius asked my father for letters of recommendation to high officials in Mediolanum. My father doesn't do such things lightly, but he owed this man a favor or two. He wrote me that I could expect to hear Dynamius refer to such references. This is his letter.'

Junius pulled out a folded piece of second-quality military paper and gave it to me to hand to Apodemius. We read the father's affectionate message describing Dynamius' request among other assorted fatherly updates of Silvanus' campaign in the north.

'Dynamius turned up in Mediolanum?'

'Yes, but he has not presented these references to any of my father's friends.'

'He found employment elsewhere?'

'Not at all. He lingers around the court.'

'There is more. Why are you worried, son?'

'Because I saw those letters of reference, or rather I saw a packet of letters, on the desk of the Prefect for Gallia, Lampadius. I saw my father's green wax seal, but it doesn't make sense. I don't believe my father addressed any reference letter to Prefect Lampadius. Lampadius hates my father's success in Gallia. He would do no favors for the Silvanus family.'

'That snake Lampadius showed you the letters?'

'No, of course not, *Magister*. Malarichus, the Frankish commander of the *Gentiles*, sometimes takes me on his rounds through the palace.'

The *Gentiles* were one of the divisions of the three thousand five hundred court troops, or *Scholae Palatinae,* ranked *protectores, domestici, gentiles, scutarii* and *armaturae*. Malarichus would have to be tough to manage his contingent: *gentiles* included hardened cavalrymen recruited from Scythians, Goths, Franks, and other *Germani*.

'Malarichus stopped into Lampadius' office to ask about the role of his guards during the coming synod. Lampadius got angry at the interruption. While he told Malarichus to bother Florentius Nigrinianus instead, I snuck a peek at the pile of letters the prefect shoved out of sight in such a suspicious manner.'

I interjected: 'Junius has been a hostage in that court for so many years, he's convinced that nobody notices him or what he does.'

'For the sake of his wellbeing, let's hope the boy is right. In other words, Junius, you suspect Lampadius of stealing your father's letters from Dynamius?'

'Why would he do that? Dynamius could just ask Silvanus for replacements,' I said.

'I know *something* wrong is happening, but I don't know what,' Junius protested.

'But you can't be sure, son. After all, the letters haven't surfaced yet to any purpose, not even Dynamius' advancement.'

Apodemius' placid reaction provoked the hotheaded youngster.

'I know more, *Magister*. Your *Ducenarius* Gaudentius doesn't tell you half of what you should hear. Arbetio and Lampadius not only tried to have Ursicinus arrested the other night, but they also want my father out of the way, permanently.'

'Your father is holding the weakest stretch of the Western Empire's border. He is an important man. And to be an important man is to be a powerful man and to be a powerful man—' Apodemius hesitated.

'Makes him dangerous?' Our young Junius wasn't slow. 'If the Empire loses its two strongest military heroes, Consul Arbetio controls both the civil service and the army. Arbetio and his creepy *consistorium* will rule the Empire behind Constantius' back.'

Apodemius scratched his scalp through his fluffy hair. 'My, my, Numidianus, I was impressed with your recruitment of the loyal Meroveus, but now you seem to have unearthed the Frankish people's first Olympian-grade political strategist.'

Junius leapt off his stool and wrapped his cloak around himself like Julius Caesar's statue. 'I may be young, but I'm not here to be ridiculed, even by you. I overheard the Lord Chamberlain say your *schola* is a spent force.'

'Oh, sit down.' Apodemius said.

He pulled one of his swollen ankles up to rest on the edge of his worn-out seat cushion and rubbed a foul-smelling paste on the pained joint. After a few minutes of tense silence broken only by Junius' sneezes, the old man put his slipper back on and riffled through notes on his desk.

'The leading Franks in court are your patron Malarichus, Commander of the *Gentiles*, and the *dux* Mallobaudes who served Constantius as *tribunus armaturarum* in Gallia. Why haven't you asked either man for help?'

'I trust no one in that court, except my mother. She's terrified of retribution against the family if I stir up any trouble. We Franks are as ambitious and competitive as anyone else.'

'True. Even our name for you, *Franci*, comes from your own word for fierce and free. Your mother's a prudent woman. So who *exactly* is this friend who advised you to trust Numidianus?'

Junius Silvanus fiddled with a riding blister on his palm. 'A woman.'

'A woman?'

'Named Roxana.'

Apodemius gave me a knowing smile. 'Your father's mistress.'

'Yes. She and I correspond.' He tossed us an anxious glance. 'My mother doesn't know.'

'Roxana corresponds with us, too.'

Apodemius lifted himself out of his chair and turned to face his great drawing of the Empire.

'There may be things even you can't hear from behind pillars, Junius. Four years ago, Emperor Constantius invited hordes of Alemanni tribes across the Rhenus River to attack his challenger Magnentius from the rear. It was a pincer movement that helped to defeat the Usurper. As part of a dirty deal, the Emperor gave these new arrivals a treaty for good land on the left bank of the Rhenus. He regrets it now—regrets it bitterly. Alemanni barbarians are burning and pillaging peaceful Gallo-Roman communities from here,' Apodemius laid his hand east of Treverorum, 'all the way down to their normal sanctuaries in the mountains to the south, here. Longstanding estates are ravaged. Cities are pillaged. Despite your father's gains, much of Gallia remains a land in chaos.'

'Everyone in Mediolanum praises my father's success up there.'

'Your father found Agrippina in ruins. He cleared out the Alemanni looters and rapists. He restored the city to civilized Roman control.'

'Roxana writes me that Agrippina is now a thriving, secure city.'

'She gives us slightly more detail.'

Apodemius stood and fingered the colored pins around the northern German capital marking the forces under Silvanus's command, including the ferocious twin *auxilia palatina*, the Cornuti and the Bracchiati.

'Silvanus led a small force of only eight thousand soldiers through territory occupied by thousands upon thousands of savage Alemanni. Your father is an experienced soldier but he and all his men were lucky not to have been outnumbered and slaughtered before they re-established control within Agrippina's walls. He pushed back the bagaudae bandits flaring through here, in central and northern Gaul. More controversially, he drove the *Germani* tribesmen back across the Rhenus by bribing them with the taxes he collected from the Gallo-Romans.'

Apodemius ran his knobby fingers through the middle of Gallia and up the line of Rhenus river garrisons to Colonia Agrippina sitting on the left bank near the delta on the German Sea.

'Now, tell me, Junius, whose idea was it to send your father to such unsung feats of heroism as the *Magister Militum per Gallias*?'

'Constantius, of course.' Junius said with a confident nod. 'My father knows the Frankish federate leaders in the north. They hold him in high regard, not only as a military commander but also as the noble son of Bonitus. My father departed Mediolanum saying it was a privilege to serve the Emperor's orders—'

'Wrong. Wrong. Wrong. It was the Emperor's order but it was Consul *Arbetio's* idea,' Apodemius said. 'Arbetio counted on seeing your father take a barbarian's axe between the eyes long before tonight.'

Droplets of nervous sweat breaking out on Junius' unlined brow caught the light of an oil lamp on Apodemius' desk.

'Now we know the Prefect for Gallia Lampadius fears the rise of Franco-Roman talent up north, personified by your father. But do you know why *Arbetio* especially wants your father killed by Alemanni?'

'I told you, he wants Ursicinus out of the way, too!'

Apodemius sighed and slumped back down into his chair with a groan. 'We must forgive a virgin's naiveté, Numidianus. No, Junius. Because your friend, the lovely Roxana, rejected Arbetio's bed. She shunned his silken sheets and perfumed bathroom to join your father in the frozen wilds of the lower Rhenus valley.'

'Arbetio and *Roxana*?'

'A match not favored by the gods or . . . let's just say, not by Roxana. Wouldn't you say that's quite a snub for the hero of Lake Brigantia, fresh from letting his tribunes die fighting the Alemanni so he and the Emperor could romp home with all the credit?'

I was as stunned as the hostage boy although, unlike Junius, I knew Roxana's addictive charms from personal experience.

'If you want to make a habit of listening at keyholes, Junius, start with the bedrooms,' Apodemius smiled. 'Now, the question is, what can we do? You must retrieve those letters back from Lampadius and destroy them. I agree this affairs smells of rancid fish sauce.'

'Can't you warn the Emperor that these men aren't trustworthy?' Junius asked.

'The court is full of our *schola*'s enemies. Both Lampadius and Mattyocopus were in the council chamber the day Numidianus and I reported the execution of the Caesar Gallus. All the councilors heard the Emperor say he had rescinded that death order. They witnessed our dismay and his dissembling. They heard that his message had not reached us in time. *If the Consistoriani wish,* they could at any time allege we'd ignored

—THE WOLVES OF AMBITION—

Constantius' change of heart for our own purposes. To this day, we do not know if the Lord Chamberlain Eusebius, to whom Constantius claims he addressed his imperial pardon, held back that message in order to trap us into acting the assassins.'

'Did the Emperor send such a message?'

'We will never know, son. But we operate with one hand tied behind our back.'

'So the court rumors are true. Your *schola* is powerless.'

'I didn't say that, but in short, those councilors have witnessed our weakest moment. We need more evidence against them or we may fall into another, deeper trap. We need to see someone tip his hand.'

'And just wait? Do nothing?' Junius' voice cracked.

'Watching, listening, and recording is not *doing nothing*,' Apodemius retorted. 'It's all we do. And so far, it has saved our Empire from self-destruction. Now go with my secretary, Junius. He'll get you a place to sleep until your return to Mediolanum.'

We watched the boy escorted away by the secretary waiting outside.

'Is Roxana happy?' I asked.

'She's contented with Silvanus. She'd be even happier were it not for the other woman in his life.'

I thought of the middle-aged biddy chasing after her son Junius in Mediolanum. I would have gladly assured Roxana she had no competition in that court.

'Did she locate Meroveus' family in Toxandria?'

'Yes, but she has got no further.' Apodemius said. 'Take the boy back to Mediolanum by the end of the week.'

'But I have my work here! Gaudentius should handle this!'

I thought of the analysis of reports from Britannia I was drawing up, a job that used my brains at last. I still faced the private headache of hiring Leo's teacher. I had no wish to return to Mediolanum. No matter how perfumed with cloying incense, a sewer of sadism lay below ground.

'Gaudentius has his hands full watching Eusebius and this damn religious convocation. My files on emerging theological alliances are pitifully thin.'

'But Catena—'

'—missed his chance, for now. So watch your back after dark.'

I said nothing, which was the best I could manage through my frustrated anger.

Apodemius peered at me hard. 'I don't care if you still hate Silvanus. He's holding the Western Empire together and your allegiance is to Roma. Take the boy up there and stay at his elbow. Our little hostage is in greater danger than he realizes. Watch them. *Watch them all*—the councilors, the Franco-Roman officers, and Eusebius. Someone is plotting to use Silvanus' letters for his own ends. I doubt if it's the Emperor's little baggage-handler Dynamius. He's as stupid as the pack animals in his care.'

※※※

Kahina had told the cook to warm up a hearty breakfast to hold me in good humor for a few hours. But now I was on Teaching Candidate Seven and my stomach was starting to rumble. Back at the Castra, Junius was waiting around for our departure.

Leo could see my patience was wearing thin. He made a preemptive move. 'Don't hire the last one,' he said, his little jaw set as firm as the old Senator's. 'He has nasty dandruff and sweaty palms.'

'Any of the others?'

'Are all private teachers so smarmy?'

'Possibly. Are all Roman seven-year-olds so impertinent?'

Dandruff aside, I was finding it all too easy to eliminate most of them as underqualified. I received each man in the Senator's dusty study and asked him to flesh out his resumé with comments on the old man's valuable library. As each 'scholar' surveyed the shelves, I could tell they felt overwhelmed or even bewildered by so many unfamiliar titles. They had arrived thinking that a few quotes from Plutarch and a glance at their old geometry books would suffice.

Not for the Manlius heir.

Candidate Eight was faring better. A fair-haired man of twenty-five raised in Augusta Taurinorum, he'd taught in elite

Roman households now for three years. After Kahina ushered him into the study with her vacant smile, I watched him tour the bulging shelves. He glanced at me for permission before thumbing through the Senator's copy of *The Lives of the Twelve Caesars* of Suetonius.

'I tried to find this at the bookseller's down in the Subura,' he smiled. 'My father had an excellent copy but it was lost. Good editions bring a high price these days.'

'Your references are good. The Tremellius family seems satisfied.'

'Their firstborn, Albanus, is going on to legal studies.'

'Does the Empire need yet more lawyers?'

He laughed with a conspiratorial shrug. 'At least it's a profession. Albanus was a good student, but he won't challenge Cicero's reputation. Meanwhile, their second-born has chosen a career in the Church. He was keener on the writings of Tertullian and Origen of Alexander than the old pagans.'

A raised eyebrow betrayed me.

'You don't practice the state cult?' he asked. 'That's up to you, of course. But I've observed that all the clever sons of Roma are concentrating on Christian studies—if they seek a career in government, that is.'

'I gather so. But it's not what we want for Leo.'

'I'm sorry, but you are who, exactly?'

'I was named in the old Senator Manlius' will as Leo's *tutor legitimus*. I am the trustee of his financial affairs until he comes of age and in charge of his education.'

I could not tell anyone that I was also Leo's father, both for the sake of Kahina's honor and the child's legal position as Manlius heir.

'But I just met his mother outside—'

'We *both* desire a classical education in Greek and Latin Greats, the usual philosophical subjects—including mathematics, and geometry. The Bible won't be necessary.'

'You are a freedman?'

I resented his implication that my instructions weren't final. I suspected that Kahina was conducting quiet conversations in the atrium outside the study, vetting the candidates for their Christian sympathies. She'd nearly died as a virgin martyr years before down in our native Numidia Militaris. Her close shave with death had cured her fanaticism. Yet I worried when I noticed she had recently hung a large crucifix on her bedroom wall.

'Antonius Drusus, our Leo is a boy *who is encouraged by praise, delighted by success, and ready to weep over failure. Such a boy must be encouraged by appeals to his ambitions.*'

I confess my fancy description of Leo was a test. Perhaps I even hoped to eliminate Antonius Drusus from consideration. He was starting to remind me of all that I was not—a full Roman citizen, a true scholar, and a personable young man free from the Castra's merciless marching orders.

'You paraphrase the rhetorician Quintilian, *Biarchus* Numidianus, the teacher of both Pliny the Younger and Tacitus,' the young man said without affectation. 'If Leo has grown up around such erudition, his teacher's job is only that much easier. Quintilian said a child should be surrounded by good speech from birth.'

'I cannot say much for the diction of *Dispensator* Verus, but Leo recognizes good speech from bad.'

'But as I'm sure you know,' he parried, 'Quintilian teaches us that correct speech is not complete without music, because he has to discuss meter and rhythm; nor can the child understand the poets without a knowledge of astronomy, since poets often use the risings and settings of constellations as indications of time; nor again should he be ignorant of philosophy, because of the numerous passages in every poem that depend on intricate points of natural science. Eloquence too is needed, and in no small measure, to give a proper and fluent explanation of the various matters mentioned.'

'Yes, of course,' I said, not a little irritated. 'The Emperor Vespasian made Quintilian a consul to underscore the importance of education as a means of creating an intelligent and responsible ruling class. No one needed the Bible in the first century to produce an upstanding Roman.'

'I would instruct young Leo according to your exact wishes,' Antonius said. 'I have long heard of your household's position in the old *ordo Senatorius* and especially the rhetorical heights of the late Senator Manlius.'

'How flattering.'

—THE WOLVES OF AMBITION—

'It would be an honor to have access to this library and to share its riches with Leontus Manlius Gregorius.'

'Yes, it would.'

'Then I have the position, *Biarchus*?'

I hesitated. How could I refuse?'

'Yes.'

We left the study and introduced Antonius Drusus to a suddenly shy Leo who stammered hello and went to fetch his wax tablet. Anything was better than returning to the expensive Sabinus School at the foot of the Esquiline Hill to be tormented by the scions of other great families.

'Antonius Drusus will be Leo's teacher,' I told Kahina.

The two of them exchanged polite small talk while I went to leave Leo with clear counsel. He must study hard while I was gone—or it was back to the brutal free-for-all of *Magister* Sabinus' open-air classroom down the hill.

When I returned, Kahina was showing Antonius Drusus around the reception rooms, recently refurbished at great expense, and briefing him on the household routine.

'Hsst, hsst! Marcus! Are you sure you knows what you're doing?'

It was Verus, sweeping a superfluous broom around the spotless floor of the entrance hall, his wrinkled eyes supervising the goings-on.

'Antonius' rates are fair and he knows his Quintilian, old man.'

'He knows a lot more than that, we'll wager. Single, good-looking, and fishing for a fine future in the Eternal City,' Verus said, peeking at the scene unfolding in the *triclinium*. 'But if he treats our Leo right, you won't hear no complaints from us.'

It amused me that the only two people of my acquaintance who used the imperial 'we' so often were the Emperor Constantius II and the crusty majordomo of the Manlius townhouse.

৵৵৵

Arriving back in Mediolanum, Junius and I reported straight to Gaudentius under the cover of darkness. The *ducenarius* had just finished exercising his considerable brawn in the Palace Gymnasium and was changing into a fresh tunic for the night.

He was relieved to see Junius, sunburned and blistered, volunteer himself for return to palatial detention. He was much less pleased to see me. Until further notice, I was to share his quarters, convenient for planning and sure to forestall any future 'social visits' from Paulus Catena.

Before Junius presented himself in his mother's suite in the main building, we three whispered by the light of a single oil lamp.

'I shall ask Dynamius whether he has had any joy of my father's references,' Junius said. 'He knows he was lucky to get them in the first place.'

Gaudentius scratched his stubbly scalp. 'No. As a Frankish hostage, you're an important political piece in the game, but a passive one. That wispy caterpillar on your lip hardly qualifies you to question an adult on his career plans—even a baggage-handler.'

'I agree, Junius. The less you draw attention to yourself, the more useful you are.' I turned to the grim-faced Gaudentius. 'But mightn't it be natural for his mother to inquire?'

Junius rolled his eyes. 'Only on one condition would my mother leave the safety of the ladies' wing to accost any official.'

'That is?'

'To prevent me from poking my nose around,' Junius reasoned. 'She'll do anything to keep me safe on her leash.'

'Then ask her now, in the full flush of her gratitude for your safe return,' Gaudentius said. 'And mind no one observes you leaving this building.'

'I told you. No one notices me.' Junius pulled his green cloak over his boyish features.

'You'd be surprised, son.'

Junius' mother did as he predicted. She searched out the *actuarius* before noon the next day.

Junius reported back to us the next night. 'Dynamius told mother that father's reference letters were mislaid.'

—THE WOLVES OF AMBITION—

Gaudentius nodded. 'Those letters are still in Lampadius' possession. We must recover them and return them to Dynamius.'

'Why trust Dynamius?' I asked. 'Apodemius has a low opinion of the man's intelligence. He is clearly just a game piece in some plot. We should return them to General Silvanus himself.'

'I'll steal them from Lampadius!' Junius said

'Excellent idea,' Gaudentius said. 'There's a *consistorium* banquet tonight. The councilors will feast in their *triclinium* until late. The guards will stand down at midnight. The main office wing should be deserted.'

'Yes? What do I do then, *Ducenarius*?' Junius' eyes danced with the excitement of carrying out secret orders from the intimidating Gaudentius.

'That's when you'll go to bed and Numidianus will steal the letters.'

Chapter 6, An Emperor at Prayer

—MEDIOLANUM PALACE, THE *TRICLINIUM* OF THE *CONSISTORIANI*—

The councilors' banquet dragged on. Some twenty men languished on their couches, replete with olives and salted dogberries, chicory with horseradish, cheese *moretum*, and eggs cooked in ashes. A few of them were still mopping up the last of the roast hare in anchovy sauce. Quinces, pomegranates, apples and old wine—the first of two *mensae secundae*—were still to come.

The wall torches burned lower in their sconces, casting shadows on the floor where real fruit rinds and animal bones mixed with fake scraps depicted in mosaic tiles and semi-priceless inlaid stones. The large candles in the corners of the room had melted into hillocks of wax tended by drowsy slaves.

Prefect Lampadius had not yet even arrived.

The desultory conversation fell on the subject of wolves—their habits, habitats, and wiles. In the shadows, Gaudentius rolled his eyes with irony. These diners were as vicious, sharp-toothed, and bloody-pawed as any voracious *lupus* prowling the dark northern forests.

Gaudentius and I listened to it all from an alcove for the slaves who kept out of sight between serving and clearing. Unseen by all except these workers, we *agentes* dodged the small tables, platters, and pitchers swinging past our weary brows.

Aedesius, Master of the Rolls, prodded the post-prandial chat along: 'If the wolf is such a dangerous predator, Arbetio, why does Roma boast its origins in twins suckled by a she-wolf? Why did our ancestors worship at the paws of a bronze monster?'

The tired Consul stretched his arms into the air. The centuries-old rituals of formal dining—the poems, riddles, songs, and philosophical arguments—were obligatory, but no less fatiguing after a day of political battles.

Yet Arbetio seemed disinclined to retire before any of his fellow councilors—perhaps for fear of idle conversation behind his back? Or because the Prefect for Gallia had not yet fulfilled his duty as a guest to show up?

Gaudentius and I had sat quiet for many hours now. Where was Lampadius? How could I burgle his office if Gaudentius didn't have the snake pinned down safely under his gaze in the dining room beyond?

'You mistake the tale of Romulus and Remus for a charming folk legend,' Arbetio said at last.

'Isn't it?' That was Florentius, prodding Arbetio on so the rest could finish their dessert in peace.

'No. The story of the she-wolf proves that we Romans imbibed wolfish ferocity with our mother's milk,' Arbetio answered. 'Barbarians should remember that when they steal our Gallic towns.'

'They had you on the run up at Lake Brigantia,' Florentius said so quietly, Gaudentius leaned forward to catch it. 'You lost the noble Seniauchus.'

'It was a difficult situation,' Arbetio said with a deep breath. 'We left the Emperor and personal guard at Camp Canini on the lakeshore. I led my troops up into the mountains. We were on the alert for the entire march—the Lentienses tribe can be the most vicious of all the *Germani*. They decoyed us into an ambush. We had no chance but to scatter along the narrow mountain paths in the dark. By morning, I'd recollected our forces together, but ten tribunes and their units were lost.'

The diners glanced at each other, waiting.

'Of course,' Arbetio said with a defensive air, 'that only emboldened the bastards. They attacked our palisade next morning—swords drawn, teeth gnashing. The *scutarii* targeteers took them on, but were driven back to a standstill.'

'Where were you, Consul?' Florentius asked from under half-closed eyes.

'I hesitated at the risk of losing more men, of course. Then Arintheus, lieutenant commander of the heavy-armed bodyguard, Seniauchus, and his squadron of household cavalry, and Bappo, an officer of the veterans all advanced—without my orders, Florentius. They routed those savages in a series of swift skirmishes, but as they returned to us, they exposed their backs. The barbarians cut them to pieces.'

'Then at last, you gave the command?' asked Aedesius.

'There was little need,' Arbetio said. 'When the men saw their officers laying there, horse and man stuck fast together in death, they poured out of our camp and trampled the horde to death.'

The image of those three self-sacrificing heroes taking charge of Arbetio's timorous command settled like a guilty miasma over the carcass of the banquet.

'So which would you rather face, Arbetio—a pack of wolves or a pack of Alemanni?' Aedesius asked.

In our alcove, Gaudentius shook his head. When would Lampadius show up?

'A pack of barbarians, of course!'

'Why?' Mattyocopus asked through a mouth full of bread.

'Barbarians have no plan, no second strategy. When Romans are on the back foot, we fight all the harder and use discipline to regain the advantage. Roman resilience shatters the enemy's resolve. Even when barbarians have enjoyed the upper hand, they suddenly flee.'

'And wolves?'

Florentius clapped his hands for the last dessert—nut cakes and honeycomb. Lollianus started up from his old man's slumber.

'Barbarians fear us. Wolves do not. Man is the wolf's supreme prey. The wounded horse that lures the wolves is fatal to his rider. The horse is no more to wolves than those *gustatio* starters were to us. A man lost alone in the woods is the *mensa prima*.'

A hush fell over the diners. The shadows of their half-drunken torsos loomed on the alcove wall behind my head.

Arbetio murmured. 'The wolves fight like Romans in disciplined packs like a trained cohort. The gods gave these animals supernatural senses.'

'Surely not supernatural!' Florentius scoffed.

Arbetio pointed a finger in rebuke. 'The scent of one drop of blood sets them on a man's path. They track him hour by hour, watching him with eyes of ice.'

'Surely they kill what's easiest and stop hunting when they're full?' Aedesius said. 'There's ample game in the great forests to satisfy them, even if they number in the millions.'

Arbetio paused before answering. 'No, *Magister*, the *Germani* know wolves are wanton killers full of bloodlust. They salivate through jaws that can consume twenty pounds of flesh in a single meal. It is a pleasure in itself, beyond hunger or appetite. They are insatiable conquerors, like ourselves—but even more dangerous.'

'How so?'

'They howl messages from one pack to another. They play possum to escape danger. They've been seen pulling up fish lines set in the ice to steal a fisherman's dinner. Whole packs will fill their mouths with snow when stalking so their breath does not steam in the cold and alert their prey.'

'But surely a man has arms to defeat an overgrown dog?' asked Mattyocopus, still slurping up scraps within his greedy reach.

'It's not a question of weapons. They run as fast as a horse and keep going hour after hour, chasing and chasing until their quarry drops.'

Arbetio's voice fell away, as if he were talking only to himself. 'You listen to the heartbeat from far away and judge the exact moment that fear has petrified your victim. Only then do you make your move.'

The room turned chilly. No man broke the silence to ask why Arbetio had switched to talking from the wolf's point of view.

Lampadius appeared at last.

Gaudentius nodded to me. I made for the officials' wing on the other side of the reception halls and imperial family's suites.

I walked quickly by the light of a four-inch palm-lamp protected by a flame-guard. Gaudentius' copies of keys to the offices hung in a small sack off my belt. I kept my special swivel knife hidden in my boot cuff.

As Prefect for Gallia, Lampadius and his staff enjoyed the use of three connected offices. I waited at a safe distance from his first door until a pair of guards quit the last shift. One passed less than a foot away from the wide column hiding me. He smelled of leather, oil, and sweat. The second man sauntered away, testing each door to make sure the wing was secure.

—THE WOLVES OF AMBITION—

The banquet was all but over. It seemed doubtful Lampadius would return to work before morning but instinct told me not to dally.

Only his private chamber interested me. I eased the first door open and slipped inside, locking it behind me. I bumped into a row of copiers' tables. Lifting my feeble light higher, I squirmed between a clutter of desks and stools, worn-out wax tablets, bent *stili* and rolls of ageing papyrus.

Lampadius' reputation for stinginess with everything except public credit to his name seemed well deserved. He even hoarded a pile of special gums and cloths for erasing vellum for reuse.

I overturned a stool before I reached the innermost chamber and sent a tabletop's worth of writing tools rattling across the floor. I jumped quickly behind the door to the third office and waited for a full five minutes, heart in throat. No one came. The guards were gone.

I needed a much stronger lamp to read anything. Anyone looking up at Lampadius' window might spot a flickering flame but it was a risk I had to take.

I pulled the ornate damask curtains closed as far as they would go, and used my palm lamp to light the wick of his desk lamp, a double-nozzled model with two thick wicks. The pottery lamp was still warm to the touch.

My neck hairs prickled to think that Lampadius had been here less than ten minutes before, skipping his meal to complete some more important task.

Two braziers sat on delicate tripods. There was a wide-armed chair, a footstool in the corner, and a stack of files on the floor waiting for the prefect's examination.

I made my way to the large desk near the window where half a dozen document boxes stood stacked and waiting.

I opened one document box after another, searching for the green vellum packet bearing Silvanus' seal. In less then five minutes, I'd rifled through them all without success. Perhaps during that unwanted intrusion by Malarichus and Junius, Lampadius saw the boy notice his father's letters. He might have removed them to a more secret hiding place.

A key turned in the first door two rooms back. I snuffed out both lamps, slipped to the back wall of the office and crouched behind a row of shelves loaded with *codices* and scrolls.

The door opened. The sinewy Lampadius stood in the frame and hesitated, perhaps scenting a stranger. To my horror, a tiny wisp of smoke rose off the desk lamp and threaded across the sliver of light left by the drawn curtains. If I could detect the smoke, so could he.

Then he hurried forward in the dark—as if he was more fearful of being discovered in his own office than I was. Instead of moving to his desk, he went to a third incense burner hanging from a chain in the corner of the room. He lifted the bronze cover and then put it back. The burner swung slowly, sending a whiff of sandalwood up my nostrils. I fought back a sneeze by pulling my tunic up to my nose and holding my breath. Any instant he would turn and see my belt buckles glistening through the gloom.

Then he was gone.

I had to decide—to stay and continue my frustrated search or follow Lampadius. Not for nothing are we *agentes* cursed by civilians as '*curiosi.*'

I checked the incense burner and found it lined with a rag of Egyptian cotton instead of ashes. I pulled off my boots, stuffed them inside my tunic, and dashed in my woolen socks down the office corridor on Lampadius' trail.

His own sharp soles clacked on the mosaic stones and slate flagstones as we traversed the length of the bureaucrats' wing, crossed two large reception halls, skipped the *triclinium* where the dog ends of the banquet were still underway, and moved on toward the imperial residential suites.

Someone else was on our heels. Before I could shout, he'd laid a hand across my mouth in warning. It was only Gaudentius. He had heard Lampadius make his excuses to the gathering in the *triclinium* and was coming to protect me.

We'd be stopped in our tracks soon enough by *domestici* guarding the imperial residences. Already I had seen one guard on duty straightening up at the sight of Lampadius coming through the moonlight across the open parade ground.

Gaudentius waited while I laced my boots back on and we two switched to a casual stride, ready to play drunk if questioned.

—THE WOLVES OF AMBITION—

But no one stopped us. Keeping a good fifty feet between the prefect's thin silhouette and ourselves, we realized where he was headed.

Lampadius swung open the tall and narrow door of the Emperor's private chapel. He dared to breach the threshold of Constantius' most personal retreat from all his troubles and crimes, the sacrosanct altar at which he prayed for forgiveness and guidance. It was the only sanctuary the Emperor dared visit alone when the community of courtiers, guards, women, children and slaves had retired. This was a fact known only to the few men trusted with his personal security.

A set of high windows lined the chapel building's stone side. Vaulting myself up to a perch on a low wall, I peered from the shadows into the chapel in time to see Lampadius inch down the central aisle toward Constantius. The Emperor lay, prostrate and still, his imperial forehead pressed against the cold granite.

Lampadius stopped a few yards away and said something. He must have surprised the sovereign deep in prayer, because Constantius leapt to his feet and reached for his ceremonial *spatha* in fear of assassination. It was outside just such a chapel that his brother Constans had fallen to my own dagger.

The two men exchanged few words. Lampadius reached into his tunic and handed a bundle of vellum to the Emperor.

The packet bore a thick green seal.

※※※

Florentius Nigrinianus summoned Gaudentius and myself at dawn. We met him on the steps of the great palace, his face the same lifeless gray as the morning light stealing across the colorless slate.

'The Prefect for Gallia has reported a plot by General Claudius Silvanus to usurp the throne,' he said.

Gaudentius laid a weathered hand across my sword belt to cut off my surprised protest and said, 'As far as our information goes, Silvanus is the most loyal of commanders, devoted to the imperial couple and the survival of the Empire, *Magister*.'

'The Imperial Post is the responsibility of your *schola*. Then explain why Silvanus wrote treasonous letters.'

Gaudentius could not silence me. 'I cannot believe it!'

Florentius ignored my outrage. 'You know too well, Gaudentius, from your own reporting of Africanus' fateful dinner party in Sirmium, how jests at the expense of our *Imperator* lead a man to the cells below. Silvanus was always too confident. He should have been more careful.'

'With his only son a hostage here? It's unbelievable! Show us this proof!'

Florentius shrugged. 'Paulus Catena always finds what he seeks as proof, does he not?'

My mixed feelings for Silvanus aside, the image of a man so charming in society and courageous in the field being wound around one of Catena's 'toys' made me so queasy I could have vomited on the priceless mosaics underfoot.

Florentius lowered his eyes as he told us, 'Once a defector, always a defector, is the accusation. Silvanus' success in subduing the chaos up in Gallia impressed us all, but perhaps he boasts too much. Some say that he bought back Gallia with payoffs of gold by the sackload to the Alemanni looters.'

'Thus saving lives—'

'—every *solidus* taxed off Gallo-Roman estates.'

'As they are first to benefit.'

Florentius heaved a sigh. 'You'll hear the Emperor call for the named conspirators to be delivered before him. Have your couriers ready to ride out with these summons.'

'The *Magister Officiorum* should be here,' Gaudentius replied.

'He is too ill. I'm acting for him,' Florentius said, 'but things have gone too far for me.' He locked eyes with the powerful *ducenarius*.

'If the weather holds, our *Magister* could be here in a week using relay horses,' Gaudentius said.

Florentius jerked his chin. Gaudentius dashed off to code an alert to Apodemius in time to give it to the first southbound rider out the Porta Romana.

I followed Florentius into the *consistorium* as a stentorious secretary read out the charges of treason to some fifty or more assembled courtiers. Constantius had not slept all night. He still wore the simple night robes in which we'd seen him praying only hours before.

Horror ran down my spine as I recognized names of Silvanus' trusted army associates—brave and useful men who always served the Empire well. No such tremors troubled Arbetio, Aedesius, Lampadius, Eusebius, or Mattyocopus, and the others assembled in front of dozens of other heads of departments and their deputies.

Many were honest men, including those most intimately connected with the imperial household or *dignitates palatinae*, the Minister of Finance, or *comes sacrarum largitionum*, the Minister of the Privy Purse or *comes rerum privatarum*, the emperor's legal adviser, the *quaestor sacri palatii*, and the prefect of Mediolanum.

The ink on the Gallus convictions had hardly dried. It seemed impossible that these busy men could digest this latest turn of events. But some would accept such accusations at face value, I realized. My hopes for Junius and his family plummeted.

The only participants allowed to sit during such solemn proceedings were the banks of sweating *notarii*, scribbling secretaries, and stenographers. Their *stili* raced across their tablets, recording the names and charges for distribution and filing near and far.

But one set of listeners did not stand impassive or impartial during this morning's droning recitation of alleged conspirators.

The two most important Frankish officers at court, the native king Mallobaudes and Tribune Malarichus, were fuming. I had seen Mallobaudes once before, in the shadows of a dank prison cell in Pola. He was the most upright of Constantius' three envoys who had witnessed the interrogation and execution of the Caesar Gallus. The other two men—the eunuch Eusebius and the notary Pentadius—enjoyed far lower standing in my eyes.

This morning Mallobaudes stood braced in front of four ranks of *Gentiles* officers, most of them Franks. These fighters wore longer hair than the Romans. Many had the flowing moustaches favored by warriors from the western banks of the Lower Rhenus. In a room of saffron, purple, gold, sky blue, and ivory linen, they stood apart in their long woolen *paenulae* dyed pine, moss, or field gray-green, all fixed to their powerful shoulders with elaborate silver buckles and oversized *fibulae*.

Their towering height, greenish garb and glistening light hair reminded me of the cold, sun-topped forest climes in which these formidable men grew stronger with each passing generation as our Roman allies.

Mallobaudes shook his head in visible disbelief at the names called out. From time to time, he cursed under his breath. His hissing drew the Emperor's steely eyes to his corner.

These accusations against Silvanus endangered every man under Mallobaudes' command in Mediolanum, but the hostage Junius most of all. The boy sheltered behind the broad right shoulder of his Frankish *dux*. The trembling clasp of his weeping mother reined in his adolescent indignation.

I gave the boy a shake of my head to caution him against any explosion.

'We question this evidence. We question this procedure,' Malarichus shouted before the scribe had finished his roll call.

He swept into the center of the room and braved the angry glint lighting Constantius' otherwise heavy eyes.

'*Imperator*, our great Empire can't fall victim to the wiles of divisive cliques. I demand a commission to fetch Silvanus to clear his name. I offer my own beloved family as hostages. Tribune Mallobaudes will remain in charge of the heavy-armed guard as surety for my return.'

Arbetio took a step out of the ranks of courtiers. 'Silvanus and all his co-conspirators named this morning will defend themselves here soon enough. We have our evidence. He has plotted to overturn this throne.'

Malarichus leapt forward and spat with contempt within inches of Arbetio's boots.

'We've all seen the peculiar "justice" handed down by this chamber. I warn the Council that should you send an outsider to Agrippina, our noble General Claudius Silvanus, being by nature justly apprehensive of the deceit and dishonest that infects this court—even when there is no cause for alarm—might upset the peace.'

Malarichus added, 'And I declare I would deem it not strange if General Silvanus reacted badly to these lies, after the extraordinary services he has rendered in Gallia.'

—THE WOLVES OF AMBITION—

Without kneeling or prostrating himself to kiss the purple, Malarichus walked straight up to Constantius. The burning pride of the elite Frankish contingent seemed concentrated in the audacious confrontation by this one man, his face as purple as the Emperor's hem.

'Silvanus? *Silvanus* a traitor to your throne? You believe *Silvanus* would do such things that these plotters and their abettors allege? Your most loyal Silvanus?"

Malarichus leaned even closer to Constantius' impassive face. Only inches below that jutting jaw, he whispered upward, 'Would you believe *anything, Imperator*?'

Constantius was unmoved. 'We've read his letters, full of strategies for stealing this chair out from under our sacred body.'

'Then send me to Agrippina before it is too late, for I fear Silvanus' rage at such injustice will provoke his noble spirit past breaking,' Malarichus said.

Mallobaudes joined his fellow Frank at the foot of the dais. The two barbarian noblemen now knelt with ill-disguised contempt and waited for the Emperor's instructions to recall their chief.

Constantius' eyes were dead with exhaustion. He lifted himself to his feet. 'We are sending an impartial representative to summon Silvanus to trial.'

He waved the two Franks back to their places in the corner but they had turned their backs on him already without apology.

'This procedure resumes as soon as all the accused present themselves here for formal arraignment according to correct procedures. General Claudius Silvanus should be escorted here in person at the greatest speed—by the *Magister Agentium in Rebus*.'

Florentius gouged his elbow into my ribs I took my cue. Within seconds, I prostrated myself inches from the Emperor's polished boots.

'*Magister* Apodemius is already en route from Roma as we speak, *Imperator*.'

☘☘☘

The Frankish tribunes, whose contingents normally guarded the vast imperial property, were themselves now cordoned off from all authority across the entire palace. Junius and his mother were under twenty-four-hour surveillance. Until Silvanus was delivered by our *schola* as Roman law dictated, no Frank at court was free of suspicion.

Within the week, the palace corridors assumed the air of an ornate and aromatic jail.

Despite his advanced age, Apodemius was still capable of riding on little sleep for days on end. I knew from our nightmare dash from the dungeon of Pola Istra to the court in Mediolanum in 354 that the *Magister* was hardy enough to ride a *Cursus Publicus* relay horse literally to his death—just to meet an imperial deadline with Constantius II.

But he could not fly. Waiting for Apodemius, Gaudentius and I avoided each other as much as possible, but I felt safe from Catena only in the company of my fellow *agentes*. Even an *equitor* or *circitor* would do.

One night after a quick supper snatched with some of the riders at the gatehouse, I dashed back through a summer downpour to Gaudentius' rooms to discover the old man's snow-white head snoring on my makeshift bed.

His worn-out goatskin boots, spattered with mud, were still laced around his arthritic ankles. I even noticed the outline of the knife he carried in a concealed sheath underneath his old-fashioned long robe.

Our Frankish recruit, *Agens* Meroveus nodded hello from the corner of the room where he was sluicing off the mud of the road with hot water from Gaudentius' basin. For the first time, I saw his bare torso. The last traces of the overfed Eastern ladies' doorman were gone. He had worked himself back into fighting shape in the Castra's gymnasium in Roma.

Meroveus grunted as he swabbed himself dry. 'The old man thought a Frank on our side might come in handy.'

'He's right, Meroveus.'

'But you and I must ride north with Gaudentius and the *Magister*, no?' Meroveus said, eyes clouding with worry. 'Our service up the Rhenus is sporadic at best. Communication lines from the river border inland to Treverorum are unreliable. There are large stretches of that route that are nearly impassable because of sneak attacks by the Alemanni, even for a full patrol.'

'Then speed will be our only advantage, Meroveus. And four men are safer than one.'

Meroveus could handle any gang of Alemanni ambushers, yet I detected reluctance. I guessed his fears were more personal. No companions on the road could help him once we reached our destination so near his former village in Toxandria. According to Apodemius, Roxana had located the Frank's estranged family, but he'd postponed any reunion with the excuses of training in Roma and minor tasks that took him in all directions but north.

I didn't blame the eunuch. His awful fate had happened to thousands of Roman prisoners-of-war but that didn't make his state any easier to bear. Roxana had conveyed back no message of welcome or acceptance from the poor man's wife.

'Silvanus is at the height of his success,' Meroveus said after an awkward silence. The anger of the Franks here at court is beyond measure.'

I answered. 'I can't understand how simple letters to fellow Franks at court recommending a grasping *actuarius* for promotion could be copied into the court records as proof of treason.'

Apodemius soon set off with Gaudentius to a brief audience with the Emperor. They returned half an hour later, faces drawn.

'We must return with Silvanus in under two weeks,' Apodemius announced. 'Catena is to question him.'

'How can that be?' I demanded. 'General Ursicinus got a fair and public hearing. Though he brushed off all charges of disloyalty, there was no further interrogation. Why should Silvanus be treated any worse?'

'It was Arbetio's suggestion,' Gaudentius said.

'Don't we have a right to examine those letters?' I asked.

'Yes, as postal officers, it's a technicality we could insist on,' Apodemius said, rubbing his white stubble, 'but I doubt it would be of any help. Are we calling the Emperor's own judgment into question?'

'We know they're a packet of lies,' I said.

'They must be a packet of distortions, but how?' the old man answered.

Someone was at the door. I unbolted it to the shivering Junius out in the open corridor standing between two sentries. His cloak dripped with rain.

'Welcome, young man,' Apodemius said, taking custody of the boy and closing the door against the miserable weather. 'I hadn't thought we'd meet again so soon after Roma, nor under such appalling circumstances. I suppose it's no comfort to congratulate you on your fine political instincts for danger.'

'You're too late,' Junius said, darting a sullen glance at me.

'Too late for your father, perhaps. Let's talk of you.'

'What about me?'

'You must leave Mediolanum tonight.'

'My mother didn't tell me we were leaving!' He pulled his wet cloak tight around himself.

'Your mother doesn't know, son.'

'I can't abandon her again! Not now!'

'They're watching her, but no one suspects her, not really. She'll be fine.'

'I'm all she has,' he whimpered.

'Yes and you are in mortal danger.'

Apodemius pulled Junius closer. With both hands laid on the boy's shoulders, he spoke in a slow and solemn voice.

'One of the sharpest accusations against Ursicinus has been that he promotes his son as heir to political power in the East. You are as much the heir to a rising Roman general as that full-grown Potentius. You risk being eliminated from the field of ambition by torture—on the trumped-up excuse of seeking information which any sane person knows you don't have.'

'Innocence never stopped Paulus Catena,' muttered Gaudentius.

'Exactly.' Apodemius said. 'Now, where can we hide the boy?'

In the silence that followed, we listened to the dripping of Meroveus' wet towel onto Gaudentius' floor.

None of Junius' fellow Franks at court could protect him now.

Beyond the city walls, we could not trust any Gallo-Roman nobleman not to curry favor with the Emperor by handing Junius over. The bitter reckoning of the civil war had only just settled down. Many proud homes had been caught supporting Constantius' opponent Magnentius and lost everything. Political suspicions still lurked and the survivors rebuilding their estates had a lot to prove.

Even the Castra was too busy and public a place to secrete a missing imperial hostage.

'I know,' I said, hiding my reluctance from the boy. 'An old townhouse on the Esquiline Hill behind high decaying walls covered by the branches of a fig tree. If I order it, our house manager Verus will lay down his life to protect you.'

Apodemius nodded. 'Good. Then the boy rides out after dark for the Manlius House with—who's on southbound duty next, Gaudentius?'

'Cassius or Rufus. Send Rufus—'

'Crooked at dice—' I said.

'But a Mercury in the saddle.' Gaudentius could not brook a slap at any rider on his team.

'Then as soon as we finish here, Junius, Gaudentius will take you to Rufus. You will ride with him to the Roma.'

'But—!'

'You ride just as you are. Don't say good-bye to your mother or anyone else. I'll explain everything and she will thank me.'

Having settled Junius' welfare, we four *agentes* then discussed which northern route up the Rhenus would deliver us fastest to Silvanus. Junius listened, but his expression drifted off to his own mounting woes, starting with his third marathon ride to Roma.

Meroveus rose from his stool and reached for his coarse brown tunic edged with red wool stitching. He pulled it over his wiry hair.

'Before we set out for the north, I make a personal request.'

Apodemius rubbed his throbbing temples. He looked old and tired. 'What is it, Meroveus?'

'I wish to be freed.'

Gaudentius looked taken aback. Apodemius gave his head a shake as if his white-haired ears had trapped a flea.

I was stunned. No one at the Castra had cared about Meroveus' status when I recruited him. As far as our *schola* was concerned, his capture, castration, and enslavement were things of the past.

'Don't be an ass.' Gaudentius was curt. 'We have important business right now. Minutes count.'

Meroveus yanked hard at his mane. 'I want to hear it. I *need* to hear it before my first mission to the north. Properly done.'

'We don't have the requisite seven witnesses,' Gaudentius said.

I laid a cautionary hand on the *ducenarius*' arm. I had lived this myself—an uncontrollable craving for recognition as a freed man. Although Marcus the slave and bodyguard to a prominent commander had enjoyed responsibility, education, security, and even affection, I had wanted more. And I had risked blinding and branding, not mention been whipped raw, shackled, and hunted—all to finish the mission that won me my liberty.

Meroveus was right. For whenever justly invoked, Roman law protected every one of us, or protected none.

I spoke up for the Frank. 'Then four will have to do. Who will do the honors and say the words?' I looked at Apodemius.

Meroveus pointed at Junius. 'I want him.'

'Me?' Junius squeaked from his corner.

'You are the grandson of the revered Bonitus, are you not?'

Gaudentius grabbed his razor from the basin and slapped it into the boy's palm. 'Don't waste any more time. Shave his hair off, right down to the scalp.'

The young man shaved away Meroveus' reddish mop with shaking fingers.

Meroveus shook himself free of the clumps, straightened his shoulders, and joked, 'Now I look as ugly as you, Gaudentius.'

I gave Junius my *petanus* to place on Meroveus' raw scalp. 'To take the place of the ceremonial *pileus*,' I explained.

'And you will do it in my own language,' Meroveus insisted.

'In both languages, Junius,' Apodemius interjected.

Junius hesitated, digesting the unexpected responsibility his nobility had handed him.

He placed my riding helmet on Meroveus and whispered, "*Liber esto.*' His childish voice cracked.

Then for the first time I heard the boy speak his grandfather's tongue.

—THE WOLVES OF AMBITION—

'*Maltho thi afrio lito.* I free you, you who are half-free.'

Meroveus threw back his head and with eyes welling with tears, he embraced the trembling boy.

'Now we go fetch your father—to clear the name of all Franks,' he said.

Chapter 7, The Broken Lands

—The Pass to Lake Brigantia—

Torrents of snowmelt swirled around our horses' hooves. Mine reared up, his forelegs numbed by the freezing water. We retreated a few steps, pushing the other three *agentes* back along the narrow trail.

After five hours of relentless climbing in pounding summer rain and hail, we confronted a formidable barrier. On our left, the mountainside dropped hundreds of feet into a tree-covered ravine below. On our right, a powerful river of icy water surged from over the steep cliffs above our heads. The waterfall crashed onto the paving in front of us and rushed downward with a roar. This deadly cascade barred us from the other side of the narrow *Cursus* route through the vertiginous mountain pass.

Almost a year before, Constantius and his forces had marched up this road during their autumn campaign to push the Alemanni back out of Roman lands and into wild Germanic territory.

But they'd been luckier than us. They'd crossed these heights at their driest. This was no week to challenge the barbarian gods still shedding the long winter's white cloak off their Olympian peaks.

Forced by the wretched weather to cut our speed by half, we had picked our way in single file up the steep road from Comum. Now and then our horses trod on traces of Constantius' expedition—bits of broken leather, discarded scraps of metal, and a broken saddle hook or two.

We'd been on the road for almost two full days, resting the night after Comum for a few hours in an abandoned shepherd's hut after climbing the pass cutting toward Curia. By rights we should have been able to do a *mutatio* for fresh horses and food before now, but at the last state stable, we found neither horse nor man. Perhaps there was a reason the road had no other official traffic fighting this weather—or at least none we had passed.

Gaudentius had decided we couldn't afford another full night's sleep in our race through Curia to reach the fortress in Brigantium. But we needed shelter from this downpour for the sake of the horses. With sheer rock faces on either side of us, there was none to be had.

So on we climbed, our soft leather helmets and waterproofed riding cloaks pelted with hailstones, and our horses' noses bowed so low, they nearly scraped the slippery paving stones slanting steeply upwards ahead of us.

If this route up the contested valley was the fastest way to Agrippina, it was also proving the most treacherous for man and horse. I cursed its narrow twists around jutting boulders that pushed me close to the very edge of the precipitous drop. Or the sharp dips and rises in the uneven paving that could trip up a tired horse. Even in peacetime, we would hardly expect to find friendly faces among people wild enough to live at these heights. They probably survived on the same grasses they fed their animals.

It was hardly civilized compared to the western highway via Divodurum I'd taken years before up to the court of Treverorum. But the court stood burnt and emptied and the city had bolted its gates against more depredations.

The waterfall's thunder was deafening. I couldn't hear the neighing of my mount or the shouts of Gaudentius behind me as he pointed up at a dangerous boulder balanced overhead.

The long summer light had offered us the vain hope of enough time to crest this demonic pass and reach one of the state *mansiones* on the final lap to the garrison at Lake Brigantia.

And now we faced this deadly cataract.

I was worried and I could see Gaudentius was weighing turning back. On this stretch of the Cursus cut between towering slopes, we were sitting ducks for any determined Alemanni bandits perched above.

We must have overestimated our mileage or lost the right road in the mists of the storm. We were within no sight of the *mansio* marked on our *schola*'s courier guide. We should have reached it some two hours before this.

I dismounted, determined to lead my horse through the cascade. Once we got the first animal through, the others would surely follow. The frothing water swelled up nearly to my knees, knocking me back for a second. I braced my thighs to hold steady against the icy pressure of gallons of water. My legs went numb within seconds.

I pulled at the end of the jingling harness and yanked the horse toward the freezing deluge.

'Move it,' I shouted at him. '*Move!*'

He bucked and tugged back. He was no obedient cavalry fighter, this thickset animal doomed to climb and descend these passes his entire life between the two sides of the Alpine route.

I pushed myself into the waterfall, blinded by the flood drenching my *petanus*. Balancing one hand on the wet rock face, I pulled again on his reins. White foam dancing off the cold rocks splashed the bronze *phalarae* decorating the straps across his withers. Mud off the cliff wall above me spattered my face, his saddle, everything. He was surefooted enough for a post horse, but terrified by the hailstones. He braced himself, as stubborn as a mule, and would not brave the rushing water.

I was just as jumpy. We were pushing our luck to keep going as darkness fell, but I was desperate to reach the open flatlands beyond the lake's thick forest where we could finally pick up relief horses and ride north at full tilt.

'Go on, you brute!' Gaudentius whipped his rear. I didn't blame him. I could have thrashed the horse myself but unlike Gaudentius, I wasn't sure harsher treatment would help us make the last leg to somewhere safe. The Alemanni would just as likely steal him for food as to rob and kill me for money.

The paving underfoot was slippery and broken in many places.

The ice water hit my groin like a slab of ice. In fury, I shouted to the gods in agony and yanked the reins again and again until I felt the stolid block of animal flesh start to move forward by inches behind me. We had only a few more feet to go when I felt him shiver and slip. For a searing moment, I knew he was going to tumble down into the rocky ravine below us, hundreds of feet, pulling me to my death. I almost dropped the reins. Then he righted himself and giving himself a sudden, jerking bolt forward, leapt right past me and onto the safety of the sodden banks ahead of me.

I sighed with relief, and hanging on to those leather cords for my own safety, finally got hold of one of his harness disks and pulled myself up and out of the rut that was deepening into a dangerous groove with each minute of rushing, cutting water.

Gaudentius was already off his horse and ready to follow. He glanced up and his eyes widened with alarm. He'd heard something that I'd missed in the roar all around me. The flooding was loosening the steep slope above our heads.

Behind me, two enormous boulders tumbled through the gushing water. One of them bounced like a Cyclops' toy ball down into the ravine. But the other, nearly the height of a man, fell onto the *Cursus* under the waterfall and blocked the road.

I was cut off from the others. I waited for some minutes but there was no communication between use over the roar of the torrent and the unyielding bulk of rock. After ten minutes in the hellish storm, I decided to wait for them at whatever rest stop next presented itself.

The horse jerked away from me with a limp. I could not afford to ride an animal with a strained leg muscle. We stumbled on in the storm for another hour until we could only feel the road underfoot. I was about to abandon myself to another night on the road under my cloak as a tarpaulin. Now that the worst of the cliffs was behind me, I looked for a suitable tree to use as a roof over our heads. Then I saw one of the makeshift huts the Alemanni used for summer herding.

I was in luck at last. The roughhewn door was unlocked. I tethered the horse to a tree near a deep cleft in the rocky slope where he could rest his shivering flanks.

There was nothing inside but a long, wide bench and a stool. At least here I could light a fire, dry my cloak and trousers, eat the dried flatbread and withered fruits we'd rationed for this day, and wait out the storm for a glint of dawn to start forward. All I had to do was reach the next *mansio* in hope that they had a fresh horse and a glass of wine for me while I waited for the others.

—THE WOLVES OF AMBITION—

My fire lit, I hung chilly trousers over the stool, laid out my worn bedroll on the lumpy bench, and stretched myself out for a deep sleep.

☇☇☇

I awoke to a silence broken by the sound of a few last raindrops plunking from the makeshift roof overhead onto the dirt floor next to my boots. I must have slept for some hours, as the entire shed was now visible in a dim slate-gray light.

No.

There was something else.

A soft footfall outside and a jingling of harness had me on my bare feet and out the hut in seconds.

At the sound of my step, a man turned, my saddle in his thick arms. He wore a mix of unbleached sheepskins and the rags of Roman army gear. I recognized the insignia of a *signifier* of the dishonored legion, the rebel *Magnentiaci*, on his filthy tunic.

He was an Alemannus, with a wide face almost covered in reddish-brown beard. His wore his greasy hair twisted into a fiendish knot pinned like a doorknob over the right ear.

But there was nothing comic in the way his deep-set brown eyes burned from under his low brow. There was an indentation the size of an onion between his left eye and temple. Some missile had gone deep into his skull but he had survived.

I took the measure of him in a glance. He lurched back, favoring one leg and gave me a weird and sudden smile that told me he was too dangerous to live among women and children. Warfare made him one of life's scavengers living from hut to hut as an outcast. If that tunic wasn't stolen, he was a veteran of battling our side or battling for our side as a *laetus*.

I gripped my *spatha* in the right hand and my *pugio* in the other. I told him to clear off. He grunted at me in a guttural dialect full of throat-clearing. He wasn't having any Roman clemency. I didn't blame him for his barbarian manners. I was almost as hungry as he looked. Perhaps he wanted my money and food, but before or after killing me, I wasn't sure. The only communication possible was by a contest of arms.

He dropped my saddle and pulled out a vicious dagger of sorts—longer than my *pugio* but nicked, rusty, and bent. If I survived a thrust from that blade, I'd die of blood poisoning a week later.

We squared off. All I thought of was recovering my boots and bedroll and clearing off without doing the man further injury. Then he lunged at me and I dodged, bracing for his second try. He lunged again but I saw that each lunge left him rebalancing for a second on that weaker leg. I retreated, feigning resignation. I even let him think he was backing me up against the slope of the hill behind the hut where rivulets ran down in dozens of tiny icy fingers.

Keeping him off balance would give me the advantage. So I started to slide sideways, first three steps to the right and then three steps to the left, making him stagger unevenly, trying to figure out when to make his third thrust at my unprotected chest.

We lurched back and forth this way for many long minutes as I gauged the weakness of his weaker limb. He was slower than I was, but a life foraging in the Alpine valleys had toughened him. I would be nothing once I was at his mercy.

Then without any warning, I used the cliff wall behind me as leverage with one foot and with a great push off the stone, launched myself headfirst like a *ballista*'s dart, tackling his weaker knee. When my right shoulder came slamming into his leg, I heard it snap. He howled, cursing me in his rough-throated tongue.

He sprawled on his back underneath me. I pinned down his knife arm and stabbed my *pugio* deep into his sleeve and thrust my *spatha* hard down through the trouser of the injured leg for as long as I needed to get to my saddlebags. He flailed in pain, then got himself under control, and tried reaching for the blade and kicking with his good leg to get himself free.

I pulled on my trousers and boots. Returning with a length of rope meant for crossing flooded streams and other emergencies, tied his wrists together and dragged him to the nearest tree. I tossed the rope over the closest branch within reach and pulled him half off his feet, then strung him up with a series of taut knots.

—THE WOLVES OF AMBITION—

I wasn't going to hurt him any further, but one good scavenge deserved another. I took his knife and boots off him in what was still a fierce struggle, despite the agony of his leg. His nasty blade would spare my better weapons some rough chores on the road.

I left him some food. It might be days before friends, if such a man still had any, found him there.

I checked the regulation padlocks meant to protect imperial deliveries in my saddlebags. I'd caught him in time. He hadn't got anything valuable.

The horse's leg was better. I rode off and didn't stop for the first four hours of the day, other than to let him drink and graze in a sunny clearing full of wildflowers. At last, the slopes began to fall away from me. My worn and stony trail crossed other, better roads. A haven must be near.

The sun was halfway to the meridian when I heard the moan of an echoing mountain horn, low and insistent, blowing across the heights behind me. I hastened my descent. It had not taken as long for the scavenger's Alemanni brethren to rescue him. They were signaling each other to hunt me down.

I leapt back into my saddle and forced the horse onwards.

I never risk stopping, even to let him drink but forced him all the way to Curia where I changed him over at last. It was nearly dusk when I gazed at an enormous dark blue lake gleaming in the distance. At the far end, a wide river rushed into the waiting waters. From where I strained in my saddle to get a better look, the river cut with such speed and power through the lake, it showed as a visible line of dark current heavy with tumbling mud through the stiller waters on either side.

As my eyes roved the miles of forested lake coast, I made out the welcome shape of the garrison of Brigantium, the last secure Roman fortress before the ravaged Rhenus valley plains.

I hastened toward its gates and flung myself with relief at the *riparienses*' chief officer, a weathered tribune holding down the beleaguered walled encampment.

He offered me ready food supplies, a change of horse, and some mixed news.

Despite Constantius' 'successful' mopping-up campaign, Alemanni insurgents still infested the territory surrounding the lake and harassed the mountain passes, making communication and deliveries erratic.

Unfortunately we could expect little better in the devastated Gallo-Roman fields ahead to the north.

'The highway running north is open, but that's the problem. Any barbarian can race through Gallia on solid Roman paving stones. The Gallic hamlets that expected protection from our troops are left hungry and vulnerable by our retreat into the garrisons. They curse Constantius for letting the Alemanni cross the Rhenus in the first place, just to defeat Magnentius and then stay on to steal good land.'

'At least you still have good wine to drink,' I said, lifting my empty cup in a grateful toast.

'I'm sorry I can't spare you an escort.'

'That's all right. Just sketch me a reliable map. I had no idea the *Cursus* was in such bad condition up there, either washed out or buried under snow and silt.'

'You took a wrong turn after Comum. You lost the modern road. You were trying to cross over the ancient route nobody uses anymore. Your fellow *agentes* retraced their steps and found the good road an hour or so back from the boulder crash.'

'So they're ahead of me? No one said anything in Curia.'

'You talked to the wrong shift. I have no doubt your companions have reached the river valley plateau beyond Augusta Raurica by now.'

'I'll have to catch up. Will it be safer going on a flat road alone?'

He shrugged. 'Flat, yes. I don't know about safe. Good Roman citizens are starving down there and squabbling over whatever the Alemanni left in their wake. Farmers only feel safe sowing crops within their town wall.'

He poured me more of his excellent wine. 'Only a decent harvest and more welfare shipments this autumn will stabilize the situation.'

'And they talk only of religious questions at court these days.'

He grunted. 'The only people making any profit from our horrors are the churchmen. They save souls with one hand and take tithes and property deeds with the other.'

'So the civil war is still exacting its price.'

—THE WOLVES OF AMBITION—

He nodded. 'If over the next two days of hard riding, you survive the Alemanni preying on parties traveling up this road,' he said, 'you'll catch up with your *magister*. They beat the storm, but planned to lay over at Count Maudio's up north for a day or two for illness.'

'Who's sick?'

'Your boss himself. Wracked with stomach cramps and unable to eat a thing, much less ride. Vomiting up his guts. I must admit, he's a hardy old curmudgeon. He cleaned out our dispensary of medicines, but I can't promise that even a sackful of tonic will get that old coot to Silvanus alive.'

⚔⚔⚔

The Brigantium tribune had overestimated the energy of the barbarians pillaging hamlets between Augusta Rauricum and the fortresses of Concordia and Tribuni. The Alemanni in the *vici* I passed were starving and hostile but passive. They saw little profit in impeding the hard-riding *agens* with his lean North African cast of feature.

All along the battered *Cursus* loitered ragged Gallo-Roman refugees pushed off their estates. They emerged from their pathetic lean-tos and huts at the sound of a horse clattering past. The adults hung back, sullen and watchful. Only the bravest or hungriest of the children mustered the strength to stand dangerously close to the verge and hold out their hands in mute appeal.

I'd now reached territory where Roman cremation was disfavored and burial preferred. More than one cemetery stretched out on the slopes overlooking the river valley. Raw wooden crucifixes and freshly hewn stones stood bare over newly dug mounds. No wonder those Gallo-Roman bishops were rushing along safer roads down central Gallia to get to Constantius' groaning buffet tables.

By the time I thundered into the gates of the old fortress in Argentoratum, I began to hope I would reach Apodemius, Gaudentius and Meroveus in time. But the officers in charge here gave me no warm wine or fresh stew. When I went to change over my relief horse for a fresh mount, I saw only nags and veteran battle steeds well past their fighting years.

Shoving Constantius' imperial summons under the nose of the *tribunus stabili*, I overruled the deliberations of his conniving cavalry master and grabbed the sleekest racer in his care over his threatening protests.

Thanks to their obvious hostility at losing the best horse in the paddocks, I completed that particular *mutatio* in record time. This animal was everything my other horses weren't—sure of foot and keen on feeling the wind in his mane.

I would push him until the *mansio* signaling a changeover half way, if there was any. Otherwise he was stuck with me for the entire next stretch. We raced with the early afternoon sun warming my right shoulder. I was sure we could do another fifty miles and reach the fortress in Mogantiacum before midnight—even though it meant eating and napping in my saddle to break all records.

※ ※ ※

My racing horse was unlucky and I was merciless in driving him on. There was no *mansio* still in operation anywhere where I could trade him in for a fresh animal. I had to rest him en route more often than I'd hoped. We plowed on past midnight, cantering by moonlight. I lost track of time, measuring only the arc of the constellations passing over my helmet.

It was by the first steely gleam of dawn that I spotted the ancient Nemetae fortress glowing faintly in the mist blanketing Mogontiacum. I'd envisioned a real sanctuary from the dangers of the road harking back to its founding by Augustus' commanders four centuries before.

Instead all I saw was a charred and chilly ruin of walls and potholed towers poised on a high wedge-shaped bank.

I trotted the exhausted horse down the last few hundred yards and waited outside the huge bolted gates until someone extended a torch over the walls and peered down at me.

'I'm carrying a message for General Silvanus,' I announced for the dozenth time of the journey.

—THE WOLVES OF AMBITION—

'I supposed you'll want to join the *Magister Agentium in Rebus*,' the sentry replied.

My heart leapt with the relief. I followed my sullen guide across a cold and gray parade ground. A strong premonition of danger and death emanated from the untended clutter of disorderly and ancient buildings we passed. On an upper floor strewn with detritus from previous occupants, I reported to Gaudentius who guarded Apodemius' door. Meroveus had gone to refresh our supplies for the final leg to Agrippina. We had to let Apodemius rest as well as he could through continuous cramps and fever.

I took my first real breakfast in days—a northern repast of forest berries, dried venison, and a strange rough porridge, in the comforting company of Meroveus. The Toxandrian and I then mounted the parapet to watch the dawn come up to reveal the true power of Rhenus River flowing past.

Meroveus did not know the history of this haunted place. Almost three hundred and fifty years before, the original fort had been Roma's base for conquests across the Rhenus and had once housed five hundred infantry.

In the horrific barbarian massacre of Teutoburg Forest, Roma had lost three of her famous legions out of twenty-eight—fifteen thousand soldiers—but not her imperial spirit. We had built a second fort on this site as part of the Rhenus reorganization.

Our imperial forefathers had quelled the tribes of the Nemetes, the Vangiones, and the Triboci into submission. The fortress, expanded thrice, was abandoned by auxiliary troops advancing across the water to conquer more of *Germania*. Those who stayed behind preferred life in the thriving market town of Nemetae outside the old fortress' walls.

Any *agens* could discover Nemetae's lost glory from studying the travel handbooks of the last century—*The Antonine Itinerary* or the road chart, the *Tabula Peutingeriana*.

Nemetae had once been a lively administrative hub with a vast market plaza, public buildings, living quarters, temples, and even a theater. That was long over.

Where once five hundred Roman legionaries had prepared for advance marches into hostile territory, a skeleton guard of fewer than two hundred held this garrison fast, locked up, and braced for the worst. A little over seventy years before our time, the lively market town under the fortress gates had fallen to Alemannic rape and arson.

We Romans gave it the town. There hadn't been anything left to pillage by the time our current nemesis, King Chnodomarius, led the Alemanni in attack yet again. The Alemannus giant had been burning homes and enslaving citizens for years now while his erstwhile 'ally,' Emperor Constantius, turned a blind eye.

Back home in Roma, young Leo was settling down to Plato or Plutarch with his teacher Antonius Drusus. What did those dead men tell him of a Roman world still fighting ignorance, brutality and destruction at every turn? Should the boy be learning to ride and fight instead? Or would my beloved city always sit safe on its graceful hillsides under the gaze of statues and pigeons?

The scars of border warfare lay all around us, but this morning, the fortress basked in a calm of birdsong and rustling treetops. North of here lay the safer *praefecti laetorum*, some dozen prefectures governed for Roma by our Frankish confederate military officials recruiting for the army and collecting what taxes they could.

But the ruins scattered around these walls, the wagon tracks leading away from the gates but overrun with weeds, and the wooden stumps of burned foundations sticking like rotting teeth where the confident town had stood for hundreds of years warned me that the Alemanni would be back.

The Empire could not afford weakness, neither in its borders nor in its leadership. Apodemius had to convince Silvanus to defend himself and return in honor to restoring Gallia to prosperity.

'What's wrong with him, Meroveus?'

'I don't know. Gaudentius has poured every potion and painkiller we could requisition down him, just to get him this far. You and Gaudentius should ride on with the summons. I'll stay here with Apodemius until your return.'

I glanced askance at Meroveus. I knew he cared about the welfare of our *schola* master, but was he also looking for an excuse to avoid facing his estranged family farther north?

—THE WOLVES OF AMBITION—

Apodemius called for me as soon as he awoke.

'I'll be ready to ride north in a day,' he whispered.

'Surely not in this condition.'

'Count Maudio's attendants gave us strong medicine. I'll be fine.'

The *Magister*'s appearance appalled me. He'd lost at least ten pounds since his arrival in Mediolanum. His room stank of digestive chaos. Only the rapid assistance of an orderly kept his cell bearable.

Gaudentius hovered over Apodemius' bed. Where I expected to see anxiety or sadness, his expression betrayed nothing.

Since the day I first met him in a North African study belonging to a retired *agens*-turned-oil-trader, Apodemius had seemed ageless. The white-haired stranger had grilled me, tested me, and even given the nod to whipping my back raw—just to consolidate my cover as a runaway slave.

I owed this old man everything. He had rescued me from a forsaken life as a freedman beholden to an angry, resentful sire. He'd overseen my training and promotion in the service from a rookie rider on the Sirmium postal loop to *biarchus* in seven eventful years. I hadn't always excelled in my tasks. He'd even kept me on the payroll during those long months of war shock from the Battle of Mursa, when the carnage left me a trembling, sleepless wreck.

Of late the *agentes*' chief had kept me deskbound with analysis work. I enjoyed the quiet respite from investigations and long distance missions. Perhaps it was his tacit acknowledgement that my presence in the old capital city was the last lifeline for the struggling remnants of the great Roman aristocratic House of Manlius.

Gaudentius shook his head. He mixed another solution of medicine with a goblet of wine and put it to the *Magister*'s parched lips. Within a minute, it surged back up into a pottery bowl.

'Is there no *medicus* here?'

'None of any use, it seems, just surgeons and orderlies used to sewing up robust fighters.'

'You need some rest,' I told the *ducenarius*. 'I'll watch him.'

Gaudentius would not leave Apodemius' side. 'If he dies, he dies under my watch.'

I went back outside to find Meroveus in conversation with a scrawny officer with a neck too long for his narrow shoulders topped by a wobbly-looking head.

'I'm Proculus, the adjutant,' he said. 'My patrol and I will escort you up to Agrippina.'

Meroveus took me to one side. 'This Proculus doesn't look like he could protect a kitchen pail from a pack of hungry puppies.'

'I'll ride with him, gladly,' I said. 'But Apodemius can't believe that he's fit to continue north. He's lost his mind, not his appetite.'

Meroveus looked at me with a strange cast in his green eyes. 'If something happens to the old man,' he whispered, 'who becomes *magister*?'

'The Emperor would appoint a new man, preferably someone we could all stomach,' I said. 'Why?'

'Nothing.'

Meroveus tossed a worried glance behind his shoulder. 'Since the investigation and torture of Governor Africanus' guests, the *agens* most by the Emperor is . . ?'

I took a deep breath, unwilling to point a finger at Gaudentius. 'Appointments are by seniority. There have been other senior *agentes* promoted years ago as *princeps officii* to various prefectures. One of them might wish to head up the *schola*.'

'What fool would leave such a cushy position to come back to run the Castra?' Meroveus said. 'Those lucky dogs know they're well off with a juicy income. Every time a prefect signs a document, his *princeps* has to countersign. Every signature carries its fat fee. Just one year as *princeps* guarantees you a nice retirement.'

'Then,' I said with a cautious nod, 'yes, the man Constantius might want to be our new service chief is someone who has stood at his side through recent difficulties. The Emperor would want a tough and astute political player who could weather the intrigues at court.'

—THE WOLVES OF AMBITION—

Meroveus lifted his Pannonian cap to scratch his raw scalp in thought. 'Gaudentius is an ambitious man who spies on people and then turns them in for treason straight to the throne instead of going through the Castra hierarchy, like any *agens* is instructed. Convenient for some, isn't it?'

I was left alone with anxious reflections. I'd thought that as soon as we caught up with Silvanus and brought him back to court, we would have saved the Empire from civil uproar. All our troubles would be over.

Instead it felt like they were just beginning.

Chapter 8, Roxana's Plea

—COLONIA CLAUDIA ARA AGRIPPINENSIUM—

After so many days of hard dashing up the river bank, the last stretch to Agrippina felt like a sluggish parade saunter. Apodemius was now too weak to stay upright in his saddle. I bought a Gallo-Roman farmer's battered *cisium*—more flaking wicker than leather and wood—for the rest of the journey. We reached the suburbs of the colony at last. Gaudentius and I had failed to persuade the old man that he should slow his journey as we passed the comfortable estates of various Gallo-Roman families.

With a strange pallor and hoarse voice, he insisted he would continue on to brief Silvanus in person, at length and in full. Gaudentius ministered to him, pouring what seemed to me to be useless tonics, in an effort to keep the Magister going.

Meroveus had made friends among the Franks on patrol. To listen to his happy gargling of those strange Germanic consonants was almost more than my Latinate ears could bear.

Proculus wanted to hear all the gossip of Constantius II's court. Given his insinuating and persistent questioning, keeping the problems of his commanding officer confidential was difficult. What Proculus lacked in physical stature, the natty little supply officer made up for in canny political instinct. The Roman might be half a foot shorter than his Frankish colleagues, but I could see why he was stationed close to Silvanus' side.

'You rode all the way up the Rhenus to tell us "no news, good news"?' he wisecracked. 'The *Magister Agentium in Rebus* himself lies in that carriage back there like a common Christian pilgrim suffering tummy trouble—all for nothing?'

'Constantius seeks reassurances from such a troubled region,' I said. 'The Emperor spends long nights alone in his chapel, praying for peace.'

'I had a dream last night,' the adjutant said, after a thoughtful pause in his banter.

'Tell me your dream!' I joked, anxious to change the subject from Silvanus.

Proculus' expression darkened. 'It was a nightmare, my friend. I couldn't move my arms or legs. Something was tearing at my flesh. I screamed out in pain. I shouted for help. But no sound came from my throat. All the same, I knew that if I said the right thing, I would be freed. Only what? The torment was beyond anything I'd ever known.'

'Why didn't you just wake yourself up?'

'I tried, I tried! But I couldn't. A greasy gag muffled my screams. I was supposed to lie. Only if I lied, would I gain relief. Screaming alone would not wake me up. But I did not lie.'

'You're lucky it was only a dream,' I said. 'In Mediolanum we hears the screams of men under torture every time they air out Catena's interrogation rooms.'

'Service up here is harsh, but we're all lucky to be well clear of that man's cruelties.'

'No one is safe, Proculus,' I said, shaking my head. 'No one is ever safe.'

The adjutant was silent for a few minutes. We were less than an hour now from our destination. His patrol's pace quickened, despite Proculus' stately discipline.

'They say dreams foretell our future, Numidianus.' He shot me a wry glance.

'If that's true, I'll spend my future with a sexy woman, built like *this*, offering me delights I'd blush to describe, even to a man of the world like yourself, Adjutant,' I laughed. 'But it's not going to happen.'

'The question is, are we masters of our dreams or are we slaves of Fortune foretold by our dreams?' he mused. 'One thing I know, I stayed master of myself in my nightmare. I did not lie and until I finally woke up, I clung to the truth.'

I prayed to the gods Proculus would never know for himself how hard that feat proved in the cells of Paulus Catena.

—THE WOLVES OF AMBITION—

We rode on until at last we saw military exercise fields

Gaudentius assisted Apodemius off the *cisium*'s rustic cushions and onto his feet, as the patrol dismounted to admire the army games underway less than half a mile from the crest of the hill where we had halted.

More than a thousand men pounded away in lines and circles as they trained, making of the former pastures a sea of green, gray, and silver set against the glossy browns of their cavalry mounts and shining auburns and golds of the Franks' flowing hair.

We gazed beyond at the rebuilt walls of the great Colonia Claudia Ara Agrippinensium, a city teeming once again with trade and comfort. The hill on which the *Cursus* had deposited us offered us a sprawling view of the colony's streets, basilica, temple, and colonnaded semi-circle of stalls behind the imperial parade ground. Fullers' racks on flat roofs all across the city caught the bright sun on their long lengths of bleached wool. There was a tannery just visible outside the city wall, next to the Rhenus.

'Do you see General Silvanus over there?' Proculus pointed to a slope on the far side of the melee of exercises. We saw a command tent flanked with banners. The red cloaks of centurions and gleaming gold of expensive helmets marked a group of officers standing or sitting on campstools while their adjutants ran up and down the slope with instructions.

'Which is the man?' Apodemius asked.

It shocked me to realize that in all these years, the *Magister* had never laid eyes on the charming hero of Franco-Roman military repute. What could be clearer proof of how long and hard Silvanus had stayed operational in the field, mopping up and swabbing the Empire's civil wounds, far from Mediolanum and the likes of throne-lickers like General Arbetio?

In that respect, Claudius Silvanus resembled his rival, the embittered hero of our Eastern defenses, General Ursicinus.

'He's the tall man with the curly chestnut hair, locked in conversation with the light-haired centurion in the red cloak,' I said. 'Just . . . there, rising now and mounting his horse.'

'Yes, I see him now,' Apodemius panted. 'He's a more dashing version of his handsome son. I begin to understand.'

He was thinking of Roxana, in thrall to this married officer and lost to the *schola* as Apodemius' best and only female agent.

'He's seen us,' Proculus shouted from his conference with a greeting party sent up the hills to the roadside where we rested. 'He is riding to greet you in person, *Magister* Apodemius.' We watched as the General exchanged some last words from his saddle with a tribune in charge.

'What are they doing down there, Meroveus?'

I directed the Toxandrian's attention to six rows of men some hundred feet apart with their backs to each other. Each row was practicing throwing a whirling object away from their ranks, but it wasn't clear to me what was turning, slowly in a circle, through the air to land safely away in the distant grass.

'They're honing their *francisca* tossing,' he said with a shrug.

'What we call a *securis*?'

'Close. It's the Franks' weapon of choice. Their axe head is heavier than a normal battle-axe and should turn only once in flight before striking its target. That's what they're perfecting right now. Then it bounces in a deadly and unpredictable fashion to trigger panic in the ranks of disciplined men only accustomed to the direct assault of spear, dagger, or *spatha*.'

'Good thing they're on our side,' I muttered.

I'd seen the Franks fight for the Emperor Magnentius at Mursa in close and ferocious combat with no chance to employ this particular trick. But I'd known that they differed from traditional Roman soldiers in favoring a formation that sent infantry speeding into the assault right between the horse legs of our cavalry ranks. They used these axes to lame the horse and slaughter an unseated enemy rider under the belly of his animal.

'When we've settled in, I'll show you the advantages of our barbed spear, the *angon*.' Meroveus promised.

'I can't wait,' was my dry reply.

We placed Apodemius back on his horse for dignity's sake. We sidestepped down the slope and once on the plain, trotted past watching Frankish onlookers to meet General Silvanus halfway. A gaggle of some fifty young women and older children watched the exercises from a safe distance, cheering on the soldiers.

'It looks like military exercises up here are more like games of skill than painful routine.'

'Even during training, the Cornuti and Bracchiati compete against each other for money and women,' Meroveus said with a laugh. He gestured at the pennants of those two *auxilia* flapping in the light breeze. The first had a double-headed dragon's head against a saffron background and the other a similar twin-headed dragon against a blue background.

'Frankish women are worth competing for,' Meroveus added with Germanic pride. 'But I wouldn't meddle if I were you, Numidianus. A fertile Germanic girl is worth a *wergild* price of three hundred *solidi*, three times that of a freeborn man, and matched only by a loss of a Frank in the *trustis*, the royal retinue.'

'What's a Frankish freedman worth?' I asked out of personal curiosity as a manumitted slave.

Meroveus put me in my place. 'Maybe fifty.'

I surveyed the smiling ranks of lively females as we rode past. They were tall and long-legged with lithe, wide hips outlined by gorgeous belts. They set off their thick braids of shining, fair hair with wide bands of embroidered cloth circling their unlined brows.

Even in early August sun, they wore light green woolen mantels with red or green hem bands, secured to both shoulders with unusual twin brooches shaped like silver cones. The *fibulae* were linked across their pert bosoms by exquisite chains. They wore their necklines cut lower than decent women in the great cities to the south, but I knew this was a tease, not a promise. Though these Germanic beauties did not enjoy the freedoms or rights of sophisticated Roman society women, they were all the more monitored and prized as vessels of their families' pure bloodlines.

There was a market-day atmosphere of celebration to the exercises. The girls cheered our little party as we passed. It was hard to believe that the so-called 'great' Constantine had tossed their grandfathers to the beasts of the Treverorum Circus behind their princes, Ascaricus and Merogaisus, in the notorious *Ludi Francici*. Legend held that the Frankish victims were so numerous and so ferocious in their defense, for once the great beasts ended their slaughter exhausted and satiated and had to be carried out of the arena.

We had the political canniness of Silvanus' father Bonitus to thank for the alliance we enjoyed today.

One girl of about sixteen or seventeen even tossed me a cocky wink. Her hair was a shade of red so light it was almost gold glinting rosy pink. A color I'd never seen in my life, completely unlike the fiery Celtic red I seen on many northerners. This girl's face was as pale as milk, sparked by cheeks slightly reddened by the sun.

I touched my *petanus* in salute.

'Welcome to Agrippina,' Silvanus shouted to Gaudentius and myself as we finally reined in mid-field. Apodemius held steady, but was dramatically reduced by his week of illness. I enjoyed the privilege of formal introductions. At the name 'Apodemius,' I detected wariness skitter across Silvanus' handsome face.

For all his straightforward welcome, Claudius Silvanus was one of the Empire's most famous political survivors while Apodemius was—pure and simple—the Empire's most famous spy. The old man's appearance was as clear a danger signal to the general as a *cornu* sounding attack in the middle of a still night.

He gripped all our hands again and gave me an extra slap on my back with the heartiness I recalled from the heady days of his rebel conferences with Magnentius and my father back in Aquileia.

His appearance up close startled me. The clean-shaven Roman I'd known as hardly distinguishable from my own Commander Gregorius or the other officers serving Magnentius had succumbed to the vanities of his father's roots. He wore his thick curls combed longer and stroked a moustache combed in the northern fashion.

'Don't stare at me, Numidianus,' he laughed. 'As they say, when in Roma . . . the men up here like to follow a Franco-Roman general who looks like a man, not a bathhouse lizard.'

'Was it on your instruction that Junius is working on a bit of upper lip fuzz himself?'

'Shaving already?' Silvanus took a sharp breath of longing for his hostage son. 'Is he all right?'

—THE WOLVES OF AMBITION—

'I will explain his transfer to Roma when we are alone,' I said in a low voice.

He shot me a worried glance, but said only, 'There is a lady waiting in the palace who will be overjoyed to see you, Numidianus.'

We trotted behind his stallion back up to the *Cursus* and reached the city walls. Skirting the riverbanks, we turned our backs on the massive bridgehead linking the old colony to Constantine's Castrum Divitia across the water. We proceeded through the city's fortified gates to follow a grand boulevard of busy shops and state buildings. Silvanus had worked quickly to restore peace to the city he'd recaptured less than a year before—abandoned by invading Alemanni who burned and carried off as much as they could. The quick eye picked up lingering traces of their destruction—a chimney reduced to charcoal here, a crumbled wall or market stalls under repair there, or a stretch of rubble where a line of elegant apartment buildings had stood.

Silvanus would not entertain a word of business until he had extended his hospitality to us. He thereby underscored that in Agrippina, only the roof of the Governor's Palace and his blooded troops protected us *agentes* from the secrets of the hostile forests on all sides.

He hosted us at a long single table set with benches and stools northern style, rather than couches or chairs. While only two of his senior officers stayed in our company to represent the Cornuti and Bracchiati troops, Silvanus warned us that our dinner party was not yet complete.

For it was not he that was hosting this banquet, but someone 'far more important.'

Our hearty toasts to each other's health were just underway when an old woman of about fifty years entered the dining hall.

Apodemius emitted a quick gasp, and for a moment we thought he was too sick to remain, but he shook his head and whispered, 'It is Evochildis of the Salians.' This formidable *matrona* was none other than the legendary widow of Bonitus who had witnessed the great Constantine forge peace with the Franks.

Two Franco-Roman females, plain and functional in dark heavy robes followed her. All three women wore heavy, ornate crucifixes on their breasts.

When the introductions and salutations had died down, we all took our seats again. While we were admiring the first platters of fresh food we'd seen in some time, a young woman slipped into the room and took a discreet seat nearest the wall behind the other women. She was so graceful and beaming, so bejeweled and yet refined, I reeled in sheer delight at seeing my old friend and one-time training rival so restored to health and spirits.

Roxana wore a robe of light blue silk, washed so soft it pooled like shimmering water around her ankles. A Frankish headdress circled her brow and pinned a lighter blue silk veil to the back of her intricate hairdo that floated down her back and brushed the heavy cloisonné belt slung around her hips.

Chains and bracelets of topazes and garnets sparkled in the early evening's torchlight.

Her robust complexion, always darker than Roman fashion dictated, had paled a little, but this evening's meeting set a deep blush streaking across her cheeks—fleshed out by love for Silvanus or hearty northern food—who could say?

Never had I imagined the ambitious, athletic young agent I had tussled with both in bed and field years ago would ripen into this gentler, softer woman.

Over a year ago, I'd watched her sad, solitary figure ride away with my boy Leo from Constantinopolis, ferrying the child to his mother's arms in Roma. Roxana had been determined even then to seek Silvanus out, but I'd warned her that the married hero could never make her happy.

This evening in Agrippina she gave me a wide and triumphant smile of welcome. It appeared my well-intended advice had been wrong.

The welcome meal the General's staff had mustered for his unexpected visitors was almost too rich and lavish, a gesture honoring Apodemius as a *vir illustris* equal in rank to Silvanus, the *Magister Militum per Gallias*.

The sauced venison was too heavy for the old man's troubled entrails. He shook his head when offered the tree fruits of the high season on honeyed platters. I watched with deepening concern as he passed up the roasted hare and river fish as well. He was almost too faint to continue the meal but could not continue to live on scraps of flatbread and dried olives for many more days.

To my distress, Silvanus gave an order and two hefty Cornuti went to our *magister*'s chair to help him to his room. But Apodemius waved them away, yet he ate nothing and said nothing. We finished dining in sober silence broken occasionally by the heavy-browed Evochildis asking polite questions about the state of the *Cursus* between the court and ourselves.

At last Silvanus signaled the ladies to leave our company and his *trustis* of officers to return to their duties.

'But stay, Roxana,' he added. When I saw the warmth of their gaze as she round the long tables to sit nearer him, I knew I had misjudged his feelings for my friend.

The dishes of silver plate were cleared away and Silvanus asked us to state our business.

Apodemius was too weak to prevail.

I rose and delivered the imperial summons to the head of the table.

Still smiling, Silvanus broke the seal and read the imperial summons to himself. His face drained of all color and his left hand strangled the heavy blue glass goblet so hard, I feared it would crack.

Gaudentius summarized events in Mediolanum, omitting no details known to our service. He summarized the main testimonies of the 'Gallus Trials'—among them, the questioning of chamberlain Gorgonius, General Ursicinus, and finally, the Emperor's own cousin Julian. The rough Neapolitan was no rhetorician. His flat recitation failed to convey the atmosphere of intrigue and terror stoked by screams rising from beneath the palace courtyard stones.

Gaudentius ordered me to add what I had personally witnessed—the underhanded transfer of Silvanus' letters of reference from Lampadius' office brazier to the Emperor in the seclusion of the chapel.

'You pay a price for your heroism and honors, General,' the *ducenarius* concluded. 'We are here to escort you back to the court for questioning.'

Silvanus brooded in silence. He'd kept dinner conversation light and general, biding his time until the hour for plain speaking had come. But he was not prepared for the awful object of our trip.

'Who spoke for me?' he asked us at last.

'Your fellow Franks Mallobaudes and Malarichus and not least your own son,' I said. 'But his position as hostage jeopardizes his life. He now hides in the Manlius townhouse in Roma.'

'I thank you for that much, Numidianus. I know you risk the charge of co-conspiracy for sheltering Junius. For the Frankish officers to defend me is as much as should be expected. A slur against my loyalty is a threat to their own authority over hundreds of guards.'

He frowned and ran his meat knife back and forth across the thick linen tablecloth.

Who among the Romans defended me against these slanders?'

The shrill and heavily accented Latin of Evochildis broke our telling silence. She had been eavesdropping on our conversation from the shadows of the hallway leading to the outer reception room.

She emerged into the light cast by a heavy wall torch. She was handsome for her advanced years, but frightening. The deep wrinkles in her weathered skin made her face almost as masculine as her son's. The beauty that had held the great Bonitus to her bed had hardened into a mask of regal pride.

Her thick eyebrows met as she burst out at us: 'Expect nothing, nothing from such reptiles!' she said with a shake of her pristine linen coif.

She turned on Apodemius. 'Did you see how the men in the field today worship my son?' Could you feel their loyalty to *him*? Does anyone *love* Constantius so? The Emperor needs Silvanus. Does Silvanus need that Illyrian clan and their court full of envious cowards?

'Mother! Silvanus shot out of his chair. 'Constantius is our emperor, Mother.'

'Arggh! Who is Constantius up here in the great delta? Is he pinning down the Alemanni to the south? Keeping the Quadi,

Chamavi, Chattuari, and Salii across that river, only miles from that bridge, divided against each other? Who else could keep a peace negotiated between their warring *reguli* and *sub-reguli*? Who else but you, my son! Who is commander north of Argentoratum?'

She turned her burning eyes on Apodemius. '*My son!*'

Fear flickered across Roxana's face. Suddenly I understood Apodemius' comment that Roxana would be perfectly happy with her hero, were it not for *the other woman*. This dragon Evochildis was the other woman—not Junius' twitching mother closeted away in Mediolanum.

With the Franco-Roman noblewoman in charge of Silvanus' reputation, we would never get the *Magister Militum per Gallias* to Mediolanum. Each day he delayed would strengthen his enemies Lampadius, Arbetio, and the others.

I rallied, '*Matrona*, you must see—'

'I see that Constantius cannot fight the Persians and hold the Western borders without the help of Silvanus. He should waste his time in groveling down to Mediolanum to explain this crime against his spotless reputation! My son is no supplicant! Your summons is an outrageous insult!'

Apodemius wrapped an arthritic hand over his dizzy eyes. 'His reputation is no longer spotless, *Matrona*. You must excuse me, General, I must lie down.'

Two *domestici* supported Apodemius off his seat and limping away to his room. At a glance from Gaudentius, Meroveus went with them.

'I think there is no harm in spending a few days in consultation with the Emperor, General,' Roxana said in a loving voice. 'Constantius can only be comforted by a careful briefing of your heavy burdens in this campaign and your plans to remain in the north for as long as imperial security demands it.'

But Silvanus was still the same, a man who hesitated and weighed the forces for and against. I saw in his downcast silence the same man who prevaricated in his loyalties on the very eve of the Battle of Mursa. That was the cursed night when Silvanus, counseled by Constantius' envoy Flavius Philippus, had betrayed his comrades with his sudden defection to Constantius' side.

Now he had to weigh the risk of refuting his enemies' evidence in Constantius' court against the dangers of standing resolute, proclaiming his innocence from a safe distance.

'I am going into the chapel for guidance—alone,' he said. 'Hours of vigilant prayer may deliver the answer I need.'

He turned to Gaudentius. 'I would ask that you consider any deliberations as delayed by your *Magister*'s illness,' he suggested, 'as well as my late arrival back to this palace. I will not ask you to lie for me, should it come to that, but I beg you for more time to take in these terrible sins against my record.'

He didn't wait for an answer, for he knew no *agens* would distort a written record of events under oath. He had asked for what he could and left it at that.

His mother rushed after him, but in the shadows, he directed her down another corridor and proceeded off to the chapel alone.

In a swirl of blue silk, Roxana rushed to our side of the table and knelt before us. Taking both Gaudentius' beefy hands in hers, she asked, 'You see who is the ruler here, *Ducenarius*? Give me a day or two. Tend to Apodemius' sickness while I persuade the General of the urgency of clearing away all these ugly accusations. I know this Arbetio too well. He must be stopped cold. This will not be his last attempt to unseat Silvanus while he is still Consul so that when his term is up, a better soldier than he will have fallen away from his path.'

'I will do what I can, Roxana, for his sake,' I promised. 'Tomorrow morning, I will request a private conference with Evochildis.'

'You are too junior, Numidianus.' Gaudentius stood up and left Roxana kneeling before his empty stool. 'And I will not interfere without Apodemius' say-so.'

I had no choice but to appeal to the bull-headed Neapolitan's vanity.

'You and Apodemius were both born in Italia,' I said, lacing my words with admiration. 'You remind Evochildis too much of the high standing of our imperial authority.'

Gaudentius conceded as much with a condescending nod of agreement.

'Whereas, I am only the child of a far-flung province, an ex-slave from a conquered and colonized people. I represent the new blood of the Empire. Evochildis may not trust senior officers of Constantius' court. When tempers have cooled, she may listen to a Numidian.'

※※※

Did Silvanus realize the dangers of delay in responding to Constantius? The Emperor's message required immediate acknowledgement, even thanks—given the signature of 'Our Eternity, The Lord of the Entire Universe,' the Emperor.

Yet Silvanus had not jumped to the obvious—that nothing less than a full prostration in spirit and person would secure him from disaster. And even if his God told him to race to Mediolanum, his mother, the uncrowned Christian queen of these Romanized Salians, was capable of holding him back. Her fierce pride in her son and outrage at his treatment by Constantius' *consistorium* had extinguished all reason tonight.

Tomorrow it was my turn to heal open wounds. I tossed and turned under the light summer covers and listened to sounds of a city waiting for the reluctant summer sunset to relieve us all. It was no good—the northern light was still too bright even at this evening hour for me to sleep.

So I slipped out into the corridor, past the rooms assigned to Gaudentius, Meroveus and Apodemius and set off to find Roxana.

The palace was shaped with three sides looking out on an interior courtyard. Roxana's rooms were as far from ours as possible, in the wing facing directly across the courtyard.

I straightened my wrinkled travel clothing and cut across the empty yard to the entrance to her wing. Slaves directed me to her suite of rooms. I knocked with my toe, as was polite.

A rosy-cheeked Frankish slave opened the door and ushered me through a small, neat sitting room. Even before I reached Roxana's innermost room, I heard a man's deep, wracking sobs. I sensed my timing was bad—then saw why it was awful.

Between the maid and the half-open door, I spied Roxana fresh from her bath in a modest, bleached *tunica*. She was sitting on a low couch, her head bowed.

She was not alone.

Meroveus knelt at her side and hung like a huge toy in her comforting arms. His brawny torso shook with anguish. His face was buried in her bosom. She stroked his shaven head and rocked back him back and forth as if he were a heartbroken child.

She glanced up at me, her widened brown eyes streaming with silent tears. She shook her head to silence me. I slipped back to my room, my heart pounding with pity at the poor man's distress.

For it was obvious what had happened. Roxana had no doubt done her best to locate Meroveus' wife and family to warn them of his castration and later humiliations as a chamber slave in the Antiochene palace.

If anyone could have convinced the Toxandrian wife that a man with such great heart and formidable fighting prowess could manage with what he had left to make that woman safe and happy again, that person would have been Roxana.

It was obvious Roxana had failed.

Chapter 9, A Frankish Queen

—The Governor's Residence of the Colonia Claudia Ara Agrippinensium, August 7, 355 AD—

I slept fitfully through rest of the short night. When dawn cracked the black sky covering the high pines of the forest beyond, I sent a slave with my request for an audience with Evochildis to the women's wing. The first hour of the working day had come and gone. I could be sure General Silvanus was already breakfasting with his officers.

I went to the palace baths where attendants scraped and shaved off a week's worth of Gallic dirt. I ate a light breakfast of hard northern cheese veined with green and tart blue-black berries coated with thick honey.

The slave returned to inform me, only too soon, that Evochildis would receive me.

There were five main buildings in the Agrippina provincial governor's headquarters—a three-storied reception house facing the bridgehead flanked by two long office buildings facing each other across the first courtyard. Through an inner gate into the parade ground behind, there was the palace with its two wings where we were housed. At the end stood the semi-circle of stalls backed by a rear gate into the city.

I marched after a soft-slippered Frankish slave with swinging hips along richly painted corridors protected by summer hangings against the humidity of the nearby river. Superb mosaics covered the floors of every room—portraits of the gods or scenes of rich life indoors and invigorating sport out of doors.

Sadly, there was scarcely a stretch of ten feet of cracked *tesserae* that wasn't stained by blood or fire. Signs of clumsy repair and make-do were everywhere. What had started as a military garrison three hundred years ago had risen into a bustling imperial capital for northeast Gallia. Then brutal barbarian attacks a hundred years ago had damaged the fortress and cut the population down to a mere twenty thousand souls.

In a sense, Agrippina had been fending off barbarian destruction ever since.

Within its ancient walls, the city comprised some fifty to sixty square blocks of Roman-style construction. Constantine's original bridge still stood proud, but its former polish was forever gone. The scars left by barbarian warfare—damaged stonework, charred timbers, and many empty spaces only recently cleared of rubble—were obvious. Since the determined ravages of its latest *Germani* raiders, Agrippina was once again struggling to recover its air of confident northern power.

The Empire could thank Silvanus for that.

Throughout many years of *agens* duties, I had seen a number of imperial suites occupied by empresses, *augustae*, and lesser court females. I'd grown accustomed to their theatrical entrances amid gelded sentries and ladies in attendance.

A powerful woman likes to make a strong first impression, all the more so when she's intelligent enough to resent her weak position relative to imperial men.

I straightened my belt and helmet as the Frankish sprite escorted me into Evochildis' reception rooms on the upper floor of the official residence.

Although she held no rank in our Roman eyes, Evochildis received me in the manner of a renowned provincial governor's wife or the queen of a tributary state.

She remained seated in the company of some half dozen ladies on a raised floor at the far end of her long public room. A couple of heated braziers on tripods warded off the early morning chill. Perhaps incense was too 'Eastern' for these hardy women. Only moldering wood chips and fresh flowers scented the air.

Even by stark daylight, I could not pinpoint her age. She had tucked her hair to the last strand under a veil fastened so tight across her brow, it was as if someone had pinned her face taut to either temple.

Large silver hoops set with garnets pulled down her earlobes until they drooped like a newborn puppy's. She lined her eyes with imported black charcoal as favored by current fashion but the creases in her cheeks were too deep to enliven with rouge.

—THE WOLVES OF AMBITION—

Like any wealthy woman past her prime, Evochildis employed all means to offset each wrinkle with some distracting drape at the neckline or swinging embroidered sleeve. The confidence of former beauty lingered in embellishments that graced her sagging figure.

This doyenne of the Salians gestured me to stand closer, below the dais. She sat on a low but expensive stool vertically grooved in the *Germani* style and covered with an otter skin cushion. She had been working on a large needlework frame stretched with bleached linen.

Men were at a disadvantage here, from the start.

Her ringed and freckled hand wafted a strand of violet silk in my direction.

'You slept well, *Biarchus*...Marcus...Gregorianus... Numidianus?' she asked, giving me a withered smile. With each careful syllable, she had stressed the links that brought me into her presence. I was there as an agent answering to the most powerful espionage master of the Empire. I had once been a lowly slave. I was the bastard son of her own son's rebel ally, then enemy. And my existence was somewhat like her own—a consequence of the Empire's extraordinary reach from the frozen seas north of Agrippina down to the edges of the Numidian desert south of Carthago.

In short, Silvanus had briefed her well.

'Thank you for receiving me, *Matrona*.'

Evochildis presided over a glittering court of her own, a distaff Franco-Roman *consistorium*. Ladies of varying age and attraction sat on chairs and stools in a semi-circle facing the main doors. I noticed again the fashion for large silver tubular *fibulae* connected by decorative chains that pinned down each lady's bodice fold below collarbone. A ball-shaped amulet of silver or crystal dangled from a second chain off every heavy belt.

Each woman worked with an embroidery or darning needle on an item of linen, hose, headpiece, or tunic trim. Each gave me a perfunctory nod with a head weighed down by heavy braids trailed by a silk veil down her back.

But I wasn't fooled. Their graceful summer costumes served as showcases for the brilliant gold cloisonné work that *Germani* artisans were famed for. Their slaves spent hours on their elaborate coiffures. But these privileged ladies were no mere gaggle of northern fashion plates or gossiping housewives. Underneath those elaborate crimped curls and hair buns, they listened well.

They reminded me of Constantius' expressionless scribes working their *stili* back and forth over wax tablets in Mediolanum—all ears but no opinions. They were no doubt as loyal to Evochildis as the armored *trustis* was to Silvanus. I remembered how the Caesar Gallus' boy *domestici* had driven me toward a violent death in Constantinopolis, forcing my reluctant steps forward with dozens of pricking stabs from their golden parade daggers. Were these tall, fair-haired Frankish ladies just as capable of setting on me like a flock of deadly birds, stitching up my eyelids and killing me with a thousand jabs of tiny pins?

My discomfort must have showed.

'Offer our guest some wine, Clothild,' Evochildis said. None other than the strawberry-haired girl from the exercise field rose from a low stool at the back of the group to play *pocillator*. She poured thick *merum* from a great purple and white porphyry beaker into a heavy white wineglass splotched with blue and green.

I took no more than a polite sip. The drink was unfiltered and crude, hardly diluted enough for civilized tastes. Was this a calculated insult?

We waited through a pregnant silence for the widow to begin. Her tone would signal to the others whether I was a friend to their hero Silvanus or not.

'You *agentes* bring bad news,' she said in thick, heavy Latin. She punctured the tight cloth and threaded her needle to the back of the frame. Then she tightened the thread with quick jerks of her free hand. She punctured again, pulled, punctured, and pulled.

'Silvanus will be his own best advocate against the envy of lesser men. He must return with us to Mediolanum without delay, even though it seems the charges are false.'

Her dark, thick eyebrows shot up. 'Of course the charges are false. My son is the Emperor's most loyal military officer, more distinguished than Arbetio and Ursicinus combined. He has reclaimed north-eastern Gallia, revived this fallen capital, and driven the Alemanni away from the ravaged estates of the Gallo-Romans to the west and south.'

'The Empire acclaims his success but—'

'Which is why he attracts envy and deceit.' She tugged at a stubborn knot before continuing, 'Your *schola* should have investigated these charges without prejudice. That was your job.'

'Apodemius' job is to question, not to trust. Right now, he is far too ill to be guilty of anything, much less prejudice. Once he has recovered and returned with your son to the court, he will make a fair and unbiased report to the *Magister Officiorum*.'

'Including the names of the leading *consistoriani* who presume to sit in judgment of an innocent man?'

'Only the Emperor will judge, *Matrona*. He admits that he consults the Praetorian Prefect Lampadius, Master of the Rolls Aedesius, the Lord Chamberlain Eusebius and certainly General Arbetio, currently Consul.'

'Oh, yes, General Arbetio will have an opinion.' Evochildis gave a bitter twist to her violet wool. She snipped it off at the knot with a tiny pair of silver scissors. She threaded the needle into the margin of her fabric to keep it handy with a rank of other needles, all trailing a rainbow of threads.

'Lampadius brought your son's letters to Constantius with the support of Mattyocopus, who is as greedy for approval as he is for honeyed sweetmeats. But I should stress that Arbetio's hand is nowhere to be detected in this affair.'

'No, he would be too careful for that.' She shot me a chilling smile.

'I am an outsider to the court, *Matrona*. But this helps me see how your son's situation is muddied by so many ambitious voices. Surely a bold and confident Frank can easily silence them. You yourself call these men cowards. None has the courage to clarify your son's position as well as he himself. It will be an official honor to escort the General and his chosen officers back to Mediolanum. But it will be a personal pleasure to see justice prevail.'

She licked the frayed end of a strand of silver silk, twisted it into a point and threaded it through the eye of a fine needle.

'I do not agree. I do not agree at all. My son's loyalty to Constantius is as clear as the blue sky over that river out that window. His duties lie here.'

Tactful as the ex-slave I was, I passed over the facts, as our great Cicero would say, that first, the sky outside was a leaden gray threatening rain and second, that Evochildis' suite enjoyed no view of the Rhenus but only of the parade ground.

'His presence in the court will also strengthen the Frankish *gentiles* under Malarichus and Mallobaudes who have stoutly defended him.'

'And why shouldn't they? We are all tied together by blood. Those Franks at court may answer to Constantius but they are also loyal scions of Frankish *reguli*. They would never fall for this clumsy political trick.'

'Indeed, *Matrona*, but the temporary loss of the west to Magnentius was a blow from which Constantius has not yet recovered. The failure of Caesar Gallus has left the East in greater confusion. The Emperor is keenly alert, perhaps overly alert, to all weaknesses in his empire or in his subjects.'

'Do not waste our time! Investigate these charges and tell the Emperor on your authority that he has nothing to fear from Silvanus—'

'—who should prostrate himself, proclaim his loyalty, and kiss the purple hem whenever asked. I speak as one employed to serve imperial communications and to speed the truth from one ear to the next, but it is no disloyalty to the service to admit there are limits to our *schola*'s capabilities. In the course of my duties I have observed the confusions created by geographical distance and the pitfalls of misunderstandings between our various Roman peoples. Only a swift renunciation of all such ambitions by General Silvanus in person before the assembled councilors can put these troubles to rest—once and for all.'

Her ladies glanced at each other over their stitching.

'I am an African, *Matrona*, of bastard Roman blood but honest Numidian breeding. I know well the society of which I speak. Silvanus' speedy and fearless rebuttal can lay these suspicions to rest.'

'Do not lie to me. You yourself have good reason to hate my son,' she said suddenly. The needles around her hung in the air, waiting for my answer.

'His betrayal of the military reformers—'

'His wise defection from the rebels—'

'His unexpected switch to the Eastern army led to the death of my former Commander and grievous harm to the Manlius name.'

Evochildis worked a silver thread in and out, in and out. From time to time, the resistant linen made a popping sound as she forced her needle into the thick weave.

'So you are honest enough to admit that, at least, Numidianus. Perhaps I start to trust you. Are you honest enough to admit that your personal revenge would be to see my son tortured, convicted, and executed on false charges?'

I placed one boot on the edge of her dais. 'Your accusation is unfair. I speak for all just men who believe in the truth.'

'Then you can't speak for Constantius.'

'No, *Matrona*, of course I do not—'

Now she rose to face me and clasped her hands around the ornate buckle at her waist.

'And I can speak as one who personally knew Constantine. That Illyrian was wise and respectful.'

'We are talking of his son.'

'Indeed. This Constantius is a fair commander of armies, but no judge of men. He wants to keep the Empire united and strong, but he listens to a council that is divided and weak. His court is full of honest Franks, hundreds behind Mallobaudes and Malarichus, but none sits on his council. Why not? Northern Gallia has many *tribuni* proud to be both Roman and Frank.'

'The Frankish officers are much respected, *Matrona*—'

'Do you know what I think, *Biarchus*? I think we Franks of the Roman Empire have become too educated, civilized, skilled, and Christian for their taste. In short, we have become too Roman. Now they fear us. I can smell their fear from here. The greater the distance between that *consistorium* and ourselves, the safer we Franks are.'

'If the others are so fearful, let Constantius hear a strong and honest man for a change.'

'Let our victories over the Empire's enemies speak for us.'

She spoke as if, by wielding her silver scissors aloft, she had personally led the skirmishes against the Alemanni.

'*Matrona*, General Ursicinus understands that victories in the field guarantee no protection from political schemes. He squashed accusations of conspiring with Gallus with a confident rebuke in court. I witnessed his testimony.'

'So Ursicinus has now returned to the East, exonerated from suspicion, and decorated with fresh titles for his victories against the Jewish rebels and Persian armies?'

'Not yet, *Matrona*.'

She smiled to herself and sat back down to her work.

'No, I thought not. Ursicinus is kept lingering around Mediolanum with his reputation still under the shadow where he loafs, waiting for the next councilor-dog to snarl at his heels.'

'The Empire will not destroy the men it most needs.'

'You have great faith in our Empire, Numidianus?'

I nodded. 'It is the Empire that I serve, *Matrona*.'

'You think Silvanus should leave his army in the hands of his Cornuti and Bracchiati officers here and spend weeks or months down in Mediolanum?

'Yes.'

'With no guarantee of return?'

'His innocence is an unassailable defense, *Matrona*.'

She took a deep breath but argued no more. The proud old woman finally understood. Now all we needed was get Apodemius strong enough to travel.

'Come. See my work.' She gestured for me to mount the dais and admire her embroidery.

I looked down on a busy picture that must have taken months to stitch, even at her fierce pace. The cloth showed where this formidable woman's loyalties lay. She was illustrating a scene overlooking the Rhenus from the vantage point of the outer city walls.

My confidence in my powers of persuasion vanished.

Behind Commander Silvanus on his mount, Bracchiati and Cornuti troops spread in ranks across the sandy peninsula fronting the main gates. Silvanus' hand was raised to accept obeisance from Frankish tribes filed four-by-four back along the long bridge to the old fortress on the opposite bank.

A little flock of Franco-Roman ladies in gold-threaded finery exchanged comments behind white hands covering modest blushes. An Arian bishop raised his hand to bless them all.

Presiding from the upper center of the cloth was none other than a longhaired Frank in rough northern fighting garb but wearing a Roman helmet and, feet planted astride, wielding a *spatha* in his right hand. This must be Bonitus, for beside him was a younger version of his beloved Evochildis, pictured here with flowing chestnut hair.

Like two Christian saints, father and mother beamed down over their famous son.

The Roman eagle was nowhere to be seen among the banners and pennants stitched in bright reds, blues, saffron, and black. A token Roman adviser who looked something like Proculus, noticeable for his short hair, rounded shoulders, and clean-shaven face, stood isolated and ignored on the far margin of the cloth. He bent slightly at the waist in a posture of submission, his hands pressed together in supplication for attention no one bothered giving him.

The imagery bordered on the treasonous.

'Your skill is impressive, *Matrona*,' I said.

'There are many empires, now Numidianus,' Evochildis said. 'There is an Eastern Empire. There is a Western Empire. Perhaps you begin to understand that we Franks maintain a northern empire in all but name. My son is pressed *on all sides* by well-meaning agents of Roma but I am sure they do not put his interests first.'

I suspected Evochildis was including Roxana in her allusion to importuning Roman agents. I even detected a frisson of animosity toward the beautiful, but unnamed interloper spreading among the listening attendants.

'I can only implore you, *Matrona*, to support our invitation to General Silvanus to speed to the court. He should confer with the Emperor as to his plans for Germania Secunda, just as Bonitus supported Constantine against Licinius. Such collegiality will put to rest all of Constantius' doubts.'

The widow shook her head. 'I can warn you in turn, Numidianus, that my son is a friend of the Empire, but it is also important that the Empire remains a friend of my son. Today is payday for the troops. At noon you will observe for yourself my son's loyalty to Constantius, but you will also see the love of the soldiers for my son.'

'*Matrona*, what soldier doesn't love his commander on payday?'

She frowned at my feeble joke.

'Please tell Constantius this from Evochildis: to give even five minutes' credence to these slanders is treason itself.'

She waved me away with a strand of that eloquent, brittle silver thread.

'You will return to Mediolanum as soon as your *magister* is well enough to travel.'

Perhaps I had been wrong about imperial women. I'd just met one who received you in state and formality—not to disguise any weakness—but because she was simply the person in charge.

The same strawberry-haired Clothild who had caught my eye during military exercises outdoors escorted me out of the widow's quarters. I suspected this flirt was as curious about me as she was assertive.

Her father was a high-ranking Cornuti officer, she said, one Tribune Bainobaudes.

'Evochildis is strong and proud,' she said in a strongly tinged Latin. 'She is *ric*, meaning powerful in our language, as well as *bald*.' she clenched her small white fist to show *bald* meant daring.

'She is a stupid old crone blinded by pride. She underestimates the envious tongues in Mediolanum set against Claudius Silvanus.'

'She underestimates *nothing*,' Clothild retorted. 'We women must fight battles too, *Agens* Numidianus. Christian or pagan, Frankish leaders take many wives. My mistress was neither the first nor the second consort of *Magister Militum* Bonitus but she is the woman who outlasted all others. She herself survived the poison of envious tongues.'

'I am here to advise her on imperial power politics, not bedroom rivalries.'

—THE WOLVES OF AMBITION—

She tossed me a flirtatious smile as we walked side by side. 'You think there are no politics in the bedchamber? Evochildis is a politician.'

'A politician? She's a faded beauty surrounded by pretty women.'

'Thank you, *Biarchus*, but I will not be deflected by compliments. You do not know who she is.'

'What do you mean?' I halted our rapid march away from the ladies' wing and faced her.

'Evochildis is the granddaughter of the Frankish king Ascaricus whom Constantine threw to the beasts. Her ancestors were among the Franks who devastated Gallia all the way to Hispania during the reign of Gallianus a century ago. Yet it was Evochildis who advised Bonitus to ally his Frankish warriors behind the old Constantine. It was she who raised her son to be a Christian Roman commander.'

'So she reserves the right to withdraw that fealty if the family's loyalty is abused by Constantine's son?'

'It would be *treason* to say that, *Biarchus*! I just want you to understand that Evochildis underestimates nothing. If anything, it is Roma that underestimates Evochildis.'

※※※

I raced back to confess my failure to my fellow agents. The largest of the rooms we'd been allocated belonged to Apodemius. Gaudentius barred me at the old man's door.

'He's too sick to receive you,' he said. There were deep circles under the agent's eyes. He still hadn't changed his riding clothes for something clean.

'Has he eaten anything at all?'

'He can get a few sips of soup down, but that's not enough to sustain life. His breathing is thick and labored.'

'Have you found anyone to consult here?'

'Silvanus' best *clinici* just left. The *medicus* said they could do little more than give us this painkilling medicine.

I scrutinized Gaudentius' expression for evidence that Meroveus' distrust was justified. I saw nothing but deep concern.

The *schola*'s survival during these unsteady times depended on the recovery of the traveler lying at the edge of death behind that bolted wood. Even the cold, ambitious Gaudentius must have the wisdom to see that running the imperial intelligence service was beyond his capabilities.

'This isn't good enough, *Ducenarius*. Silvanus' staff treats gaping war wounds or minor skin rashes in young and otherwise healthy men. He needs someone skilled in the internal sicknesses of the old.'

'I refuse to leave his side. That's the most I can do,' Gaudentius said. His stony expression warned me that I was inching toward insubordination.

'I'll try and get someone,' I said.

It took me a little time to find my way through the Agrippina headquarters, with its two residential wings facing each other behind a pair of great reception halls, various military shrines, and bath installations to return to Roxana's rooms.

I couldn't help but notice that Silvanus maintained his mistress in these three chambers as far across the empty parade ground from his mother's domain as possible.

Roxana scolded me with a forgiving smile.

'Marcus, you should never visit me alone. We are old friends and there are tongues in Agrippina eager to wag at my expense.'

'Where can we go?'

'Let's walk past everyone's noses toward the church buildings a few blocks away. There our innocent conversation will be all the intimacy any busybody can report.'

She donned a summer cloak against the threatening rainclouds. We walked in suspended silence out the two-story building and toward the great horseshoe of stalls that faced the inner gate of the official residence.

'I can't wander about, Roxana,' I explained. 'I came for an expert healer for Apodemius.'

'I know someone,' she said, 'but there's no guarantee. Frankish herbs and potions are different from ours. Much of what they call medical care seems no more than barbarian spells and magic. The barbarians across the river still offer human sacrifices to their gods.'

'We must try. And one other thing. As long as Apodemius lies on that sickbed, there's no one to influence Silvanus but his stubborn mother. She doesn't comprehend how venal his enemies are.'

'And I do,' she said with a wry twist of her soft lip. 'But this blow has left Silvanus both angry and bewildered. It seems the more he hews to Constantius, the deeper the Emperor's distrust. He spent many hours last night alone in the chapel, praying to his God for guidance.' She sighed. 'He often finds comfort in religion these days.'

'Every hour he delays, the *consistoriani* fill Constantius' ears with more rumors and lies.'

She raised an eyebrow. 'And knowing that the Emperor is such easy prey to their schemes, you still advise Silvanus to throw himself into that arena?'

'Only he can clean off the filth collecting around his name. You must make him see he has no choice, Roxana.'

'You might not believe it, my old friend, but there are limits to my talents. *She* opposes whatever I suggest, on principle.'

'You were never so timorous before,' I said. I was not ashamed of the hoarse affection in my voice.

'Love can make you stronger and readier to fight, Marcus, but it can also make you weak with longing and fear,' she answered in a quiet tone.

We walked a few steps through the busy street before she asked me, 'You once loved Kahina like that. Perhaps you still do?'

'Kahina is no longer Kahina since her harsh enslavement in Hispania. The scars of the whips and shackles have healed over but her innocent African sunniness is a thing of the past. The iron weights on her spirit are permanent—invisible, heavy and cold. I left her in the care of Verus and a smart new teacher for Leo. If only one half of her former spark returned . . .'

Roxana squeezed my arm to ease my despair. 'I know you can never forgive Silvanus for betraying Gregorius and the others,' she said. 'The rebels would have held their own. Kahina would never have been captured.'

'Silvanus tried to make it up to me the day after Mursa by lying when Catena told the Emperor I was Constans' assassin. The

Emperor's blade had even scraped the hairs on the nape of my neck when Silvanus intervened.'

'Then remember his goodness in that, Marcus, please. You know that if anything happens to Silvanus, there will never be another man for me.'

'I've never seen you so vulnerable, Roxana. You were the mistress of deception when I first met you. Of all the first year recruits in our class, you were the toughest. Surely you haven't forgotten all your Castra training?'

'No Castra training can hide love in my eyes. Evochildis sees it and she sees weakness.'

'Surely she loved Bonitus just as well. Shouldn't she love you for your attachment to her son?'

'After Bonitus there was no other man for Evochildis. Instead, she became a man herself.'

Her angry eyes warned me off discussing Silvanus any further.

'And Meroveus? What news for him?' I asked.

'A Toxandrian woman living here said she knew his village. I explained Meroveus' capture, enslavement, his wounds, his courage, and his promising standing as an *agens* in Roma. This Ragamunda carried the news back to his family, but she returned with a hard message, Marcus. His wife wants nothing to do with him.'

We'd reached the wall of the church.

'Return to Apodemius now. Marcus. Tell him I have gone farther into the city to find the healer. I'll be back as soon as possible.'

'His injuries have exhausted him. His lungs and abdomen have succumbed to the chill of the northern storms on the *Cursus*.'

'Marcus, Apodemius can't live forever. Who knows how old he is? The *schola* must prepare for another *magister*, sooner or later.'

'Then we must make sure it's later,' I said, wondering in my heart if Gaudentius felt the same way.

Chapter 10, A Roman Payday

—Agrippina, August 7, 355 AD—

I splashed myself off with water from the basin in my sparsely furnished room. A wave of shame overwhelmed me as reviewed the morning's debacle.

Last night I had boasted I could convince the proud old Evochildis of the dangers gathering around Silvanus. Perhaps she would have believed threats coming from a hard-faced man like Gaudentius. Certainly Gaudentius would say so now.

Each hour passed in Agrippina left me imagining events back at court: the barren Eusebia retiring at night to defend her precarious position as imperial consort and Constantius prostrating himself before dawn, pressing his inscrutable features against the mosaics of his candlelit chapel as he prayed for relief from his crippling fears.

I imagined the streams of bishops still pouring through the city gates each sunrise, submitting themselves to the deceitful ministrations of the eunuch Lord Chamberlain. The poor fellows in their ecclesiastical getups thought they'd come to debate only the nature of their Savior.

I knew Eusebius better than that.

The Lord Chamberlain's mounting interest in theology didn't fool this pagan. The fawning rotund eunuch would comb his devout guests for information and ply them with favors in return. He would have every single cleric in his debt by the synod's conclusion at the end of August. He would trick them into acting as his unsuspecting agents as he stitched together a new intelligence web independent of the Empire's official network under Apodemius.

Meanwhile, the other backstabbing *consistoriani* were jockeying as hard as ever for Constantius' ear, hedging their bets and measuring their exposure to the accusations against Silvanus.

We had to get Apodemius back on his feet. We had to get Silvanus to Mediolanum just long enough to eradicate once and for all the jealousies bringing the Empire closer to self-destruction every day.

The Manlius household had only just survived one civil war. It could never survive another.

I glanced out the window. Roxana appeared in a long hooded green cloak from the building opposite. She waited in the shadows of the parade ground. After a few minutes, a bent and ragged Frankish woman hurried with a shuffling step across the pounded earth of the square under military escort. The two women spoke for a minute and then hurried toward our wing.

I found Gaudentius mixing the last drops of his ineffectual tonic into a watery wine. He lifted his stubbled face up to me with impatience at my interruption. 'This is the last of the medicine from Count Maudio's villa.'

'Roxana is bringing the barbarian healer now.'

'I pray to the gods she's on our side,' he mumbled.

The women's footsteps echoed down the stone corridor. The old woman bustled past us straight for Apodemius' chamber. As Gaudentius opened the door, a gust of foul air told me the old man was still failing. I could barely see his head, so gaunt on the pillow. A soft blanket covered the rest of him. His distended knees made two hard knobs under the wool. His eyes were closed and his forehead moist. His shallow breathing crackled, like pebbles running down a tiled gutter.

The old woman opened his eyelids to check his pupils and then laid a finger on his pulse. She thrust her hands under the blanket and palpated his chest and stomach, moving her strong fingers up and down the *Magister*'s belly.

She frowned and muttered in Frankish.

She unrolled a long strip of stained linen, pocketed with individual compartments stuffed with twigs, leaves, dried berries and dark, thick pastes.

'I will try cramp bark on him,' she muttered in broken Latin.

'That's a woman's drug,' Roxana said.

'To ease the stomach pains. But the problem is down here.' She laid her hand on Apodemius' lower chest. 'Does he have pain in legs and arms?'

'He has suffered from joint pains for many years,' I said.

'Coughing? Spitting?'

'Foul and yellow. But there's no food left to come up, so he seems to be vomiting up nothing but white globules.' Gaudentius said.

'His own fat. Bad sign. The body begins to devour itself,' she said. 'We stop that.'

The healer woman started selecting leaves to soak in the boiled water Roxana poured into a fresh cup.

'What are these large red berries?' I asked, touching some vivid fruits rolling out of their pouch.

'Don't touch those!' The woman pushed my fingers away. 'Deadly poison.'

'The tree of the *Eburones*?' I asked.

Could these smooth red berries come from the famous *taxeus* tree? In his Gallic Wars, Julius Caesar wrote of Catuvolcus, chief of the Celtic Eburones, who poisoned himself with yew rather than submit to Rome. And one of Senator Manlius' favorite historians Florus said that when the Cantabrians were under siege by the legate Gaius Furnius in 22 BC, most of them took their lives either by sword or fire—or by poison extracted *ex arboribus taxeis*.

'Yes, she grunted. 'The fruit of the *iwa* is harmless but the brown seed inside is fatal. A tea from a single needle-leaf kills baby in its womb. Death to all animals but deer.'

'Deer?'

'Deer can pass the seeds without danger. They eat their fill as a delicacy. The birds spit out the poisonous cone.'

'Then why do you carry it?'

She squinted up at me from her preparations. 'I have seen a great healer cure a woman's diseased breast with a constant treatment using bits of fungus from scrapings of this tree mixed with wine—tiny, tiny bits over many months.'

'Why so little if it works?'

'Woman's hair fell out. Nails fell out. She lost weight. But four or five months after, her breast was cured. Now leave me to my task.'

The woman kept on working with fingers stained by years of crushing and mixing her dark ingredients. We could do little more than watch her try.

Army horns sounded in the distance from the sprawling camp surrounding the city walls. Gaudentius ordered me to represent our *schola* at the long-awaited payout to Silvanus' troops about to begin on the exercise field.

I was reluctant to leave Apodemius' side, but Gaudentius didn't have to tell me that this was the best chance—perhaps our last chance—to change Silvanus' mind. The General had asked us for time, but time was the one thing we couldn't give him.

※※※

The sun had burned off the river mist and left a crisp blue horizon over ten thousand troops gathering for their *donativa*. The Bracchiati and Cornuti regiments were assembled in full. The Batavi, Regii, Petulantes, plus mounted troops, including the *equites Bracchiati* were forming into ranks. Treasury representatives of *limitanei* and *riparienses* units along the recovered sections of the border as well as officers from the Primani legion stationed elsewhere in the province had arrived on schedule.

Military pay in debased *denarii* had meant little for some years now. But the commander's bonuses and gifts in reliable *solidi* would last these soldiers for the coming year. Spirits among the men would be high today. I tried to shake off the gloom of Apodemius' sickbed as I hurried to locate Adjutant Proculus.

Meroveus joined me. We walked the three city blocks of boulevard that led south. On our left was the smaller courtyard surrounded by administrative buildings leading eastwards to the elongated peninsula on which the bridgehead stood.

We emerged out the southeastern-most city gate to admire the procession of troops that had fought with Silvanus through hostile Alemanni territory now marching beneath their banners from their camp into the exercise field.

Some of their fellows had been installed in fortresses along the Rhenus to the south of us, but these lines of defense were still thin and ill protected. The once-grand fortress and base of the *Legio XXX Ulpia Victrix*, Tricensimae, had been lost to Frankish marauders four years ago. What remained standing waited to be reclaimed, if only Silvanus had the regiments here to do it. The brave 'Thirties,' heirs of Trajan's own *Legio XXX VI Victrix* of two centuries ago, were now off fighting the Persians in the East.

Red-cloaked centurions and a more senior officer in bleached white galloped back and forth calling order into loose order formations with shouts of 'Move, move,' but the atmosphere among the men was festive and impatient. The centurions were laughing and tossing jokes down at their subordinates. With ringing voices, officers called the rolls out and hundreds upon hundreds of voices eager for their chance confirmed, '*Adsum!*' These professionals took little time to find their places to the order, '*Ad signa.*' After half an hour, hundreds of officers' voices fell silent. The brisk roll call was completed.

Meroveus had disappeared from my side without explanation and I could not find Proculus anywhere. I presumed he had been swallowed up in the crowd of Tribunes of the Treasury busy finalizing their accounts with the payroll masters whose aides were lugging forward the padlocked *aeraria*, full of coins, to weigh and count out.

Meanwhile, at the signal '*Laxate,*' one group of Franks did more than stand 'at ease.' They moved into a mock 'castle' position in a confident, playful mood. Raising their shields to their mouths to amplify their voices, they indulged in a holiday version of their *barritus*, the *Germani* war cry.

They fell into their unsettling battle dance, the three-beat *tripudium*, swinging their shields from side to side and stomping their boots to the rhythm of their chant. These coordinated gestures chilled the bone marrow of our enemies but today, our warriors were only showing off for their fellow soldiers assembled across the rolling fields.

Step, step, forward, thrust, step, step, forward, thrust they pounded—though instead of climbing on the enemy's shield on the third and forward step, they lifted their weapons, threw back their heads and crowed.

I watched these Franco-Romans with awe. Whatever their jests today, they'd passed through a Hades of ambush threats and skirmishes for weeks of patrol just to recapture this bastion. They looked so tall and golden in the clean summer air, with long strides and flowing hair—so *ric,* or powerful as my new acquaintance Clothild would say.

No wonder the rest of us Romans had taken up this tactic after centuries of so-called 'disciplined' warfare. How many Roman lives had mastery of this 'barbarian' style of attack saved since?

The Cornuti were renowned 'buck warriors,' and the horn-like feathers thrusting up from their leather helmets were no laughing matter. These were the military heirs of the men who had won the decisive Milvian Bridge for Constantine forty-three years ago.

The Bracchiati might have abandoned their wolf skin capes of old for modern tunics, but like their ancestors and brothers-in-arms on Trajan's column, they still fed their aggressive spirits with images of animal ferocity. Once again, I was struck that centuries ago, the original men of Gallia assigned to this *auxilium* had been nicknamed for their trousers or *brachae* and were now known for their metal armlets or *bracchiae.* Their trousers had since become as Roman as had their *Germani* neighbors' wild *barritus* cry and for good reason.

I spotted Proculus in the crowd at last. His skinny form hurried forward across the field in the company of a senior tribune of the Cornuti whom he introduced as Bainobaudes. So this striking man, tall and ramrod straight with reddish-gold hair, a fighter still in his prime, was Clothild's father.

'Where's Silvanus?' I asked them. The soldiers were already filing past us to receive their money and sign receipts in whatever fashion they'd been taught.

'He'll be here for the salute when we're finished and make a short speech,' said Bainobaudes over Proculus' head. The tribune looked as though he could have carried the skinny adjutant a mile or more without breaking a sweat.

'May I see him first?'

— THE WOLVES OF AMBITION —

'No,' Bainobaudes stopped me. 'He's at prayer.'

'I must talk to him. We must all convince him to return to court to confer with the Emperor before it is too late.'

'I'll see what I can do,' Proculus whispered behind the great Frank's massive shoulders.

A roar went up from the ranks.

General Silvanus rode out the southeastern gate of Agrippina, followed by his personal guard. He carried his parade helmet under his left elbow and a light breeze lifted his long brown curly hair as he galloped forward.

The army sent up a cheer, swinging their money pouches, sagging or full, around in the air. On either side of Silvanus, standard-bearers raised their banners in reply.

From a distance, he was the same Claudius Silvanus I remembered from that long-ago season of deliberation and desperation among the reformist rebels before the civil war broke out. If only Silvanus joined their side, they reasoned one night, the usurpation had a real chance of success. Only at the last minute, after many weeks of uncertainty, had Silvanus suddenly appeared in the torch-lit archway of Magnentius' headquarters to join the rebellion. Even then, he'd teased and cajoled them as if the insurrection against the free-spending and dissolute Constans was no more than a game. His lighthearted confidence had charmed us all during all those months of strategizing at Magnentius' side.

Silvanus was always the careful and levelheaded voice among the rebel officers.

All would go well for the reign of Magnentius, to hear Claudius Silvanus tell it.

And then, without any warning, the dashing Franco-Roman was gone, trailed by his thousands of cavalry.

And all went wrong.

As he galloped toward us now, the former Roman Silvanus became the new, with irrefutable echoes of his Frankish forebears—the shoulder-length hair, the long-tipped chestnut moustache, the wide jewel-studded belt, the large silver cross bouncing on his chest, the garnet hilt of his sword, and the ornate silver pommels of his saddle.

He reviewed his waiting officers and spotted me from his saddle. That beaming countenance brandished to meet the gratitude of his army faltered for a moment at the sight of the Roman *agens* still carrying gross charges against his honor.

Anger flared up in his eyes and then died. His practiced amiability eclipsed his hidden resentment.

'Numidianus,' he called, 'is the *Magister* better this morning?'

'No, General, but your lady has found us a wise woman who may help.'

'I will provide an entire *ala* to speed him south to the skills of court doctors.'

I crossed the few yards of pounded grass and in a discreet voice, punctured the bonhomie of his greeting.

'General Silvanus, the only traveling companion we seek is yourself. You must come with us to answer these accusations face to face. You must confront the *consistorium* and expose their lies to Constantius.'

'I wrote simple letters to my Frankish associates. What is the treason in that? Where is the ambition in that?'

'I beg you to imagine the consequences of staying here. Even innocent hesitation carries heavy risks.'

'I have not finished my deliberations, Numidianus. What honest man would not see a trap in your invitation?'

'It is not an invitation, General. It is an imperial summons.'

'How can lies be manufactured from nothing? How can a reference for a baggage chief become an assault on the *cathedra* on which that man sits even now?'

Bainobaudes came up to us. 'The distribution is complete, General. The men are ready to hail their commander.'

'Thank you, Tribune.'

'General Silvanus, we have known each other for many years. I have known you to be vacillating in your loyalties, even perfidious to your closest comrades-in-arms. But I never thought you were a coward.'

'How dare you! I saved you from the Emperor's sword!'

'Then let me save you now. General Ursicinus bravely answered the Emperor's summons. He left the Persian front and crossed the breadth of the Empire, a journey of many weeks.

Within minutes of entering the *consistorium*, he had shamed the Emperor and his accusers into silence.'

'My men are waiting for their pay.'

'Are you not as brave as Ursicinus?'

Silvanus wheeled his horse away and galloped to the front of the ranks. A *cornicen* blew his horn for silence. A hush fell across the troops as sunrays stroked the feathers, horns, *dracones*, and pennants rustling in the breeze sent up by the nearby river. Centurions positioned themselves as required to relay Silvanus' message deeper and deeper into the assorted ranks. From where I stood on a small rise to one side, I could hear every ringing word.

'Brave fighters! Loyal Romans! Receive what is your due in the name of Emperor Constantius II, the son of Constantine and the grandson of Constantine Chlorus. The Emperor values you, each and every warrior of the Empire standing here today. He holds you in high esteem for your skill, your strength, and your courage. Today the Emperor rewards you because he values you . . . while I, General Claudius Silvanus, I love you as my brothers!'

A roar went up anew to the slamming of shields on knees in approval. The standards swung side to side in answer. The neat lines turned into a shambles, as men embraced the companions of his *contubernium* standing on either side and swung their remunerations high.

I could do no more here on the field. I left the slope and turned back toward the city gates. I told myself Silvanus would see reason once the excitement of the day had faded. That final speech had sounded promising, almost a farewell to leave ringing in their ears before he departed.

Proculus caught up with me. His puny face flushed and his shallow chest pounded away under his tunic.

'The General has called an urgent meeting of the tribunes and *ducenarii*, all provincial civil servants within reach, and his *trustis* tomorrow at midday. All in your party are entreated to be there.'

'Then he is taking counsel, then. I am glad to hear it.'

'Even if you cannot persuade him, then this is your chance to persuade those of us who care about him, Numidianus! In the provincial governor's main council room, don't be late! Tomorrow, midday!'

I was not up to making more speeches that would be pierced by the *angon* of Evochildis' scorn. I prayed that this sudden summons was Silvanus' face-saving gesture before departing with us for Mediolanum. He would protest that he could not abandon his command. Then he would listen to each officer's entreaty, one by one, to his common sense.

There was Meroveus, standing on a low bluff overlooking the emptying field. He hardly acknowledged me. He looked dazed.

'Coming back?' I asked him, barely halting my stride.

'Not right away, Numidianus.' The Toxandrian's steps did not fall in with mine.

'What's wrong?' I turned around and scrutinized his odd expression of dismay mixed with elation.

Meroveus could not find words, though his mouth worked away to no avail. After a long minute, he got it out.

'I saw a youngster wearing the insignia of an infantryman pass by with his companions. I grabbed his arm on impulse. I startled him but I could not help myself, Marcus.'

'I believe you, Meroveus.'

'He reminded me so much of myself before... It was like gazing into one of Roxana's bronze mirrors. Then I thought to myself, this boy and I might be kin. I asked him if by any chance he knew of my family, my hamlet, or my children... I'm afraid I asked him if he knew my wife.'

'And did he?'

'Marcus, he told me that he knew my *widow*.'

'Good gods. The shitty little *sterculus*. I hope you flattened him.'

Meroveus shook his head as slowly as a sleepwalker. 'I was too stunned to move. My tongue stuck to my mouth. He disappeared into the ranks. I lost him, Marcus, I lost him.'

'Too bad. If we knew the little runt's name, we could find his unit by checking the rolls and hunt him down. Teach him a lesson.'

'You don't understand, Marcus. He told me his name—Grifo. Of course he resembled me. He was *my own son*.'

Chapter 11, Across the River

—Facing the Castrum Divitia—

'The *Magister* any better?'

Gaudentius shook his head.

Meroveus and I had been unable to find Adjutant Proculus for help in locating Grifo's unit. I had kept the miserable Toxandrian company over a silent supper and then taken a tray of spelt bread and meat stew for Gaudentius.

The *agens* had camped outside Apodemius' room since our arrival and guarded the *Magister* like a rangy, snarling Cerberus. His tunic stank and his leg bindings hung loose and sloppy over his riding trousers.

'The healer woman is with him,' the Neapolitan said. 'His breathing is quieter. His vomiting has slowed. But he's weak and confused. She says until the fever breaks, he's still in danger.'

'You can't go on like this,' I told him. 'Get some sleep or at least a bath and a shave. I'll stay here. I'm only good for sentry duty now. I caught Silvanus out on the field, but he gave me indignant protests, nothing more.'

'You failed again.'

'Not quite. He's calling a council for noon tomorrow. Apodemius and you should be there.'

'Apodemius can't even sit up.'

'Then you'll be our senior representative.'

'Senior enough to arrest a *Magister Militum* for his own good and haul him back to court? Only Apodemius has the authority to do that.'

'You can at least threaten Silvanus with more seniority than me. I told Silvanus just now that he should show as much bravery as Ursicinus and defend himself like a man. Perhaps that prompted tomorrow's meeting. As for the mother, that damn old woman believes that I *want* to see Silvanus strapped onto Catena's rack, as personal revenge for betraying Gregorius and the others.'

Gaudentius rose from his stool to confront me. His shaved pate shone with the sweat of his long vigil. He flexed his stiff shoulders as if rousing himself from a dark meditation.

'Do you?'

He had had too much time to ponder whether I was the right delegate to argue Silvanus' best interests.

'I resent that. I'm as committed to my duties as you are.'

'I've heard different. When you were dismissed from your *schola* duties at Mursa, you hung around the battlefield. Then you flung yourself into combat like some *tiro* hungry for his first blood.'

'Wait! You don't know—'

'—Apodemius told me it took you months to recover from battle trauma. Maybe that old harridan Evochildis is right. You're too emotional, Numidianus, like a woman.'

'I couldn't stand by.'

'*Agentes in rebus* are supposed to stand by. We don't take sides. We report the truth. We deliver new information. We investigate the dishonest. We escort the indicted to judgment. We're not trained by the best experts in the Empire to muck in with foot soldiers and get ourselves killed. You forgot what you owe our *schola*.'

'You weren't there.'

He sneered, 'You rushed in behind your former master like the sentimental, indebted freedman you will always be.'

'With respect, go to the baths.'

'No, because unlike you, I don't leave my post.'

'What are you afraid of?'

'Apodemius is a man with many enemies in every corner of the Empire. There are many men who would like to send him a "visitor" as he lies in there to finish him off.'

'Surely you trust your fellow *agentes*?'

He stared hard at me. 'In my experience, every man has his price.'

I paused for an instant to check my temper. 'Then let Meroveus and myself relieve you as a two-man team.'

He saw I had swallowed his insulting insinuations for the sake of Apodemius' welfare. He relented: 'Perhaps later. Go find that woman Roxana. See if she can get anywhere with Silvanus. Toss her a warning that arriving in Mediolanum under arrest isn't the best start to a general's defense.'

'Gaudentius, you need some rest.'

'I never rest. And if I were in charge, you'd be on your way back to Roma.'

'You're not in charge.'

'Not yet.'

※※※

I found Roxana darning by the sun's slanting rays on a bench in the corridor outside her suite of rooms. The early afternoon warmth poured through a high open window and lit up the crown of her brown hair coils. She wore a wine-red *stola* over a tunic of thin wool hemmed with wide gold embroidery. She'd taken up the northern fashion for low-slung hip-belts and even had one of those round silver amulets dangling at the end of a chain.

'What is this bauble I see bouncing off every lady's knee?' I asked, fingering its filigree contours.

'A Frankish fertility charm.'

'You're keen to have children?'

'I'm keen to blend in.'

'You'll never become one of them, Roxana. You belong back at the Castra, using your talents.' I brushed her rosy cheek with the back of my hand in affection. She took my hand and placed it back on my knee.

She raised one eyebrow. 'And be as alone as you? Speaking of alone, where's Meroveus? He should be helping you.'

'Back with the army clerks, searching the army rolls for his son's name, Grifo.

'There are more than ten thousand men out there. There must be many Grifo's.'

'Just as well. I would be careful before chasing down someone who wants me dead.'

Roxana laid her darning in her lap and shook her head. 'I don't understand it, Marcus. I sent word to his family that Meroveus only wished to see them. He desired nothing more than that. My messenger woman returned saying that they did not want him back. It was heartbreaking to tell him once. I don't want to see him rejected twice. If his family has told the world he's dead, they must have good reasons. He must accept it.'

'Just as Silvanus must accept our summons!'

'Give him time to come to a decision.'

'Time has run out, my dear old friend. You've got to persuade him.'

She shook her head. 'I won't see him until late this evening—if at all. Be patient. Even the *Magister Militum per Gallias* must make a show of consulting the doyenne of the Franco-Romans, not to mention the opinions of his *trustis*. But in the end, he'll have his own way.'

'Which is *what*, exactly?' I grabbed both her hands from her infernal darning. 'He's using his mother's counsel as an excuse to nurse his own outrage, Roxana.'

'Silvanus is wrestling with his pride. To leave his command to prostrate himself in front of Arbetio and the—'

'He's too proud for my taste—too proud of his Frankish lineage, his Roman education, his military rise, and his personal following. His hubris will cost him dearly.'

'You've always been untouched by his good points. Is it possible, *dear old friend*, that you feel some jealousy?'

I resented her allusion to our former recreation in bed.

'Don't flatter yourself so much, Roxana. I'm not the only one losing patience. Gaudentius is threatening outright arrest.'

'Can Gaudentius do that?' She looked alarmed at last.

'I'm not sure. Officially speaking, he hasn't been appointed acting *Magister Agentium in Rebus*, but remember that Gaudentius did Constantius a personal favor some months ago. He turned in the disloyal Sirmium governor and his chattering dinner guests without going through the proper channels of our *schola*.'

'Emperors don't return favors.'

'I meant that Constantius won't worry over silly procedural complaints if he has Silvanus lying on his stomach below his dais.'

Her thoughtful brown eyes narrowed with displeasure at the image.

'If it comes to arrest, Silvanus is well-protected.'

'Gaudentius will convince the *trustis* that their heads are at stake if they disobey an imperial order to deliver up the General.'

'Shush, Marcus, someone is coming.'

The charming Clothild rounded the corner.

'Oh, there you are, Roxana. The healer woman sends for you. She needs someone to fetch more of her medicines and save her a trip into the city. The stupid biddy can't write. Can you help?'

'I'll go now,' Roxana said. She wrapped up her half-finished sock and collected her *paenula* for the walk across the parade ground.

I found myself alone with Clothild for the second time in twenty-four hours.

'This is something of a coincidence, *Dominula*.'

'Not really, *Agens* Numidianus.'

She lowered her eyes in a becoming way and asked, 'Shall we take a walk?'

'Aren't there rules about such things among you Frankish ladies?'

'My father is a high-ranking officer. I do what I like.'

I would have thought that a prominent offspring would have been far more constrained in good society than any floor-scrubbing slave girl, but I didn't argue.

Clothild was a member of Evochildis' distaff *trustis*. An *agens* never knew where he might stumble on useful information. The daughter of a Franco-Roman tribune might know useful things, possibly even hand me the key to unlocking Silvanus' resistance.

'I don't need any more trouble,' I warned her. 'Perhaps another lady should accompany us for the sake of propriety?'

'Oh, I won't give you any trouble, I promise.'

She tossed me a knowing glance with those cornflower blue eyes. They made a lively contrast against her pinkish strawberry hair coiled in a loop at the nape of her neck and finished in a circle around the crown. Her earrings were gold and her twin *fibulae* linked by an impressive string of chained *cloisonné* disks set with garnets.

An *agens* is trained to observe things ordinary men overlook, but with Clothild, who needed special training? There were many lovely things even a blind man could report back to the Castra. She smelled of lavender oil harvested in the south of Gallia. The swishing of her hems hinted at expensive undergarments of silk. The traders of ladies' finery had a good customer in this fetching girl. Her slippers were of sturdy leather that made delightful squeaks on the flagged corridor. With every light step, her hips gave a jingling sound. Silver adornments shaped like the animals of the forest dangled from her belt.

Her own fertility amulet was of the usual silver but studded with sparkling tiny blue stones that reminded me of a ring Kahina had once owned. Kahina's fertility had needed no such charms to conceive the strapping Leo after only a single night of innocent lovemaking. This Clothild exuded a dangerous air of ripeness herself, garnished with just enough quick intelligence to attract me—despite my professional misgivings about her age and status.

We strolled side by side out the inner gate of the Governor's Palace and across a main boulevard that slashed through the city parallel to the riverfront. We crossed the outer courtyard flanked by the two administrative buildings. The river waited for us through the front gates of the city walls.

Clothild's flushed cheeks, lighthearted wit, and graceful gait lifted my gloom. Apodemius, Gaudentius, Silvanus, Roxana, and Meroveus—these troubled souls began to fade from my thoughts.

At the water's edge she turned right, toward the south of the city. But I knew that way already. It led to the exercise grounds and the vast camp of Silvanus' troops, thousands of men and tents ranked behind sturdy palisades.

'The field camp is of no interest to us. You'll only be a distraction. They've got their money and they're busy right now. Some of them are preparing to march back to their bases in Traiana, Novaesium, and Bonna.' I said.

'So which way?' she said, a little frown creasing her snow-white brow.

'Let's go this way.' I directed our steps across a small ramp that connected the left bank to the flat peninsula where the charred remains of six low-rise guard buildings bore sad witness to Alemannic savagery. Gulls pecked at dried out ropes of weed twisting around the old pilings.

'No, not that way, please,' she said, taking me by the hand. 'Let's walk in the other direction, then, to the flower fields north of the city.'

She wrinkled her nose when she smiled, but she was too insistent for my taste.

'No, I want to see Constantine's old fortress. Shall we?' I started to cross the sandy peninsula for the bridge.

Across the low wide river, the border guards of the *milites riparienses* were going about their duties in the Castra Divitia. I started across the impressive stone bridge that spanned the Rhenus and stopped halfway. I leaned against the parapet and waited for her to catch up—partly out of curiosity and partly to challenge this playful female. I liked her twinkling eyes, but not her overconfident manner.

Pouting, she hung back on the peninsula and called, 'The other side of the river? Do you want to leave Agrippina—or the Empire itself?'

'I just want a look around the old defenses. Why not? You can see for yourself the guards are on duty.'

'But the Franks on the other side are savages. You know they take prisoners for human sacrifice to their god Wotan, don't you? Roman officers like you are their favorite victims.'

I checked my weapons as the sentries on the Agrippina side receded inside the Castra Wall. But I grew all the more curious to test her exaggerated reticence. I moved farther along the bridge. She followed me in silence but clutched her cloak around herself. She stopped midway at the pedestrian alcove over the cutaway piercing the cold waters beneath.

'That's far enough, *Agens*.'

'Come on! Don't be such a little girl! I want to see the old defenses. The ramparts are full of our men. Surely you've crossed this bridge before?'

I relished the wind brushing my brow and the cool broad stones underneath my feet. The August day had turned warm. The sky's lowering clouds had blown off, leaving a steely blue mixed with gray wisps. There was a pleasant freshness to this climate, though nothing would ever delight me as much as the blinding light burnishing the snowcapped Atlas Mountains of my birthplace.

With obvious reluctance, Clothild followed me across the rest of the bridge to the gates of Constantine's old Castra on the barbarian bank.

The forty-five-year-old fortress was a wide, walled square marked by sixteen round towers that marked the exit from the Empire and entry into the land reclaimed by the Frankish tribes. A couple dozen guards stood sentry in the towers but the atmosphere was relaxed enough. Sentries took a glance at my *schola* insignia and nodded. We two passed the Via Sagularis, the road that always spaced the residential quarters from the protective wall, and went on into the main court. At least a hundred men were posted there. They watched us from their work or rest inside the fortress.

But Clothild took little notice of their admiring gaze. She looked preoccupied. What was it about a little jaunt across the river that made her so nervous?

I led her past the rear gates leading into the wilder land beyond.

'Let's turn back,' she said, grabbing my arm. 'I want to turn back.'

'Have you never walked here before?'

'Yes, of course I have. Many times. I'm not a cooped-up child.'

'Don't you ladies take walks in the forest?'

'Sometimes. The women of Evochildis' court spend too much time in each other's company. We had to follow the General from Treverorum to reclaim Agrippina, but life here is too slow. There's no entertainment to speak of, no games, no festivals, and no visiting circus bringing us animals from Egypt or acrobats from Crete.'

'You do walk here with friends? So I'm right—it isn't so dangerous.'

'Not if we stay within sight of the Castra. The Franks on this side of the river are too busy fighting each other to harass the fortress. But there's nothing here. Let's go back.'

From under a sea of overgrowth what had once been a sturdy Roman road cutting through well-tended fields begged for repair.

—THE WOLVES OF AMBITION—

Untamed greenery was in late bloom, with feathery white fronds promising root vegetables that would rot for lack of harvesting.

Clothild dragged behind me as I walked the broken pavement.

'So you've been this far before?'

'We sometimes meet a trader here who sells us furs for the coming winter. He might not like our snobbish ways, but he likes our coin.'

I kept going, always slightly ahead of Clothild, seeking the darker reaches of thick forest lying ahead.

We reached the high-roofed wall of trees and I plunged ahead, leading her by the hand into a natural cathedral of barbarian wilderness. A dried blanket of fallen leaves crunched under my boots.

She halted to catch her breath. 'We must turn back, now, *Agens*. I was told—I mean, I wanted to walk with you in the open fields.'

'Isn't it beautiful here?' I gazed up into the sunlight twinkling through the canopy of treetops, unwilling to let this girl dictate to me. She'd been easy enough to detach from the official residence, but now the forest made her tremble. This outing had been her idea. What was bothering her so?

'Don't worry, *Dominula*. You're safe with me.'

If there was anything to be gained from a light flirtation, my training was certainly up to it. I ran a cautious finger along the pink fuzz lining her graceful nape. She shivered and laid a hand on my shoulder and smiled. I leaned her against one of the wide trunks and gave her a deep and convincing kiss. I enjoyed the tentative press of her full lips.

The girl was barely over half my age. Yet she began to respond. I sensed the young lady had done this before, although I would never be so impertinent as to compliment her skill. Germanic women were famed for their chastity and demanded more respect from their men than their Roman sisters.

'There, no one saw that, Clothild. Will no one miss you?' I planted small kisses around her neck and then licked her earlobe. She shivered with pleasure.

'Not even that formidable mother of generals, Evochildis?' I whispered, putting my arm around her slender waist. Her fertility amulet jingled a dutiful warning.

'She's in conference with General Silvanus,' Clothild whispered. 'She dismissed her ladies to amuse ourselves as we liked. I went looking for you and was ordered by that horrible *ducenarius* to fetch Roxana instead.'

A conference between mother and son was bad news. It would be all the harder for Roxana to undo in one romantic rendezvous an entire day's lobbying by the willful widow. Did Silvanus have no levelheaded officers to make him see sense?

Perhaps Clothild knew more, but how to tease it out of her?

'Let's be glad it's so private here. Surely your father would not like to imagine you letting any *curiosus* kiss that lovely face,' I said. She started stroking my back. Through my tunic, her fingers explored the thick whiplash scars that crisscrossed my shoulder blades like oxcart tracks.

She took a deep breath between kisses. 'Fathers never like to think of such things,' she said with a flush. 'Besides, he's too busy right now to worry about me.'

'Exercising his troops? Logistics with his officers? Payday is a good chance to collect news from the paymasters of other forces stationed around the province.'

'No, nothing like that.' She nipped my ear. 'You ask too many questions, Numidianus.' Both her hands were cupped around the back of my head. She pressed her hips into my thighs.

'Please, *Agens*, let's go back now. It's cold in the shade. We can drink some wine in the palace together.'

I gave up. I would learn nothing from this tease.

'You're right. I wouldn't want your father to find us here.'

'He won't be back until nightfall.'

'Oh? He went somewhere?' I ran my hands from her waist to a few inches below. Her rump was full and firm underneath all that imported silk. I pulled her tighter toward me as we took some steps back.

'Um, um.'

'He left Agrippina?'

'Let's not talk about my father.'

'He went to another garrison?'

—THE WOLVES OF AMBITION—

'And leave his command? Not the great Bainobaudes,' she scoffed.

We kissed again. I inhaled her mix of lavender and amber oils. As the kissing deepened, I had the feeling that she was softening toward me more than she had intended. Our caresses were having a worrying effect on my nether region.

I stopped for a moment to cool down. She knew nothing useful.

'You're right. Let's go back. I'm in no position to explain this to your father.'

'He won't know.'

She tried kissing me again, but I straightened up and now stood too tall for her lips to reach mine.

'I told you, he won't!' Frustration made her irritable.

Something was wrong with her erratic manner.

'I'd feel a lot better if I knew where your father was.'

'Stop going on about my father! Bainobaudes is with Tribune Laniogaisus deep inside that forest now.'

'What are they doing there?'

Her cheeks flushed. 'Nothing.'

'What are they doing, Clothild?' I squeezed her arm very hard. She squirmed.

'They're meeting the *reguli* of the tribes this side of the riverbank. They're not expected back until dusk. All right, are you satisfied?'

I pulled away. 'You said your father is with a tribune named Laniogaisus?'

'Yes. What of it?'

'Did this Laniogaisus once serve under Emperor Constans in the court at Treverorum as a *candidatus*?'

Clothild turned petulant. 'Let me go! How would you expect me to know what Laniogaisus did then? I was just a child living with my grandmother during Constans' reign.'

'Where are they now, exactly?'

'Well, by now they've reached the *vicus*, I suppose. He and the *trustis* have gone with that pathetic adjutant, Proculus.'

So that was why Meroveus and I had failed to find Proculus with the army officers.

'Why?'

'I don't know *why*!'

'Which *vicus*?'

'It's nothing more than an abandoned army camp occupied by dirty Frankish hunters. You won't find prettier girls waiting for you there, I promise you.'

'How far is it?'

'About fifteen minutes along this road, I think. I've never gone past this point.'

'I'm going to find them. Thank you, Clothild. I enjoyed our walk.'

'Wait, you can't!' she yelled at my back. I left her there in the middle of the potholed road, her rosy mouth hanging wide open, her cheeks beet-red, and her skirts caught on the high weeds. The still forest beckoned.

I recalled a certain Laniogaisus, one of the 'favorite' Frankish prisoners so loyal to Constans until the anguished end, when the doomed young Emperor left his contingent of good-looking playmates on the border between Gallia and Hispania in his desperate flight.

That day had ended badly for both Constans and for myself. Seconds before he could kill my commander Gaiso from behind, I had plunged a dagger into him. Only a blatant lie from Silvanus later had saved me from Constantius' sword slicing through my neck.

Obviously the handsome barbarian Laniogaisus had thrived since his capture so long ago. He was now a valued Roman officer and advising the most powerful Franco-Roman of the Western Army.

What was he doing with the Tribune of the Cornuti, Bainobaudes, in some wretched settlement on the wrong side of the imperial border? I prayed I was not too late. Strange politics were afoot behind my back.

※ ※ ※

I plunged through the deeper shadows under the leafy canopy. If only I had had a horse to speed me toward their meeting place. I didn't expect a warm welcome when I intruded on their secret meeting. Mine was probably the last face they would want to see. My only comfort was that Silvanus had been sensible enough to include the steady, modest Proculus as part of his delegation.

Clothild had said from the first that our encounter outside Roxana's rooms was no coincidence. Gaudentius, Apodemius and Meroveus were otherwise accounted for. Only that *agens* Numidianus was idly nosing around Silvanus' court. Clothild had been told to distract the nosy North African while Silvanus sent his trusted advisers across the river.

Now I understood why she was willing to lure me in any direction but that of the forest. How ironic that Clothild had failed in her 'mission' to keep me pleasantly distracted and out of the way for the afternoon.

Other suspicious things also made more sense now. Silvanus might be loyal to the Emperor, but his confused and prayerful indignation was something of a feint. In the end, he was still the coolheaded man I knew from years before. As before, he was weighing every single one of the odds, for and against, before he threw his dice.

But this time, he was playing a deadly game with Constantius.

I trotted along the neglected road until the woods opened onto a sunny clearing. The rotting palisade of an abandoned Roman camp marked out a large square. Within the enclosure, some twenty crude huts sunken halfway into the ground sent smoke into the sky through holes in their shabby roofs. A dozen horses stood tethered outside what was left of the original barricade trench. Four barefoot boys loitered around the Romans' animals, examining their shiny harness disks and sturdy saddles.

'I bring an urgent message for the tribunes.'

The boys didn't understand my Latin, but pointed out a large hut, no less mean or muddy than the others. Unlike good Roman surveyors, these Franks didn't have the sense to position their sewage downwind. The settlement reeked.

As I passed the deep-set hovels on my way to the meeting, sullen adults peeked out from behind doorframes or turned from grinding, cooking, or potting to add my features to their memory of Roman faces penetrating their enclave. The summer air shimmered with hostility.

A butcher had just planted his boot on a dead hare's long ears. With both hands he ripped the fur free from the carcass and tossed it into a pile. His eyes followed me as I nodded to him, but he did not return my greeting. As a matter of training, my mind registered that, of all the faces that scowled at me in passing, only the butcher's was male.

Were the men of this *vicus* included in the conference with Frankish leaders? I reached the large hut and listened. Through the door, I heard excited exchanges in a guttural Franconian dialect.

I announced myself and a Frank standing inside grabbed me by my sleeve and pulled me in. He slammed the door behind me with a gruff Latin, 'Here's one more.'

It was hard to say whom I had startled more—the dozen or so rough Frankish *thunguli* or the nine Franco-Roman visitors in their spanking trimmed tunics and polished armor.

'Spying on *us*, Numidianus?'

The challenge came from Proculus, squeaking in Latin from the periphery of the tall, somber-faced officers. Bristling with weapons, the gathering stood braced in the middle of a tense exchange.

A glance at their insignia, features, and dress told me that Proculus was the only man here beside myself who was not of Frankish blood. These were indeed men of the *trustis*, Silvanus' private Frankish bodyguard *cum* council embedded into the ranks of his military staff.

'Not spying, only party-crashing. This is no time to keep secrets from men trying to save your commander from further danger.'

'There's nothing for you here,' the tallest of them said to me, sticking to Latin. As the circle parted, I recognized Laniogaisus, positioned in the center of the rigid circle.

'Do you remember me, Laniogaisus? On the Hispanic border, hunting for your former sovereign?'

'Better than you might want to be remembered,' he said. 'Go back to the river. This is none of your business.'

'Don't you men trust a fellow Roman?'

'We'll have to for the moment,' Bainobaudes said, with a restraining hand on Laniogaisus. 'Stand over there, *Agens*.'

They resumed their conversation with the tribesmen. The atmosphere was hurried and impatient.

Laniogaisus shook his head in frustration and pulled Bainobaudes aside for a hushed exchange. Sword hilts were clutched. Nervous fingers fiddled with dagger sheaths. Something had gone wrong.

On their side of the dark, dank hut, the Franks counted on their fingers. They shook their unkempt manes in disagreement. They haggled among themselves without success. I'd seen less sinister behavior in ravenous cats lurking in Roma's great amphitheater after midnight.

Laniogaisus raised an objection. A Frank who almost matched him in height and muscle returned the retort in dismissive, brutish tones. Most of these men had fair-complexions. Their ruddy faces shone red with the heat of determined bartering.

Proculus understood enough Franconian to know why things were going badly. He inched over to my side.

I bent down and whispered in his ear. 'What's going on, Adjutant?'

'Silvanus sent us here to test the waters. Laniogaisus is a native of these parts, raised not far from this settlement. Yesterday he sent word to the local *reguli* to send their most trusted deputies to meet us here today.'

'Why?'

'To ask if the leaders would accept Silvanus into their territory.'

'Is that a joke?'

'Hush. Being the son of the legendary Bonitus, Silvanus expected to hold sway. But these Franks represent different rival tribes and they don't like the idea. Not one of them brought an invitation to make Silvanus the dominant *rex*.'

'So our hero is not welcome?'

Laniogaisus gave an outburst in thick-throated Franconian. The knuckles of his fists clenching his sword belt turned white.

The Franks retreated to their far corner of the hut and resumed arguing. They braced their boots far apart and faced off, interrupting each other first, and hissing at each other in threatening tones next. They seemed to enjoy no better terms with each other than with our general's envoys.

Proculus whispered, 'Silvanus gave us a position to fall back on, to offer them bribes, just like he paid some of the Alemanni raiders hard *solidi* to retreat back into the mountains.'

'So the Gallo-Roman taxpayers' resentful rumors are true. But it doesn't look like these men are to be seduced by gold.'

'Oh, you're wrong, Numidianus.' Proculus took a deep gulp. 'They've just pushed up the Silvanus bid as high as Laniogaisus dares go.'

'So we should leave.'

Proculus was listening hard. 'Wait. Now they're weighing the price of Silvanus' offer against the ransom they would get from Constantius for his head.'

'They *told* our side that?'

'Of course not. That's why they're bickering over there in the corner. We're not supposed to figure that out.'

'They would sell his head to the Emperor?'

'Of course. The problem, as usual, is that they can't agree among themselves which tribe gets to decapitate him.'

At the mention of ransom, my scalp prickled with an awful premonition. If Silvanus was worth a fortune in ransom, a tribune or two with the elite of the *Magister Militum*'s council wasn't exactly a dog's meal. We were all in danger.

'If the deal is off, Laniogaisus should signal our retreat.'

One of the Franks had subdued the others with a decision.

I heard the telltale jingle of a belt buckle just on the other side of the door behind me only a second too late. The Franks were going to make their move, and it had nothing to do with offering General Silvanus sanctuary in their forests.

That was why there were no men working in the hamlet, minding their own business.

Like Silvanus, they too had a backup plan.

I drew my *spatha* and *pugio* at the sound of scraping blades outside. Laniogaisus stopped arguing with the lead Frankish tribesman and stared at me.

'Ambush!' I yelled.

—THE WOLVES OF AMBITION—

The Franks shouted to their henchmen lying in wait on the other side of the hut walls. The door burst in. Within seconds, Laniogaisus had lurched forward in an attempt to take the lead Frank as his hostage. But it was obvious that taking one Frank was perfectly fine with the others.

We were Romans and we fought then as Romans, always aware of each other in the middle of sudden and violent mayhem.

The Franks were better prepared than we were, and vicious to boot. Grabbing a stool for a shield, I took on one of the shorter Franks. Against his swinging axe head, my *pugio* was of no use. I lurched forward with a confidence I didn't feel as he reached over his head to plunge his blade into my forehead. I jammed him between the stool legs against the mud wall and plunged my *spatha* deep into his unprotected groin. The deadly axe fell from his grip.

I stuffed it into my belt and made for the door. Poor Proculus was on the verge of meeting his death, but the Frank swinging his *francisca* straight for the adjutant's waist didn't see my sword stroke coming down on his forearm. He screamed as I sliced through to the bone.

I pulled Proculus through the door just before Laniogaisus and his enemy locked themselves into a death grip in its narrow opening. I yanked the tribune free. He rammed his dagger with an upthrust into the barbarians' entrails.

Still fighting off Franks, we stumbled in clusters through the low doorway. Out in the open was hardly better. The *vicus* had known all along what to expect.

A gang of villagers waited for us outside, led by the butcher himself, still wearing his apron smeared with hare's blood and fur. Despite their motley appearance, these villagers wielded sharp blades of solid Frankish workmanship.

The women, hidden in their miserable huts, peeked out at the bloody chaos through mean little openings cut into their wattled walls.

Laniogaisus gave the order for us to move into a tight defensive wedge against a mob that assumed they'd outnumbered us. But they underestimated coolheaded Roman training. One after another fell to our blades. Now they saw that in our expert formation we could fend off triple their number and still make steady progress to our horses.

Their wounded captain shouted to them from the doorway where he clenched his midriff and leaned—helpless and dying. He was calling off his fellows. Their ambush had failed but they kept up their raucous threats as they retreated.

I got the bleeding Proculus up on his saddle and, leaping onto a Frank's horse, raced us both out of the *vicus*. The adjutant was losing blood but not mortally wounded. We galloped behind the others down the potholed road for the safety of the Castra Divitia.

The Franks didn't follow us. We had our territory and they had theirs. Silvanus had just made a mistake thinking they wanted to share.

He'd played his Frankish trump card behind Apodemius' back but had lost the hand. The delaying was over for our general. Our mission would be carried out, Silvanus' innocence made plain, and political calm restored to the Western command. Without Laniogaisus' barbarian sanctuary, the *Magister Militum per Gallias* now had no option but to answer Constantius' summons to clear his name.

Or did he?

Chapter 12, The Only Course Left

—The Governor's Palace, Agrippina, August 10-11, 355 AD—

Proculus wasn't fatally hurt but needed his wound cleaned and bandaged. After delivering him to Silvanus' *medicus*, I rinsed myself off and devoured my evening meal in ten minutes. The palace servers gave me a glazed bowl of river fish steamed with barley and some spelt flatbread to take to Gaudentius. Surely he would relent now and let Meroveus and myself relieve from his watch.

The *ducenarius* was sound asleep. His head lay flopped onto a makeshift pillow fashioned by scrunching up his dirt-spattered traveling cloak. This time he put up no resistance. Meroveus hoisted Gaudentius over his shoulder and slung him onto his own bed next door.

The healer woman took Gaudentius' bowl and downed it with a grateful grunt. No one had looked after her until now.

'Is the *Magister* any better?'

The windows were shuttered against all drafts. The air in the room was fuggier than ever. I peered down at him through the dim light of the single oil lamp at his bedside.

Apodemius' white hair caught the gleam of the flame. I leaned close. His wheezing still rattled like pebbles on a seashore. His face was flushed and wet. His nobbled limbs rested like fleshless rods underneath the limp blanket.

The healer woman shook her head. 'My medicine should have worked better. Two medicines are sometimes not as good as one. Ordinary people never understand that the balance of the body is delicate, like a gold merchant's scale.'

'Two medicines?'

'That man out there gives him Roman tonic mixed with wine. Fights my root tea.' She jerked her head at the corridor where Gaudentius' stool sat empty.

She shook her head again. 'That man has no trust.'

She'd laid aside her coarse cloak and sat on a stool near Apodemius' knees, never taking her eyes off the *Magister*. Her complexion was as wrinkled and cushiony as a centurion's saddle padding. She had thrown back her *palla* and exposed coarse gray hair twisted into a thin braid with a length of faded yarn. My first impression of a desiccated crone diminished. I noticed the clarity of her blue eyes, the set of her strong jaw, and her high, intelligent forehead.

'Get more hot water,' she said.

Meroveus sent a slave running for a pitcher.

'What's your name, woman?'

'Guntheuca.'

'Where are you from?'

'I came from the other side when I was a young and beautiful girl.' She chuckled. 'I was war booty.'

'Who freed you?'

'I freed myself, Roman. A woman with intelligence and courage always finds a way.' She nodded at her pouch of powerful drugs.

'Has your tea saved a man as old and sick as him before?'

'I treat many old people now. Roman army doctors only fix the young—soldiers full of blood and fight, young men with something to live for.'

'Oh, not everyone in the army is twenty-five.' I was starting to feel my age, almost thirty by my loose reckoning.

'This man is tired, very tired.' She shot me a warning glance. 'Perhaps he does not want to live.'

'Nonsense! He's got to live! If you can't save him, confess it. We'll get someone more skilled.'

'Now you sound like that other one. There is no one better than Guntheuca between here and Mogantiacum.'

The slave came running back, splashing boiling water all over the stone floor. Guntheuca measured powdered roots into her palm, sifted them through her fingers into a cup, poured the water over, and blew on the surface to cool it.

'What is this medicine?'

'Some call it *Odenkopf*. Others call it *lugenwerz*. My grandmother called it *beinerwell*.'

'Did you tell Gaudentius his wine tonic might be fighting your treatment?'

'Of course.'

Yet Gaudentius has gone on with the drink that made Apodemius only sicker. I sat in silence. Should I trust the ambitious Gaudentius with the survival of our *schola*? Or should I trust Roxana's barbarian healer? She carried no fancy surgical instruments. She quoted no Galen. She measured with her fingers rather than the precise spoons of Roman physicians.

I knew the prejudice Gaudentius felt toward this somber creature, with her bunches of dried twigs and linen packets of powders. Gaudentius might be wrong to continue slipping Apodemius that syrupy red potion, but what would I do in his place?

The camphor-like steam rising off her tea bit my nostrils. She lifted Apodemius gently into her arms without any difficulty and passed a sponge dipped into the tea between his lips. After a few minutes of this, she had squeezed half the tea down his gullet. She laid his featherweight shoulders back down on the pillow.

He seemed hardly conscious.

'Is the fever bad?'

'Fever is good, Roman. Fever means he is still fighting. If we keep him off that man's tonic for just one night, the fever will build and the crisis may come. The cramping has eased. The fat no longer comes up with his vomit. He might battle it out. The fever will rise tonight—that is normal in the evening—but he has to break it himself. The old man must fight.'

I left the emptied supper tray outside the door for a slave and brought in Gaudentius' stool for myself.

'Take a rest now, Guntheuca. Meroveus and I will watch him. Use my bed next door. I will call you if there is any change.'

She rose, her eyes turning on me with a wary glint.

'Do not give him anything. Put that cool cloth on his head from time to time as the fever mounts. I will rest for an hour. No more.'

I opened the shutter a crack to release the horrendous stench. The sun was lowering over the horizon, bestowing a northern summer dusk of haunting softness. I gazed at the glistening fields far beyond the pastureland full of army tents, banners and standards, ox-wagons, and stables. The cleared land ended at wooded foothills lining the distant southwest. Any minute now, the great orange disk of Apollo would drop out of sight behind that dark, continuous line of impenetrable forest.

The oil lamp sputtered and went out.

I sat in the darkness with Apodemius lying there, both of us helpless. The rattle and hiss of his lungs, working in and out, in and out, in their fight for life filled the dark void. That thin crack of fading light between the shutters shot into the room, like an archer's arrow piercing my hope of saving the old man.

I bolted the shutter shut against the evening draft. When I heard the slave recovering the supper things outside the door, I told him to fetch me a fresh lamp.

Sitting in the dark felt like abandoning myself to despair. I laid my palm on Apodemius' forehead. His skin was as hot as a brazier and as dry as the flaking papyrus files cluttering his Castra office. Could any brain burn that fiercely and still survive?

The slave was already at the far end of the echoing corridor. 'Wait!' I called after him. 'Fetch us two or three lamps. We'll need more light to watch by.'

I went back to the *Magister*'s bedside and found the basin of cool water and a towel. I soaked, squeezed, and patted. I continued to do this, many times an hour, as the needle of sunlight piercing the shutters' crack faded slowly away.

After two hours or so, Meroveus took his turn, and I rested outside in the corridor, waiting for my next shift and thinking.

Silvanus had exhausted his choices. If he left tomorrow for Roma, I would persuade Gaudentius that it was his privilege, not mine, to escort the General's party. Gaudentius knew he had the Emperor's favor. He knew he had made new friends at court as fast as Apodemius made fresh enemies.

Gaudentius had every reason to wish Apodemius dead. I must be the one to stay behind to help Guntheuca bring the *Magister* back to health.

—THE WOLVES OF AMBITION—

In the end, Gaudentius trusted Meroveus to guard Apodemius while we answered the General's general summons at noon. Claudius Silvanus gazed around at the men gathered in the provincial governor's great reception chamber. I took note of their insignia as Gaudentius and I passed their ranks to join Proculus. The adjutant was freshly bandaged and standing in his proper position with the rest of the military staff.

Thanks to the salary handout, many of the legions and *auxilia* of the Western Army under Silvanus' command still had officers present in Agrippina. The room was full and yet dozens more were trying to squeeze in through the wide doorway. After almost an hour's wait, some two hundred army officers and a few municipal bureaucrats drawn in from across the city stood waiting to hear Silvanus' reason for the meeting.

Slipping between armored shoulders in the jostling crowd, I spotted the insignia of the *Legio Primani* as well as the *auxilia* Batavi, Regii, Petulantes, Bracchiati, and Cornuti. Features of all kind bore testimony to the mix of bloods that made the Roman fighter of our times. In the end, whether our grandfathers were Celtic, Frankish, Alemannic, Gallic, or even Numidian, we were bound together this bright August day in spirit, training, and self-discipline.

We were all imperial servants.

From the officers' calm and congenial expressions, I deduced that the secret of Constantius' charges had been kept a close secret by the *trustis*. How different this gathering was from the *consistorium* down in Mediolanum! How virile their stance! How straightforward their glances of concern and readiness! I saw no eunuchs or torturers, only honest, eager men by the dozens.

Laniogaisus signaled the assembly to order. Silvanus wasted no time coming to the point.

'I speak to you today as loyal officers of the field army and the *auxilia palatinae*, of the *riparienses* who have suffered such grievous losses during recent border assaults, and most faithful bodyguards of my *trustis*, you men who serve the Empire well. I value you on this day perhaps more than any other.'

The officers' expressions shifted from congenial to curious.

Silvanus spoke to his men as officers, not slaves—none of Constantius' imperial mask of 'we or us.' He said 'you and I' as if to brothers-in-arms.

Moreover, instead of secreting his women behind ornate grilles like an Eastern potentate, General Silvanus had this morning included the leading ladies of his headquarters as equals in this audience. Looking regal in her long green plush tunic and overtunic of silvery silk, Evochildis presided from a wide *cathedra* surrounded by that same cohort of stern-faced attendants, fair and steely-eyed.

Roxana stood to the other side of the room, accompanied by a few comely slaves and younger companions, including the sly Clothild, now draped in a burgundy and gold brocade too stiff for her youthful frame.

Had Silvanus already bid his family circle a private farewell? I was still *agens* enough to examine the women's faces for clues. Roxana disguised her swollen, red-rimmed eyes behind a thin veil. She avoided my questioning glance. She might be happy that Silvanus had found the courage to defend himself in Mediolanum but her situation in Agrippina without his protection would soon become precarious.

Evochildis, on the other hand, looked far from displeased that Silvanus has decided to take up the reins of his future at last.

'I regret to tell you that I, General Claudius Silvanus, *Magister Militum per Gallias*, who so recently paid out imperial gold in the name of Constantius II, I stand accused of treason against that same Emperor.'

'Treason on spurious grounds!' One of the Petulantes' officers stepped forward.

Silvanus raised his hand to cut off the inevitable outflow of protests.

'On spurious grounds, indeed.'

He gave a wry, almost bitter smile. 'Since the Battle of Mursa, never did I harbor treasonous thoughts or swear allegiance to any other than our Emperor.'

'Then what's changed, General?' asked one of the Cornuti leaders. No one stood on ceremony with the commander they trusted and served.

—THE WOLVES OF AMBITION—

'Some of you may have remarked over recent days on the presence of unusual visitors, none other than the *Magister Agentium in Rebus* from Roma and three subordinates. They delivered the Emperor's charges. I have considered their invitation to come to Mediolanum and face these unexpected accusations. They set before me the example of General Ursicinus, the Commander of our forces in the East, no less redoubtable for his victories . . . and no less doubted in court. He answered the Emperor's recall from the East and appeared in Mediolanum to rebut such slurs.'

'So answer such charges with our own victories as proof!' cried a muscle-bound logistics officer from the Primani.

'Our victories? That is the problem, *Actuarius*. I have intelligence enough to conclude that these accusations were triggered, not by my disloyalty, but by the *success* of each of you in the field!'

Silvanus moved among them, turning to one officer after another as he drummed home his argument.

'It is *your victories* that feed the envy of cowards back at court. Whatever I say, these are men ready to corner me with yet more lies and forgeries. Mere words will not wash away villainy so well prepared by powerful personages.'

The rumble of protests fell silent. The clever Silvanus had blamed his predicament on their bravery and loyalty. He had tied them to his fate. Now it dawned on me that Silvanus might not intend to obey the Emperor's summons just yet. I suddenly found myself the object of dozens of anxious and angry glances as hardened men searched my eyes for confirmation of Silvanus' doom.

Silvanus gave them a bitter chuckle. 'Don't stare at *Biarchus* Marcus Gregorianus Numidianus as if he were an oracle, men. He's done his duty and no more!'

Proculus spoke up, 'The truth is your best defense, General. You must face these lies.'

'It is important to learn from one's fellow soldiers,' Silvanus answered. 'If the man next to you falls because his grip on his *clibius* was weak, you hold yours all the tighter. If you see the enemy is lying in strength on the right wing, you ambush his left. Is it not reasonable I should study the experience of General

Ursicinus? He has answered similarly unjust charges, but is he returned with full honors to active duty? No, he remains detained at court and unable to return to his command.'

'What are your choices?' one of the Batavi asked.

'Like any experienced soldier caught in a narrow ravine, I considered a strategic retreat.' This drew an appreciative chuckle from his uneasy audience.

Silvanus nodded to Laniogaisus, who then took the floor to reveal his secret 'negotiation.'

'Yesterday, the General sent a small party of us to ask for temporary sanctuary with the Franks on the other side of the border.'

'That's no choice!' protested one of the Petulantes centurions. 'That's defection and flight! We deserve better than such ignominy for serving under your standard!'

Silvanus jerked his head up to look over the heads of so many fellow Franco-Romans to answer this daring challenge from the very rear of the chamber.

'Then you will be pleased to hear what happened, good Ruricius. Continue, Tribune Laniogaisus.'

'All we asked of the tribes was time enough to use our own trusted sources in court to investigate this conspiracy. Mallobaudes and Malarichus have already protested but only been confined for their pains. Those wretches across the bridge pretended they would offer the General sanctuary, but for a price. We were prepared for that. We haggled for more than an hour. The price steadily rose, as each man saw the consequences for himself if another tribe pocketed more *solidi* than his own.'

The officers nodded to each other.

'The Franks began to quarrel. Then it turned uglier. We overheard their foul alternative—to seize our general and his gold, and then sell him for ransom to Constantius—alive or dead.'

Laniogaisus shook his head. 'We failed in our mission and barely escaped imprisonment—or worse—ourselves.' He pointed at Proculus' fresh bandages.

Silvanus took over. 'Not for the first time since these *agentes* delivered their summons, have I spent the night kneeling deep in prayer in that chapel next door. I have asked God what is the best for us all. I face a web of lies as coiled and barbed as a wolf trap waiting for my foot to step into it. I have sought help and fellowship across the river, beyond the Castra Divitia, but found only greed and division.'

Silvanus paused. In the many long years since I had first seen him—jovial, confident, and bold that night among the rebels—his face had grown leaner from hardships in the field. His once dancing eyes now gazed out at us through dark rings of sleeplessness. His voice was calm, but weighted with resignation and regret.

'I have asked you here, my fellows-in-arms, to tell you how God has seen fit to answer my prayers. He has pointed me away from Mediolanum's judgment. He has saved me from our Frankish cousins' treachery. There is only one course left to me.'

So here it came—finally—his hard-won capitulation to the *agentes*' appeals. It would be humiliating for him to prostrate himself under the satisfied gaze of Arbetio and Lampadius, but Constantius would see reason once Silvanus was staring down their deceit in person.

Silvanus braced his shoulders and paused for an instant, then took the plunge.

'It is with doubtful jubilation and deep humility that I find myself issuing a general muster of the entire Western Army to join us here in Agrippina as soon as they can.'

'I call upon you, my noble companions in battle and fellow defenders of the Empire, to acclaim me as your Emperor of the West.'

A thrill of astonishment gripped the assembly. Spines straightened. All eyes fixed on Claudius Silvanus. Not one man wanted to say years hence that he had not imprinted on his mind this scene, this moment the *Parcae*, those great Fates, whirled their spindles of destiny, twisting Silvanus' life into an unexpected skein of purple.

There was a horrible, terrifying silence, through which only Roxana's stifled sobs were to be heard. Evochildis frowned at this and rose to her feet. She lifted her magnificent profile to direct all observers to hail her son.

But before anyone could recover his voice, a Bracchiati tore one of the imperial drapes off a window and, ripping it in half, wrapped it over Silvanus, adorning him with imperial colors.

'*Imperator!*' cried a tribune at the front of the chamber. Laniogaisus fell before Silvanus' boots, prostrating himself at full length.

Hundreds of voices rose up.

I had just time through the crowd to see Roxana collapse into a flood of tears and flee the great chamber. We had both failed in our mission to deliver Silvanus back to the court, but legal procedure was the least of my distress.

I had failed my friend Roxana in leaving her lover to his own folly.

Mayhem engulfed us *agentes* as Silvanus' officers rushed forward to congratulate their commander. Deputies raced out the double doors to deliver the momentous news to the vast army camp outside the city walls. Any minute now, an order would reach the hundreds of *cornicines* spread across the vast field of tents to blow the signal for assembly.

Silvanus marched in triumph out of the residence to receive the expected acclamation of thousands. Before my eyes, pennants torn and flags in any color that approximated purple waved above the heads of tribunes and centurions.

Gaudentius and I lingered on the steps of the governor's great reception hall. We had witnessed the excited clamor erupting around us. We had watched the excited stream of red-faced officers trail Silvanus down the steps of the great palace like unstoppable Vesuvian lava.

Within minutes the beaming Claudius Silvanus had mounted his stallion and ridden between the horses of Bainobaudes and Laniogaisus toward the encampment beyond the gates. He passed out of our sight to lead his procession down the southbound boulevard and into the embrace of his faithful troops.

The tumult that had drowned my shock faded away. There was a long silence broken only by the clanking of spear and buckle as the last *domesticus* left the hall behind us to resume his duties.

'He has lost his senses,' I said.

Gaudentius turned on me with features distorted by rage.

'The fool! The idiot! Don't tell me this was the answer from his Christian God. Silvanus has done this out of fear, pride, anger and loyalty to that dragon of a mother. Now he's counting on more time to collect his forces before Constantius' sword comes down on his neck.'

'He certainly won't want Constantius to hear this news until he's ready. But if the Fates are on his side, he has—'

'—time we must not give him.' Gaudentius pounded his fist on the pillar.

'It will take him time—to summon the legions spread out across the province and confirm their support, to test the support of civilian leaders across the province like Count Maudio, to take control of the mint—'

'It's our duty to deliver this news before Constantius hears rumors.'

'I saw no man there this morning who did not rush to join his triumph. Only our *schola* stands apart from the army—'

Gaudentius stopped his cursing and looked hard into my eyes. 'That's right. Only we stand in judgment today. As soon as that blasted banging of shields dies down, Silvanus will remember we are here. He'll put us *agentes* under guard—at the very least.'

'In that case . . .' I wavered.

'Collect your things, Numidianus. We might have no more than an hour before this delirium in Silvanus' head clears and he remembers we're still here—independent witnesses to his crime. His tribunes will be coming for us soon. You must be the first to deliver this news to court.'

'Without Apodemius and yourself?'

A deafening thunderclap from a sea of shields and men's bellowing roars hit us then and nearly drowned out his command.

'I am ordering you, *Biarchus*! Hurry! *Escape Agrippina now!*'

Chapter 13, One General More or Less

—ONE WEEK LATER, MEDIOLANUM—

'It was just as the Tribunes Mallobaudes and Malarichus warned, *Imperator*. Silvanus received your summons with indignation and confusion. He protested that he was his imperial sovereign's most loyal servant.'

'You are saying we made a mistake, *Agens*? Yet you yourself now deliver the ultimate proof of the General's treason.'

'There had been no intention to claim the diadem for himself before the accusations were laid at his feet, *Imperator*. We arrived to see him pay the army in your name and to dedicate their victories to your eternal reign. I witnessed the distribution of the *donativa* myself. Even after he knew of these charges, he debated for many days how to defend himself. On August 7, he was *Magister Militum* of your army in Gallia—no more and no less.'

The Emperor's heavy jaw jutted upwards. 'And on August 11, as if by some deranged miracle, Silvanus elevated himself to our equal,' he intoned.

The route south had proved as hazardous as ever, but I'd been lucky to catch a cavalry unit with fresh horses and a taste for speed halfway down the river valley plateau between Mogantiacum and Augusta Raurica. They left me in the foothills below Curia where I hesitated, reluctant to cross the Alemanni-infested passes alone. I waited for half a day. Just as I was about to accept I had no choice, a military convoy fresh from delivering arms and clothing to the fortress in Brigantium started up the foothills.

We made excellent time. The summer floods had cleared. Some of the *mansiones* dotting the route were resuming halting service. I'd ridden my relief horses hard enough to make the journey in record time. This would no doubt pour yet more oil on the inflammatory accusations that *agentes* were barbaric in their treatment of equine state property.

Waiting for a groom in Curia to bring my fresh mount, I snacked and stretched my legs with a five-minute walk along a mountain path behind the layover station. I picked miniscule strawberries that burst in my mouth with a tingling sweetness. Just as the groom called me back to my saddle, I spotted more appetizing red fruit. I was just on the verge of swallowing a handful, when my greedy hand froze at my lips.

These berries were like smooth and shiny cylinders with a knob of a brown seed peeking out. There was a strange obscenity to this. I realized with a chill that this might be Guntheuca's deadly drug. I wrenched off a short branch with dozens of the suspicious little fruits and crushed it into my satchel to send to the healer as a gift.

The minute I had arrived at court, I had sought out the deputy *Magister Officiorum* to demand a private audience with the Emperor. His arms overloaded with religious documents to distribute, Florentius huffed with impatience. He himself would hear me out only after the synod's heated debate.

'Use that time to clean yourself up. You look a mess, entirely out of keeping with court protocol.'

'I can't wait—it's for the ears of the Emperor alone.'

'Really, *Agens* Numidianus, your *schola* oversteps itself. Perhaps you are not a Christian, but surely even you understand, within that room is the most important convocation of powerful theological authorities held in years. They are determining nothing less than *the true nature of Christ!*'

'The true nature of the Empire is at stake.'

'I'm afraid the Empire will have to make way for God, at least until sunset,' Florentius said.

'You can't afford to obstruct me, Florentius.'

Florentius scrutinized my weary face still streaked with the sweat and dust of the road.

'You have five minutes with him in the small reception room adjoining the large conference chamber,' he said. 'If a *biarchus* has forgotten his place in the scheme of things, there had better be a good reason.'

—THE WOLVES OF AMBITION—

My exhausted mind lost track of time. I waited for over an hour, perhaps almost two. The drone of argument and counter argument, bouncing between Greek and Latin, filtered through the heavy doors to the conference hall. I almost dozed off when a break in the proceedings startled me back to attention.

Constantius burst into the room in full imperial regalia, as ornate and stiff as the hundreds of bishops ranked on the other side of the heavy oak doors. Indifferent to my purpose, the imperial bodyguards at his heels kept their eyes fixed on my weapons. I was still wearing my dust-covered riding cloak and mud-covered riding trousers. I removed my *petanus* as he entered, but he saw it bore a telltale feather, that signal to all *Cursus* relay staff that I rode through on state business of the greatest urgency.

I prostrated myself at Constantius' spotless boots and spoke into the grouting of the tessellated mosaics.

'On August 11, General Claudius Silvanus assumed the purple to the acclaim of the officers of the Gallic Army.'

I was almost grateful my nose was pressed flat against the stones. I didn't have to witness the first shock register across his granite face.

'Rise, Numidianus. Who knows of this?'

'Silvanus was mustering the forces as I left, *Imperator*. By now the news must have traveled across northeastern Gallia and followed me south, nearly as fast as my own horse. All Mediolanum may know by tomorrow or the day after, at the latest.'

'Report to an emergency meeting of the *consistorium* at midnight. Until then, divulge this to no one.'

Rising to one knee, I reached to kiss the sweeping purple hem again but missed—his flight from the room was so hasty. My stomach churned at the thought of delivering this catastrophic news to the leering *consistoriani*.

I cursed Silvanus for falling into a trap laid for him here at court. There must be some way to unravel these knots of lies and misjudgments coiling around the security of the state before disaster turned to tragedy.

How best to use the hours until midnight?

With Silvanus' Junius hiding in Roma and my three colleagues trapped up in Agrippina, I had no ready ally for any investigation in Mediolanum.

I decided to enlist the cautious Florentius, though the danger was obvious. Even if I sought to uncover the truth about Dynamius' letters of reference, Florentius' loyalties during these uncertain times lay neither with the indignant Franks nor with my *schola*. His career depended on keeping order in the palace and protecting the civil service from disruption.

When it came to resolving Silvanus' disaster, all I could insist was that Florentius follow the letter of Roman law.

Within the hour of my unhappy announcement to Constantius, I moved quickly on that point. The sinking sun had not yet touched the high city walls. The inner courtyard still bustled with power merchants moving between their cluttered offices and the crowded baths. Outside the entrances to the furnaces, slaves unloaded wagons of fresh wood to feed the fires that filled the *caldarium* with suffocating steam. A flock of Greek priests fluttered past in their dark robes for the baths' entrance. It seems that deciding whether Christ was merely a godlike man or divinity-made-human was sweaty work.

I finally found Florentius in the great bowels of the palace kitchens. A fat man in a wide apron was thrusting a plucked crane by its limp neck into Florentius' face. This choleric official was Constantius' head chef. Few courtiers dared enter his empire of a thousand cooks, servers, and slaves roasting away in their Hades of spitting fires and ovens. The two officials were shouting at each other over the earsplitting racket of pans and ladles.

Florentius saw me and broke off yelling. Neither man welcomed my interruption of their row over the safety of meat supplies in the August heat. Apparently the droopy crane was just one of many spoiled specimens.

'Sorry. I have had my interview with the Emperor, but my mission is not yet complete. There is more business that concerns you, Florentius,' I lied. 'My *Magister* Apodemius ordered me to inspect the letters containing the evidence against Silvanus.'

'You're too late.' Florentius shrugged me off.

—THE WOLVES OF AMBITION—

I raised my palm in the sweaty chef's face and gave Florentius a polite but firm smile. 'I don't think your office has any right to deny this to our *schola*.'

A tick of his cheek betrayed some doubt as to the procedure in question.

'Where are these letters, exactly?' I pressed him. 'In the Emperor's possession?'

'No, *Biarchus*. Evidence of that kind is a legal matter for the Quaestor.' He waved me away. 'The affair is out of my domain—and yours.'

'Then take me to the Quaestor ... now, Florentius, please. I'll wait for you outside, for five minutes but no longer.'

I waited for thirty minutes instead of five and then gave up. Perhaps Florentius' freedom to cut off a tirade from the Imperial Chef about depleted salt supplies was limited. Or perhaps he had decided to call my bluff.

I retreated to the outer courtyard gatehouse to discover Cassius waiting for the late afternoon rider of the day to gallop through the inner gates. The *circitor* soon rode into view, dismounted and dumped the familiar sacks of imperial mail from parts south and east into our postal gatehouse. We sent him off to rest and cleared off the long worktable.

'It's your privilege to check the registry,' Cassius said giving the enormous pile a doleful once-over.

'There's more than enough here for two men.'

'The synod tripled our workload. Surely you have better things to do. What exactly happened up there in Agrippina? Why didn't you all bring Silvanus back to face trial?'

'Let's get through this together.'

We worked away in silence, separating normal bureaucratic mail and synod communications from private imperial mail and registering each item in our official records.

Being *agentes*, the mountain of synod mail contained potentially useful intelligence for our *schola* about affairs and alliances in distant province. Cassius and I could play the game of intrigue as well as the Lord Chamberlain Eusebius. Cassius showed me an impressive registry of bishops' names and their correspondents that he'd compiled since the start of the synod. We laid aside anything else that interested us for secret copying and resealing as part of our information-gathering responsibilities.

Most of the rest of the packets were standard reports from provincial offices and military garrisons governed by the Mediolanum jurisdiction.

I had just finished reading a particularly aromatic missive full of family gossip from Macedonia addressed to the lovely Empress Eusebia.

'The Empress thinks her two brothers have the makings of consuls,' I was saying to Cassius, when a thick packet caught my eye.

The envelope of *emporitica*, coarse brown packing paper, was addressed to 'Malarichus the Frank and Tribune of the *Gentiles*.' Malarichus was hardly a man I associated with epistolary pastimes.

The sender was the Tribune-in-Charge of the Cremona Armory. I recognized his name. As of last week, this unlucky official stood accused as a co-conspirator of General Silvanus—though the poor man apparently had not yet realized it when he mailed his appeal.

'You keep on,' I told Cassius. 'This one's mine. Close the shutters for a minute.'

We locked ourselves away from any prying intruders passing through the gates outside. I sat down at the table and lit a second lamp. As I'd been trained back at the Castra, I worked at separating the letter from the wax seal, keeping the seal whole and bending the vellum away from the disk. I prayed it wouldn't crack; otherwise it would be necessary to produce a similar new seal with one of our duplicates held under lock and key for just such underhanded occasions. My luck held. After ten minutes of patient fingering, the seal fell off intact.

Inside the packet I found a piece of cheap writing paper, the same *taeneotic* sold by weight that Apodemius favored, folded around a square of expensive vellum.

The Cremona armorer had scrawled, '*Honorable Malarichus, I have received the enclosed communication in the name of General Claudius Silvanus and yourself, admonishing our factories to "prepare everything with speed." I forward this letter to your good offices in all confusion and innocence, for as you know or should* know, there has been no previous instruction from General Silvanus or yourself received by me before this. I am in no way privy to your designs and require further elucidation.'

The simple man had misspelt 'elucidation.'

His letter continued, '*Being a somewhat rude and plain citizen, I fear I cannot make out what might be obscurely intimated. If there is any order or orders of which our armory should be aware, then please make things plainer by the earliest post. Otherwise, I transfer this letter to your noble hand in good faith that only you can explain how such an instruction came to be sent over your signature . . .*'

I put this heartfelt message aside and examined the pricey vellum enclosed. I had read only a few words when the hair on my neck prickled in shock.

The letter bore the familiar, bold signature of General Silvanus.

'Cassius. Look at this.' I pulled out of my belt sack the folded letter Silvanus had sent Junius months ago. I thanked the gods the boy had forgotten to ask for its return.

'This is General Silvanus' own letter to his son Junius.'

'Yes. So what?'

'Now, look at the writing over his signature on this.'

'A different hand, I swear, or I turn in my insignia,' Cassius muttered.

We were staring at a bold forgery—a phony letter. Only the decent common sense of a plain-speaking Roman armorer trying to do the right thing had delivered it into our hands.

But was it too late?

'Are you going to give it to Malarichus?' Cassius whispered. 'We can copy this letter but it's against the law not to deliver it.'

'Malarichus may thank me by the end of the day for showing it first to Florentius. You are my witness that no one else has tampered with it.'

We locked up the postal office and set off for the main official wing. This time we gave Florentius no choice but to take us into his private office, sequestered out of earshot from his school of curious scribes and slaves. He pretended surprise that we'd lifted the seal, but after the requisite show of bureaucratic disapproval, he read both letters.

'Summon Malarichus here,' he told a *domesticus* standing sentry in the corridor.

Once the most trusted official on Constantius' palace staff, Malarichus arrived guarded on each side by four mute Scythians. Clearly, the Emperor was taking no chances in a court with five hundred or so *Germani* loyalists armed to the teeth. I bit my tongue, still under orders not to reveal to Malarichus the fateful move Silvanus had made up in Agrippina.

Florentius kept the intimidating Scythians out in the corridor.

'You have some mail in today's post, Tribune. Please read Malarichus his letter from Cremona,' Florentius told me. As I started to read out loud, Malarichus' truculent expression turned to bewilderment.

When I'd finished reading, Florentius asked the Frank towering over him, 'Do you know this armorer?'

'I have heard of him. He is an honest man and I am honest enough to say so.'

'Have you ever written to him?'

'Never.'

'Then if he is as honest as you say, why would he be asking through you for General Silvanus to clarify such instructions?'

'I cannot believe this letter. Show it to me.'

I showed the bogus letter to the tribune, carefully folding it between my fingers so as to conceal Silvanus' signature and obscure the noticeable difference in height and slant of the letters.

'This is a copy?' Malarichus asked Florentius.

'Why a copy?'

'That is not the General's hand. What trick are you playing, Florentius Nigrinianus?'

'Would you know the handwriting of General Claudius Silvanus?'

'As well as my own,' Malarichus growled.

Florentius nodded to me, 'I am now ready to grant your earlier request, Numidianus. I will alert the Quaestor.'

Cassius, Malarichus, and myself waited in nervous silence, prisoners of the Scythians blocking the doorway of the cramped inner office. After some twenty minutes of suspense, boots clattered back along the corridor. The Quaestor's secretary, accompanied by half a dozen *scutarii*, appeared with Florentius.

'Here . . . they are,' the secretary said in an anxious whisper. He untied a bulging leather dossier and pulled out the green-sealed packet of letters Gaudentius and I had witnessed Lampadius give Constantius in the private chapel.

Cassius and I spread out the letters one by one under the stern eyes of the court watchdogs. One glance through a single paragraph was enough to send up alarm. Silvanus seemed to be planning weapon transfers, secret passwords for amassing distant legions, and the quicksilver seizure of key departments and archives in Mediolanum, Trier, Sirmium, and even Constantinopolis. Occupation of the state mints was a high priority, so new coinage could proclaim Silvanus as imperial ruler as soon as possible.

Florentius and the Quaestor's secretary sat down. By the light of three oil lamps held close to each letter, they examined the ink and surface of each vellum piece in turn.

'Get the Chief of the Scribes,' Florentius ordered the senior *scutarius*, through gritted teeth. 'We need the Emperor's best expert to confirm my suspicions. If I'm not mistaken, a previous message is faintly detectable in the pores of the vellum. Silvanus' original content has been scrubbed almost clean but not quite.'

'The family has always insisted these were innocent letters of reference to Frankish compatriots recommending the capabilities of Dynamius the *Actuarius*,' I said.

'I believe they once were no more than that,' Florentius said, his face drained of color.

We stood, speechless, staring at the now-familiar hand of the forger, consistent from one letter to the next, each message of treasonous strategy finished off with the bold, hurried flourish of Silvanus' own hand. When peering just inches away from the calfskin, I thought the vellum did indeed seem to hold traces of ink where none should be.

The Chief of the Scribes arrived, all swishing robes reeking of incense and ambergris bath oil. He lifted the lamplight close to the vellum, sniffed and rubbed. He took a *stilus* from his belt pouch and, laying it perpendicular to the handwriting, compared the slant of the letter's text to the slant and height of Silvanus' signature.

'I believe this letter to be a forgery,' he said at last.

I thought Malarichus would erupt like Vesuvius.

※※※

Not for the first time, I admired Constantius' imperturbable expression. If Malarichus looked ready to use his blade on the entire Council, the Emperor and his *consistoriani* kept their composure at Florentius' startling revelations. Never popular at the best of times, I remained standing in the obscure shadows of the chamber, mindful of Eusebius' hatred of my *schola*'s interference.

'I know nothing of these letters, but what Mattyocopus told me,' Lampadius told his fellow councilors. 'But as a sign of good faith, I offer myself for suspension during a commission's investigation into this unfortunate matter.'

'We suspend you from service,' Constantius replied but he did not deign to turn his head in the sinuous prefect's direction. Silent glances around the table congratulated Lampadius for the triumph of getting away with nothing more than mere suspension.

'We have heard testimony and also clear the Master of the Rolls from all suspicion,' Constantius added. It was true that nothing presented in the packets linked the forgeries to Aedesius.

Aedesius' cohorts visibly refrained themselves from patting the quaking official on the shoulder.

'But in the end, we have no choice but to submit Eusebius Mattyocopus to further questioning.'

'No, no! I beg you, *Imperator*, I know nothing whatsoever of these forgeries. I only saw these letters briefly! Where is Dynamius tonight? Why is the Emperor's Baggage Handler not brought forward?'

'You forget, poor Mattyocopus. The *Actuarius* Dynamius was not long ago promoted to Corrector of Tuscia Umbria,' Arbetio said. The Consul then turned his back on trembling Mattyocopus to confer in a whisper with the *cubicularius* eunuch, the Lord

—THE WOLVES OF AMBITION—

Chamberlain Eusebius. For one adept at orchestrating far more successful conspiracies than this, the wily Eusebius hung back from this forgery affair with manifest contempt.

Mattyocopus' flabby shoulders began to shake. A stream of hot urine ran down the greedy ex-treasurer's trouser legs of bleached goat suede. The rest of the *consistoriani* twisted away with revulsion.

At a summons from the Emperor, Paulus Catena entered the room followed by four others, all a head taller than the 'notary' himself. Mattyocopus started to whimper.

I suspected the reptilian Lampadius must be at the heart of the conspiracy against Silvanus. I recalled his outer office full of tools for erasing vellum. But I stood silent, knowing there were many 'truths' lying here, still veiled and neglected, before the assembled courtiers. There might be *some* truth to Lampadius' claim he'd obtained the Dynamius references from the scapegoat Mattyocopus, but these *consistoriani* had not seen Lampadius' suspicious movements that night Gaudentius and I had spied on his journey to Constantius in the chapel.

In not reporting that Lampadius had hidden the letters in his office brazier—an act that spoke of the prefect's dishonesty and guilt—I was letting poor Mattyocopus take all the blame. If Lampadius was not as innocent as he pretended, perhaps Mattyocopus was not as guilty as accused. The shrieks of the pudgy man condemned to the waiting arms of Catena's henchman were sadly convincing to me.

I noticed Catena's misshapen little mouth smirking with relish. He escorted the fallen official out the great side doors and down the stone steps leading to his cells to begin his work afresh.

It seemed Catena never slept. Did he, too, fear the tongue of Marcellus, the Count of Dreams? Or did he fear his own nightmares? It was all the same to me. I had a horrible moment when it seemed the gods whispered a warning that sooner or late, we would all fall to that sadist's whims below the grand state rooms.

But there were other important issues at stake tonight.

The urgent meeting disclosing the forgeries to the Emperor had lasted until well past midnight.

The Emperor laid his head back, closed his eyes, and sighed. 'The question before us, Councilors, is what do we do now? We know that Silvanus is innocent of treason and that perhaps these forged letters drove him to a public act of desperation that is, however, impossible to forgive. We admit, we are sorely grieved by this chain of events.'

'Why did the *agentes* not succeed in bringing the General to us?' Arbetio smiled at me. 'All this could have been sorted out among loyal citizens. All here tonight have only the interests of the Empire at heart.'

'General Silvanus had not yet completed subduing the Alemanni raiding parties infesting the western bank of the Rhenus between Augusta Rauricum and Bonna,' I said. 'For the good of the Empire, he is reluctant to abandon his command.'

'Nonsense,' Arbetio said, 'Silvanus is a guilty coward. Now we understand why, don't we, my fellow councilors? Whatever the explanation behind these stupid forgeries, Silvanus' true ambition has surged to the surface in their wake. He has revealed his true nature. He has taken the purple. He must be dealt with.'

'But how? By whom?' Constantius muttered to himself. The Emperor stared at the flickering torch sconces lining the opposite wall. The shock of Silvanus' acclamation had struck deep.

'You have another general still at your disposal, *Imperator*,' Arbetio said with a sly expression. 'Call in Ursicinus. He's still in Mediolanum, waiting for your favor to restore him to full esteem. This seems the perfect opportunity.'

'Ursicinus? No.' The Emperor shook his head.

Constantius' last interview with the hero of the East had left that formidable military hero insulted and simmering with resentment.

'We have seen that General Ursicinus is a proud man,' said the Master of Admissions, rising to his feet. 'I offer to sooth his pride by summoning him, here and now, with all pomp and formality. After being cast as the Maelstrom of the East and a nepotistic military upstart, nothing will be more flattering to Ursicinus than to be announced with full honors as a most politic leader and mighty fellow soldier worthy of Our Eternity's trust in so delicate a matter.'

I tried not to gag. No wonder this flowery-mouthed character had risen to his post in charge of imperial ceremonies and appointments. His verbose suggestion hung in the air like sickly perfume.

By the light of the late night's glowing lamps, knowing smiles curled across many faces of the *consistoriani*. The use of Ursicinus suited any expert in daring moves on the *latrunculi* board. Despite the warm night air, I turned cold as I watched Constantius' mind chew on this insidious solution.

In short, one fearsome general could be pitted against another.

If Silvanus was destroyed as a rebel, fair enough. It was no more than his precipitous folly deserved.

On the other hand, if Silvanus eliminated Ursicinus, no one in this room would weep. He was still suspected of promoting himself as ruler of the East with Potentius as successor in all but name.

Remembering my boyhood slave days of reading out loud to Senator Manlius from that bombastic historian Publius Annaeus Florus, I thought of the summation of Caesar's defeat over Cassius, Brutus, Pompey and the rest of their republican faction. Antony's survival had been described as an obstacle to Caesar's consolidation on ultimate power. Antony had been 'a rock in Caesar's path.'

I watched, suspecting that Constantius could not resist the temptation set before him. There were two 'rocks in his path' to unchallenged power. A rare hint of a smile passed his lips as he reviewed this question—of one general more or less.

'Then summon General Ursicinus to this chamber, Aedesius,' the Emperor said. 'Apologize for rousing him at this late hour. Pay him every respect. Convey to him the news that—not for the first time—the safety of our beloved Empire rests in his unequalled hands . . . and do not stint in your flattery.'

We waited in exhausted silence as the Master of the Rolls ran off to fetch Ursicinus from the military accommodations of the court.

Aedesius' honeyed invitation had caught the great fly. The hero arrived this time without his son or trusted tribunes-at-large. He prostrated himself, kissed Constantius' hem, and rose again to his imposing height.

'I welcome this chance to clear my name, *Imperator*. I trust this body of upright men is ready to restore me to the Eastern command.'

Constantius waved a jeweled hand, as if the outraged soldier had insulted his audience by asking for a renewal of a *Cursus* travel permit.

'We implore you to forget your preoccupations with your own reputation for the moment. This is no time, General, to resume your defense of a disputed case when the urgency of pressing matters before us must be mitigated before things grow worse. Let all parties proceed now with our former harmony.'

Ursicinus struggled to hide his confusion. So the charges against him weren't dismissed? Or even to be discussed? Wary of a new trap, the grizzled veteran took a step back,.

'Listen carefully, General. We are deliberating a matter of supreme urgency. General Silvanus, whom we held to be no poorer than yourself in loyalty and service to our wishes, is a traitor. He has assumed the purple.'

'If I may add as consul, *Imperator*,' Arbetio rose to his feet, 'our council has decided that you, Ursicinus, are the best man to resolve this emergency.' He glanced down at his doddering fellow consul. On cue, the ancient Lollianus Mavortius nodded his consent.

Ursicinus knew as well or even better than some present tonight that power in the Empire resided, in the end, in the common soldiers' hearts. Whoever commanded their love commanded the Empire.

'Have the forces in Gallia acclaimed Silvanus in full, *Imperator*?'

'Our information is that he is mustering the entire Gallic army to his side as we sit dawdling,' Constantius said through clenched teeth, his eyes darting to me standing hidden in the shadows.

'Even with the Council's unanimous support, I'm in no position to argue with fifteen thousand men in place,' Ursicinus said. 'And to summon my own forces westward poses a delay which would be fatal.'

'Therefore, General, we must arrive at a more subtle—let us say, diplomatic—solution,' Arbetio said.

Constantius asked, 'Can we not agree that, following the discovery of these unfortunate forgeries which cornered Silvanus against his nobler inclinations, we should be all the more careful in how we approach him now?'

'Forgeries?' Ursicinus glanced at the faces around the table.

'Yes,' Eusebius said. 'It seems that before August 11, Silvanus was innocent of conspiracy. But he could have refuted these spurious documents at any time in person. Instead they triggered his precipitous and criminal claim.'

'His inner greed for power merely dropped its veil prematurely,' Arbetio said, 'for no man claims the purple who does not dream of it beforehand.'

Constantius rose to his feet. 'We need ambitious men, Arbetio, but men ambitious for a stable empire, not their own elevation. Silvanus is far away and vulnerable to distrust and bad counsel. He may deserve a path for escape, like a valuable hunting dog whose disobedience has landed his paw in a trap intended for the fox.'

This did not satisfy the leading councilors, but no one dared interrupt the Emperor when he continued. 'We are tired. We face another long day of overseeing the debate of our ecclesiastical delegates.'

The Emperor stepped down from his dais. He placed his heavy hand on the General's braced shoulder.

'We propose this, Ursicinus. No violence. No cavalry assault. No shots fired over the walls of Agrippina. We will write a letter to Silvanus pretending ignorance of these slanderous rumors. You will carry this letter to Agrippina with a small party of men—all family or friendly fellows-in-arms.'

'My son Potentius? Adjutants Ammianus Marcellinus and Verinianus—?'

'As you choose. No more than ten. We cannot afford to alarm Silvanus further. We do not know how he will receive you. You will announce yourself as his replacement in charge of the Gallic command. You will lace him with compliments. You will pay all respects to the misguided officers who rushed to his standard. You will urge Silvanus to speed to our side to receive all due accolades for his victories and instructions for his new responsibilities with us here.'

The *consistorium* adjourned for the night. My presence had been superfluous, but instructive. I had observed the fate of Silvanus batted back and forth like one of Leo's featherweight toys.

As the councilors filed out after the Emperor, I remained behind, watching the unholy partnership of General Ursicinus and Consul Arbetio bend their heads together in conversation.

'Florentius!' I whispered. 'I cannot go into the secretariat unnoticed. Please follow those two and tell me what they are cooking up—quick!'

Florentius' attitude toward me had changed after the day's unholy revelations. Without a moment's hesitation, he lifted his long robe and scuttled after the Consul and General.

I waited on a stone bench in an unlit part of the long corridor outside the Council chamber. There was nothing left of the night's dramatic events, but the sounds of the palace at rest, broken only by the patter of slippered slaves moving here and there, the grinding of bolts and locking of doors, and the smell of candle wax dripping on wall sconces.

I heard distant basilica bells chime out the small hours. Whatever the time, it was still my job to know what this game consisted of—especially when Arbetio's hand was in play.

A dark figure slipped through the shadows where I waited. It was Florentius.

'I am sorry, *Agens* Numidianus. All I caught before they parted for the night was Consul Arbetio saying, "Ursicinus, this is your one and only chance. Don't waste it".'

Chapter 14, The Death of Hope

—WITHIN THE GATES OF MEDIOLANUM—

Chance at what?

I thanked Florentius, slipped out of the palace and headed back to the Financial Building. Still clutching Arbetio's troubling phrase to my bleary mind, I kept a low profile as I sneaked across the shady courtyard. I hadn't forgotten my beating at the hands of Catena's thugs.

The Empire's dilemma had seemed clear enough earlier tonight without layering on yet further conspiracy. General Ursicinus would surely relish assuming Silvanus' command in the West. Indeed, Silvanus would well be advised to grab a seat at the consistorium table in Mediolanum. He could even try to replace Arbetio as consul next year—if his coming reconciliation with Constantius was a success.

And then, yes, only then, I *realized* where the 'rock' in the road lay, and *for whom*. Arbetio hated Silvanus as much as ever—hated his success in both battlefield and bedroom. Geographical distance between the two men had given Arbetio ample room for his deceitful ascent. Having Silvanus sitting next to him at the table where all imperial power sat concentrated threatened the eclipse of his long career.

Something more was in play here.

I found the key to Gaudentius' rooms along the dank covered walkway along the side of the Finance Building and let myself in.

I stopped at a snuffling noise, as if the rats that plagued the kitchen alley were slumming in the *agentes*' quarters.

I struck the flame for the oil lamp and stepped back. Another man lay curled up on Gaudentius' mattress and next to him on the floor, sat an overturned beaker with wine dregs in the bottom. I could have used some drink to help me sleep, but this rascal had left me nothing.

Worse, whatever his rank, he was a disgrace to our *schola*. He'd gone to bed in his travel clothes. His scrawny legs were swamped in borrowed riding trousers many sizes too long, his feet were still tied into city sandals instead of proper travel boots, and his snoring face was covered by the hood of a shabby riding cloak. He had no weapons, sword belt, nor satchel for his private papers.

He snorted in his dreams and rolled over. For the gods' sake, it was old Verus sleeping off a lone journey from Roma.

'Verus, old man? What are you doing here? What's wrong?' I poked his ribs and held the lamp closer to his wrinkled face.

'*Queecumjwkej.*' Nothing but gibberish and spit.

'Verus! Wake up!'

'What? What?'

'It's Marcus. What are you doing here? Is the family all right?'

'Oh! Marcus! I've been waiting up for you all night.'

I turned his empty wine cup upside down. A single drop of wine fell on the stone floor. 'Yes, I can see that. If there's bad news, don't keep me waiting. Is Leo all right? Kahina?'

'Yes, yes, they're all fine, all good and fine.'

He rubbed his stubble and blinked at the bright little flame. Then he leaned over to stare at me.

'But you look like something that's climbed up the well from Hades, son.'

'What are you doing here, Verus?'

'Oh, I brung some important papers to sign. They're over there, on the table. But more important, I promised I would hand deliver this.'

He wiggled his wiry eyebrows at me with sleepy glee. He dug out a folded piece of paper, the first-class stuff made of quality papyrus the Senator had once imported for his official documents.

'It's his first letter he ever wrote and he's written it to you, Marcus. That Antonius Drusus helped him a bit with his spelling, but the letters is all his—no helping him with his handwriting. What's more, he's told me to wait for you to answer it and he's going to read your letter back to him all by hisself without anybody's help! What do you think of our little lad now, hmm?

Oh, ain't we proud of 'im, Marcus. He's taking to his books like a real little sculler now, just like his grandfather.'

I took the precious paper into my hands and patted Verus' knee.

'Where's your fancy-schmancy toilets, lad? Apollo's Balls, I feel an imperial shit coming on.'

'Outside right and down the covered walkway along this building, then past the statue of Trajan, next to the entrance to the baths,' I said. 'Don't get yourself mugged and don't get into any gossiping,' I warned him. 'You can't trust even a latrine pest in this court.'

'Well, at this hour, I'm not likely to be making friends, is I, lad?'

Verus slipped away on his bowed legs. It was kind of him to let me read Leo's first letter alone, to let me shed a tear or two that it was not I, his own father, who had helped him dilute his ink so that it didn't clump in a glob at the end of his *stilus*. The little mite had even copied the style of one of the Senator's massive histories by borrowing red ink for the opening greeting, as if his little note were a substantial new entry into the Roman law books.

Salutations, Marcus Gregorianus Numidianus! I send you my wishes for your good health. Please return home soon. My studies are going well. I have finished ~~reeding~~ reading half of Plutarch. I am not good at geometry but very good at sums. Verus says someday sums will be more useful to me than Plutarch to add up our farm profits. Should I listen to Verus? What do you think?

Antonius Drusus says my Greek is better than his was at my age. Antonius Drusus is kind and patient. He is also kind to my mother. She is better and sends you her fond greetings. Antonius Drusus says someday soon he will marry. Perhaps Mother and he will marry each other. Perhaps they will marry in the autumn when his friends return from their holiday villas. Is this a good idea? What do you think?

Please return to Roma soon. I pray for your health.

Leontus Manlius Gregorius

I tucked the letter into my travel satchel and exhaled a long shudder. Conflicting emotions swamped my heart. Leo's handwriting was regular, his tone respectful with a hint of humor at Verus' expense, and his style devoid of the pretentious flourishes that I knew precocious Roman schoolboys sometimes adopted to impress their elders.

What did I think? Could any appeal be more direct?

Verus returned from the latrines, still adjusting his worn-out belt.

'Verus, how's Kahina?'

'Well, well, you know, Marcus, one doesn't like to get up hopes, but the other day, I heard the *Matrona* laughing.'

'Really?'

'Yes, *really* laughing, not that imitation noise she makes when she thinks somebody made a joke she don't understand.'

Try as I might, I had not been able to reignite the light of Kahina's old personality. Years of cruel abuse as a war captive in the vast Hispanic prisoner farm had left us only a shell of a woman.

I was almost afraid to know more, but I pretended indifference, asking, 'What made her laugh?'

'Well that teacher fellow has a way of making the hours pass, I admit.' Verus looked around the room, 'Any more of that plonk for a tired traveler?'

'No, you sot. What are these papers you want me to sign?'

'Oh, permission to shift some of the oyster beds away from dirty sewage. And there's replacing some of them Falernian vines where rot set in. And sale of the bee farms in Hybla. Kahina spoke to the manager come up from Sicily with his deliveries. He says he'll give us more than a fair price if we leave him all them hives and queens.'

Maintenance and upkeep were to be expected but I did not like the sound of that last item. Constant devaluation and silver dilution made me distrust coinage. The Manlius estates had only survived the recent civil war because our managers, slaves and household in Roma had lived off the food and goods from our properties and bartered the surplus produce in town.

'Kahina is thinking clearly enough to suggest a decision like that?' The Kahina I'd left behind couldn't have followed the fluctuations of the honey auction market.

'If you don't want to sign that one there, I'll just take it back. I'll tell the manager myself that's how we sees it. He needs your signature, no matter what Kahina says. There's no getting around the wise old Senator's precautions.'

He rolled over and pulled the cloak back over his head.

'Verus?'

'Yes, Marcus?'

'Leo writes that his teacher hopes to marry.'

'Well, don't say I didn't warn you.'

'You didn't.'

'I did too.' He yanked the cloak off his face. 'I asked you, as plain as that insignia on your tunic, whether you knew what's you was doing the day you let him cross our threshold. I can always spot a young man on the make—not that I hold it against him.'

The old man began to hum himself to sleep. He thought he had me fooled, but he didn't. Leo wasn't just talking to Verus about the utility of adding up harvest profits someday. The child was worried about changes at home.

Was the letter even Leo's idea? Or did it come from Verus? Or even Kahina?

'If Antonius Drusus makes Kahina laugh, then he should stay,' I said, hating every word coming out of my mouth.

Verus shrugged. 'If you say so.'

'I don't like to think of her alone, week after week, perhaps longer, especially if I'm posted again outside Roma. She deserves good company and moral support. This Antonius Drusus has nothing against him, does he?'

'It's not my place to say, son. If you think that's what's best, then you think it's what is best. But I say, if you don't trust the man, Marcus, maybe it's not what you feel is right is really right.'

I could make no sense of his drowsy rambling.

'Kahina must get better, for Leo's sake, as well as her own.'

'You're still thinking like a slave, son, like that little Numidian still living in the back room of his mind. *Biarchus*, humpf!'

'The *back room of my mind*? What in Hades do you mean by that, Verus?'

'I've known you since you was little, Marcus Numidianus. You caught that vicious squirt Clodius stealing your sandals, but you thought it wasn't best to tell on him. So you didn't squeal, even though you knew it wasn't right.'

'I was a *slave*, Verus. I didn't want to be a troublemaker. I wanted my mother to live in peace.'

'She suffered all the same.'

'And anyway, how do you know Clodius stole my sandals?'

'Because your mother borrowed offa me to buy you a new pair, didn't she?'

※※※

I tussled for hours with my doubts. Before I slipped into a fitful sleep on the spare mattress next to Verus, I'd resolved to return straight to Roma to relieve my fears. What was best for Kahina was whatever she wanted—no more and no less. But if Antonius Drusus was courting her, the House of Manlius had to take stock of his ambitions regarding Leo's inheritance. Perhaps there was no connection whatsoever, but the proposed sale of the Hybla bee farms was too much of a coincidence to leave unquestioned.

Sometime before dawn, I heard a single, quiet toe tap at our door.

It was a *domesticus* from the main building.

'You're summoned to the *consistorium* side chamber.'

'What time is it?'

'Fourth shift.'

Dawn was about an hour away. 'I'm not shaved or washed yet. Isn't it too early for another council session?'

'Hurry up.'

The imperial bath slaves were just opening the wide doors to the day's fresh towel deliveries. A handful of bishop-delegates loitered outside for opening hours. No doubt they hoped to squeeze in an early soak in the *caldarium* pool before the heat of the August morning matched the passion of their celestial fistfight.

I splashed off my face, brushed off my riding trousers, and buckled all my gear back on, glancing with regret at the snoring Verus, so cozy under his cover.

To reach the same anteroom where I'd broken the bad news to Constantius the day before, I had to pass through the great reception hall where the bishops would convene after breakfast and then the empty *consistorium* chamber. There were no scribes or sentries preparing that room.

There was no council meeting this morning.

Dressed in a richly embroidered tunic and a wide belt studded with garnets set in gold holding up fine goatskin trousers, Constantius worked at an ornate desk in the confines of this semi-private room. Only Florentius Nigrinianus and one other man stood at his side, watching him review documents for the day's theological arguments.

The Emperor seemed fully restored to stiff semi-divinity from the night's political shock, though so few were here to fully appreciate it. Hearing me arrive, he waved off the ritual prostration. I waited at attention.

Wall sconces and oil lamps lifted the gloom of dawn just enough to read by. I scrutinized the man standing next to Florentius. He was of middling height and had Italian features that reminded me of someone. I noticed also his polished sword pommel, impeccable belt buckle with carved gold attachments, a bleached tunic of fine-gauge wool and a heavy mustard-colored cloak.

He looked like a Roman of the old school. In fact, so much care had gone into the old-fashioned touches and good taste that I suspected he was a new-made man. No genuinely aristocratic Roman would have decorated his tunic with those two huge *orbiculi*, great roundels stitched in thick red and gold.

Constantius finished reviewing the synod agenda.

'We'll hear them out in that order, Florentius. Tell the Lord Chamberlain we want no more speaking time allotted to the Athanasius clique from today on. We've heard far too much about the piety of unwashed Egyptian monks.'

'Yes, *Imperator*.' Florentius hurried away to start another sixteen-hour day of ecclesiastical headaches.

'*Agens* Numidianus. You will recall the late Flavius Philippus, Praetorian Prefect of the East until 351, our envoy during the failed negotiations at Mursa?'

'Yes, of course, *Imperator*.'

Flavius Philippus had been a self-made son of a Roman sausage maker. He had risen from notary to senior military officer under Constantius leading the Eastern forces against Magnentius. Indeed, I remembered the imperial representative Flavius Philippus well. He was not the stranger who stood in front of me.

The Emperor had entrusted to Philippus the vital task of crossing enemy lines during the standoff of the divided Roman army to negotiate with the rebels. Philippus had outlined Constantius' generous compromise offer to Magnentius—nothing less than the chance to rule the West as Caesar, freeing Constantius to return to the East to see off the Persians.

Philippus had begged Magnentius' troops not to continue with civil war. For his efforts, he'd been detained against his will. He'd died within the next twenty-four hours, trapped behind our lines and felled in the slaughter along with so many tens of thousands of brave soldiers.

Magnentius had been an idiot to refuse Philippus' offer. It was sometime before the rebel emperor died for his greed for more power, but it was refusing Philippus on September 27, 351 that sealed the rebels' fate.

At first Constantius had condemned Flavius Philippus for his failure to prevent the bloody debacle at Mursa. It had been none other than General Claudius Silvanus who related for the Emperor the ringing plea for peace the imperial envoy had delivered to the thousands of Magnentius' troops standing poised for battle.

It was Silvanus who had cleared Philippus' posthumous reputation. As a result, the dead envoy now had statues raised to him across the Empire.

I also knew it was the same Flavius Philippus who had persuaded General Silvanus during crucial minutes of hurried conversation in a battle tent behind Magnentius' speaking podium to defect with his troops from the rebel forces overnight. It was Philippus' honeyed promises of speedy promotion in exchange for betraying men like my father Commander Gregorius that had won Silvanus' force—and the Empire—for Constantius. It was Flavius Philippus who had shot Silvanus on his path to *Magister Militum per Gallias* only hours before his own death.

Thus the Fates had entwined the destinies of Claudius Silvanus and Philippus Flavius.

—THE WOLVES OF AMBITION—

'Yes, *Imperator*, I do remember the late Philippus Flavius well.'

'Good, Numidianus. This man is his brother.'

Only a complete dolt would miss the implication of his presence. Silvanus had restored honor to the family name of Philippus. And today a member of Flavius Philippus' family was in private conference with the Emperor, debating Silvanus' fate. Philippus' brother was here to repay the family's political debt to the Franco-Roman in trouble.

'Numidianus, we recall you have come close to the sharp blade of justice yourself, more than once. It was General Silvanus himself who cleared you of accusations by Paulus Catena the morning after Mursa. We also recall that you witnessed the sad confusion leading to the execution of my cousin, the Caesar Gallus. You will now demonstrate your fidelity to our throne and your debt to General Silvanus by carrying out a difficult mission.'

'My duty and my privilege, *Imperator*.'

The Baiae oyster beds and Hybla bee farms would have to wait. And Kahina and Leo's teacher, Antonius Drusus? I swallowed my anguish over this delay in my return to Roma.

'You know the journey to Agrippina. How long will it take General Ursicinus and his men to reach Silvanus?'

'It's hard to say, *Imperator*. The journey is more than five hundred miles, taking up to ten days in ideal conditions but longer in bad weather and uncertain times. The Alpine stations between Comum and Curia are barely re-established. Only thanks to your autumn campaign against the Alemanni, could a company of a dozen stout soldiers get through the Lake Brigantia region safely enough. We had a bad time going up with just four *agentes*.'

'Can you ride ahead of Ursicinus if you leave immediately?'

'Not to any profitable distance, *Imperator*. You've crossed the mountains yourself with troops.'

'That journey by horse relay once took as little as one week in good weather.'

'We have known better times, *Imperator*. That assumes fresh *riders* as well as fresh relief horses and complete control of the western bank between Augusta Raurica and Mogantiacum.'

'You made the journey well enough just now.'

'I attached myself to various convoys riding south.'

The Emperor tapped an impatient finger on his desk. 'You've been trained for marathon rides, Numidianus. Your journey with Apodemius back from the execution of our cousin broke all records.'

We had also ridden one horse to its death and nearly lost the second.

'Are you asking me to make the journey to Agrippina alone, *Imperator*?'

'Yes. I want no one to see you, no one of any consequence.'

I would have told anyone else to make the journey himself if he thought it so safe. We had seen for ourselves going up that the *mansiones* between Cambete and Confluentes were not yet re-secured. The Alemanni raiders had come to value the rich farmland inside our borders, those fields Constantius exchanged in exchange for harassing Magnentius' forces from the rear. It was proving impossible to double-cross them and wrest their hard-won territory back. A lone Roman rider on the *Cursus* stretch running up that disputed valley was nothing more than unprotected bait.

Constantius sensed my silent alarm.

'Let us explain ourselves, Numidianus. General Ursicinus is a good soldier.' His heavy-lidded eyes narrowed at the thought of the powerful emissary. 'But we cannot afford any more misunderstandings between ourselves and a man as valued as Silvanus.

'Of course not, *Imperator*.'

Constantius gave me one of his stony gazes: 'So you will ride alone, as far as possible ahead of General Ursicinus, and draw no attention to yourself. The General's delegation leaves tomorrow morning. You will leave today. You will not sleep until you have informed Apodemius that the name of Claudius Silvanus has been cleared of all suspicion.'

'Apodemius is very ill, *Imperator*. His life is in danger from an illness contracted on the *Cursus*.'

'We are distressed to learn this. Then we leave it to Gaudentius and you to explain to Silvanus that his patience with this sordid forgery affair will be generously rewarded with a seat on the *consistorium*. You will relay that to no one but Silvanus in person and alone.'

'Yes, *Imperator*. But is this not the same message General Ursicinus will deliver on my heels?'

'Let us hope so, Numidianus, let us hope so.'

Philippus' brother gave a nod to wish me well. I took my leave to pack up my few belongings.

The Emperor's order to traverse the disputed wilds of Gallia at such speed was practically impossible. The Emperor well knew it. With great loss of life, he'd campaigned in the same Alpine region beset by marauding Alemanni less than a year ago.

Was Constantius merely making me a victim of his 'show of justice' for Flavius Philippus' brother to witness—and no more? Or had Constantius tired of his officers' lies and conspiracies and sent me ahead to make sure the message Ursicinus delivered to Silvanus was the right one?

I could only think of Constantius' mysterious 'rescindment' of orders to execute his cousin Caesar Gallus—orders sent via the Lord Chamberlain Eusebius which had failed to reach Apodemius and myself in time—if they ever existed.

With a generous bribe to the *tribunus stabili*, I chose the strongest horse in the stables. The kitchens gave me as much dried food as I could pack to avoid any unnecessary stops in the mountain *mansiones* en route. Even state accommodations along the *Cursus Publicus* that were back in service fell prey these days to lightning raids and other depredations from barbarian bands.

Heaviness flooded my heart.

True, I owed Silvanus for saving my life that day in Constantius' tent on a hill overlooking the massacre of Mursa. But I still hated the man every time I remembered the excruciating last hours of Commander Gregorius' life. Only the kindness of the Fates had led me across his path on the dark battlefield. I found him sliding on his belly in agony through the upturned mud trying to reach the medical triage tents. He had died in my arms, my master, and only with his last breath, acknowledged that I, the little slave *delicatus* of his dining room, was his bastard son.

As I prepared to ride again for the north, I could not even bring myself to say goodbye to Verus. I fought off my desperate wish to be going home to Roma instead of over the Alps yet again. I left a message for him with Cassius at the gatehouse to explain that the letter answering Leo would have to wait for my return.

I was ready to leave within less than an hour.

Malarichus was right. What would Claudius Silvanus do when he learned that Constantius had allowed forgeries to taint his name and push him into this deadly corner? Would he accept the *consistorium* seat? Or would he use his hardened troops against both Ursicinus and Constantius?

My sworn duty was to risk my life for the next few days to prevent another political debacle.

My proud Manlius soul thought of all the suffering and loss Kahina and Leo had suffered from the civil war. Despite my upbringing, I felt deep anger push away every fine feeling I had learned as a boy in Roma. I felt the death of something I could not name.

I almost hoped I would be too late to save any of them from themselves. These imperial giants, with their rivalries and deadly prevarications, their see-sawing from one alliance to the other, from truth to deceit and back again, these imperial *dwarfs* had pulled the ancient house of Manlius to its knees.

I rode out of the gates and took one last glance back at the hard stone city walls with their unblinking towers and formidable gates. I knew that Ursicinus' party would certainly take their leave the next morning with more pomp and preparation than my scrambling departure.

Then I found the words for what I felt—about Kahina and Antonius Drusus, about Roxana and Silvanus, and about Arbetio, the Consul of Machinations and Misrule.

I felt the death of hope.

Chapter 15, The Wounded Must Die

—THE *MANSIO* JUST BEFORE CONFLUENTES—

I rode off at full gallop, aiming to cross the rest of northern Italia and reach the foothills by midday, change over to a mountain-hardy mount in Comum, and conquer the first half of the steep pass by dusk.

This route through the Alps had become familiar to me and I paced my horse better. I knew where he could drink from streams of fresh snowmelt. I remembered a glade where we could stop for ten minutes to eat.

It would be slow going to reach the other side of the narrow crossing in less than two days but a successful changeover in Curia by the third day would ensure me a critical advance on Ursicinus.

The wildflowers blanketing the high valleys were dried out by now. The slopes of green grass had turned ochre. As I rode my horse through the stiff overgrowth, his footfall snapped tall weeds into hollow stalks.

This time I travelled unprotected by any *schola* companions or military convoy. I approached the first valley settlement of Alemannic *laeti* settlers. I allowed precious time to pass as I watched from the shelter of a bluff overlooking the valley for any signs of brigands. I detected no threat, so I moved in closer and saw that hovels we'd passed on the trip north were abandoned. Anxious not to lose any more daylight before reaching the next safe *mansio*, I cantered without incident through pastureland dotted by a few ragged shepherds tending scrawny flocks.

As I'd hoped, the *mansiones* between Curia to Brigantium were back up and running. Newly arrived units of *limitanei* guarded each station to protect state traffic along the border between Italia and the lake fortress. They reassured me the rest of the descent was safe from Alemanni molestation—for the moment

I didn't relax my guard.

Finally, my horse rounded the last abutment overhanging the border between Roman territory and barbarian-contested Rhaetia. Lake Brigantia's glistening water beckoned. The Rhenus' silt rushed into the lake, pushing a distinct line of brown through the tranquil blue-black waters. Its long arm stretched northwest into Alemanni-occupied land.

The Brigantium officers made sure I got fresh food and a leaner, faster horse for the river valley plateau. There were still many hours left to the third day, so I continued on the *Cursus* due west. By the fourth hour, sweat poured down into my eyes and I tied a thin towel around my brow under my *petanus*.

Fatigue was starting to bite. Halfway to Augusta Rauricum, I stopped at a small relay station where the twisting Rhenus came back into view and rejoined the road.

I wouldn't have even stopped then, except the horse was run out and my own thirst was mounting faster than I'd hoped. I was out of fresh water, and I felt the lightheadedness of sleeplessness alter the grip of my seat. Marathon rides were normal for an *agens* rider, but that didn't make them easy. I shook my head at the stable boy's offer of a cup of watered wine and plunged my dusty head under the gushing fountain in the stable yard.

I said little to the friendly *manceps* in charge of this modest *mansio* hardly worth its state license. He was desperate for reassuring news about the security conditions along the *Cursus*. He even offered his one serving girl to me 'for a trade' but the information I carried wasn't for barter. I wanted him to see only a *biarchus* racing like some rookie circuit rider with his first feather in his *petanus*, not a man with the future of the Empire's political balance nipping at his heels.

Once I had my hands on his best horse, I tipped him enough, but not too generously. I didn't want him to remember me that well when Ursicinus showed up.

I was aiming to reach Argentoratum by nightfall but it looked like I might not make it. Along this stretch the road turned again and paralleled the river northwards as it flowed through a wide valley plain. Here was the fertile land Constantius had promised years before to the *Germani*. Insatiable barbarian bands were still seizing once-comfortable Gallo-Roman farms and sending captive citizens to slave in their strongholds on the other side of the border.

I caught up with a convoy of ox-drawn wagons jamming the road. The soft fruits of a meager harvest—blackberries, red berries and peaches—jiggled in their baskets behind the nervous drivers. Mounted army veterans escorted the farmers, —or were the farmers themselves—battle-scarred fighters retired by the state with land pensions. They weren't about to hand their hard-earned profits over to foreign plunderers without a fight.

A gruff Illyrian wearing the frayed insignia of the *Legio Petulantes* hailed me down to give a friendly warning. The Alemanni chieftain Chnodomarius was last heard to be using a settlement poised on the right bank facing Argentoratum as his headquarters.

Chnodomarius had reason to be angry. He'd told his followers that their bargain with Constantius—to harass the rear of rebel forces under Magnentius in exchange for land inside the Rhenus border—was permanent. Silvanus' field army had driven them back towards the Rhenus and our reconstituted *riparienses*' defenses thwarted their attempts to return to their Roman settlements. They felt abused and cheated.

Supreme among the self-styled kings of the Alemanni, Chnodomarius waged a campaign of stop-and-start assaults across the water from his redoubt. He was testing Roman defenses without committing himself to an all-out attack.

'I wouldn't want to fight any frontal invasion led by Chnodomarius,' the veteran-turned-farmer added. 'That Alemannus has learned good Roman tricks from us. From what I hear, the last skirmish felt like facing our own trained troops.'

'Barbarians always learn fast,' I said. 'Julius Caesar praised the Nervii for fortifying their camp in imitation of the Roman troops they were fighting.'

I smiled to myself, thinking of my Numidian blood lost in the mix of Roman and Gallic Manlius heritage. Wasn't I the kind of fast-learning mongrel the Empire took to its bosom? The gods help us if Ursicinus or Silvanus triggered another civil war, because these outsiders might be the only winners.

So far Gallo-Roman defenders had one lucky advantage on their side—Alemanni kings, such as they were, hated each other almost as much as they wanted coveted Roman land. They'd made gains as a wedge between two Roman armies at civil war, but surely a re-united Roma was impossible for ragtag barbarian forces to defeat.

It was impossible to stick to the Emperor's delusion that anyone riding through these fraught regions could travel 'alone.' Would my few discreet conversations en route betray my mission to prepare Silvanus?

But no one molested me or queried an *agens*' right to thunder past their rattling wheels. I kept my horse on the soft dirt verge of the route to protect his hooves while they rattled in a sullen file over the paved stones.

The one thing I told myself during the long hours of wiping burning grit from my sleepless eyes was to keep my face forward, forward, always forward. I feared I would lose my stamina and courage the moment I looked over my shoulder and saw General Ursicinus' standards racing up behind—erect and confident.

I thought of Orpheus, ordered by the gods never to glance back at his precious Eurydice as he led her out of Hades. Torn by love and anxiety, Orpheus turned around. The gods took back Eurydice forever.

Had Ursicinus and his dozen riders stopped over in Curia or were they already at the fortress in Brigantium? They traveled with their own spare military horses. I calculated that if they rested nightly, they'd reach Agrippina between August 27 and 28. I would need a decent night's sleep soon, but if I only allowed myself one long rest in Mogantiacum—the last fortress before crossing through eastern Belgica—I'd reach Silvanus perhaps a day ahead of the General.

I needed those crucial hours to overturn the simmering cauldron of pride and ambition that threatened imperial peace.

A soft summer's dusk bathed the Mogantiacum ramparts in a pinkish glow as my horse fairly staggered through the gates the next afternoon.

'What's the road like ahead?' I asked a logistics officer after securing fresh food and a stronger horse. The last one had suffered badly in the heat. I suspected the stable boys at the *mansio* two legs back of reserving the better horseflesh for some local official's private use—or a bigger tip.

—THE WOLVES OF AMBITION—

'Should be all right. The worst is behind you, as far as raiders go. Silvanus has stationed divisions down to Divodurum and up to Bagacum, although most of them are heading right now to Agrippina.'

He wrapped up salted river fish, flatbread, and dried apricots for my satchel.

'You've heard the news, right? Silvanus has grabbed the purple for himself. He's calling in the whole Gallic field army for his *ad locutio* of acclamation!'

'Yes, I've heard. By the way, is a senior officer named Barbatio still serving up here?'

I was hardly a friend of the former Master of the Guards, but since our fortunes clashed in Antiochia, he'd tried to square our differences.

I'd disliked him as lieutenant in Numidia under Commander Gregorius and I'd detested his actions in the East, but the brutish officer had made good on recovering Kahina from her hellish imprisonment on that vast *latifundus*, a slave estate, in Hispania. For getting my son's mother back alive, I would forget the rest.

After dabbling in the crime of trafficking in Roman citizens and at risk of losing his career over his role in the Gallus affair, he'd accepted a demotion to the north. Barbatio might be greedy, ambitious, and more than a little thick, but during troubled times in disputed territory, any old acquaintance might come in handy.

'No, that hairy bastard bribed his way out of here,' a sentry said. 'He got himself transferred earlier last spring to what's left of Treverorum. He's in charge of military liaison with the legions to the northwest.'

His companion gave a bitter chuckle. 'No rough and tumble skirmishes with devious Alemanni ambushers for Barbatio. There was no way someone like him was going to spend another frozen winter in this gods-forsaken outpost.'

I shrugged it off and saddled up.

'Keep your eyes and ears wide open until you reach Franco-Roman territory,' said the logistics man. 'Yesterday some two hundred Alemanni attacked the bridge over the Mosella at the Castellum apud Confluentes and were spotted near the second *mansio* afterwards, about twenty-five miles north.'

'I heard they burned out the bridge,' said the sentry.

'The bastards.'

The grooms called me away. I bundled up my food and drink for the last and hardest push to Bonna and finally, Agrippina. The summer nights were short but I'd allowed myself four hours of sleep. Apart from the logjam of harvesters' wagon convoys, I'd been lucky with the weather and the stations and made good time.

The rim of the sun peeked over the treetops beyond the Rhenus on my right. I kept my eyes trained on that eastern bank, looking for any traces of recent Alemanni crossings or fresh settlements.

What I didn't expect turned out almost as bad. The gates of Constantine's old Confluentes fortress were bolted tight against visitors. Along the six-meter high walls, archers and weaponry were positioned from all nineteen round towers to repel any repeat attacks. The wooden bridge across the Mosella was indeed burnt out. Charred piles pierced the air like rotten teeth. A couple of well-guarded engineers had started surveying for repairs, but the timbers were still smoking. No one had re-started ferrying rafts for fear of more attacks.

'You'll want to get into the fortress or move on fast,' one of the engineers shouted.

'I'm going on north. How do I cross the water?'

'Is your horse up to tackling that bend, way up there?' a surveyor asking, pointing at the river. 'There's a natural embankment of silt that's collected about a quarter of a mile downstream. The water level is low for now. The last time I looked, there was footing at least halfway across. You can try fording the rest if you're in a hurry.'

I would do just that. Within fifteen minutes, my horse was inching his way across the muddy beachhead of silt and weeds caught in the bend. We were lucky that this time of year, the water level was at its lowest. The flooding had stopped. I reckoned there were only fifty feet of deeper current to swim across.

I dismounted and held the satchel with my valuables—*agens* and *Cursus* papers, food bag, flints, and waterproofed cloak—on my head with one hand, leading the horse deeper into the water with my other. I wasn't the most confident of swimmers—no child of the Numidian desert raised as a slave on the Esquiline Hill was—but I managed to fight the current accelerating in a powerful rush as it rounded the narrow strait.

—THE WOLVES OF AMBITION—

The horse followed, jerking its heavy body forward until, suddenly, he yanked the reins right out of my grip and heaved away, knocked sideways by a massive tree trunk half-submerged in the muddy water's rush.

I lurched and caught one of the reins out of the water, just as he flailed for his footing, rolling farther from my reach. I lunged for him and pulled his harness hard. He faltered and neighed, floundered and kicked, swimming to save himself but jerking his head and curling his lips back in distress as the rough bark scraped his hide.

I felt riverbed underneath our feet again and stumbled onto the northern bank. I led him up through thick, mucky reeds to grassy safety.

He clambered away from me and his shoulder sprouted bright red. The trunk's splintered end, like a fistful of pointed daggers, had jammed right into him, gouging his flesh. A deep wound the width of my hand span streamed with fresh blood.

An *agens* rider always carries acetum and a fresh bandage in case of injury, but to dress an angry horse's shoulder was another matter. I did my best, but when I remounted, he bucked in agony and finally reared high, trying to throw me off.

I tried re-cinching the saddle but no matter how I adjusted its position, the wood under the right front horn pressed deep into his wound.

I had no choice. I would have to walk him to the next *mutatio*, a journey of no more than twelve miles in any developed part of the *Cursus*, but possibly much farther in this war-ravaged terrain.

The sun's rays lengthened as we plodded along. I couldn't stanch the flow of blood. My impromptu bandaging was already bright red.

I surveyed the horizon for the telltale chimney smoke of any hostile settlements. Instead, a flock of crows streaked across the sky, darted, and dove toward a nearby line of trees, then sped up again. Their strange dance diverted me for a moment or two as we plodded forward.

They weren't crows, but ravens, entertaining themselves with some teasing, pecking game. My clothes dried off after a couple of hours, but still there was no relay station to swap my injured animal. I strained to see what was ahead along the road and searched the surrounding slopes for a friendly Gallo-Roman *vicus* or hovel—anywhere to bargain for a fresh horse.

Instead the object of the ravens' amusement was a large dog on guard for some shepherd, watching my progress along the road. He stood there and just when I thought I'd left him and his flock far behind, I made the mistake of glancing back to check the empty fields dotted with clusters of abandoned apple trees surrounded by rotting fruit.

There was no sign of Ursicinus, but glancing back, I spotted the canine again. It was large, with a long and narrow head, two upright ears close together, a mane around its neck and a thick tail that dragged low. It watched my injured horse with interest.

I picked up my pace and jerked the reins to urge the limping horse along. I glanced back and saw the cur follow us, keeping his distance but watching us as if he had nothing else to do.

The flock of ravens followed him. My anxiety grew. I tried to remember this part of the *Cursus* and wondered whether, if I forced myself on the horse and compelled him to ride through his torment, we might reach help all the sooner. I tried to remount, but he dodged me from one side of the road to the other, again and again, and once I almost lost hold of him entirely.

I trotted on foot as fast as I could get the animal to go. The warm colors of the summer fields began to soften into the monochrome of twilight, lit only by the sun's streaks of red and orange in the western sky. I glanced back with foreboding and was relieved to see that the wolf—for my hackles had shot up at the realization that he might be nothing less—had given up his game.

I breathed easier now, but still longed to find a station around each bend in the road. At last I spotted one, but instead of a friendly chimney spouting smoke behind a busy stable yard, only the silhouette of a charcoal ruin stood in the dusk.

I had been warned. This was the second *mansio* after Confluentes that had been attacked. Two walls of what had been a two-story building stood exposed to the sky behind the well in the courtyard. The stone foundation had survived the flames and marked out the rectangle of the *taberna* rooms on the ground floor.

I led the horse toward the ruins, then unsaddled and tethered him under the shelter of wooden and plaster flooring that jutted out from the remnants of the upper story. It made a triangular roof over our heads for the night. I wanted to change the bandage drenched with coagulating blood, but I found I'd used up all my linen the first time around.

In what had been the back rooms, a couple of serving girls had once shared their favors with men riding through. A graffito read, 'Heredis earns her freedom here. A golden wreath around each erection, Priapis.' A glob of Heredis' thick rouge tossed aside by the invaders stuck to my boot.

Where was Heredis now? No bedding had survived the Alemanni torches. I found nothing like a sheet or garment for a fresh bandage. A scrap of rough blanket feathered away into gray-white strands when I picked it up.

There was nothing to eat for either horse or man in the yawning stone ovens or charred shelves. Everything was covered with ash, including the incinerated grill studded with bits of blackened meat.

I moved some loose floor stones to make a crevice and started a fire from twigs gathered nearby. I dug out what was left of my flatbread and apricots. I filled a battered bucket water from the well for the horse, but he was too weak from loss of blood to drink much. When he flopped down on the flagstones, he sent up a choking cloud of gray ash. I drank deep of the wine I'd cadged in Mogantiacum, too lazy and dispirited to water it down. I needed to sleep.

Beyond all imperial admonitions or self-discipline, I needed oblivion.

I'd just let my eyelids drop when I heard a gentle footfall. I leapt up and retrieved my *spatha* and satchel, braced for the appearance of a leering Alemannus.

Instead there was dead silence—no barbaric yowl and no clatter of badly armored mountain thugs.

I had imagined it. Then there was the faintest crunch of dried leaves. It was just the crackle of the fire. A few sparks flew and then my little fire settled down again to a warming glow, I listened. There was nothing but the friendly snap of the flames.

The horse suddenly jerked alive and struggled to his feet, pulling at the leather reins, jingling his harness disks, and tossing his head with a shrill neighing that jangled my nerves.

I jumped up again and, lit myself a torch out of a dried branch and peered past the ruins into the black night.

Two icy eyes gazed at me from the shadows, my torch flame reflected in expressionless pupils. Then the animal lifted its muzzle to the moon and sent up a heart-freezing howl, long and piercing.

My horse turned frantic. The wolf watched us with inhuman poise. Its nostrils flared wide and sniffed the night breeze. My horse's bleeding wound had led the predator to us as surely as if we had leashed him to my saddle.

He sat on his haunches a good fifty feet away, but I wasn't taking chances. I thrust the torch at him, hoping fire would warn him off. He didn't budge. Stepping back, I tossed my belongings out of the way onto the broken floor above my head and unsheathed my *spatha*. I thrust the torch at the wolf again, moving forward, step by slow step, to show I wasn't afraid.

He took a few prudent steps backwards and snarled. I bucked up my courage and thrust at him again, from less than six feet away. He never took his eyes off me, but backed away again, and turning, suddenly trotted way into the darkness beyond.

I grabbed more dry branches and stoked the fire to keep it burning strong. An hour passed. The wolf had given up but the horse was still jittery. I calmed it with soothing words as best I could.

I dozed off beside him and dreamed of water, bright desert sun, and Leo. He was no longer a little boy but a young man, startling me with his height and breezy confidence. He said he had news that would make me happy and asked me to come home. Something woke me up before I knew what it was.

My sense of wellbeing vanished at a long howl in the distance and then a second, and a third. Suddenly a chorus of weird whelping howls filled the starry sky. The wolf was lying in retreat just out of sight beyond our ruined walls and the circle of firelight.

I knew because he answered his fellow wolves with a summons long and haunting—and very close by.

He was calling them to the feast.

I wrapped my cloak tight around my left forearm. Holding the flaming torch in my outstretched left hand, I inched forward with my *spatha* in my right. I stepped to the front of the fire and placed myself between the injured horse and the wolf waiting to lunge at us out of the darkness. The rest of the pack sounded miles off. If I managed to silence this one before the others arrived, we might have a chance of escape.

I waited and watched, scanning the void, trying to detect anything that might move. Finally I spotted a shifting shade, a mere phantom of a dark form, moving forward. At last he stood just outside the flickering light. His fur was colored ochre, almost golden, and tipped with black.

His eyes locked onto mine.

I moved forward, fighting down my fear, my sword primed to plunge into his belly the instant he reared. But he just stood, fixed and patient, as the flame of my torch moved closer and closer to his unblinking gaze. The black strip running between his close-set eyes made him seem displeased, no more. He bared his fangs, as if to test them and gave a low growl.

There was going to be only one chance at this. I raised my sword slowly. With the torch on one side and the sword swinging down on his neck from the other, I hoped to trap him, but he merely stepped back, again and again, leading me in a stately progression deeper into danger.

I heard a sudden growl and looked left with barely a second at a second wolf already on its hind legs and coming down on me, its long fangs whiter than my fire, its pink gums salivating for my flesh.

My swing was too late. Powerful jaws closed over the waxed wool circling my arm. The weight of the animal as it tried to tear my arm away was ferocious. I nearly dropped the torch as I swung my sword hard at the animal's neck and instead sliced into its left leg pawing the air to gain purchase on my chest. It howled and loosened its bite, but the first wolf was racing at my legs. The head twisted for purchase on my calf and I slammed down the burning branch to sink its fiery nob into the animal's right ear.

It squealed. The smell of singed fur bit my nostrils. The two wolves drew back for a moment, the one limping only slightly, circling around, preparing to come at me again, and the leader furiously shaking away the scorching pain.

The horse was whinnying in terror. I caught the stench of his bowels emptying with fear. This was no battle hardy warhorse or stubborn, canny army mule—just a *Cursus* runner who sensed death moving in.

I backed into the shelter of the walls. The wolves moved forward in tandem this time, right up to the rubble of the stone foundations. My torch was burning low. I had to save myself. My only safe retreat was the jutting platform of what was left of the upper story hanging over the bucking horse.

My satchel and riding cloak were already overhead. Though no circus acrobat, I could hoist myself up. I could just manage to lay my sword and the torch onto the protruding planks. It was a risk to take my eyes off the wolves, much less turn my back on them, but I grabbed on to the edge of the broken floor and jumped.

Burnt wood crumbled under my weight, breaking off in charred pieces and covering my hands with grimy splinters. Weaponless, I sprawled on the floor and felt the terror of easy prey.

The wolves watched, unsure of the torch, but hoping I'd turn my back again. They inched forward, their eyes just level with the ruined foundation wall.

The horse kept twisting, pulling at the reins knotted tight to a pothook in the wall. If he kept at it, he would snap the leather cords or break off the hook and make a futile run for it. Would they chase him or trap me here?

I had to get up above the wolves before they took their next leap at me. I looked at the steep drop of the ruined walls on either side and gauged which one offered better purchase.

Aiming as high as I could, I leapt up and grappled the ragged mix of burnt wood and plaster and swung myself side to side by one hand and then the other, higher and higher, until I got my left fingers worked into what felt like a crack in sturdier planks above and out of sight.

I pulled myself up to safety just as the wolves stepped through what remained of the tavern portal. I watched, breathless, as one wolf minced forward, nursing his cut leg with determination. He limped closer and closer. My horse kicked and bucked to no avail.

The wolf lifted his muzzle and sank his teeth into my horse's belly.

The horse screeched, his anguished grimace painful to witness. He flailed in agony, trying to throw the beast off. The wolf became a tossing mass of white, black, and golden fur, but its jaw held fast.

The horse reared, but now the first wolf, forgetting its singed ear, aimed its foreclaws straight for the horse's wounded shoulder.

—THE WOLVES OF AMBITION—

I shrank back into the corner of my retreat, knowing the wolves could smell my sweat and fear, but hadn't the power to leap that high. I rescued the flame that was creeping fast to the edge of the floor that supported me and kept my sword near my right hand. I wrapped the cloak around me and stared out into the friendless night.

No sound seemed as terrible that night as the crunching, smacking, snuffling noise of the two greedy wolves.

But I was wrong.

Their feasting was nothing to the song of triumph and brotherhood that erupted from one of the animals below my trembling legs. He lifted his blood-covered nose to the night sky and howled.

Nothing echoed from the hills beyond. But my relief lasted no more than five minutes.

There was the soft swish of dry brush. Into the diminishing circle of firelight stepped the most terrifying sight yet; a pack of wolves, too many to count in the shadows, advanced toward the ruin's walls. An army of icy eyes gleamed from the shadows at the waiting banquet of equine meat. My heart beat as loud as an intentional call to supper.

The newcomers waited in silence as the moon scraped across the sky. Entrails slithered across the floor beneath me. The singed wolf reappeared from underneath my platform, retreating to savor a leg bone near the ovens.

His withdrawal was an invitation to the others. In less than a minute, I had by my count more than fifteen wolves young and old devouring the horse underneath my crouching knees.

I might be up here for another day—another day I couldn't afford to lose. I recalled overhearing Arbetio say that banquet night in Mediolanum that he feared wolves' incomparable hunting skills and insatiable appetites more than a contingent of screaming barbarians. The horse would not satisfy them. Once they had finished with his carcass, I'd be next.

I thought of Silvanus, wounded by slander and soldiering on to disaster, his honor and impetuous pride luring his wolfish rivals on his trail.

How did one kill a pack of wolves with a single sword and a dying fire? I wished the horse were not so appetizing and its blood not so rich and warm.

I wished I could turn that meat from good to bad...

I opened my satchel and by the light of the torch, removed the branches of the yew I'd saved for Guntheuca. Surely wolves knew not to touch the bright red berries—nature's signal of poison—but what if I extracted the deadly seed?

Ignoring the hellish noises beneath, I spread my cloak and wiped my hands clean of ash and blackened wood. Only now did I notice the circles of blood staining the left sleeve of my tunic.

I had at most fifty berries. They didn't look like much piled together. Using the swivel knife hidden in my boot cuffs, I extracted the knobby brown seeds from their red cones. They'd dried out during the long, hot ride, which was lucky for my purposes. Using the tin cup from my satchel and the butt of the knife, I pounded until I had a precious pile of coarse powder the texture of ground peppercorns.

I lay on my stomach and inched myself toward the precarious edge of the charred floor. I had to position myself directly over the dismembered horse without tumbling headfirst onto the corpse. The wolves were a mass of bobbing ears, snarling teeth, and expert paws working away in savage harmony. A part of the floor broke off underneath my right shoulder and nearly tipped me into their banquet.

I said a prayer to the gods and dribbled a bit of powder, only to see it waft right over the animals and float back to the walls. I had to cut the draft as much as I could. I draped my cloak lower and lower, and tried again, sprinkling it onto the bleeding mess of flesh between their heads, here, there, now here and now there again, trying to lower my hand just enough to get most of the poison into the path of their bloody red tongues. I wiped the last traces of powder from my fingers, knife, and cup.

They had already eaten their way into the horse's belly, scraping at ribs, tussling with sinews, and scooping out the growing hollow of the horse's rib cage. The sounds of the gushing organs were ghastly. Finally the bigger beasts had had their fill. A few pups got their chance at the miserable leavings.

—THE WOLVES OF AMBITION—

It seemed for hours that nothing would slake their bottomless hunger, though they took it by turns, some of them ripping a chunk for themselves to eat apart and other snuffling and bumping their noses against each other.

I accepted defeat. The branch had not been yew after all. My mystery spice had only made the horse all the tastier.

The only good thing seemed to be that they had forgotten me for the moment.

My arm had stopped bleeding. The foul smell of the abattoir filled my nostrils. I wrapped myself tight in my cloak and pressed myself into the angle of the walls. My torch was going out. With my satchel for a pillow, I felt myself nodding off.

I must have dozed like that for hours, one part of my mind remembering I must not roll forward off my planking. In my fuzzy half-dreams I heard the wolves squabbling over scraps until their growls seemed to turn into birdsong.

I opened my eyes and clutched my cloak in panic. The sky had lightened over the trees along the road into a peach haze spreading across the gray horizon.

Below my perch stretched the remains of the horse—his head at one end, almost entirely detached from the throat pipe and long white spine to his discarded tail pointing to the opening that had once been the doorway to the station.

And scattered between the head and the tail and beyond the station's walls and as far as the edge of trees within my sight lay the bodies of wolves.

They were not sleeping. They were not even breathing.

I heaved a sigh of thanks to Guntheuca, and was about to clamber down when my heart stopped at the sound of one low, rumbling growl.

I was halfway off my ledge when from behind the stone foundations limped my attacker with the singed ear, set on revenge. He had eaten first and finished first, devouring a leg across the room while I poisoned the rest of the carcass. He had watched his entire pack sicken and die around him.

He was now going to take his revenge.

Chapter 16, Friends True and False

—THE ROAD TO BONNA—

The wolf's steely gaze fixed on me as he licked his fangs clean. I fought off a way of panic, telling myself he couldn't possibly be that ravenous. He'd eaten the horse's rear left leg and thigh. In a filthy corner of what had been the *taberna*'s kitchen only a blood-smeared hoof remained dangling by a rubbery sinew off the end of a well-licked gaskin bone.

Did I just imagine it was pure hatred lurking behind his frosty eyes? I'd been trained to read men, not four-legged predators. Unlike imperial *consistoriani*, this mankiller's expression gave away nothing.

My legs were stiff from huddling on the platform all night. I measured the drop over the rear of the walls and considered making a run for it. But when I picked up my satchel and sword, the wolf growled and walked right up to the remains of the horse. He stepped over the barrel of ribs, and positioned himself under the charred and broken beams jutting into the open air only inches from my boots.

He was long, lean, and strong. He sat down on his haunches and waited just below me. I hardly breathed. Perhaps he would lose interest in me and abandon this theater of carnage for fresh drama elsewhere.

I underestimated his impatience. He reared up on his hind legs and pawed at the air, trying to catch hold of my ledge. He missed.

He rose up again, and this time, his claws caught at the most burnt section of the wood. This time, his bloodstained paws scraped the most burnt section of the wood. Shards of blackened beam broke right off, scattering charcoal ash into his cold eyes, and sending him crashing to the floor in a cloud of velvety powder.

He reared up a third time and pawed at me again. He caught the most fragile part of the platform to my right. A portion of the ledge broke off and dangled by mere splinters of wood. He smelled success and tried again and again, each time breaking away burnt pieces of planking.

I inched back, knowing I could stand secure on the unburnt section of the flooring, but realizing that the wolf would keep working away at my perch until he'd reached my legs.

The triangle of ruined wall above my head wasn't thick or high, but its precipice of broken plaster and stone roofing was my last resort. The lower edges that were within my reach were the sides that reached down to join the weakest parts of the flooring.

The animal snarled at me, expelling a gust of foul breath. My stomach churned with hunger and fear. He lunged deeper. The force and weight of his heavy body broke away another chunk of my refuge.

He panted as he fell back on all fours and watched the burnt wood swing back and forth in the air, still hinged to the floor jutting above his head. I prayed to the gods that the worst was over. Most of the charred flooring was gone. The few square feet that had supported me all night were solid.

But the wolf knew better. He had me standing with my back pressed right into the angle of the remaining walls, my boots within his reach, if only he mustered the force. I watched his long back twisting beneath as he circled, snorting and panting. His right ear was raw and blistered.

With a hesitant forepaw, he tested the width of the rear tavern wall that led up to my sanctuary. A cat would have had no problem, but he was enormous. After the balancing on the first stones, he fell back to the ground.

He turned his back on me. Threading his way between the bodies of his fellows, he walked to the opening that had been the *mansio*'s front door. I sighed with relief. It was as I'd hoped. He'd grown bored with me.

Then he turned. His silvery eyes glinted in the rosy dawn shadows. The rising sun outlined his fiendish form.

—THE WOLVES OF AMBITION—

He dashed forward and threw all his power into a mighty lunge, soaring up, up, up into the air in front of me, his great mouth twisting open to sink his fangs into my ankle and drag me down to my death. I felt his teeth clamp around my left boot, pressing in to puncture the leather.

I grabbed the top edge of the wall behind me just as he kicked at the platform with all his might to bring me down.

There was a strange, thudding crack. The wolf's head flew back and his body gave a violent jerk underneath the ledge. He dropped back to the floor just as a spear flew into his side. It bounced up and down, its long iron shank reverberating with the impact.

Two men in helmets and fur shoulder capes stood just outside the ruins, shaking their heads. One man stepped forward, avoiding the mess of horse guts and wolf corpses, to recover his *francisca*, the axe that had brought down my enemy. He wiped it off and slung it back under his belt. Then he yanked out the long barbed *angon* and handed it to his companion.

'I am a lucky man today,' I said, faint with relief.

'I suppose you also want us to share our breakfast with you,' he said, shaking his head at the bloodbath strewn across the blackened flagstones.

'Well, there's always roast wolf,' said the *angon* owner.

'I wouldn't eat any of that if I were you,' I said, dropping to the ground. 'It would be a once-in-a-lifetime recipe.'

※※※

Rathar and Leudast were advance riders for a regiment of Bracchiati answering Silvanus' summons to the formal acclamation in Agrippina. Their breakfast turned out to be diluted wine, dried venison, and smoked river fish.

'It's all right, finish it off,' Rathar said.

'No, it's good, but somehow I'm starving and off my feed at the same time.'

'I don't blame you, watching these monsters gorge themselves all night.'

'Anyway,' Leudast said, picking at his teeth with a fish bone, 'There'll be a celebratory feast after the religious ceremony and the wine will be flowing.'

'More than fifteen thousand soldiers to feed in one go! I wouldn't count on getting a second course.'

'Silvanus has always looked after his men, Rathar. We just got our pay on time, for what that's worth, and now there'll be more—much more.' Leudast shook the money purse hanging from a silver circle on his belt. 'The General looks after us, we'll look after him, won't we?'

Leudast looked like a man who had spent his thirty or so years counting his blessings in coin. His turnout was fastidious, with the Frankish weakness for silver garnet fixings on his buckles and sword belt rings, finely embroidered boars running around his tunic hem at the knees and gold and red stripes attached at the shoulder and sleeve hems. His cloak was attached over the right shoulder by a conical *fibula* of silver. I was surprised to hear such a well-turned-out soldier was only a senior scout.

Rathar shook his head and handed me more of his wine. 'I don't swing my standard between emperors that fast,' he said.

We sat in silence, digesting our meal. The morning sun had risen above the treetops running over the slopes on the far side of the road.

'You have any choice?' I kept my tone indifferent.

'No choice about being a soldier, that's for sure.' Rathar gave a bitter laugh. 'That's Roman law, isn't it? Father a soldier, son a soldier. But my father fought in the front lines of the *comitatus* for old Constantine against Maxentius in the Battle of Verona in 312. Loyalties to the imperial family should die harder than that—' he gestured northwards toward Agrippina.

'And be rewarded better!' Leudast sneered. 'My father fought at the Milvian Bridge but was I promoted any faster for it? Who's going to punish us if our officers and *praefecti* tell us to serve the wrong man?'

'Look what happened to the legions Magnentiaci and the Decentiaci—the ones who followed Magnentius and his brother,' Rathar said. 'They're roasting on the Persian front now for their service—if they're still alive.'

—THE WOLVES OF AMBITION—

'You got paid well enough only a few weeks ago,' I said to Leudast. 'I see from your tunic you're a *duplicarius*. Double pay can't be bad.'

He pulled out his purse and turned it inside out. The poor man had only a few coins left.

'And lost a year's wages to some bastard *veterinarius*. I swear he was playing with loaded dice.'

'Were they ivory with gold and blue spots?'

Leudast stared at me. 'Yes. How did you know?'

'Because I've been bankrupted by a set just like them down in Mediolanum,' I said.

'Nobody gambles away his *donativum* in one night except you, Leudast,' Rathar scoffed.

'One of these days I'll be scooping up my winnings and buying myself a farm in Aquitania,' Leudast said.

They bickered like this as we packed up. It was a gruesome walk past the battlefield of dead wolves to recover their horses still tethered fifty feet away. We decided which horse could carry two men instead of one up to Bonna. I listened to them squabble and thought of the rivalries fracturing the Roman command all the way to the court in Mediolanum.

I'd lost an entire day's riding to the wolf attack and almost lost my life, but as far as Rathar and Leudast had heard, there was no imperial party dogging my tail. They planned to wait in Bonna for the rest of their unit to catch up. I would plow on in exhaustion to try to reach the governor's residence in time to deliver my private warning to Silvanus ahead of Ursicinus' arrival.

As we cantered north, I took one last glance at the burnt-out *mansio*. Deep under the angle of the ragged platform, the wolf pack leader lay bleeding to death. He hadn't fought to eat me, just to exact revenge.

Perhaps wolves showed each other more loyalty than men.

※※※

I'd watched Magnentius amass the Western Army to challenge the Constantine family's hold on the imperial throne.

I'd once seen the combined Illyrian legions under General Vetranio's command stretched across the Danubian valley.

I'd seen the entire Eastern army under Constantius positioned outside Mursa.

So I should have been prepared for the miles-long crush of files of infantry, cavalry horses, and military wagons moving up the river route toward the gates of Agrippina. They had been arriving for days and the fields sprawling to the east of the main road had no more open space left for *francisca* practice. Instead, the horizon was filled with serried ranks of thousands of tents set up by the arriving legions.

Pennants, eagle standards, and *dracones* snapped in the breeze coming off the cool river. Tribunes hurried through the palace gates with news of fresh arrivals while others emerged, flying back to field headquarters with fresh orders.

At the center of this orderly excitement was one man—the self-declared Emperor Silvanus.

I had no time to spare for this bottleneck of disciplined military to make way for a single *agens*. I borrowed Leudast's horse—at a price—and sped around the western corner of the city walls, circling past two towers to the first of three back gates and entering the city from the rear.

I rode up the five long blocks of the colonial city to the back of the market stalls and into the parade ground behind the governor's residence.

My first duty was to brief my superiors. To see Gaudentius still at his station outside Apodemius' room was already a welcome relief but from the end of the corridor I saw in time that four sentries guarded our rooms. If I appeared before them, I'd fall prisoner as well.

I covered the telltale insignia on my tunic, circled back, and dashed across the parade ground to the women's wing. I sent word by a passing *Germana* slave to tell Roxana that I would wait for her at the nearby basilica.

The city streets were in fresh tumult, exhilarated by the promise of profit and entertainment from thousands more soldiers come to acclaim a new emperor. No one took any notice of me. When I entered the great basilica, the noise of the city faded away to the sound of echoing stone.

—THE WOLVES OF AMBITION—

The church was dark, cold, and musty, smelling of incense and beggars. Roxana slipped through its great oak doors at last. She wore a light summer *palla* with a hood pulled low to her brow. She lifted it to search for me in the obscurity of the murky gloom.

'Marcus! What are you doing back here? Silvanus detained Gaudentius until the Gallic forces are under his complete control! Meroveus and you will be arrested!'

'Meroveus?'

'He disappeared the same morning as you.'

'He never left with me. That's why I need your help, old schoolmate,' I said.

'What's happened? Why are you here?'

'Sent by the Emperor himself. General Ursicinus is on my heels. He'll arrive any minute now with a traveling party of a dozen or so family and friends.'

'Ursicinus? Traveling without the legions of the East? I don't understand.'

'Neither do I, not everything. Ursicinus remains under suspicion of high ambition himself. Constantius has sent him up here with a letter for Silvanus—to tell him Ursicinus is now taking over as *Magister Militum* of Gallia. Silvanus was cleared of all charges—'

'That's wonderful news!' She let out a gasp of pent-up anguish.

'—and he will be invited to join the *consistorium*.'

'Why were the charges dropped?'

'Because I exposed forgeries written over Silvanus' signature on the letters given by Dynamius to Mattyocopus and Lampadius.'

Her large brown eyes blazed glints of hazel-green as she spit out, 'How did they dare?'

'They would have succeeded except that an armorer in Cremona wrote to Malarichus with too many questions about alleged weapons orders Silvanus never placed with his factory. He included a forged letter from Silvanus in the mail packet.'

'And Malarichus reported it?'

'No, I found it in the court postal office first. And compared the handwriting to a letter your friend Junius showed me on your advice, thank the gods.'

'Silvanus will be forever in debt to your *schola*, Marcus. But it's too late! Silvanus has declared!'

'It's more complicated than that. Constantius' letter to Silvanus doesn't reveal that he knows about the acclamation. He's allowing Silvanus a chance to back down and turn himself in for promotion. Ursicinus will deliver it with a straight face and send Silvanus back to Mediolanum.'

'Silvanus must back down. He must!'

'And you must tell him, Roxana. Ursicinus might arrive as soon as tomorrow. Silvanus has to call off this circus and send these legions back to their positions.'

'You must tell Silvanus yourself!'

'And risk detention with Gaudentius? I have to get back to Roma as soon as possible. Kahina is about to marry Leo's teacher and I'm determined to get back before she makes a mistake or give her my blessing. Either way, I can't risk more of these delays. Even if Apodemius is still alive, he's in no condition to call off this crazy usurpation.'

'At least the worst is over.'

'I don't believe the worst is over, Roxana. The Emperor doesn't trust Ursicinus to recall Silvanus to court with honor. Neither should we. Arbetio called this Ursicinus' "one and only chance." Some unseen danger lies in Silvanus path, I'm sure of it.'

'Marcus, what happened to your ankle?'

I had ignored the throbbing as long as I could, but I needed a dressing and acetum to make sure the wolf's bite wounds didn't fester. Roxana went off to beg fetch bandages and hot water from the deacon. I was left alone to consider my next action.

I couldn't bring myself to believe Roxana capable of convincing Silvanus to be on his guard from Ursicinus. She'd already failed to persuade him defend himself in court. Instead, the simmering ambitions of Evochildis, combined with the hostile greed of his Frankish cousins across the border, had trapped him just as the lead wolf had cornered me.

If he'd been so deluded as to believe he could survive as co-emperor, then he would be eager to believe any blandishments coming out of Ursicinus' honeyed mouth.

Even supposing Roxana could convey a warning to Silvanus and supposing I managed to explain to Gaudentius what Florentius and I had uncovered in Mediolanum, I knew anyone would hesitate before hanging personal survival on a single phrase caught in a dash down a corridor well after midnight.

Only I knew how sinister Arbetio's face had looked that night. Only I could guess whether Constantius meant that last gesture of conciliation by sending me ahead or merely intended it as a charade to impress Philippus.

Who and what could we believe?

Until now, my duty to Silvanus had meant trying to get him to face Constantius in person, to stare down the bared gums of the hounds around the *consistorium* and to prevail. If he'd listened to me, he would have been in the court to enjoy vindication at the discovery of the forgeries. He could have pressed home charges against his enemies then and there.

If Ursicinus brought an invitation to Silvanus to swap his post for a seat on the *consistorium*, did I have enough to accuse him of deceit? If Constantius meant for me to sweeten the invitation with secret blandishments against Ursicinus' possible double-dealing, was there reason to trust the Emperor this time?

I had to talk to someone close to Silvanus—closer even than Roxana. Laniogaisus? Bainobaudes? Proculus? Or even Evochildis? Whom would Silvanus trust? No one.

Roxana returned with bandages and a vial of vinegar. I cleansed the puncture wounds and bandaged up my shin. It didn't look too bad, but as the day had worn on, it hurt to walk.

'Roxana, you're right. I must talk to Silvanus!'

'Even if he puts you under guard? I'm not sure he won't execute you all for treason once he's sure of his authority over Gallia.'

'*Agentes* can't be charged or tried for anything performed in the course of duty. That's Roman law.'

She shook her head. Silvanus had already moved himself beyond the protection of Roman law and might take us all there with him.

'He's receiving all the *praepositi* and *tribuni* paying their respects,' she said after a pregnant silence. 'How do I interrupt that?'

'Tell him I carry a warning on which his entire future hangs. I pledge my honesty on the memory of Commander Atticus Manlius Gregorius. Until he finds five minutes for me, I'll hide in your chamber.'

I waited most of the remaining daylight hours in that modest room. After my night on the ledge, I enjoyed nothing more than to wash myself clean in her basin and stretch out my cramped limbs on her fragrant bed. I slept long and deep. I woke up to more hours of waiting, with nothing to read or distract me from a sense of losing valuable time while Ursicinus rode closer and closer.

The pristine room was small but comfortable, with a view over the city rooftops. It wasn't hard to imagine the tired Silvanus retreating here to this feminine redoubt to confide his doubts and dreams in loyal Roxana's arms.

Her garment trunk overflowed with Frankish-style dresses. Vials of scented oils and other toiletries stood near a basin mounted on a tripod of enameled iron. Silver tweezers, antler horn combs, ointments, and pastes lay scattered around an ornate vanity box covered in semi-precious stones. Lengths of embroidered trim and heavy pieces of silver jewelry betrayed how hard this Mediterranean was trying to refashion herself to northern tastes. The rough and tumble *agens* who'd once seduced me in little more than linen gauze and cheap massage oil had acquired all the trapping of an imperial mistress.

Nonetheless, I worried for my old friend and rival.

Silvanus might cherish Roxana's affections. I valued her intelligence, courage, and generosity. I could guess that it was his mother Evochildis who guided his loyalties, tying them tighter and tighter to the hallowed memory of Bonitus.

Roxana returned at last, breathless and unsmiling. Making sure she wasn't followed, she closed the door behind her and whispered, 'Now. He's seen everyone who arrived today and gives you ten minutes while he readies himself for the banquet of welcome for all the commanders. He's waiting for you in the residence halls on the other side of the parade ground, in his mother's private chamber.'

'That's no good. I want him alone.'

'That's the best I could do.'

'All right. Lead me to him.'

※ ※ ※

Roxana left me at Evochildis' door and disappeared back to the modest comforts of her rooms. I announced myself and entered. This time I faced no squadron of needle-wielding ladies surrounding the formidable Frankish matron.

Mother and son sat opposite each other over a heavy oak table scattered with military papers. He was rolling these up to entrust to a military scribe standing by. There was every reason to assume he had just given the doyenne of Frankish women a summary of his position as Gallia's new emperor.

'Marcus Gregorianus Numidianus. I am much relieved to see you. I sent men to search for you and now you come out of hiding to present yourself like the straightforward man I know you to be.'

'You put Apodemius and Gaudentius in detention. Our third man has disappeared altogether.'

He gave me that same wide, ingenuous smile that had once beguiled the hardened rebels eagerly waiting for him in Magnentius' council.

'I only feared you and that bald Toxandrian had raced off to Mediolanum before I was ready.'

'I don't know what happened to Meroveus. But I did just that.'

Silvanus' practiced smile dropped away. For the first time, he looked his age to me.

'You have already been to the court and back, while I've been gathering the troops here?'

'I have.'

'I see you're limping.' He allowed himself a sour smile. 'Surely you didn't run all the way?'

'I was unlucky with a horse.'

'That must have slowed you down. And to think Roxana once told me you were a rider with a lot of *stamina*.'

I ignored his vulgar gibe. 'The message I bring you from Constantius is for your ears alone.'

The shock in his eyes was obvious.

'Leave us, Mother.'

Evochildis rose from her chair with a deep heave of her bejewelled bosom. 'Let nothing sway you from your purpose,' she told her son.

He nodded like a sleepwalker. When she'd gone, he gave me a stiff command to continue.

'First, General, you have been cleared of all charges, following my investigation of Dynamius' reference letters carried out with the assistance of deputy *Magister Officiorum* Florentius. Lampadius, Mattyocopus, and others are under investigation for passing forgeries. Rejoice you have a valuable friend in Cremona, General Silvanus. The tribune in charge of the armory there is a man with a nose for the reek of conspiracy.'

All color drained away from Silvanus' handsome features. He had given up hope too soon. If he had trusted his political talents as much as he trusted his field skills, he could have been present in court to see himself reinstated in the Emperor's favors.

'I see. Go on, Numidianus. What else?'

'Second, General Ursicinus is en route to Agrippina, perhaps mere hours away, carrying a letter from Constantius. The Emperor orders that you hand command over to Ursicinus and report to Mediolanum.'

'Hand over command? Does the Emperor not know I've declared myself his challenger?'

'His letter doesn't speak of this. He is, in effect, allowing you the chance to dismiss these forces back to their previous positions, to cancel your acclamation banquet, to toss off the purple, and return unscathed to his side.'

'Ha!' Silvanus tossed back his head in disbelieving laughter.

'And third, I deliver a private message from the Emperor himself. I beg you, Claudius Silvanus, listen well.'

'Oh, I'm listening, have no worries about that.' He paced back and forth across the wide room.

—THE WOLVES OF AMBITION—

'The Emperor instructed me to add his promise of a place at the high table of *consistoriani*, the same table where Arbetio now presides as consul over Lampadius, Aedesius, Eusebius the Lord Chamberlain, and even the elderly Consul Lollianus Mavortius who was Urban Prefect of Roma while your father still lived. Such men hold the Emperor's ear. You are invited to join them.'

Silvanus collapsed into the chair where minutes before his mother had no doubt been urging him to march on Roma with the entire Gallic Army.

'Is there anything else?'

'Yes. This comes from me. I beg you to add this to your weighty considerations. Only minutes after he received his commission from Constantius to travel here with his small and unassuming party of family and trusted colleagues, General Ursicinus was joined by Consul Arbetio. Florentius Nigrinianus eavesdropped on the two of them as they walked down the corridor. He overheard Arbetio whisper to Ursicinus, "This is your one and only chance. Don't waste it". Florentius is an honest witness.'

'And yet all I will have in writing is the Emperor's letter asking me to relinquish command to Ursicinus?'

'Yes.'

'Nothing else is on the record? That I am to have a place on the *consistorium*?'

'The brother of Flavius Philippus was witness to Constantius' promises.'

'But not witness that Arbetio has won Ursicinus over to some fresh conspiracy against me?'

Proculus arrived to tell Silvanus that the commanders were gathered in the vast governor's *triclinium* for the banquet to begin.

'We have prepared a proper purple garment for you to wear at last, *Imperator*,' he said.

As soon as the door closed behind the adjutant, Silvanus asked, 'Why should I trust you—of all people—Numidianus?'

'You know who I am and what I was—once a slave bodyguard, a simple *volo* serving the Commander Atticus Manlius Gregorianus. I have no wish but to serve my *schola* and to be a credit to the House of Manlius.'

'I betrayed your Commander,' he said.

'You saved my life when Catena would have had me in chains for the death of Emperor Constans.'

'You were only doing your job that day, defending Lieutenant Gaiso against a sneak attack by a disgusting coward.'

'That is why you should trust me now. Because I do my job, no matter how nasty. I've delivered my messages. You can detain me with Gaudentius and Apodemius now. The "bald Toxandrian" has disappeared.'

We heard boots running to the door and this time the scrawny Proculus flew unannounced back into the room.

'*Imperator*! General Ursicinus is on his way to Agrippina! He's less than a mile away, with a dozen officers including his eldest son, Potentius. Only the crush of legions is slowing him down.'

'We were expecting him.' Silvanus said, as if he'd issued the invitation himself. 'Go lay on all the honors. Go, Proculus, *go*!'

He turned back to me. 'Aren't you the one with the fancy Roman education from old Senator Manlius? Remember the old saying, *Non decipitur qui scit se decipi?*'

'*He who knows he's being deceived is not deceived.*'

'Exactly, Numidianus. According to you, I know now that I'm being deceived. Does Ursicinus know you met the Emperor in private?'

'No, I don't think so.'

'Good. Then I will deceive Ursicinus. I will accept the Emperor's disingenuous letter with all disingenuous gratitude. I will watch to see which way Ursicinus falls.'

'You are not going to arrest me, then?'

'You can be detained indefinitely with your troublemaking *schola* colleagues until I've decided your fates—if you choose.'

'Or?'

'Or you can prove your suspicions that Ursicinus is up to something. You can do your job again as a loyal servant of your *schola*—with one difference.'

'Which is?'

'As of today, you report to my court and no one else. From now on, you spy on Ursicinus—for me.'

Chapter 17, Two Generals Meet

—Agrippina, August 29, 355 ad—

I had now failed Emperor Constantius not once, but twice. Silvanus showed no interest in rescinding his bid for imperial status. He made no move to call off this evening's circus.

The flood of legions answering his summons must have gone to his head. Thousands upon thousands of soldiers were still arriving at the gates of Agrippina to acknowledge him as the supreme commander of the Gallic forces.

In his haste to end our interview, he'd forgotten to forbid me to consult my superiors. Perhaps he assumed I would avoid Gaudentius and Apodemius out of eagerness to prove myself to his new regime. In his betrayal of oaths to the Constantines, he underestimated the bonds of my own *schola*. Certainly for one *agens* to be left roaming free while the others remained under guard was an awkward situation. But to have my superiors' blessing to follow Silvanus' command would solve one immediate problem.

I hunted down the weedy Proculus. After all, he owed me for getting him out of the ambush across the Rhenus.

He was lost in a sea of logistics officers trying to sort out which legions had priority over others in access to food, water, and field position.

'So you've come out of hiding, have you?'

'I need to report to my *Magister*,' I said.

'Silvanus doesn't trust him, sick or healthy,' the adjutant said. 'He remains under guard, just like your *ducenarius*. I'm surprised you haven't been dragged to join them. Where's the other one, the Toxandrian?'

'I have no time to look for him. Silvanus and I are old acquaintances,' I said. 'He's given me a new set of instructions. But first, I must have secure access to Apodemius.'

He shrugged. 'I'm too busy.'

I grabbed his wounded arm and squeezed the bandage just enough to focus his mind.

'All right,' he said, shaking me off. He escorted me to the sentries posted outside Apodemius door. I knocked and entered, expecting to see Gaudentius or Guntheuca, but the old man lay unattended, breathing normally, in a deep sleep. I laid my hand on his forehead. His temperature felt normal.

'How long has he been left alone?'

'Since yesterday,' the sentry told us. 'Gaudentius was exhausted. The healer woman says her work is done.'

Proculus was getting impatient. I knocked on Gaudentius' door and found him shaving at his basin. Before departing, Proculus told the guards that I, and only I, was free to leave.

'What are you doing here?' Gaudentius' tone was surly. 'Now you're stuck with the rest of us while chaos reigns outside.'

'I have a new assignment,' I said, 'from "Emperor" Silvanus himself. I came to report to Apodemius and you before Silvanus could stop me.'

I overlooked the resentment flushing the *ducenarius*' weathered face while I brought him up to date: on the forgeries exposed, the *consistorium*'s decision to send Ursicinus with the disingenuous letter proposing an exchange of posts for the two generals, and my suspicions that Arbetio and Ursicinus were up to more.

'What does Silvanus expect to gain by pretending he believes Constantius is still in the dark?'

'Time, Gaudentius. Time to pretend to Ursicinus that he believes he is safe from the Emperor's wrath. Time to luxuriate in the knowledge that the Emperor's secret message is more reassuring than Ursicinus knows. Time to test both men, to see where the next trap lies.'

Gaudentius shook his head. 'Our *schola* can't afford to get entangled in these double-dealings. Silvanus is a usurper at worst and no more than another general at best, a general who's *still* disobeying direct imperial orders to return to Mediolanum.'

'This is the third time I've seen Constantius offer compromise to a usurper, Gaudentius. Only old Vetranio was wise enough to kneel in contrition. Magnentius kept fighting out of sheer military habit. He knew nothing else. Silvanus is holding out from nothing more than injured pride.'

'Each man has his Achilles Heel, Numidian. It is our job to make sure the Empire doesn't trip over it.'

'If you knew that Arbetio, Lampadius, and their fellow conspirators were plotting against you, would you race out those gates leaving all your defenses in a rival general's control? Especially if that general is under just as much suspicion for limitless ambition?'

Gaudentius dried off his shaven scalp and pulled his tunic back on.

'I don't care. Our *schola* answers to the office of the *Magister Officiorum* in Mediolanum and he answers to the Emperor. You delivered Constantius' message. You're done.'

'I'm not done.'

'I order you to stay here with us. Silvanus can hold us here by force, but under Roman law, he has no authority over us. As soon as Constantius has dealt with him, our detention will be seen for the insubordination that it is.'

'If Apodemius were awake, he'd tell me to get back out there and discover what's going on.'

'I'm ordering you to stay here, bastard. If anyone reports events up here, it's going to be me—and not to Silvanus, but to Constantius.'

'When Apodemius wakes up, tell him I've left, but not because I'm loyal to Silvanus or to any other man. Because I'm loyal to the Empire. I'm going to do what I was trained to do at the Castra—find out the truth.'

I left him standing in the middle of the corridor, held back by two guards and powerless to stop me.

☧☧☧

I marched out between the remaining sentries and headed for the banquet hall before Gaudentius had time to rip the *agentes in rebus* insignia off my tunic. We had different ideas of duty, I told myself, but I expected I was going to pay for my insubordination later. It was all well and good to invoke

Apodemius' well-known love of gathering intelligence by any means, but Gaudentius didn't share the old man's love of disguises and double agents, unorthodox chains of communications, and human sources. Gaudentius trusted only brute force and crude blackmail.

I shuddered at the idea of Gaudentius promoted to *Magister Agentium in Rebus*, a man with so little education, sensitivity or imagination. He showed a lot of gall trying to pin me down with protocol and hierarchy. Hadn't he himself jumped the queue to report Africanus to Constantius, just to curry favor from 'Our Eternity'?

The entrance to the banquet hall overflowed with hundreds of officers—tribunes, prefects, centurions and their staffs. There wasn't enough of the former governor's furniture to accommodate so large an army of hungry stomachs—neither couches with individual tables for dining in the 'old' style or benches and long tables in the northern, Frankish style. The *triclinium* was a bustling jumble of slaves and servers running this way and that under the frantic eyes of Silvanus' *trustis* and their deputies. I understood their anxiety. As a favorite child slave in the Manlius home in Roma, I'd been the *pocillator* pouring the wine during many a formal meal for the Commander's military cronies.

The atmosphere among the new arrivals was excited and loud, but also watchful. I overheard snatches of conversation between army professionals struggling with their loyalties, their alliances, and their obligations to their troops to take the wisest course. General Silvanus had wrenched half of Gallia back from barbarian depredations and earned their respect. There was less talk of civil war than hope of some concession from the Emperor.

After all, hadn't Constantius II shared the Empire with his brothers, and then his cousin? Hadn't he even offered the West to Magnentius, who was a far less brilliant example of imperial assimilation than the handsome and well-spoken Franco-Roman Silvanus?

In my eavesdropping on this crush of hearty men, some still injured from fighting their way through Alemanni-held lands, I heard one name repeatedly—Ursicinus.

—THE WOLVES OF AMBITION—

They all knew he was on his way. They did not know of the letter, of course, but they knew Constantius was a cautious man. Would Ursicinus issue some kind of signal of conciliation from Constantius? Or would he arrest Silvanus on sight? Whatever he did, I intended to be within reach of his every move, to stand within earshot of his every utterance. I would not choose a seat for myself until I knew where Ursicinus and his party would be settled.

Silvanus, now changed into a purple-hemmed cloak fastened around his shoulders with eagle-shaped gold *fibulae*, would take the center of a long table commanding a view over the long hall. As he strode in to accept a formal salutation from the assembly, Tribune Bainobaudes, earmarked for glory, came in next, followed by Tribune Laniogaisus leading the rest of the *trustis* in the new lineup of imperial command.

I awaited the one person who had more reason than all these towering Frankish officers to relish the satisfying culmination of this day.

Evochildis now entered in full state, followed by her ladies. They wore extravagant multi-layered tunics of emerald, azure, dove gray, all set off by burgundy, gold, or silver trims. Agrippina's seamstresses must have worked long nights to produce this flock of silk veils and trailing silks. Their jewelry jangled as they eased into their places of honor among the officers squeezed from one end of the hall to the other. I searched among them for my friend, surely the lady on whom all eyes tonight should fall in admiration.

But Roxana was not in their company.

Bonitus' widow was not about to lose this valuable chance to tighten the bonds to her late husband had forged with generations of Franco-Roman soldierly. Before taking her chair, she worked her way around the room, granting this man or that a greeting, or query about the health of his family and the prospects for a son, or a salute to the memory of a late officer loyal to Bonitus.

When it came to imperial matrons, Augustus' great Livia herself would have admired Evochildis this evening.

The first dishes borne high by kitchen slaves landed on the tables—river fish, salad, spatchcocked pigeon, fattened goose, and even peacock roasted with the feathers reinserted back into crispy, salted skin—all accompanied by white wine from Mosella vineyards lucky enough to have survived Alemannic depredations.

In the fields outside the city walls, the lower ranks were drowning in cheap red *fundanum* spiced with herbs. If they didn't want wine, there was *cerevisia* from fermented rye and *aqua mulsa* from fermented honey, and as much game stew and fresh bread as they could swallow, not to mention slatherings of butter for those who had the northern taste for such grease, followed by the freshest fruits of summer.

I waved off offers of a place. I kept on the move and lingered in the shadows of the wide marble columns and flickering wall torches and waited for Ursicinus. Amid the gaiety Silvanus too fixed his gaze on the entrance. He scarcely noticed when his mother singled out none other than Clothild to join her father at the main table.

I was almost glad Roxana was not here to witness this annointment of daughter as well as father to the new imperial inner circle. If Bainobaudes was to serve as Emperor Silvanus' *Magister Officiorum* during the day, was his daughter a candidate to serve the new court at night as official imperial consort? Had Roxana been discarded? Was Junius' mother forgotten altogether? These Franco-Romans seemed to tailor their devotions to Christian marital strictures to suit their armor.

A gentle hand stopped my progress along the wall of columns near the rear of the hall.

'Don't feel sorry for me. That only makes it worse.'

Roxana had slipped into the crowd unheralded and unwelcomed by her lover. I could not believe Silvanus was so callous as to forget Roxana during these testing hours, but he showed no intention of flaunting her before hundreds of powerful soldiers.

'Did your meeting with Silvanus go as you hoped, Marcus?' she asked.

'If it had, you'd be dining on a modest rabbit stew tonight with your General before his dawn departure for Mediolanum.'

'I see.'

Her limpid brown eyes caught the flicker of the dancing lamp flames, the sparkle of jewels and the gleam of polished armor.

—THE WOLVES OF AMBITION—

Were they bright with pride or wet with sadness? She poured dark *Niger* wine from a jug on a sideboard into a glass goblet and started to gulp. I pulled it the empty vessel from her hand.

'That's the heavy stuff, dear lady.'

'Don't tell me what to do.'

'I may need your help over the next few days, Roxana.'

'Leave me out of it, please. I'm not who I once was, Marcus. Can't you see? I have no secret weapons against the enemies I face here.' She glanced at the radiant Clothild leaning in conversation within Evochildis.

'You're better now. Wiser than before. Come back to the service where your fellows respected you for your talents.'

'Resented me, too.'

'Are you any less resented here?'

She poured herself another drink. 'What was it that Apodemius called me, "My failed experiment?" My life as Roma's first female *agens* was something that happened to another girl, a long, long time ago.'

'The Roxana I knew could hold any man down, either in her bed or under a bare blade.'

She laughed at that. 'If I'm lucky, Silvanus will let me keep loving him in the shadows until one of us grows tired of sharing nothing more than moonlight and melancholy.'

'It might not be too late to save both of you. You're as smart as ever. Don't give up so easily.'

'You know something, don't you, Marcus? What do you know?' She gripped my arm like a Fury.

'I'm not sure. You know Arbetio better than I.'

Her eyes widened with alarm. 'Arbetio? Is he coming here?'

'No, not Arbetio but—why do you look so afraid? Does Arbetio still love you? Does he still want you back?'

'He has tried—but not out of love. I felt more hatred from him than love. Conquest is what excites him. He wants to humiliate me and those I love. As soon as I fell into his clutches, I was fighting to escape and found the safety of the *schola*. He never forgave me for joining the service, the one Roman institution strong enough to protect me.'

"Now he's set on the downfall of your lover. He has escaped censure for the forgery fiasco. He's not above using Ursicinus as his tool, just as I suspect he used his fellow *consistoriani*.'

'He thinks that if Silvanus fails, my only course would be back to him. He wants me to prostrate myself, to appeal for his mercy.'

I took her by the shoulders and pulled her out of the path of bustling slaves. 'You could always live with Kahina and Leo in Roma. The boy remembers you and loves you. Kahina needs the help of an understanding sister. I wouldn't make any claims on our old friendship. Those days are behind us.'

Roxana glanced up at me with eyes filled with wistful tears. We stepped aside to make way for a server bearing a wide platter of roasted venison in a leek-and-plum sauce.

The officers' toasts were turning boisterous and vulgar. The drinks kept flowing, the servers coming and going through the archway giving on to the corridor behind us that led to the kitchens downstairs. Soon it would be time for the dishes of fruit, nuts, and white grapes already being arranged by slaves on small dishes covering the sideboard behind us.

There was still no sign of Ursicinus. Silvanus half-listened to the chitchat on either side of him. Laniogaisus, Bainobaudes, and Evochildis were deep in private planning, their heads craned forward in conversation. Other members of the *trustis* hailed Silvanus with salutes and jests down the length of the table and got a distracted nod for their cheer.

'What did Gaudentius order you to do?' Roxana kept her voice to a whisper.

'Keep my nose out of this whole affair.'

'If only Apodemius were well again.'

'Apodemius would tell me to stick my nose in deeper. Roxana,

The evening was wearing on. What might have delayed or preoccupied the great Hero of the East beyond the gates?

'I'm worried that Ursicinus is setting up a trap outside these walls right now, Roxana. If he surrounded this hall, he'd have the entire Western Army command hostage to his orders. I'm slipping outside now to make sure we're not under siege."

'Yes, go. I've never been so nervous, Marcus.'

—THE WOLVES OF AMBITION—

She nodded goodbye with a gentle squeeze of my hand and moved off to join a group of minor ladies beckoning to her.

※※※

I slipped out of the huge dining hall and worked my way around clusters of officers stretching their legs in the large reception area near the entrance. I trotted toward the city gates and the river road. Dusk had fallen at last. It took me only a few minutes to reach the outskirts of the walls looming over the teeming camp fields to the south.

Hundreds of campfires flickered across the former pastureland. I heard only the music of normal army life, multiplied dozens of times and stretching all the way to the dark line of thick forest. This was the sound of the Roman army at peace—shouts, orders, braying mules, bellowing oxen, barking dogs, bursts of laughter, and occasional trill of a flute piercing the night air.

I discovered no secret siege. Ursicinus had not turned these forces against Silvanus. Confused, I returned to the banquet and ate cold pigeon off an abandoned platter.

I had almost finished the leftovers when shouts from the sentries were almost drowned in the festive roar.

Officers turned in their seats or jumped to their feet to see what caused the persistent commotion blocking the entrance. But I looked the other way on purpose—just in time to catch Silvanus. He checked his curiosity and fought off the impulse to rise from his chair like any ordinary officer.

He had to remember, he was an emperor now.

The crowd parted. Ursicinus, Potentius and their companions strode into the center of the room.

The Hero of the East was as imposing as ever, with his rigorous haircut, scarred hand, Persian dagger and confident swagger. He had a fresh glint in his eye. No longer the penitent hero claiming redress in a hostile court, he found himself among fellow warriors. He could claim his rightful place as an equal of Silvanus in the field.

Potentius stood behind him, one hand on the hilt of his *spatha*. He took in the assembly with a wary smile, ready to defend his father's back in every sense. A quick-eyed adjutant and ten or so *tribuni vacantes* handpicked from his trusted delegation to Mediolanum positioned themselves in a wide line facing Silvanus. One had a damaged ear, making me think of my night fighting off wolves.

So far Ursicinus had followed the Emperor's order to the letter. Before arriving in the hall, he and his party had washed and changed from travel to parade dress. They were coming to drink and dine as diplomats and emissaries, not enemies. None of them made a threatening gesture or a sudden move.

Silvanus didn't look reassured. He rose to his full height and braced his shoulders with his cloak clutched around his torso in defiance. He rounded to the front of the table to receive the imperial delegation.

Murmurs died on expectant faces around the hall. A serving girl dropped a spoon and it clattered on the floor, the only sound to break the heavy silence weighing down on the two generals.

'Mighty General Ursicinus, welcome to Colonia Claudia Ara Agrippinensium,' Silvanus said.

The crowd waited. Would Ursicinus arrest Silvanus? Would he give a speech begging him to see reason? Was there a detachment of soldiers loyal to Constantius encircling the palace at this moment, to seize the entire assembly?

I knew Ursicinus had his letter to deliver, so I was not surprised to see him reach back and receive the solid packet of vellum from his son. He did not hand it to Silvanus.

Instead he did something that astonished even the most cynical officer in the room.

Ursicinus fell to his knees, sending up a gasp around the room. He went further. He prostrated his hefty body at length before Silvanus and reached forward. With that roughened paw that had survived so many hand-to-hand duels, he grasped the edge of Silvanus' cloak, and lifted it to his lips.

Evochildis rose from her chair before Silvanus could recover from the shock. She pushed Bainobaudes away from his place next to her and addressed the entire room.

—THE WOLVES OF AMBITION—

'Come, General, you and your officers are welcome to our court. Come, sit between my son the Emperor, and myself. We have much to discuss.'

Astonishment filled Proculus' face and the shifting glances of the Franco-Roman *trustis* as they made places on the dais for their important new guests.

I was left watching Potentius settle down to his meal as I thoughtfully picked away at a bit of sauced river fish.

I was as confused as I was suspicious. Had Ursicinus gone overboard in following Constantius' order to approach Silvanus with caution?

Or had Constantius' suspicions of Ursicinus' ambition driven not one, but two generals into open revolt?

Or was there a third scheme, hidden somewhere, a scheme that would suit Arbetio better than anyone?

I was sure of one thing. For Ursicinus to acknowledge Silvanus' claim was the one move on the board nobody had foreseen.

The lumbering General Ursicinus had arrived to play a subtle, deadly game.

Chapter 18, Trust Between Heroes

—Agrippina, dawn, September 1, 355—

Given his paralyzing jitters over disloyalty and treason, why hadn't Emperor Constantius foreseen this? To force together two resentful military generals at the peak of authority over both the Western and Eastern Roman armies was courting rebellion against the Constantine dynasty. Certainly the Emperor planned that one general would replace the other. Possibly he even feared or hoped one or the other would destroy his rival—no matter what he said in front of Flavius Philippus' brother.

But why hadn't he anticipated they might band against him?

The night's festivities had lasted until dawn. Hours of sniffing around the palace secretariat and the visiting commanders' main meeting tents the next morning told me nothing. After morning Mass in the governor's chapel, Silvanus had declared a Christian day of rest and a moratorium on all meetings.

It was a tactful way to offer Ursicinus' party, not to mention thousands of soldiers, time to recuperate from their frantic race at forced pace up the Rhenus to the capital. But it also gave Evochildis, Silvanus, and the *trustis*, a needed respite to debate what should come next.

I reported before dawn on the following day to resign my assignment. Silvanus now had no need of a spy. I would demand he release the *agentes* in detention. We would return to Roma post-haste.

Proculus directed me to Laniogaisus. The Franco-Roman was already in conference with his fellow tribunes. So much for the moratorium on meetings.

'*Biarchus* Numidianus? What do you want? We're pressed for time.'

'If you're assuming the role of *Magister Officiorum* for this court, Laniogaisus, then you have the authority to relinquish my services. I respectfully resign my commission from Emperor Silvanus,' I said. 'Because of the last two days' events, an *agens* seems superfluous. I request the release of my *schola* superiors and a search for our man Meroveus the Toxandrian so we can all four return to our headquarters in Roma as soon as possible.'

Laniogaisus glanced at Bainobaudes. The other tribune shook his head. Each was reluctant to admit they were in the dark. Despite distrust of us *curiosi* on principle, they had realized the value of my inquisitiveness in the fight to escape the ambush across the river. As they didn't know exactly what my private mission from Silvanus was, could they risk annulling it?

Laniogaisus maintained his composure. 'I've got no fresh orders to change your assignment. Better you continue until the Emperor decides for himself.'

'In that case, I'll need a horse to accompany the imperial party to this morning's review of the troops,' I said.

I'd done what was correct under the confusing circumstances. That freed me to pursue one question that kept nagging at me. Why hadn't Constantius' hypersensitive political instincts warned him of this alliance against his fortunes? Something, somewhere, was ajar or askew. But it would take more digging to unearth it.

And Meroveus? If we were to leave the north imminently, the fate of the Toxandrian had to be uncovered.

An hour later, the sun rose on the two generals in full parade gear trotting out the city gates. They rode toward the field of tents stretching for miles to the distant forest on the horizon. The first joint appearance of the two commanders would be to inspect the legions carrying out their exercises in the rising August heat.

From that hour on, the Emperor Silvanus and General Ursicinus seemed inseparable.

Some fifty of us on horseback followed the imperial party's flapping pennants. I didn't take my eyes off Ursicinus but from that distance, it was impossible to spot any flaw in his demeanor. If anything, he extended nothing but excessive respect and ready candor to his new 'sovereign.' The great man even reined his horse back half a pace, an almost too-obvious show of deference for Silvanus' spanking new purple-hemmed cloak. Yet he remained within Silvanus' earshot and they seemed collegial enough from the distance of fifty feet.

Proculus had assigned me a respectable horse suitably decked out in jingling court harness and colorful silk saddle trappings but no matter how inconspicuous I was, there was no way I could tail the two generals any closer than I did without earning a reprimand.

So far Ursicinus' comportment made a mockery of my warnings to Silvanus of Arbetio's vicious scheming. I couldn't afford to become the public fool of the new Agrippina court by raising alarms over nothing. So, no matter how uneasy I felt at the sudden camaraderie between the two generals, I concealed my astonishment from the trusting Proculus, riding just ahead of me.

Laniogaisus and Bainobaudes must have worked late into the night with dozens of tribunes and prefects to prepare the reviewing spot on a slight slope facing south and to organize the newly mustered forces for this display of imperial force.

As soon as the two generals stepped up to the wooden viewing stand, thousands of excited soldiers sent up a deafening roar of approval and banged their shields on their knees to affirm the alliance.

Horse maneuvers, archery demonstrations, *ballista* and *manuballista* contests, infantry formations, and drills would last the entire morning.

The highlight of the day would be the demonstration of *francisca* throwing. Straw targets stood to the far right of the platform. With the rising sun at their backs, the best axe-handlers among the Franco-Romans would compete against each other for a generous purse. While the most senior officers had followed Silvanus and Ursicinus up onto the stand to give the massed armies the best view of their united authority, I was left with the bulk of the processional body in the shade below.

There wasn't much I could do, I thought, until I spotted one of Ursicinus' *protectores*, Verenianus, returning from a tent. He swabbed off his sweating brow with a wet towel. His left ear had been sliced into two equal pieces at the middle, as if a sharp blade had caught the lobe and pulled forward—possibly a Persian's friendly salutation.

'Verenianus, welcome to Agrippina. I would be happy to assist you if some of your officers wish a tour of the city or a visit to Constantine's old fortress across the Rhenus.'

My little speech was fatuous enough, but it broke the ice.

'Thank you for your courtesy, *Biarchus*.'

He kept his eyes trained on the wheeling horses of the Petulantes *auxilium*. That was that. I was going to make a discreet retreat when he suddenly grabbed my tunic sleeve.

'Tell me, we heard Silvanus paid his troops not long ago.'

'Yes, Silvanus distributed the *donativa* in the name of Constantius on the seventh of August.'

'We've also heard that some of the legions aren't satisfied with their coin. Have you heard rumors of discontent?'

His question put me on my guard. Perhaps Verenianus had lingered below the viewing platform for more than a drink of water. With or without instructions, he was doing a little reconnoitering himself, but I couldn't fathom his exact purpose. I was not the first officer in Agrippina he'd questioned, I felt sure.

'Have you seen the *francisca* used to such effect before?' I changed the subject. 'It's not only essential that the axe turn no more than once in the air and hit its target, but also that it bounces unpredictably off the ground to scatter the discipline of the enemy's line.'

'Yes, the remnants of the Usurper Magnentius' forces under Ursicinus' command have used them against the Persians, to greater or lesser effect,' Verenianus muttered. 'But the campaign against Shapur demands more than tricks with Frankish *angons* and axes. The Roman Army requires iron discipline. Are these legions so easily swayed from one emperor to another? Are they so content with their new *Imperator*?'

I let his question linger in the air. Just then I spotted my wolf-slayer, Leudast, down among the competing finalists in the final round of axe throwing. Knowing his precision when aiming at a lunging animal from fifty feet, I wasn't surprised to see him doing well against a painted bale flying a scarlet rag.

Verenianus was just fishing. I'd kept moving the whole previous day, my ears alert for grumbles of discontent and

—THE WOLVES OF AMBITION—

discord, or even rumors of residual loyalty to Constantius. I'd heard nothing.

Yet it was possible there were hotheaded regiments out on the field today who were practicing their skills for more than a bag of prize money. So far, the campaign to claw back Gallic territory from the Alemanni claimants had been far from lucrative for the average soldier.

I suddenly recalled how the cynical Leudast and the reluctant Rathar quarreled over how much they owed the Constantine family versus the war booty promised by the new Emperor Silvanus.

Proculus joined us in the shade of the platform and wiped sticky perspiration beads off his forehead and the inside of his helmet.

'May I have a word, Numidianus?'

I was grateful for the adjutant's interruption and happy to step a few paces away from Ursicinus' bloodhound.

'I hope your *Magister* is strong enough to travel, Numidianus. If you do obtain release for your colleagues, leave Agrippina while you can. Tempers are short. Policy changes by the hour. There's no love lost on Silvanus' part for your *schola*. He still resents Apodemius' coming here to arrest him. He's just as likely to clap you all in chains for good as to wave you down the *Cursus* with a picnic sack.'

'Apodemius seems to be out of danger but he's far too weak to ride a horse. We'd need a good, solid vehicle.'

'I'll see what I can arrange.'

'Thanks for your warning. By the way, for my money, Adjutant, that Verenianus seems too curious about discontented soldiers.'

Proculus' narrow shoulders squirmed under armor too big for him.

'It doesn't hurt to be ready for anything. You and I know General Silvanus. He backed into this without a second plan. If Ursicinus is on his side, he has landed on his feet like a lucky cat. Otherwise—'

'It's the otherwise I'm watching out for, Proculus. Don't misunderstand me. I don't think Silvanus is a bad servant of the Empire. But I've known the man since 351. He was the very last to join General Magnentius' rebels. Then he abandoned them on the eve of their victory and gave the day to Constantius. All his life, he's waited as long as he can to choose allies or switch sides. He's like a racer changing horses halfway around the *Meta*. Maybe this time he waited so long, he realizes he has no side at all.'

'But he has Ursicinus now,' Proculus said. 'Together they control the army.'

'It was too easy.'

'I had that dream again,' Proculus said, after a pause.

'Which dream?'

'I told you about it. But this time, I saw the man tormenting me, telling me to confess something that was not true. I remembered to wake myself up in time. I freed myself of my tormenter with his crooked, mismatched eyes.'

I felt a chill but said nothing. Surely his description of Catena was born of rumors about 'the Chain' that reached the north. Our nightmares were often like a soup pot, churning the scraps of unfinished thoughts and fears into a stew that made no sense.

'There's something I've wanted to ask you since you arrived,' Proculus. '*Matrona* Evochildis says that the General's—sorry—the Emperor's mistress Roxana was once a *curiosus* herself. Or should I say *curiosa*? I did not know such creatures existed.'

He squinted up at me in disbelief.

I chuckled at the idea.

'Don't laugh, Numidianus. The great lady tells her companions that Roxana has not only serviced councilors of the court without restraint, she has been tainted beyond Christian salvation by her Castra training in underhanded arts and perverted sexual tricks. She says that Roxana is unworthy to be an emperor's consort.'

'Does she? I'm no expert on our state cult, but that doesn't sound very Christian to me.'

I felt like strangling this guileless, round-shouldered messenger. He was only confirming what I had observed—that Evochildis was determined to marginalize my poor friend from her only chance at happiness.

'Come on, you would know, Numidianus. Is it true? Such a lovely, modest woman—a government agent? One shudders to think what that noble lady might have been ordered to do in the course of her service.'

'Neptune's Dick, Proculus, do you imagine our *schola* would waste time training a *woman*? Why the entire imperial postal service would shut down in protest at the sheer insult.'

'No, no, of course not. I never intended to insult—'

'I can't imagine where that arrogant old bag heard such a story—unless Roxana herself hoped to seduce Silvanus with fanciful tales of high intrigue. You're a man of the world, Adjutant. Don't you find a woman will try anything to make her bed more interesting than the next lady's, right?'

'Oh, yes, certainly.' Proculus almost blushed.

The *ballista* demonstration was winding down and the field was taken over by the archery contestants.

'I am relieved to hear it, *Biarchus*. I admire the *Matrona* Roxana for her discretion, her grace, her—'

'You know, Adjutant Proculus, Evochildis reminds me of a certain politician, one of our two current consuls in the *consistorium*. This man can't win supreme influence using honest arguments. So he stands back and sets a tableful of fearful councilors on his rival in his stead. Like a pack of snarling chase dogs, other men isolate and corner his rival until the poor victim has nowhere to turn'.

'Yes.' Proculus nodded. 'Evochildis gets the other women to shun Roxana, no matter how hard she pines to join their company.'

'Oh, sorry, were we still talking of women?' I replied, tossing him a wink as he clambered back up the steps of the platform to receive instructions.

A roar of support drowned us out. The winners of the axe throwing competition came to the foot of the platform to receive their prizes. The first two winners received their prize money with prostrations and salutes of their weapons.

Leudast had taken third. To the astonishment of the commanding officers, he tossed his little sack of coins back up to the platform where it landed with a clink at their boots.

'I got no need of trifling prizes, *Imperator*,' the scout shouted up over the clatter and cheering behind him. 'The real treasure that my weapons should win me waits in the south on the field of battle. Look behind me! The Bracchiati stand ready. The Cornuti stand ready. Lead us across the Cottian Alps and take Mediolanum now! You've gained the purple on the back of promises of more riches for all your troops. We don't want petty rewards for *tirones'* games. Every day's delay is dangerous to us all.'

Silvanus tossed the coin purse back into Leudast's chest. Centurions hustled the scout away to the clamor of support from rougher fellows in the field. Meanwhile, thousands of other soldiers were busy with their demonstrations or unsure what was happening at the viewing stand so far out of earshot. *Cornicines* and *buccinatores* blew across the fields for order and the festivities came to an end.

Verenianus still stood not far away from me, his arms crossed, his expression smug. In a few seconds he would join the procession departing with Ursicinus but first he wanted words with me again.

'So what did I tell you, *Biarchus*? There are dissatisfied men out there, men who want to fight for real profit.'

I could not let this pass a second time.

'The last thing the Empire needs is another civil war. There's no need to march on Mediolanum if Ursicinus and Silvanus control the entire army between them. If they see eye-to-eye, they're in a strong negotiating position to avoid bloodshed altogether.'

'Indeed. The two men have suffered greatly from Constantius' ingratitude. In fact,' he said with a smile, 'they talk of little else. Good luck, *Biarchus*.'

I pulled Proculus to one side. 'Did any of the troops demand that Silvanus march across the Cottians before that outburst?'

Proculus nodded and said in a low voice, 'Yes. Yesterday some officers requested permission to meet Silvanus after Mass. Please, keep it under your *petanus*. The Emperor told them to calm down until he hears how Constantius responds to rumors of Ursicinus' prostration.'

'The lower ranks don't seem so easily silenced.'

'Simple men prefer things simple,' Proculus said. 'In eight weeks our soldiers have cheered Constantius, then acclaimed Silvanus as their new sovereign, and now are expected to add

—THE WOLVES OF AMBITION—

Ursicinus into the picture when not a single one of them wants to go fight Persians in the East. They're loyal, but confused.'

'No Roman emperor in history survives in front of an army of unhappy soldiers,' I said. 'Silvanus has always waited too long. One day he'll regret it.'

At the orders from their *optiones*, the vast sea of men started flowing back into the routine of another September afternoon. Wagons of food and fodder lumbered down the long, straight lanes of the demarcated camps. Embers were stoked back into orange flames, stewpots hung up to boil, horses curried, weapons cleaned, and artillery targets stowed away.

I mounted my horse and returned to the city on my own. Now and then some outburst of belated celebration or bark of logistics officers punctuated the settling calm of the early evening. The last thing I wanted to see was this ocean of brave and eager men butchered on another battlefield like Mursa. The only hope for peace was to see unity hold fast between Silvanus and Ursicinus.

I wanted to talk to Roxana about the warning I'd had from Proculus. Halfway to her quarters, I changed course. It would only compound her sadness. Meanwhile, I had a message for Gaudentius.

I found the *ducenarius* boiling over with frustration, not even able to get a good view of the army camp from his window. The sentries guarding him looked well settled into their places in the corridor.

'Good news, Gaudentius. Proculus says we should be ready to leave right away in case my request for release is granted.'

I thought he would be pleased. Instead he scowled at me like a caged animal heading in a wicker cart toward the Roman arena.

'Meroveus is still gone.'

'But where?'

'How should I know? Apodemius is alert. He asked to see you as soon as you showed your African face.'

I rushed to the *Magister*'s chamber. He was sitting up in bed in a fresh linen tunic and sipping a bowl of broth held to his lips by a Frankish slave with long hair and ragged leg bindings. The old man waved the boy away and gave me a triumphant smile.

'I was turned back at the banks of the River Styx.' He looked like a perky, pale skeleton with wisps of white hair sticking up all over his bony skull.

'You must recover your strength as fast as possible. We may be able to leave soon.'

'Thank the gods! Such heavy food up here! All I can get down my gullet is this strange broth. Well, Numidianus. It seems I have Roxana and you to thank for finding me the Galen of Frankish sorceresses. I will reward the woman generously despite one complaint. She has utterly failed to eradicate my cursed arthritis.'

'I'm so relieved to see you better, *Magister*.'

'Are you? You disobeyed *Ducenarius* Gaudentius' orders.'

'Yes, *Magister*, but—'

'He told you to withdraw. He told you to take no action under this new "Emperor," didn't he?'

'Yes, *Magister*, but—' I braced myself for a demotion. Gaudentius would be satisfied with nothing less.

'That was incorrect of you. Gaudentius knew that our *schola* cannot be seen to take sides in a military struggle battle over authority.'

'But he doesn't—!'

'You've already spied on one usurper, I know, I know, but that was on my instructions, to the considerable profit of our service. So, tell me, what have you found out so far?'

I exhaled with relief and told him my suspicions.

'Surely you know more than that?'

'What do you mean?'

'There's more. There's always more. Think, Numidianus, think. Go back over it again. What makes you uneasy, apart from the obvious idiocy of Silvanus seizing the purple?'

I recited it all again—Silvanus' outraged pride, his justified suspicions of Arbetio and the Council, his understandable hesitation to trust Constantius, the unbridled ambition of Evochildis, the hostility of the Frankish tribesmen across the river, the tardy revelation of the forgery, the feeble punishment meted out to the most convenient culprit, the sly looks of the *consistoriani* at the thought of one general eliminating the other, and the last secret whispers of Arbetio to Ursicinus overheard by Florentius.

I told him of Constantius' orders to race ahead with a verbal guarantee for Silvanus, of my solo race up the treacherous river route, the elevation of Bainobaudes and his virgin daughter, the unexpected prostration of Ursicinus, the pregnant 'day of rest and prayer,' and now the public impatience of certain units to march on Mediolanum to unseat the last Constantine in power.

All of this took half an hour or more, yet Apodemius' attention flagged only once. I am sorry to admit he wasn't at all interested in my encounter with the wolves.

He shook his head, dissatisfied with my report.

'No, no, think hard. What's wrong now?'

I sat quietly, thinking over Verenianus' persistent curiosity about troop dissatisfaction.

Gaudentius interrupted us, unable to disguise his irritation at exclusion from my long debriefing by the *Magister*.

'If Numidianus still enjoys his exceptional freedom of movement,' he said, 'I suggest he go hunt down Meroveus and drag him back here so we can start packing. The Toxandrian coward must have seen the guards coming at some point and taken to his heels.'

'Come now, Gaudentius. Don't I recall Meroveus in detention with you just after the acclamation?' Apodemius chided. 'You don't want to acknowledged he escaped from under their noses.'

'And Meroveus is no coward,' I said. 'But I have no idea where to find him.'

'It won't be so hard,' Apodemius gave a hoarse chuckle. 'You must have noticed, Gaudentius, that Meroveus spent a great deal of time at my bedside exchanging Frankish chitchat with our healer woman. I don't speak their awful language but even through my feverish dreams, I could make out the word *Grifo* from time to time. It's obvious isn't it?'

Gaudentius and I waited for the old man to explain.

'I suspect he failed to find his Grifo in the military rolls, so he took the next obvious course—to use that old woman's network of Frankish links. If our Toxandrian *agens* has disappeared without permission, there must be a very good reason. You'll find Meroveus with his son.'

He sighed. 'I'm tired and want to sleep. Give this slop back to the sentries and get rid of this slave, Gaudentius.'

Apodemius leaned toward me, his fluff of white hair stiff with sweat like a bird's crest.

'Now, think, Numidianus. Before you follow Gaudentius, just think for one more minute.'

In the doorway, Gaudentius fiddled with his sword belt and shifted in his boots, unwilling to admit I might have learned useful information by disobeying him. I refused to let him distract me. I rose to my feet, threw back my head with eyes closed, and drew myself a mental picture of the morning's events.

Then I had it.

'Potentius. Potentius wasn't on the viewing stand. Ursicinus' son Potentius was missing.'

'Exactly,' Apodemius nodded. 'I've noticed you've said nothing about the person who might hold the key to this whole strange piece of political theater. You told me that Constantius was in such a hurry to employ Ursicinus as his delegate to Silvanus, he brushed away the general's insistence that they clear his name, once and for all. So Ursicinus still stands in Mediolanum accused of one ambition—to claim rule of the Empire of the East for his son. There must be some truth behind this charge—it's too persistent and widespread a rumor. I believe Ursicinus' heart and hope rests on the future of that young man.'

'He's the image of his father—only younger, taller, and stronger.'

'And probably brighter. Yet just when this future caesar should be currying favor with his new *Imperator* Silvanus, his eldest son is strangely unaccounted for. Silvanus has bound Ursicinus tightly to his side, but from your account, it seems possible that Ursicinus is playing a part.'

'The resentments they share are genuine enough. Constantius has treated them both badly.'

'But the ready prostration? Riding behind Silvanus in the parade?' Apodemius clucked with disbelief. 'Remember where we met when I recruited you, Numidianus?'

'In a dressing room at a rundown circus.'

—THE WOLVES OF AMBITION—

'Yes. I've always had an affinity for the illusions of public performance. I've learned that to understand the tricks, it helps to go backstage. If there is a trick being played on Silvanus, I would bet that Potentius is the magician.'

'But he wasn't even there.'

'Exactly. Because he's busy behind the scenery. And if he's busy elsewhere, then his father's abject submission to "Emperor" Silvanus is only a play for time.'

'Busy doing what? Time for what?'

'Oh, for the sake of the gods, that's for you to find out, isn't it, Numidianus? Gaudentius, give our guards a message for Silvanus' staff that I'm far too feeble to be moved, out of my mind with fever, on my last breath, writing my will—anything to decelerate our eviction.'

Gaudentius was furious. 'We are in grave danger, *Magister*. Our loyalties must remain with Emperor Constantius. When this rift erupts into violence, we will be the first targets.'

Apodemius' flushed red. 'You've forgotten your first lessons at the Castra, *Ducenarius*, and it's something I've been wanting to say to you since the Africanus affair. Our *schola* is loyal to no man, not even Constantius. We serve the interests of the Empire and if it's not obvious what those interests are, our first duty is to find out.'

There was no mistaking the irritation in his voice. To see the old man's former impatience return filled my heart with joy. Apodemius was finally out of danger—or at least, in no more danger than the rest of us.

Chapter 19, Poison Can Be Good

—Agrippina, September 3, 355 AD—

I needed Meroveus' help. To find Meroveus I needed that healer woman Guntheuca. Only Roxana knew where to find her.

Roxana wasn't in her quarters nor was she currying favor with the ladies of Evochildis' court. I barely escaped bumping into Clothild on my search of the residential wing. I guessed that Roxana would not be in Clothild's vicinity. The elevation of the blushing Frankish girl had eclipsed Roxana from public view, it seemed.

Finally, I found my friend in the last place I would have thought she felt at ease—on her knees, praying alone in the governor's private chapel. The altar was decked out in fresh purple and gold hangings and cloths, all appliquéd with the *Chi-Rho*, the first two Greek letters of Christ's name, as befitted an imperial emperor. That bevy of needle-whipping court ladies worked at lightning speed.

She pretended not to hear my steps echoing on the cool stone floor, so I stood in front of her, blocking her view of the large crucifix and her new 'savior' hanging on the wall above us.

'So you've become a Christian for Silvanus, as well? If he declared himself King of the Picts and colored himself all blue, would you rush out to buy yourself fresh paint?'

She dropped her clasped hands, but kept her gaze fixed on my boots.

'Don't ridicule me, Marcus. Remember the legend of Mary Magdalene?'

'Yes, the Commander's first wife tried to convert all her household by reading us such tales.'

'There's a great deal of good in the Christian creed, Marcus. Christ forgives a woman's past, sooner than certain so-called Christian women.'

She lifted her anguished face to me, cheeks streaming with tears, her careful Germanic eye make-up ruined. I found myself kneeling down next to her, as odd as it felt.

'Roxana, you and I are not safe in Agrippina. Apodemius is stalling, but Gaudentius is ready to get out the instant Silvanus lifts their detention. You must help me find Meroveus in time. When we *agentes* leave, you must come with us.'

'I will never leave him, Marcus.'

'Then you're a fool, Roxana. You've been many things, including a double-crosser, but never a fool. That runty Adjutant Proculus likes you enough to warn me that Evochildis is spreading the story around the court that not only were you once another man's mistress, you were even an *agens*. How did she find out?'

'How do you think? Silvanus knows everything about me—more than you, more than Apodemius. But I've done everything to prove that I'll be a good empress.'

'*Empress?*'

'Yes! He's promised nothing less.'

'You don't believe in that, do you? You can't. That's why you're in here, praying and crying, isn't it?'

'He asked me to be patient.'

'Evochildis will never permit it. I don't know what kind of a Christian she is, but she'll use your past, your present, and your future to keep you from gaining ascendance over her. She'll stop you, whatever it takes.'

She covered her face and broke down into sobs. 'He swore on his father's name.'

'He once swore allegiance to my commander and all the reformist rebels.'

I let her cry for a few minutes, until her tears subsided.

'Roxana, where is Meroveus?'

'I told you, I don't know,' she choked out.

'Apodemius says that the healer woman knows. Stop this pantomime of piety and take me to her.'

—THE WOLVES OF AMBITION—

I helped her to her feet. She gathered up her long summer blue linen *palla*, wrapped it around her hair and shoulders, and led me out the back gate of the parade ground. We hurried through busy streets, past vendor's stalls, cobblers, butchers, tailors, laundries and bathhouses, and all kinds of low-rise apartments made ramshackle by rapid repairs of Alemannic devastation.

Everyone in Agrippina seemed in a rush—anxious to move with the times, hail the new Emperor, and seize uncertain opportunities, no matter the dangers. Fresh posters, placards, and graffiti lauded 'Emperor Silvanus' with invitations to the newly arrived troops to favor this or that little enterprise or bathhouse with their custom.

We drew no notice from these city folk until we reached a more disreputable part of the capital in the northwest corner of the city walls. Roxana tapped on the door of a three-story residence, still partly rubble, surrounded by squawking chickens and blocked by street children playing a game.

'I'm busy. What do you want?' Guntheuca stuck her head through a crack in the door. 'Oh, it's you.'

She admitted us into a badly lit room dense with burning incense and chimney smoke. Drying herbs hung from the low ceiling. Pottery jars and cheap glass bottles littered a long table of rough oak. I spotted her special bag with its pockets for medicines and leaves unfolded at length at the far end of the table.

'You helped our *agens* Meroveus escape detention, didn't you, Guntheuca?'

'I gave the sentries a drink,' she said with a shrug. 'They were thirsty.'

'And on that particular night, you advised Meroveus that the sentries would grow sleepy and stay asleep for as long as he needed to get out of the governor's palace.'

'Perhaps.'

She had her back turned to us. All I could see through the low light was her sharp elbow sticking through her sleeve as her fist pounded the pestle into the mortar bowl.

'He has duties to the *schola*. I want him back. Where is he?'

'That man has suffered enough punishment for three lifetimes.'

'No one wants to punish him. I need his help. Where will I find him?'

She shrugged. 'With his son, Grifo, I suppose, in the Cornuti camp, in one of those thousands of tents.'

'Grifo's rank?'

'Trainee medical officer. What did he call it? *Discens Capsariorum*—or something like that.'

'Are you sure?'

'Not that those quacks understand real healing,' the crone muttered, her eyes still on her work. Her deft fingers separated buds, stems, pods and leaves in the bowl.

'Do you know the unit? His centurion's name?'

Roxana listened, but said nothing. Her face was puffy from weeping. Her dark eyeliner was smudged into black circles. She was fiddling with the herbs laid out on the table to dry. Her sad thoughts carried her away from the healer woman's hovel.

'No, I didn't ask,' Guntheuca said. She broke Roxana's reverie with a sharp, 'How did you come to choose that woman Ragamunda as an intermediary?'

Roxana looked up. 'Why?'

'Because Ragamunda lied to them and she came back and lied to you! Ragamunda decided for herself it was best for his wife to think him dead, and she lied when she told you his family didn't want him back!'

Roxana shook her head. 'I was told Ragamunda was an honest woman. I paid her well. Why would she do that?'

'Because she's related to a man who wants that family's farm. They need Meroveus' wife to be a lonely widow! And they say you were once an *agens*! I don't believe the Empire would employ someone so easily deceived—man or woman!'

Roxana's face drained white. If even Guntheuca had heard the palace rumors about her disreputable past, then no one in Agrippina—not even the slaves carrying night soil—would accept Roxana as Silvanus' official consort. Better a naked acrobat bouncing off the back of a horse in Flavian's great amphitheater than a member of the despised *curiosi* sitting on the new throne next to the new emperor.

I was in a rush to leave, but an *agens* is tested again and again on noticing the small things. I noticed Roxana's quick hand dive

—THE WOLVES OF AMBITION—

out of sight. She had pocketed some of Guntheuca's herbs in the small satiny purse hanging off her jeweled belt.

'Roxana, we didn't come here to steal. Put it back.'

'What did you take from me, girl? You only had to ask.'

Sheep-faced, Roxana turned out her bag. She'd pinched a handful of yew berries.

'Roxana, you know those seeds inside the red fruit are toxic. Leave them here with Guntheuca. She knows their proper use.'

The crone shook her hoary head. 'No, keep them, Roxana. They will remind you every day that some of the most colorful jewels within reach can be deadly.'

Roxana looked away, knowing full well that the wise woman was no longer speaking of plants. We thanked her with a few coins from my own purse and hurried back through the city. We headed for the Cornuti encampment buried among those thousands of tents stretched across the southern horizon beyond the city gates.

'What could you want with those berries, Roxana? Throw them away. I killed an entire pack of wolves with powder ground from the fruit of a single branch.'

She shook off my restraining hand. 'Don't ask me, Marcus. Leave women's business to women.'

Of those trainees we'd met in the Castra's poisons class, most of our more muscular fellow *agentes* dismissed poison as a woman's weapon. But dead was dead, no matter the means. And I had personal proof that Roxana was capable of any underhanded battle to emerge the winner.

She had to be stopped.

I grabbed her shoulders and pulled her up short, right in the middle of bustling strangers shoving and elbowing past us. Two men were pissing into the laundryman's waiting curbside vat right behind her.

'Roxana! Whatever your chances of keeping Silvanus in your bed, killing his mother isn't going to increase them!'

'Stay out of this, Marcus. Poison can be bad or poison can be good—that's what our instructor told us.'

'He never said any such thing. He taught us to be cautious. In case something went wrong, we were to keep antidotes handy. There's no antidote for yew poison.'

She wouldn't say any more. In antagonized silence, we pushed-and-shoved through the half dozen crowded blocks that sprawled south of Agrippina's main boulevard. I was so blinded by anger at what I feared she might do, I nearly overturned an entire cart of pristine green bottles being delivered by a bare-chested glazier to a nearby wine shop.

We emerged out the southern main gate and stopped to get our bearings. There, past the usual shacks and slums that attached themselves to any Roman city wall, stretched the perfect lines of tents and standards. But it was impossible to spot any with the twin-headed serpent shared by the brother legions, the Cornuti and Bracchiati. We'd have to tackle the camp head-on.

Roxana shook me off and pulled her linen *palla* over her elaborate court coiffure and refastened her belt so her cloak covered her expensively embroidered court dress. The camp was peopled with women enough—no Roman division occupied imperial territory for long without its common-law women and even children catching up on its tail—but Roxana was wearing a fortune in jewels and fine stitching work on her back. We had to stay inconspicuous.

Discipline with so many legions and *auxilia palatinaes* gathered in one place had to be tight, but their security measures surprised even me. The Petulantes occupied the front lines facing the city and we only got past their sentries at the first palisade and into the main lanes between tents by my pulling out my *agentes* papers. Even then, we were stuck with their double escort to navigate us through thousands of troops.

It took us almost half an hour to reach the Cornuti tents. Roxana's cloak was covered with dust dried in the August sun and churned up by hundreds of hooves and cartwheels. After only a few weeks, army boots had worn down the grass underfoot. The field was as hard packed as that priceless Dionysian mosaic floor under Silvanus' spotless soles.

'The medical tents are in that corner there, upwind of the mule stables,' a Cornuti lieutenant said, directing us to go another hundred feet or so.

For a minute, I thought we'd been sent in the wrong direction. We checked one tent after another and found nothing.

'Where are the medical trainees?' I asked a slave rinsing out tin basins behind one tent.

'Don't know, *Biarchus*.'

'He's not here,' Roxana said. 'Perhaps Guntheuca's whole story is as big a lie as she claims Ragamunda told. Sometimes I think all these Frankish types are out to show up us real Romans.'

I lifted a sardonic eyebrow at being included in the term, 'real Roman,' what with my bronze skin, dark hair, and other traces of Numidian blood mixed with Manlius Roman and Gallic features.

But I was about to agree with her, when I peered into the afternoon sun. 'No, there they are! You see them?'

Half a dozen soldiers had just rounded a corner. Headed straight down the lane toward our section, one of them was unmistakably our man—a taller, prouder and fitter version of Meroveus, right down to the thick reddish hair. His masculine grace and power was a cringe-inducing reminder of what Meroveus had lost to the castrating slavers.

'Grifo, I'm Marcus Gregorianus Numidianus of the *agentes in rebus*. I've come for your father. He's derelict in his duty to his *schola*. As his recruiter, I'm responsible. Where is he?'

The boy, now as tall as I, evaded my searching gaze.

'My father Meroveus is dead,' he said in a careful, even tone.

'Of course he isn't. You met him yourself in the exercise fields on payday.'

'The man claiming to take his place in your service must be an imposter.'

'You're afraid we'll punish him, aren't you? You're wrong. I need him. Emperor Silvanus has put our other colleagues under arrest.'

'A woman came to my mother. She said my father had been captured not far from our old home in Toxandria. He was taken beyond imperial borders as a prisoner-of-war and sold to Eastern slavers. They cut off both his balls and made him a ladies' maid in an *Augusta*'s decadent court in Antiochia. Does he owe Roma more service than that?'

The young man's eyes blinked hard with alarm. He'd given himself away. Both his passion and even more important, his use of the present tense, had betrayed his secret.

'No, Roma owes him, loyal Grifo.' I lowered my voice and turned the boy's back away from his fellow medical orderlies.

I whispered, 'The *Magister Agentium in Rebus* orders me to keep a close watch on General Ursicinus and his visiting *tribuni*. I cannot do this alone. So, I'm asking you for the last time, where is your father? If you do not give me an honest answer this time, then I will report him as absent without permission.'

Grifo turned away from me, but not before I detected hesitation.

'Where is he, Grifo?'

'Do not take him away. Not now. Not today.'

'Why not?' I grabbed his arm. 'Why not today?'

'Because he ... is ... waiting for my mother to arrive. Please, *Biarchus*—'

Grifo clutched my arm in turn with the grip of an Atlas. 'Please give him these last few hours of hope. Just another hour or two.'

'He's here, then?'

Grifo nodded.

'Then we'll wait. In the meantime, give this lady a pillow and a stool in the shade and something to eat and drink.'

It was strange to find myself inside the heart of busy army with nothing to do but observe. The high- and low-ranked alike went about their duties in the centuries-old routine now repeating itself across our vast Empire from Londinium to Aleppo to Cartago. I walked up the measured road between the tents, comforted to know that, whoever the emperor, whatever the province, however fierce the enemies ranged against us, all this— the medical tents, the munitions tents, the *signifier* polishing his standards, the *cornicen* his horn, all this was as permanent as Roma.

Thanks the gods, I thought, all this would never, ever change.

A group of infantrymen from another *auxilium* returned from their exercises beyond the tents. A munitions officer supervised the distribution of freshly sharpened swords. A teenage slave rinsed off his superior officer's underclothing behind a tent a few flaps down.

That was how I had spent my youth as a *volo*, a slave embedded deep in the fabric of the military, acting as bodyguard and trusted shadow to the Commander Atticus Manlius Gregorius. I had loved the man as hard as I served him, turning bitter only when I found out that I was his unacknowledged bastard. Instead of freeing me as my dangerous mission demanded, he had tried to keep me by his side against my will, for fear of losing his only child to the truth.

I'd pushed all that away for years now, not out of pain or anger but shame. Wasn't I doing the same to my own Leo? When was the right time to share the secret that could cost him his enormous legacy of name and fortune—the secret that I was his true father?

'Here she comes.' Roxana's gasp woke me from my rambling thoughts. 'That must be her.'

We watched as Grifo reappeared from one of the medical tents and hurried to greet a middle-aged woman in simple beige robes. She came from the direction of the southern perimeter of the camp in the company of a palisade sentry.

Grifo took her arm and tipped his fellow soldier for his pains. He relieved his mother of her travel sack. Their heads bent together in concentration. She must have arrived along one of the unpaved road leading away toward the forest and its life of small *vici* and farms. She covered the lower part of her face with her *palla*, whether from discretion or to keep from choking on the swirling dust of the day, I couldn't say.

Grifo suddenly stopped outside an ordinary tent and embraced her. She took a deep breath and straightened her *palla*, then stood stock-still. The boy lifted the flap of the tent and gave his mother a little nudge. She disappeared.

Grifo sat down outside the tent, took his *pugio* from its sheath on his belt, and drew circles in the dirt.

'Say one of your Christian prayers for him, Roxana,' I whispered. 'Such a good man deserves his family and farm back on any terms. Pray to whomever you want, I don't care. Just pray hard.'

Meroveus finally reappeared from under the leather flap of Grifo's tent just as the sun was setting on the long summer hours fixed by Roman clocks so far to the south. Roxana was dozing on a cot laid out in the shade. I was ruminating on events down in Roma and wondering if Leo had abandoned hope of my ever answering his plaintive query, 'What do you think?' about Kahina and his teacher.

'I'm ready to render myself up to the *schola*'s discipline,' he said. I noticed he had hidden his *agens* insignia away and traded his Roman riding clothes for his son's trousers and bindings under a worn-out tunic to better hide among the other Cornuti.

The poor man had been weeping. The two lines that always scored the sides of his cheeks looked deeper than ever, giving his face the appearance of a graven stone image. I had no heart to ask him why he stood there alone.

Grifo had disappeared too, no doubt to accompany his mother back to the camp perimeter and send her on her way home to their village, her sad reunion done with.

Out of respect for Meroveus' somber demeanor, I asked no questions about his absence and stuck to my business. I brought the Toxandrian up to date as we ate barley and beef stew out of borrowed tin bowls. He nodded to show he was listening, but never met my eyes. Sitting a little apart, Roxana said nothing. She took only a few mouthfuls from her share. Her expression was more desolate than Meroveus'.

'So, now we have to watch Ursicinus and anyone in his delegation like hawks. Apodemius doesn't trust General Ursicinus' acknowledgement of Silvanus and neither may Silvanus, for that matter. Potentius may be using his time elsewhere to some unknown purpose. We have to find out what that is.'

Meroveus shrugged his assent. Surely he was fighting to contain his unbearable disappointment at his wife's final rejection. I had to give him time. I gave his shoulder a brotherly pat, scraped my own bowl clean, and told Roxana, 'Let's wait over there for him while he collects his things.'

'No!' Meroveus shot up from his campstool, and then collapsed, weeping in a heap, his head buried in his lap, his wracking sobs heaving his whole frame.

—THE WOLVES OF AMBITION—

Roxana dropped to her knees and held him, not for the first time, I knew, to console him through his grief. He got out a few words of something I didn't catch. Roxana looked up, a changed expression lighting up her features.

'He's torn in two, Marcus. He doesn't want to disappoint you.'

'Disappoint *me*?'

I grabbed him by his tunic collar, shaking him out of his tears.

'You big blubbing barbarian! She's taking you back, isn't she?'

The Toxandrian's shoulders rose and fell, so overwhelmed with relief and joy that he could not speak one Latin word.

He finally collected himself. After a few last heaves, he said, 'You saved me, Numidianus. You offered me a new life, even a new family among the *agentes*. How can I turn my back on the *schola* now?'

'Where's your wife?'

'There are difficulties. She must hurry back to our village to ready things. She was on the verge of accepting a man she didn't love. Now everything has changed. She still needs a man to protect and provide for her—and that much I can do.'

'She needs her husband to love her,' Roxana added in a strange and gentle voice. 'And that you can do, too, Meroveus. Thank the gods she's wise enough to understand.'

I noticed that in the emotion of the moment, Roxana had forgotten to thank her new god of the state cult.

'I owe you my life. From the moment I came out of that tent, I've been trying to find the words to confess my disloyalty.'

Roxana burst out with a disdainful laugh. 'But I resigned from the service. You knew that!'

'Perhaps you owed it less,' Meroveus said, silencing her disbelief.

'I can accept your resignation on one condition,' I said. 'Good Meroveus, get us out of this mission in one piece by helping me with the surveillance of Potentius and the others. Then come to Roma, sign all the necessary papers, and I promise, you'll start your new life with your family with honor and Apodemius' blessing.'

Meroveus leap from his stool and squeezed me so tight I fought for breath.

'Thank you, thank you, Numidianus. Only you would understand what it feels like to be returned from slavery to life again. Thank you.'

'And I have a person to thank before I leave this camp,' I said. I slipped out of the tent and caught a passing *pedes* hurrying back to this tent to eat with his *contubernales*. I asked him where I might find Leudast, the Bracchiati scout with the famous *francisca* skills and the big mouth.

'Gambling, probably,' he said with a shrug. 'Leudast enjoys a particular reputation.'

I kept going, row-by-row, tent-by-tent, passing through the Bracchiati camp, until I heard the raucous sounds of a dice game. Following the cheers and groans, I came upon half a dozen soldiers leaning over three gamblers seated at a camp table.

One of them was Leudast. Near his right hand, a pile of bronze and silver coins made a small hill of newly acquired wealth.

'Looks like the scout is hauling it in,' I said to a rider watching from a few feet away. 'How long has this game been going?'

'Practically all day. Yesterday he lost the last of his prize money from the *francisca* contest. We all thought he'd drink it off. But he turned up again today, sober as a Vestal, with fresh stakes.'

'And dubious dice, if you ask me,' another soldier muttered from the back of the spectators. I wondered if this officer was about to break up the game, for fear of a fight breaking out among his men over Leudast's sudden 'luck.'

And a fight was indeed looming. I peered over the shoulders of the thickset bystanders. Leudast's dice were ivory with gold and blue dots.

'Who would stake Leudast all over again, with his sad history?'

'A stranger who wants a man in his debt,' said the first soldier. I raised my eyebrows, but he shook his head to signal me not to ask too many questions.

The dice kept rattling and the tension mounted.

—THE WOLVES OF AMBITION—

'Not again!' another loser protested. Leudast gave a greedy shout of victory and we all heard the chink of coins joining the hill on the table.

The mob around the table was growing too thick and the play too intense for me to thank Leudast for saving my life.

'Why don't you break it up before it's too late?' I asked the lieutenant. In the good days, before his terrible wounds turned him bitter and distant from his men, Commander Gregorius had enjoyed a knack for keeping the harmony among the ranks. Apparently, the Bracchiati cohorts were manned with rougher stock.

The lieutenant shook his head. 'The men like to sort such things without with a heavy-handed superior mucking in. Sooner or later, one of them will challenge Leudast's dice. There'll be some kind of fight. Leudast will win the fight, but he'll have to change his dice. Then he'll lose his money all over again.'

'And then?'

'He'll be in deeper debt to whomever is staking him.'

The tent was filling with the sour aroma of excited men, their eyes glazed, meals and washing forgotten. This was bound to get ugly. Leudast might have made himself the man of the hour by challenging Silvanus in front of thousands of his fellow soldiers at the foot of the viewing platform, but now he was about to lose all their respect out of stupidity and greed.

I had more important things to do. Deep in thought, I found myself trailing another man. He wasn't tall, but his erect posture, and imposing gait marked him out from the soldiers relaxing on both sides of the tent lane. He wore a long, hooded *birrus*—far too warm a cloak on such a hot late summer night.

That trick of the mind's eye that understands before it sees told me this man wasn't a Cornuti or a Bracchiati.

He stopped without warning, hesitated before choosing his tent, then lifted a flap, and dodged out of sight.

Roxana and Meroveus were ready to go. Roxana had recovered some of her spirit, despite her worries. Perhaps Meroveus' contagious happiness and relief has bolstered her morale. We needed no escort to direct our feet toward the city towers beckoning beyond the forest of banners and standards all around us.

As we passed the tent where the mysterious visitor had disappeared, I stopped.

'Meroveus, you're dressed for the part. Please go into that tent and ask your Frankish cousins for something, say, a knife sharpener or a bootlace. You lost yours in the games. Memorize the face of every man inside. Meet us behind that mule wagon ahead in five minutes.'

Roxana and I kept going at a brisk pace and then sheltered in the shadows of the mule drivers' little patch of camp. We waited for five minutes, then ten, and longer and longer. Meroveus didn't come back. After about two hours, judging by the camp's routine, we were more than worried. Roxana alerted Grifo. Should we plunge headlong into the tent ourselves?

Something warned me not to be too precipitous. The tent sat quiet and peaceful, identical to its brothers on either side in appearance.

'You've known Meroveus far longer than I,' I said to Roxana. 'What's happened to him?'

'I've never known him to lose a fight,' she said.

Grifo said, 'And if there was any serious disturbance or violence inside, somebody would have noticed by now.'

'We know there're at least two men in there, and probably more. But it's dead quiet.'

'That tent is marked out for something, I'm sure of it,' Grifo said. 'Notice how all the other Cornuti give it a wide berth?'

'So what's he doing inside all this time?'

'I think he's back on duty,' Roxana said, looking me straight in the eye. 'He's found out something worth staying for.'

CHAPTER 20, TWO MEN IN A TENT

—AGRIPPINA, SEPTEMBER 4, 355—

The eight-man tent sat like a boat becalmed in the center of a bustling fleet. A Cornuti *tiro* carried food and drink for at least four men inside. A minute later he emerged, jingling coins in his palm. Grifo tried to strike up a conversation, but the youngster brushed the medical trainee out of his path with a grunt.

Mealtime came and went, but still no Meroveus.

As sunset approached and I'd failed to report to Silvanus as promised, I had no choice but to leave Grifo on watch near the mule station.

At the palace, a self-important new 'imperial aide' told me that Silvanus could give me five minutes, but only after his post-dinner planning session with General Ursicinus.

I would wait in Roxana's quarters rather than risk the sentries who were still keeping Gaudentius and Apodemius pinned down. Grifo and I had agreed that if Meroveus returned, he should join me there to avoid trouble with Gaudentius.

Roxana opened her door, saw that I was alone, and with a worried expression went back to her silent mending. I watched her deft fingers move the darning needle back and forth across a pair of pale blue stockings stretched over a smooth cowry shell.

'Whatever happens, I won't go back to Roma with you,' she said suddenly, breaking the still of the early evening.

'You can't travel alone through Alemanni-infested territory without protection. And you aren't safe here any longer.'

'You may be right, but anywhere but Roma. That's what Arbetio wants. He thinks I won't have anywhere to turn. No matter what you say, I've lost my standing in the *schola*. Now I've shamed myself with a rebel usurper. Arbetio already imagines how he will lord it over me, taunt me, then forgive me with a sneer and—'

She looked wild-eyed into the empty corner of her small room, seeing invisible horrors beckoning.

'So I must choose either a slow death under Paulus Catena's chains and hooks for treason, or Arbetio's humiliating "protection," the rest of my life chained to a man who enjoys cruelty.'

'I told you, Roxana, hide with us in the townhouse in Roma until you find a new life.'

She gave a bitter laugh. 'Shut in like a recluse? I leave that to poor Kahina. Catena would find me sooner or later. The Lord Chamberlain Eusebius would see me as yet another pawn to trade across their table. You know me better than most, Marcus. You know what kind of woman I was.'

I had once lusted after her, admired her, and resented her privileges in the *schola*. That was over now.

She read my thoughts. 'Apodemius thought he had good uses for me, but now it's too late for all that. Nowhere is safe. I can't leave Silvanus. I won't.'

'Roxana, accept the truth. Silvanus has already left you.'

'No!' She shot up off her stool.

There was a tap at the door. Roxana opened it to discover Meroveus hulking in the corridor. She forgot her rage and pulled him inside before anyone spotted him.

He fell back against the door as if his powerful frame could brace it against some pursuing evil.

'Drink?' I handed him a cool beaker half full of *posca*.

'No, I've been fed, watered, and practically fêted until I can hardly stand.'

'Fêted? What's going on in that tent?'

'Assassination—that's what.'

'No, no,' Roxana slumped down on her crumpled bed cushions.

Meroveus had stumbled into the tent and found two Roman officers in conversation. He had thought up a better story than borrowing a knife sharpener.

He had told the two strangers that he'd tipped off someone named Drogo about a juicy bargirl in the city. In exchange Drogo had promised him a pair of leg wrappings in good condition and a second-hand red and gold *orbiculus* to sew on his ragged tunic shirt. Now he couldn't find the man's tent and he was starting to think his new 'friend' Drogo had tricked him.

Meroveus acted short-tempered, then calmed down. The two men in the tent were surprisingly friendly. They didn't seem to mind his interruption. He apologized but accepted a drink.

'So, we three got to talking. Neither one of 'em was Cornuti, that was obvious. They fell into using a few words from the East—you know, Greek words that sneak into a man's talk after a few years out there.'

Roxana nodded. In her anxiety, she pulled at her fancy braids and curls as if they were pesky gnats tormenting her brow. Meroveus took a glug of the *posca* and went on.

The two Romans encouraged him to air his grievances, take a rest, eat a snack, and drink some more. But most of all, they wanted him to talk. Eventually he found it easy to mix truth with fiction. He laced his invented poverty and resentment with genuine bitterness over his fate.

'After half an hour or so, I'd figured out what they were hoping to hear. Two smart officers from the East pretending they were passing the time of day? I convinced them I harbored no love for Silvanus or his new throne. I cooked up a story about my family's loyalty to old Constantine.'

'Did they encourage that line?'

'Oh, yes, Numidianus. They talked of how well Constantine had treated the Frankish *laeti* up here in the old days. How much families like mine owed Constantius.'

'What did you say?' Roxana's hand fidgeted with her darning yarn.

'I begged them to keep my politics a secret from my *contubernales*. After a while, I was anxious to go, but they plied me with another beaker of thick, sweet wine. I still feel sick.'

'What did you mean, assassination?' I glanced over at Roxana who looked too frightened to repeat the word.

'This is their job—to dig up malcontents and low-ranked men no one would notice to do what they called "a little dirty duty for the Empire".'

'To murder Silvanus. And they found what they were looking for?'

'They said they tried the Bracchiati first but someone threatened to report them to the *protectores domestici* here at the palace. So they moved on to the Cornuti camp where they found men easily enough. Dissatisfied veterans, reckless gamblers—you know the type, Numidianus. Hard men who prefer warring and booty to games.'

Meroveus shook his head. He'd long ago learned the high price of being such a man.

'Assassinate Silvanus?' Roxana whispered.

'Yes. They're hiring the men to do it. They set the price with each of us, one by one. None of us is a friend of the others. None of us can say much about the others or even who's hired us. Each of us to be paid separately and in secret afterwards.'

'Afterwards? Who are they?' Roxana gripped the Toxandrian's wrist.

'They had stripped off their insignia. They were careful not to use each other's name.'

'Did one of them have a slice through his ear?'

Meroveus gave a nod.

'Good work. That's Tribune Verenianus. So, that's what Potentius has been up to. Setting up a chain of anonymous assassins who can't be traced to his father even under torture, should things go wrong.'

'And they've been bloody careful,' Meroveus said. 'Must have rotated between the governor's palace, in and out of the camp, because from what I heard, there are never the same two recruiters staying in that tent long enough to be identified.'

'Where do they think you've gone now, Meroveus?' I asked. 'You might have put Grifo in danger if they can trace you to him.'

Meroveus gave a chuckle. 'I told them I went to the latrines.'

'To take the longest shit in Roman history?'

'They've figured out by now that I've run out on them. It'll be a *pugio* between my ribs if I show my face near that tent now.'

'Is a man named Leudast one of them? Did they lend Leudast his gambling stake to put him in their debt? Verenianus marked him out at the games, I remember.'

'Like I said. We don't know them or each other.'

—THE WOLVES OF AMBITION—

'And the plan?'

'I don't know. But it will be something that can't be pinned on them. They talked about "an accident".'

※※※

So now I had something concrete to report to Silvanus. Something as dark as could be, nothing less than the sad confirmation of our suspicions that Ursicinus' capitulation was a ruse. We did not know what lay behind it, however. Was the prostrating General's gambit yet another of Constantius' double games or was the General from the Eastern Army playing his own side without the Emperor's authority?

I knew one thing; Arbetio's whispered encouragement had stuck fast in the resentful General's gut like a lead-weighted *plumbata*—short, sharp and sure. I almost had a chance to ask the formidable man himself, because he nearly spotted me waiting for my audience outside Silvanus' chamber. I ducked out of sight. There was no knowing whether Ursicinus had taken in the faces of the onlookers in the Mediolanum hearing at Constantius' feet. I didn't need to put the man on guard just when I might catch him playing his hand.

'The Emperor will see you now. Five minutes maximum,' the pompous twit at the door told me.

'I'll talk to the "Emperor" for as long as it takes,' I told him.

Silvanus had stripped off his ceremonial armor and cloak during the long meal. He stretched himself out like the finest Roman aristocrat of ancient times, replete with food, drink, and good conversation. Now that Ursicinus had retired, my old acquaintance and I were almost alone.

'Numidianus? I'd forgotten about you.'

'Dismiss your attendants,' I said, 'unless you don't mind them hearing the truth.'

Silvanus' face twitched with displeasure. I hadn't used any form of polite address, much less *Imperator*, *Magister*, or even *Domine*. It took a second or two for the habitual, evenhanded smile on that handsome face to return. He read my expression and sat up straighter, alert to something more important than empty protocol.

'I'm not afraid of my old friend, Commander Gregorius' ex-slave.' He waved away a beefed-up unit of *protectores* and I waited for them to clear the room before I asked him:

'So many fresh guards? Are you afraid of your new comrade-in-arms, General Ursicinus?'

'Hardly. We've just compared notes on Constantius. We agreed that the man is well meaning at heart, sincere in his faith, and tireless in his governance. We also agreed that he is far too easily influenced by malignant, ambitious, and dishonest advisers.'

Silvanus poured himself a nightcap from a goblet of milk-white glass and filigreed gold.

'Clearly Ursicinus trusts me. Why should I be afraid of a fellow officer who fills my ears with sentiments that would be treasonous in Mediolanum? Your *ducenarius* with the big ears would have had a field day if he had heard Ursicinus in his cups tonight.'

'You should be wary, Claudius Silvanus.'

Silvanus laughed and ran his fingers through those thick brown curls grown long to suit his Franco-Roman following. He tossed his head as if to shake off the evening's labors.

'I must have drunk a little too much myself tonight. I have a headache.'

'I am about to make it worse.'

'You *agentes* can be useful, Numidianus, but no one likes your insinuating, slippery, and deceitful double-dealing.'

If ever there was a double-dealer, it was this charmer. He was a man who played the odds, not the principles. When he'd led a defection of thousands of troops that dawn in Mursa and thus doomed Magnentius, my father, and all their fellow military reformers, it was only the result of his coolheaded, final assessment of where his future lay—nothing personal.

I held my temper. After all, he'd been cornered up here in Agrippina.

'You gave me a job. I've done it. Don't you want to hear my report?'

'Yes, of course. You were always clever, Numidianus. Only, you should be far more careful who knows it.'

'One thing first. I demand you lift the detention of Apodemius and *Ducenarius* Gaudentius.'

'No. I know many men who'd like to know that Apodemius has been rendered *nullus*—even temporarily. And Gaudentius caused the death of men I liked, men who meant no harm with their late-night banter. I'm not sure which agent is more dangerous, but if either tries to leave that corridor, they die on my orders.'

'Then I withhold my report.'

'Go ahead. You won't find me the kind of emperor who trembles at every shadow behind the columns.'

'What do you gain by holding Apodemius in detention?'

'Peace of mind—for now.'

'You forget. I hold a hostage of my own.'

'You?'

Silvanus glanced to the left and right of where I stood and chuckled.

'A hostage? Did you steal a house god from the governor's atrium stile? Who is he?' He emptied his goblet.

'Junius.'

Silvanus choked on his wine, spitting it all over the Dionysian revels depicted under our boots.

'You're bluffing, Numidianus. Roxana told me he was safe, and out of Mediolanum.'

'But she didn't tell you where, did she?'

I knew Roxana loved him and perhaps in his way, he still cared for her. They confided in each other. So I had been sure not to tell Roxana where Junius hid.

'So release my colleagues and issue us *evecti diplomatae* to get us safely down the *Cursus* through the territory your troops now control.'

'I know you, Numidianus. You wouldn't harm my boy. That's not in your character.' Silvanus allowed himself an uneasy chuckle.

'I would never harm him myself. But he's still a runaway hostage of the Roman throne. Duty dictates I report his whereabouts to Consul Arbetio. And you know Arbetio's reputation—or ought to by now.'

He was no longer reclining like a satiated god, but up on his feet, his right hand drawing an imperial ceremonial *spatha* I'd never seen before. It had been welded by a skilled Frank with a knack for twisted patterns but was never intended for battle.

He laid its point on my throat. 'Where is my son, you bastard! I can torture it out of you!'

'And that's not in *your* character, General. Pride has made you stupid, but not that stupid. Torture me, you lose your boy forever.'

We heard footsteps on the flagstones. I twisted away from Silvanus' blade to see Evochildis standing in the archway leading from the dining room toward her wing.

'Put your sword down,' she told Silvanus. 'This *agens* only serves the Empire, as do we, isn't that right, *Imperator*? Give us your full report, *Biarchus* Numidianus.'

'Yes, *Matrona*. Thank you.' I knelt on one knee, only because it was such an easy way to please the vindictive bitch and keep her attention on my warning.

'Potentius rotates his *protectores*—Verenianus is one—to sit in the army camp in pairs until they find enough men willing to kill you for a bribe. They tried to hire my Toxandrian who escaped detention some days ago in search for his son, a medical trainee with the Cornuti.'

'I've noticed Potentius' absence from time to time over the last few days,' Silvanus said to his mother. 'One or two of their party is always missing from our meetings, but I never thought much of it.'

'It's too ridiculous,' Evochildis scoffed.

'When will they attempt this crime?' Silvanus was not so skeptical. He knew he claimed no monopoly on turning coat.

'Any time now. They might have as many as half a dozen signed up.'

'And where?' Silvanus listened hard now.

'We don't know.'

Evochildis lifted her long skirts as if I were vermin to be kicked away. 'Don't believe any of it. It's another trick to lure you to Paulus Catena's barbed claws and burning rods in Mediolanum.'

'Who volunteered? Silvanus asked. 'Their names? We'll haul them in. Make an example of them,' His eyes had gone blurry.

'Lowlife. The restless and the greedy.'

I didn't explain my debt to the sporting Leudast's unmatchable axe skills, nor to the reluctance of his fellow Rathar to abandon the leadership of the Constantines out of generations of loyalty. Silvanus would have no time for the politics of lowly scouts.

'They cheered me,' he said to his mother. 'Thousands, they all cheered. They were in such a rush, they draped me with shreds of purple drapery and pennants and acclaimed me.'

'Leave with us now for Mediolanum. Ride south with us tonight. Clasp the Emperor's letter in which he commands you to relinquish all this to your heart. Forget this suicidal imperial pose.'

I gestured at the elaborate trappings abandoned in haste by the governor in his flight from the Alemanni raiders.

'You would not be the first occupant of this palace to come to his senses. You are trapped in a nightmare. Wake yourself up, General!'

I saw his resistance was weakening and pressed on:

'Bring Roxana, your mother, and anyone else who needs protection from Ursicinus—Laniogaisus, Bainobaudes, Proculus, and all the others who serve you with honor. But do not delay any longer.'

'Letter? That's right. In the excitement of his prostration, he never gave me Constantius' letter.' Silvanus looked at his mother.

'I carry Constantius' personal assurance to you, General.'

My words made him waver.

He had not been emperor for even one full month. He'd enjoyed his taste of independence from Constantius, the thundering of shields in his name and the clamorous parades.

'No. No!' Evochildis turned her son away from me. 'There is nothing for us in Mediolanum but more Roman tricks and traps—all lies. You said it yourself tonight to Ursicinus, did you not? You two agreed you have all good reason to take things ill. While unworthy men are raised to the consulship and to other high positions, both Ursicinus and you have survived many dangers, only to be scorned by Constantius.'

'But Constantius himself has written his offer and even sent this *agens* to reassure me that—'

'And tonight, my son—and not for the first time since he arrived and laid himself at your feet—General Ursicinus said that you had been cruelly harassed in an unworthy controversy through the interrogation and arrest of your friends and summoned to trial for treason by that Apodemius. Did he not say that again, tonight?'

Silvanus pointed to me and said, 'If there's evidence that Ursicinus is setting his own trap—?'

'—while he himself, the greatest general defending us against the Persians was summarily called back from the East to be exposed to the hatred of those *consistoriani* cowards? Did he not complain of this himself to you, tonight?' Evochildis' shrill voice drilled home her suspicions.

Silvanus said, 'Whom should I believe?'

'My son, you think this is the same general who intends to kill you?'

Silvanus stared down at the mosaic figures gamboling across the floor.

'I hold Constantius under obligation, through gratitude for my coming to his side with my soldiers in Mursa.' His voice faltered. 'Yet the Emperor is variable and uncertain.'

I rose off my knee and tossed aside any further pretense at respect.

'It is you, Claudius Silvanus, who is variable and uncertain. You are vacillating and indecisive. Steady in battle, resolute in rebellion, but now—like a *draco* flapping this way and that in the winds of flattery.'

'Why should I trust an African freedman more than the Empire's greatest defender of the East? Why should I listen to you rather than my own mother?'

'Because my mother warned me against stubborn vanity,' I answered. 'But then, she was the daughter of a civilized colonial farmer, not some axe-throwing savage from the German forest.'

—THE WOLVES OF AMBITION—

Evochildis picked up the white goblet and threw it at my head. Its ghost-white glass shattered on the doorjamb behind my head.

'I have nothing more to report, General. I will prepare the *Magister Agentium in Rebus* and the other two *agentes* to leave Agrippina tomorrow morning. Proculus can provide us with a strong and fast carriage. I've implored Roxana to go with us for her own safety. For the sake of all that we two have shared since the days of Magnentius, I implore you to make Roxana come with us.'

At this, Evochildis threw her head back. Her eyes shone with triumph. 'What did I tell you? Yes! In the end, that woman is just another spy, like all you *agentes*. You take no sides but you stick to each other. You answer to whom? To what? You just spread your tales, and then you all fly out the gate to visit your next hornets' nest of trouble.'

She was soaring now on a windstream of hatred.

'Take her with you! With my blessing, take the Roman *curiosa* whore! And after she's gone, we'll scrub her rooms clean until there's not a hairpin or a fleck of powder left!'

There was no way I could avoid telling Roxana that I had failed for the third and final time to get Silvanus to meet the challenge of his enemies at Constantius' court. I'd never seen her look so angry as when I repeated Evochildis' curse. But it brought out my Roxana of old, my Castra student rival, armed and trained for battle, no matter how underhanded or treacherous.

She'd found her fighting will again. I rejoiced to think she would leave this Frankish fortress for Roma.

I was wrong.

Roxana clenched her fist. 'Sentries are not enough. A cohort would not be enough. They try to kill him, they kill me first.'

Chapter 21, A Barbarian at Prayer

—September 5, 355 AD—

Before dawn the next day, an 'imperial' aide appeared at Apodemius' door. As Silvanus' Magister Officiorum, Laniogaisus had issued road papers guaranteeing five agentes safe passage down the Cursus Publicus controlled by the Emperor Silvanus.

In effect, we were now free, even ordered, to leave for Roma. That included the maligned Roxana. When I went to give Roxana her *diploma*, she stayed behind her bolted door and refused to open or even speak to me.

Gaudentius was already shaved and packed, his boots laced, and helmet cleaned.

Apodemius was finally back on his arthritic feet, no less swollen than before his dangerous illness. At least his featherlight figure meant there was less weight for those wobbly ankles to bear. His wool traveling tunic had been bleached back to ivory and his travel cloak brushed smooth. A slave had trimmed his frothy white hair to within half an inch of his bony scalp.

'I can accept Meroveus' resignation,' he sighed, 'although it means searching hard for another *agens* to fill his shoes. He's been an excellent addition to our *Germani* team. He had shared his Toxandrian dialect with the language instructors, as well as his knowledge of Eastern court politics under the domination of those eunuchs.'

'He'll be relieved to know he has your blessing to stay behind, *Magister*.'

He laid a bony hand on my shoulder. 'So do you, Numidianus.'

'*Magister*?' I'd already finished bundling up my few things.

'Did you think we would just turn our backs on this political disaster?'

'I'm sorry, *Magister*. I should have known.'

'Gaudentius will accompany me only as far as Count Maudio's estate. His family offered to receive me in the worst throes of my illness and now I wish to thank them. In this case, thanking them means imposing on their hospitality and lurking in their peristyle garden while you continue this mission with Meroveus' help.'

'So you will stay within a few hours' reach?'

'Better Silvanus thinks me gone. We cannot make the journey to Roma safely without you two and it isn't a propitious time to take leave of this drama. After all, if Ursicinus does intend something devious, he's more likely to play the last act if he believes that the *Magister Agentium in Rebus*, however feeble, has left the theater altogether.'

'My presence will displease Silvanus.'

'And alert anyone else planning malfeasance. Silvanus is not to know. Lie low and watch. You're good enough at watching, Numidianus, but not so talented at lying low. Swallow your showoff tendencies for once.'

'I'll do my best, but how does one watch out for "an accident"?'

'I only wish we knew.'

⚜⚜⚜

For the benefit of the sentries and any other officials monitoring us, Meroveus and I made a public show of saddling up behind Gaudentius and the sturdy carriage carrying Apodemius.

We rode in procession out the inner gates dividing the residential buildings from the main office building of the governor's palace and then slowly turned right down the wide boulevard leading out of Agrippina. By the first pinkish light creeping up over the wide, gray river, we trotted passed the sleeping city apartments and exited the southeastern outer gates toward Bonna.

—THE WOLVES OF AMBITION—

The vast spread of army encampment on our right was already busy with pre-dawn routine. It was a disciplined hustle and bustle that had been repeating hundreds of times over for hours already, arriving with the sun itself as it spread its rays across the vast Empire all the way from the Persian front.

Thousands of Roman soldiers of all languages, appearances, and faiths summoned to Agrippina were exercising, eating, repairing their equipment, tending their animals, and busying themselves with all the other tasks of keeping fighting ready.

We rode slowly for the sake of Apodemius' painful joints and it was almost an hour before I could say that the subdued rumble of so many officers' commands and the smoky breakfast fires of the assembled troops had fallen away behind us.

At Bonna, we heard that the bridge across the Mosella at Confluentes stood repaired. The fortress gates were open again. The *riparienses* at the garrison there shared what they had to eat and drink and updated us on the conditions farther to the south.

Meroveus and I turned around at this point. We left the state road and took an unpaved track used by anyone without access to a permit. We attached ourselves to a lumbering convoy of traders' wagons delivering freshly harvested vegetables. I swallowed my impatience at their plodding pace. We wanted no one to remark on a pair of *agentes* racing pell-mell back to the provincial capital.

We slipped back into Agrippina by the rear gates after nightfall. There was only one safe place to go first. But when she saw opened her door to our faces, Guntheuca scowled.

'I have patients to care for, much work to do. Why don't you two bury yourselves in that army camp where you belong?'

'Because so many of the ranks know Meroveus' face, especially the soldiers around Grifo's tent,' I said. 'Don't worry, we're not staying long.'

And so we set up our watch. I dispatched Guntheuca to tell Roxana that we needed smuggling into the palace somehow, but not to inform Silvanus of our 'disobedient' return. To ensure we could count on her discretion, we layered our message with warnings that Silvanus' life depended on keeping our presence secret.

I disguised myself in borrowed Frankish trousers under a ragged tunic with embroidery that looked like it had travelled more miles than Alexander the Great. Guntheuca darkened my bronze curls with some herb-soaked potion guaranteed to cover any lady's gray hair. To merely smell it was to pity ageing women.

Meroveus changed out of his *agens* tunic and with a sigh of regret, shaved off all his telltale red stubble yet again. His stark white scalp gleamed by the flickering light of Guntheuca's humble pottery lamp.

Thanks to Roxana's well-placed bribes and Meroveus' convincing curses in thick dialect, we went to work a few hours later with stolen *domestici* insignia fastened to our shabby tunics. I had picked up a few words of Franconian over the previous days and now I dropped the odd *geben* and *haben* into my stilted Latin phrases. Our situation was hardly ideal but at least we were moving undetected inside the palace walls.

Meroveus and I resolved to keep our distance from each other from then on. It was important we not be caught conferring. We grabbed the first tasks at hand that helped us keep tabs on the movements of the inner circles of both generals.

We came and went for hours on end, never stopping for meals or rest that first day. Like all slaves, we became two faceless nobodies, visibly burdened and bent low by one obvious chore or another whenever we crossed paths with an officer or courtier.

It was particularly gratifying to me a few hours into the first day working the residential wing to roll a cart overloaded with stinking chamber pots right past the haughty Clothild. She lifted her heavy skirts, turned her delicate nose away from my foul presence, and hastened out of my path.

A moment later, she deigned to speak to Roxana at a bend in my route. Trained by the best, Roxana looked right through me. I kept on rolling.

For all our efforts, at the end of a sixteen-hour stint, Meroveus and I had learned nothing. From the kitchen to the dining room, while rounding corners behind carts of dirty linens past the residential chambers, or clearing away the conference room debris from a working meal, all seemed well.

But after midnight, as the palace slept, Roxana confided to me the inner thoughts of the ladies at court. She knew for certain that Evochildis had started counting the heads of Ursicinus' delegation herself, despite her avowed confidence in their

—THE WOLVES OF AMBITION—

celebrated new ally. The canny old woman had noticed the odd disappearance of first one deputy, then another.

Evochildis' watchfulness was not necessarily a good thing. Subjected to sudden scrutiny down the banquet table or on the parade ground podium, Ursicinus' plotters might realize they'd been rumbled.

Once we were keeping such close count, the consistency with which Ursicinus kept two men rotating in and out the camp beyond the city walls became obvious.

I had suspected their purpose was to keep their possible recruits among the army riffraff uncertain as the identity of the ringleader.

Now another reason occurred to me and it was equally sinister. No one in a conspiracy was safe from Catena's claws and chains unless every last man was too implicated to betray his co-plotters.

Emperor Silvanus' new *comitatus* had sat until after midnight and yet they rose again at dawn to begin planning anew. The freshest hours of that September day passed as Silvanus and Ursicinus resumed their close conference in the private reception room.

As I trundled the linen mountains this way and that, the two generals' respective staffs hurried past me. Before midday, I glimpsed Potentius waiting for a scribe who came scurrying down the main corridor toward him, his obedient arms overflowing with scrolls and messages. Verenianus kept Proculus busy reviewing the correspondence with arms factories and mints in the region, though no coin had been issued in Silvanus name so far. Perhaps the mint authorities were playing for time. They knew that once a *solidus* bore Silvanus' dashing profile, there was no turning back for northern Gallia.

Laundry duty was certainly no casual pastime, for all the minutes I spent listening and spying. Evochildis and her dozen favorites had taken up changing into ever more elaborate garments as the ostentation and formality of the costumes and meals grew to match the decorum and presumption of their new court.

Constantius must have realized by now that Silvanus had let the door of 'forgiveness' slam in his expressionless face. The general had not arrived in Mediolanum to join the *consistorium* and thus, Ursicinus had not been handed sole command of the Western Army as the new *Magister Militum per Gallias*.

Yet so far we heard no warnings of Constantius marching north. The atmosphere of excitation and nerves permeating every public room of the palace told me that the two generals felt the urgency of their situation. There was only so long one could feed and supply the bulk of the Western Army from one location, especially a region as hard hit by barbarian pillage over the last year as the northeastern provinces of Gallia.

Riding back up with Meroveus to Agrippina, we had seen that the common roads were besieged with begging widows and their hungry children. The market convoys told us of the strain the army's stomach put on this year's slim harvest.

On the second day of our secret vigil, Meroveus and I noticed nothing suspicious. We considered switching our posts over to the kitchen, but if an accident was to befall Silvanus, we had already ruled out an obvious poisoning. Silvanus had an official taster now, as befitted a Roman emperor of ancient times.

We listened, we watched, and we moved as stealthily as possible, emptying braziers, beeswaxing tables, scrubbing floors, trimming wicks, tamping and relighting lamps, cleaning the muck out of wall sconces—all without a single break. I began to know the crud and stench of the governor's residence as well as I knew the mustier corners of the Manlius villa and slaving there had been downright leisurely compared to the demands of this rundown palace.

What were we missing? Where was the 'accident' to take place? Verenianus, Potentius, that scribbling adjutant Ammianus, and the rest of the Mediolanum delegation all turned up sooner or later at regular hours, answering open summons, and debating in public what their next move should be.

I knew from my days as a youngster in Roma that people only noticed nervous servants, incompetent slaves, and prying underlings. Meroveus had done his time as a bodyguard for no less than the *Augusta* Constantia in Antiochia. He was equally adept at keeping shoulders hunched, head bowed, and eyes on his task.

—THE WOLVES OF AMBITION—

By the second night, we were exhausted, as if we'd marched fast-pace across the whole of Illyria. We treated ourselves to a surreptitious soak in the city baths for twenty minutes to compare notes in the fuggy anonymity of the *caldarium*.

'Nothing.' Meroveus wiped off his dripping pate. That red stubble would be poking back up again within the week.

'Nothing.' I sluiced off my torso from a bucket of fresh water. 'If anything, Ursicinus is more privy to Silvanus' intentions than Laniogaisus or the mother. The two heroes are inseparable.'

'But I wasn't the only one they tried to recruit. I heard what I heard. Something was afoot.'

'But so far, all they do is hold meetings, eat, and then watch the army exercise.'

'No,' Meroveus gave me a sharp glance. 'Ursicinus has invited all the leading officers to a stag hunt tomorrow morning, followed by a midday feast in the forest out beyond the camp.'

'That's a change. How many hunters does that make, you reckon? Two hundred?'

Meroveus nodded. 'Ample confusion in which anything might happen.' His honest green eyes peered into mine through the steam. 'Even an accident. What do we do?'

'I've already warned Silvanus. It must have occurred to him that it's an unusual time for something so recreational.'

'All I know is, they're getting everything ready for the hunting feast in the kitchens.'

'Why go hunting now? Unless Ursicinus proposes it as a last event before re-distributing the troops back across the provinces to secure Gallic territory? Constantius' forces might appear on the southern horizon at any minute.'

We repaired back to the vestibule off the gymnasium and reclaimed our clothes from the cloakroom boys for a small ransom in bronze coin.

We were leaving just in time. Proculus' scrawny shoulders bobbed against the rim of the central pool as the adjutant made small talk with a fat city bureaucrat I'd seen coming and going for meetings. The adjutant's arm was healing well, but he wisely kept it dry, resting it on the rim of the basin.

I pulled Meroveus into the shadows of the tall columns. We both tossed towels over our heads and shoulders. Proculus might be undersized, but he had quick wits. No bald Meroveus with a hairy red chest or dyed Numidianus would fool him up close.

When our final duties of the night were done and the palace again fell silent, I slipped off to Roxana's wing. There had been nights in the past when I would have been sure to discover Silvanus in her ardent embrace. Now she opened the door to my whisper and stood there, alone and forgotten, wearing the thinnest of tunics in the fading evening heat.

'Warn Silvanus about this hunt on for tomorrow. If there were to be some kind of accident, what could be a better setting?'

She smiled a fraction of a second with a knowing nod. 'Silvanus may not have taken all your advice, but your warning didn't go unheeded. He intends to beg off the hunt at the last minute for reasons of overwork. He and I will attend a dawn service in his chapel, well guarded by trusted sentries.'

'I'm relieved to hear it, for your sake. Goodnight, Roxana.'

She brushed her familiar lips on my cheek with a light kiss. I knew her heavy perfumes of old, irresistible unguents for professional seduction. Now there was only the faint scent of rose bath oil.

I slept ill that night on a thin, filthy pallet in the back of the kitchen. I lay among a hundred others, both men and women, tossing, turning, snoring, and sneezing in their miserable places on the floor in the meanest of servants' quarters.

Those who had more comfortable private hovels or shelters in the city had fled until dawn recalled them to their duties. Others had nowhere to go. They came from prisoner ranks of Alemanni or Franks from across the river or had pitched up from Gallic villages razed to ashes by recent warfare.

Nothing in these back halls was fit for even such unfortunates as these. The chamber pots were overflowing onto the tiles. How far we were from the ritualized Eastern comforts of Constantius' vast imperial household in Mediolanum! Over the long centuries since the founding of this garrison town, each Roman governor of Colonia Claudia Ara Agrippinensium had obviously considered his tenure as too temporary to give a Hercules' Hair how his attendants subsisted.

—THE WOLVES OF AMBITION—

For all her northern roots, Evochildis, the *matrona* of this establishment, apparently held herself aloof and indifferent to their pitiful condition.

How different *Matrona* Evochildis was from the late Lady Laetitia, Commander Gregorius' invalid wife back in the Manlius' great days. How carefully Laetitia had tended to the needs of her slaves, both before and after her conversion to Christianity. Even during her own lingering sickness, she had nursed them back to health. She had watched and listened for signs of unhappiness or need. In the end, the only person she could not make content was her former rival in love, my own enslaved mother, a seamstress in the back rooms of the townhouse.

There were, I thought bitterly, certain values of our great Roma that even garnet-crusted Franco-Roman 'nobility' with their grandiose tapestry work hadn't yet absorbed.

Meroveus was lost to me in this chaos of sub-humanity. I shut out the unpleasant crush of bodies and noises and closed my eyes. I tried to imagine what violent and unexpected misfortune was being set up for Silvanus even as I lay there powerless to stop it.

I finally abandoned sleep and returned my lice-infested matting to the slaves' storeroom. I would wait and watch—exactly as I'd promised Apodemius, for the convening of Ursicinus' hunting guests.

I climbed the stone steps up the side of the outer city wall overlooking the southern gates. Below me, sentries unbolted and swung open the great oak barriers to the new day. Within a few minutes of my settling down at an archer's spot, undetected and unsuspected, stable hands and soldiers arrived from all directions through the gloom and shadows of the fading night.

Then came the clop of hooves and jingle of harness disks. Infantrymen arrived from the depths of the army camp leading muscular warrior steeds. The night's torchlights caught the glint of precious stones embedded into the breast pieces of the better grade horses. From underneath where I hid, prize procession champions exited the city to wait for their imperial riders to emerge.

There was something fantastical about it, something almost mythical to my eyes, burning for lack of sleep. Hundreds of horses now snorted and stomped for their riders who were still dressing or breakfasting in tents and palace chambers. While miserable men and women slaves rose up in their stained day clothes near pools of their own urine, these curry-combed champions preened like Olympian mounts.

One by one, the hunting guests arrived, followed by lieutenants, aides, adjutants, and attendants. They started choosing their weapons for the hunt—bows, all varieties of spears, javelins or angons, axes and swords. One or two of the men had obviously breakfasted on a little more wine than usual. Boisterous greetings, sleepy mutterings, and impatient orders broke the stillness of the dawn. The morning sky lightened to reveal a cool September morning of fresh breezes and clear vistas. a few trees lining the horizon were turning yellow and red.

Autumn was coming. More than a thousand miles from where I crouched against the stone parapet, members of Roman society were returning from seaside resorts or cool hillside estates to assume their urban *personae* and responsibilities for another year. I remembered Leo's appeal to me in that painstaking letter pleading that I return in time to tell him what I thought of the friendship between his teacher and his mother.

Instead, I'd failed to answer the earnest child. A wedding would be scheduled any day now.

Even if the Rhenus postal links were now suspended by political uncertainty, I could have replied somehow. Surely if I had tried harder, I could have managed to get him a note, routed west to Treverorum and then safely down the secured central *Cursus* to the south?

I dropped my head onto my arms with despair.

There was a fresh commotion below—warning shouts and the pounding of boots.

I looked down just as Ursicinus passed through the gates underneath me and emerged outside.

Of course, there was still no sign of Silvanus. Mounted and ready, impatient, and proud, General Ursicinus asked the other officers where 'the Emperor' was keeping himself. The staff replied they were expecting him any minute.

—THE WOLVES OF AMBITION—

Proculus came running through the gates, directly underneath my crouching form. He darted between the dozens of horses blocking his path to find the scowling 'Hero of the East.'

As neat as a messenger in a Greek play, Proculus conveyed Emperor Silvanus' excuses on cue. The leaders of the outing inched their horses closer to hear the apology. Laniogaisus, Bainobaudes, and so many of the Franco-Roman contingent tossed their long hair and wheeled their powerful horses around and around in tight circles with visible disappointment. It was the Frankish officers' hope to best the visiting *tribuni* in the hunt's test of skill. This was, after all, their home territory. Who knew better the ways of the beasts than these sons and grandsons of the barbarian forest who still decked themselves out in horns and furs in spiritual harmony with them?

I named to myself each of the officers at Ursicinus' side. I watched them test their weapons—bows, spears, angons, and axes—any of them could fell even an emperor from an anonymous distance.

Something in this scene was troubling but, as often happens, the inner mind perceived something before my eyes understood. As soon as I realized what it was, I did not let myself believe it.

I checked again.

For, as I numbered the members of the Mediolanum delegation—man-by-man, uniform-by-uniform, horse-by-horse—I realized with a chill that what looked correct and even more than proper was exactly what was *wrong*.

For the first time since the night they arrived, every one of Ursicinus' staff was present and accounted for. Each man in his contingent would have an alibi and a witness for this moment and place. Under questioning, each officer could prove by the testimony of his fellow Roman that he was there, innocent and oblivious to—what was happening?

Meroveus had left the conspirators' circle far too soon. There had been a change of plan. There was no 'accident' in the works. Ursicinus' plot depended on a diabolical trick.

The irony had hit me too late. The 'stag hunt' had never been merely recreational, true. But they would bag a boar or stag while the true prey—Claudius Silvanus—was stalked at home.

Ursicinus had realized Evochildis and Silvanus suspected him. He had counted on Silvanus to beg off this morning.

It was the surest way to get Silvanus alone while all the Romans sported at a safe distance in the forest. All that remained was for the real 'hunting party' led by Leudast to corner its prey in his habitual retreat, the chapel.

Stumbling down the ladder running the back of the wall, I dashed to the ground and crossed the parade ground in less than a minute to warn Roxana. I reached her chamber with a chest practically bursting, my gasps throwing me against her door.

Unbolted, it swung open, pitching me into her empty room. There was nothing for me there but my *pugio* and *spatha* hidden under her mattress. I grabbed Meroveus' weapons as well. Servants and slaves didn't cart around chamber pots fully armed.

It took another precious few minutes for me to return at full tilt across the parade ground and to the back of the main building and to scramble across dozen upon dozens of sleeping servants until I located Meroveus.

I pulled him, still asleep, straight up off the floor.

'Take these. Get up. It's happening.'

He followed me as fast as he could through the daze of sleep.

The governor's chapel stood to the side of the main building, annexed by a narrow, windowless corridor leading off the most elaborate of the public reception rooms.

We got to the entrance of this long passage just as a soul-freezing shriek rang out, reverberated along the marble walls ahead, and echoed in our ears.

We were seconds too late. The third of a trio of sentries was the only one still on his feet. He was staring straight at us, grasping with futile fingers at a gaping wound in his chest spurting blood all over his boots. The blade had slashed deep into a heart beating its last right in our faces. His attacker had opened the man right up when he retrieved his *francisca*.

We sprang over his two dead fellows.

The scene before us was like a nightmarish mural painted in shades of danger and death. Only instants before, Roxana and Silvanus must have knelt side by side on cushions set at the foot of the granite altar. They looked like a frieze depicting a marriage ceremony cruelly interrupted. They were scrambling to their feet as the robes of the priest administering the Christian sacrament could be seen fleeing behind the altar for a rear exit.

Five men blocked our path to Silvanus and Roxana. I couldn't make out their features under their gear. As Meroveus rushed ahead of me, he greeted one of them by name.

The killer hadn't yet identified me. He assumed Meroveus was one of them. He gestured at Roxana. 'We'd given you up. Get the bitch out of the way.'

Silvanus and Roxana retreated up the steps to the broad altar. He shielded Roxana with his body, pinning her to the granite table with his back as he drew his sword—not his sturdy weapon blooded by years in the field, but that decorative showpiece.

He took on the two lead attackers, fighting both at once. Although he could hold them off for a moment or two, I knew they were fitter and faster than their 'Emperor.'

'Get out,' Silvanus shouted to Roxana.

Meroveus rounded on the third man, the conspirator who'd hailed him as an ally only seconds before. He rammed the startled assassin straight through his stomach. The Toxandrian recovered his blade in time to square off with the fourth of the men, who seemed undecided how to finish his powerful assailant before reinforcing his fellows at the altar.

The next surprise was mine. With a growl, the fifth and fiercest-looking of them turned and greeted me as 'friend.' I lifted my sword in defense and my blade clashed against the weapon wielded by Leudast, none other than my savior from the maddened wolf.

Startled, he jumped back and took his first swing at me, missing by several inches, but not before his eyes met mine.

There was no negotiating this fight, no matter how much I owed the scout. One toss of that axe in his left hand would bring me down, bleeding to death on the floor. It's vicious axehead dripped with the blood of the last sentry lying outside the chapel entrance.

The man fighting Meroveus darted around Leudast and tried to come at me from my left side while Leudast threatened me from the front. Meroveus swung around to the altar to pick off Silvanus' attackers and free the General.

A cry from the man coming up from behind Leudast to a gurgle as a blade from behind sliced deep into his neck just below his cheek guard. It loosed his skull from his neck bone. Nearly decapitated, the rest of his torso slumped, tumbling forward into Leudast's back. I used that instant to try for a final thrust at the scout, but he pulled clear of me in time.

But it wasn't Meroveus that had felled the dead man whose head now lolled on the stones.

Standing behind the fallen soldier, with the bloodied blade of Meroveus' first victim in her hands, was the one combatant no man had counted into this fray—the Fury Roxana, trained to the highest standards of combat at the Castra Peregrina.

Silvanus cried out behind her. His glorious imperial sword clattered down the altar steps. Roxana swung around to join Meroveus to defend him.

I wasn't stopping to see how badly Silvanus had been hurt. Meroveus and Roxana could hold off two assailants for a time and the General's shriek from the base of the altar gave me a crucial second as Leudast glanced away from me. The scout hoped his fellows had killed their prime target already and could make their getaway. That tiny break in his focus gave me the instant to thrust my sword upwards and graze his left inner thigh.

He rounded on me with his axe, lifting it high to take off my arm through the left shoulder joint. I dodged its downward path but it caught my armor padding, slicing off a chunk of thick wadding, but missing my flesh. While his right arm was still on the downswing, I had swiveled and rammed my boot right into his groin, the kind of ungallant defense that Castra spies needed more often than field weapons.

His eyes bulged out and he folded over in agony.

Leudast was out for now. Three were dead. Leaving Meroveus to finish off the last attacker, Roxana fell to her knees to tend to Silvanus. He was bleeding heavily onto the base of the altar. His right arm was sliced so deep to the bone, I wasn't sure he would keep it.

The Toxandrian had lost the slight advantage he'd enjoyed with his feint of friendliness. Despite his height and skill, he was up against a skilled soldier ten years younger who was determined to eliminate him before finishing off Silvanus. I came at the man

—THE WOLVES OF AMBITION—

from behind, but he was too quick and seemed to almost relish fighting both Meroveus and myself at the same time.

Roxana was trying to get Silvanus off the altar and to safety. She lifted him into her arms, as heavy as he was, releasing a river of blood streaming over her robe. The ferocious fighter in her had given in to wails of horror. She had almost got Silvanus back on his feet. The two of them were inching past Meroveus, trying to move back down the chapel toward the spot where the sentries lay.

But Leudast had revived. Limping on his wounded thigh, he lunged at them. I turned to tackle him and missed. There was an awful sound behind me as Meroveus lost his duel with the younger man and dropped to his knees, an axe protruding from his stomach.

I had only seconds to insert myself between Leudast and his fleeing targets.

He seized his chance and took a powerful swing into Roxana's hip. I had no time to think. I could save Silvanus or Roxana—but not both.

I dodged between Roxana and Leudast's sword and yanked her away from Silvanus. Without a pause, Leudast swiveled and ran his sword across Silvanus' waist. With an expression I hope never to see again, he sawed at the great commander's torso, like a butcher taking off a choice cut. Silvanus dropped his sword.

Roxana screamed. She clutched her bleeding hip and hobbled out of the chapel as fast as she could. Her shrieks resounded all the way down the marble corridor.

Leudast tossed me a cruel, sportsman's smile before making off behind the altar in the direction taken by the priest.

I crouched over Meroveus, sprawled across the blood-soaked kneeling cushions. I lifted him into my arms and whispered, '*Maltho thi afrio lito*. I free you, you who are half-free.'

He forced a smile. His eyes flickered. Then his breathing stopped. The noble Toxandrian soldier was, at last, truly free.

The sun had hardly risen. The crime had taken no more than five minutes. News of the chapel massacre sped through the governor's palace. A wait echoed across the parade ground from the open windows of Evochildis' wing, joined by the screams and shrieks of her female court.

In a daze, I stumbled after Roxana. When the trail of blood left by her dragging skirts petered out, I bribed servants from one end of the palace to the other to find her.

She would not turn to Evochildis for comfort—that much I knew. Where had she fled?

At last I found Proculus, the only officer not riding through the sylvan paradise after some innocent stag.

I grabbed the adjutant by his bony shoulder and begged him, 'Roxana? Where is she?'

Of all the men on Silvanus' staff, Proculus had always respected Roxana most. The bloody events of the morning had rendered him paler than the marble walls.

He seized my bloodied tunic with trembling hands and said, 'Hidden in my chamber. Find that healer woman, wherever she is. The Lady Roxana has poisoned herself.'

Chapter 22, The Mastery of Dreams

—September 8, 355 AD—

The news of Silvanus' death flew across the countryside on the freshening autumn winds blowing lifeless leaves underfoot. The wailing of women, highborn and low, never seemed to die down.

Apodemius and Gaudentius arrived from Count Maudio's estate late the next evening to find me keeping vigil at Roxana's bedside. Still in her bloodstained robe, she was scarcely breathing.

Leudast had taken a deep slice into her across the softest part of her left hip. It took Guntheuca three tries with layers upon layers of fresh-bleached linen to slow the streaming blood. I knew how an army medic would have sewn Roxana up, using boiled tools drenched in acetum to stave off the foulness that could cost a wounded soldier a leg, even weeks after battle.

But I knew better than to tell the crone what to do. I watched the Frankish healer work with her foreign treatments. She bound a foul-smelling plaster of black-brown herbal paste around my friend's wound, discoloring the pale skin over thick crusts of blood.

Guntheuca took Roxana's pulse again, and shook her head. 'We should have taken those berries away. I worried how she might use them but this was not what I feared.'

I took Roxana's limp, white hand in mine. She was wearing a blood-colored ring—red garnets fastened to a silver band—no doubt a gift from Silvanus.

Guntheuca saw me hold the limp hand with tenderness.

'*Matrona* Roxana favored few men with her conversation or time. You became friends with this lady as soon as you arrived.

How did you worm yourself so quickly into her trust? Brought her news from home? Some gift from a sister?'

'Friends? Oh, old woman, you have no idea how long it took Roxana and myself to become mere friends—years and years.'

At this the *Magister* gave a knowing sniff. How many years ago had he pitted the skills of his female agent against his clumsier Numidian decoy agent to the *schola*'s advantage?

Confused by this, Guntheuca was silent some minutes. Then she said, 'I am sorry to see her come to this. She was brave, lonely, and loving.'

Roxana's bandages were soaked through again, the dark red blood pooling across the linen.

'How bad is she?' Apodemius asked.

'I saw one other case of poisoning like this. First there were violent shakings and a racing heartbeat. Then came a complete collapse. Finally the heart stops. She has lost much blood and is weak.'

'I saw no tremors,' I said. 'Her pulse is slow. She's so quiet. How much longer?'

'Not long now. I tried to counter the poison, but no potion could bring it up.'

I'd found two or three of the wrinkled, reddish berries in the bottom of Roxana's small belt purse. I weighed them in my bloodstained palm. How harmless they looked, but I knew their power, remembering the dead wolf corpses full of ground yew.

Gaudentius interrupted our vigil, already dressed in full travel outfit.

'We must quit Agrippina again soon,' he muttered to Apodemius. 'Thanks to Numidianus, we have seen and heard too much for Ursicinus' liking.'

Gaudentius would have left town already. He was keen to be at Apodemius' side when the *Magister* reported our official version to Constantius and then be done with this messy affair.

Our journey would be a slow one. Apodemius was still not strong enough to use a saddle. And I clung to the hope that Roxana would survive and ride south in a carriage at his side.

The *ducenarius* had never liked the idea of a female *agens*. Even worse, he resented her reputation, which only grew in Castra circles the longer she'd been retired from active service.

—THE WOLVES OF AMBITION—

She'd outwitted and outfought most of her fellow students. She'd been an agent, even a double agent, and never once had she been caught failing in her mission, whatever it was. No one had ever doubted her intelligence or courage.

Gaudentius was clawing his way to the top of the *schola* and he didn't like any competition, even retired. His narrow eyes told me he would enjoy leaving Roxana to a nameless burial under the wrathful supervision of the devastated Evochildis.

As usual, Apodemius' thoughts were impossible to read. His gaze roved up and down Guntheuca's motionless patient—the woman he called his 'failed experiment.'

'I say, we leave the slut here and get to Mediolanum before Ursicinus,' Gaudentius said. 'Only a show of false condolence holds the general here. Such formalities will be over soon enough.'

'This "slut" came closer than you ever will to sitting at the right hand of an emperor,' Apodemius replied.

'She'll never wake up. We have to get to Constantius while we can. Who knows Ursicinus' next move?'

'We wait,' said the old man. He glared at Gaudentius. 'Am I not standing on my own two feet after weeks of danger?'

'Then at least we can use the time to pay our respects to Evochildis,' Gaudentius insisted.

The widow of General Bonitus sat surrounded by her red-eyed ladies at the side of a marble bier on which Silvanus' body lay in gruesome estate in the center of the main reception hall. I had seen what Leudast did to Silvanus. I didn't need to see the corpse again.

More important, I didn't trust myself to look Ursicinus, Verenianus, Ammianus, Potentius and the other Roman delegates in the eyes without giving myself away. I knew too much for my own good. My fellow witness, Meroveus, was no longer around to corroborate any accusation of conspiracy. Whatever Apodemius and Gaudentius knew was second hand.

When it came to the truth, I wouldn't have cared who confessed it. I almost missed my old acquaintance, the greedy rapscallion Leudast, but I would have bet the wily scout was nursing his wounded thigh far away by now.

'I'll stay with Roxana,' I said.

About an hour later, Apodemius returned from Silvanus' bier. He looked startled to see Roxana clinging to life with such stubborn, pale-cheeked calm. He drew me away the carved wooden bench outside. This dark alcove had basked in the motes of sunrays the day I discovered Roxana at her needlework weeks before.

It seemed another age.

'A wave of arrests will begin after the rituals have been performed. Gaudentius is right. We must leave before nightfall. That gives us at least a day's advance on Ursicinus, possibly two or three. He can't leave here without securing complete command over the legions loyal to Silvanus while they're all recalled in one place. There will be more than one tribune who balks at first.'

'I want to see Roxana's ashes interred next to Silvanus' in the chapel where they prayed together.'

Apodemius waved his knobby claw in my face. 'This is no time to be sentimental, Numidianus. That place is for Junius' mother, on some future day, gods help her. Anyway, Evochildis will decide on the style of funeral. Roman or Frankish burial, that's for her to say. I fear it may not be the Roman ceremony Silvanus would have wanted.'

Gaudentius came trotting up the corridor.

'We're too late. Ursicinus has started making arrests for treason in the name of Constantius. He's already detained ten of Silvanus' staff. He told me it's our job as imperial *agentes* to escort the accused men to trial in Mediolanum.'

Apodemius sighed. 'Well, we are lucky, then. At least on that score, the General of the East knows his Roman law. It is our duty. But we lose our chance to brief the Emperor first.'

'Who's been arrested?'

'Potentius is fanning out officers all over the province to bring in the leading commanders who rallied to Silvanus the fastest,' Gaudentius rubbed his scalp, frustrated at seeing his rapid exit turned into a laborious job of convoying top men in chains. I recalled that he'd been the cause of at least one accused man committing suicide en route to judgment. 'But he started with that squib of an adjutant named Proculus.'

Proculus, so decent and loyal, was first to be shackled.

—THE WOLVES OF AMBITION—

At that, I fled back to the bedside I cared about far more about than Claudius Silvanus' resting place. Watching Apodemius and Gaudentius cross the parade ground yet one more time, I felt hollowed out by all that has passed so quickly in only a few days. I could not remember when I had eaten last but it seemed my throat had blocked up.

The turn of events had claimed many victims, but at least there was no civil war. The Empire was still whole. Protecting the Empire, not men, was the goal of our *schola*. Apodemius even hinted that I was in line for a promotion to *biarchus, upper class*.

I should have rejoiced. Instead, I was choking. Silvanus lay dead and Roxana was dying.

The gods had granted me one private consolation. Arbetio's triumphant gloating over Silvanus would not include Roxana among his victims. But who remained to share this note of irony?

There was no one left in this wing of the palace. Attendants, ladies, slaves, and all the other factotums that peopled such vast buildings had vanished, gone to spy on the laying out of Silvanus and the wretchedness of his family and the Franco-Roman nobility. Such people reminded me of society wives craning their necks as their carriages passed some unfortunate leper or freak begging by the roadside.

The air outside Roxana's closed door filled with the stench of the latrine. I covered my nose with my sleeve and removed myself from my post with distaste. Was this the reek of death?

Guntheuca opened the door as if she were presiding over a flower garden. She gave me a broad smile, as if the cloacal stink was Frankish incense to her.

'Numidianus! I was about to send for you! No one deserves to hear this first but you. The lady will be fine. The wound has laid her very low, but she will live!'

'By what miracle of barbarian skill have you revived her?' I muttered through the thick cloth of my tunic.

Guntheuca chuckled. 'No miracle. Nature, *Agens*, nature! Her system expelled the poisonous cones whole. Look.'

She placed her crooked fingers right into a chamber pot and from that muck, pinched out the dark and deadly brown core of a yew berry.

'You see, Numidian? You see? In her haste to die, she gulped the berries down whole. They passed through her body untouched. If she had chewed—even once—she would be dead.'

'Her feeble state?'

'Caused only by her wound. She needs care and rest, but the power of her despair was her salvation.'

'And possibly her undoing,' I said.

Now Roxana faced a future without the only man that made her life worthwhile. What punishments would Catena or Arbetio prepare for Silvanus' lover? Sadly, if she had a choice, I knew which tormenter she would choose.

'Do not worry. This woman is powerful.'

'She is *ric*,' I said.

Guntheuca pushed me back toward the door. 'Hurry, call some slaves to clean her up and air out this room.'

※※※

'They put that Proculus, Silvanus' adjutant, on the rack an hour ago,' Rufus said. 'Your dice.' He handed me the cup.

Our gambling session could not take my mind off the terrible 'justice' being exacted only a few hundred feet from where I sat.

'That sickly guy? He'll be squealing before the sun reaches the edge of the wall,' said Cassius. 'And if he's like the rest of them so far, many innocent names will pop out of his dry and burning lips, just for the sake of a sip of *posca*.'

They chuckled. I could stand it no longer. Proculus had served honorably. Had he not told me twice of his nightmare in which he was forbidden while asleep to strike a certain innocent person?'

This time there was no need for the Count of Dreams to pave the way. Proculus' nightmare had already sprung to life at the hands of Paulus Catena.

I stood up from the dicing table.

'We haven't finished!' Cassius said.

I strapped on my armor, straightened my insignia, slapped my *petanus* on my head and marched unheralded up the steps of the great palace.

—THE WOLVES OF AMBITION—

I knew the entry hall, the outer reception chamber, the great reception chamber, the office alcove, the inner *consistorium* chamber with its dreaded door, the echoing steps beyond. I knew what waited below. I was walking of my own free will down the narrow descent from which no man but a henchman of Paulus Catena's ever remounted.

I knew Catena's ways. I'd witnessed his pleasure using new 'interrogation techniques' borrowed from the Persians, the Armenians, and any other foreigners who valued life and law less than Romans.

Screams warned me to turn back just as my boots touched the rough pavement of the lower regions of the palace. My eyes couldn't adjust quickly enough to the darkness. Nevertheless, I plunged forward, feeling my way along cold, dank walls. It took me time—moving through the unfamiliar little chambers in the dark, my blindness broken only by the odd wall torch—to discover Proculus lying, naked and white, on a contraption of infernal efficiency.

I did not recognize his tormenter, a tall, bare-chested wraith I hope to never see again. I showed the officer my *biarchus* badge, the *agentes*' insignia of the *schola* entrusted to escort villains, cheats, political exiles, and criminal suspects.

He thrust out his colorless lantern jaw and grunted, but he didn't challenge me. After all, why should an *agens* not share in the triumphant result of his day's work?

The reek of Proculus' loosened bowels and panicked sweat assaulted my nostrils. How could any man, even the most sadistic, endure a working day in this Hades?

'Proculus, do you know me?' I asked through the gloom.

'Don't even try. He talks gibberish,' the interrogator said. He was half a head taller than myself, as pale as his victim, but his was the spongy white of a worm crawling through a corpse's entrails. This was a man who never saw daylight.

'Yes,' Proculus whispered. 'Numidianus, the *agens*?'

'What has he confessed?'

'He impeaches no one,' said the Worm. 'But he defends Claudius Silvanus the Usurper to the last. Read it,' he barked over his glistening naked shoulder. The round-shouldered figure of a hooded scribe perched on a stool in the moss-covered shadows.

The scribe held up his tablet under a torch casting light above his head. 'Let me see... *not driven on from ambition but compelled by necessity... Four days before he assumed the badges of empire, he paid the soldiers... in Constantius' name exhorted them to be brave and loyal to their Emperor.*'

'Yes,' Proculus whispered. 'The truth. I'm witness to the truth, Numidianus. If Silvanus had planned this, he would've given the *donativa* in his own name.'

His eyes rolled back into his skull.

'Let him go,' I ordered the Worm.

'On whose authority?'

'On the authority of my *schola*.'

'Why take the responsibility, *Biarchus*? He won't last much longer.'

'Exactly. He has nothing more to tell you. I was there, up in Agrippina. I will be giving witness too. This little man took orders. Nothing more. Is this not what the others tell you—that Silvanus was thrust up to the purple by circumstances?'

'None so senior as him.'

'Has he named any plotters?'

'No one.'

'Will killing this poor sack of bones get you anywhere?'

The Worm shrugged. 'He's safer dead. That's the policy.'

'Did you take all that down?' I asked the scribe. The hunched clerk nodded.

'Who comes after this?'

'Poemenius, Governor of Treverorum—'

'But he proved his loyalty to Constantius years ago by shutting the door of the mint on Caesar Decentius during Magnentius' revolt!'

The Worm shrugged and gestured with a greasy hand toward another door, bolted and thick with iron struts that separated us from the prisoners' cells.

'Poemenius is under arrest and waiting back there.'

'Who else?'

'The *duces* Asclepiodotus, Lutto, and Maudio.'

'Is the Tribune Laniogaisus there?'

The scribe lifted a small lamp to examine a scroll unrolled at his feet.

—THE WOLVES OF AMBITION—

'No Laniogaisus listed.'

No Laniogaisus?

Silvanus' right-hand man, nominated *Magister Officiorum* for the upstart regime, cleared of suspicion? What could explain this?

'Tribune Bainobaudes?'

The scribe checked again. 'No Bainobaudes.'

The explanation dawned on me. Constantius' *consistoriani* had launched a far-reaching political purge of northern Gallic leaders. Many were Franco-Romans, but many were noble Gallo-Romans. They were being crushed for reasons unknown to me—and possibly unknown to the coterie who'd rallied to Silvanus' desperate claim.

It was no coincidence that *Lampadius* had carried the forged Silvanus letters to Constantius in the first place. *Lampadius* had drafted those phony letters and now *Lampadius* had added his personal enemies as Silvanus' 'co-conspirators.' The architect of the forged conspiracy had been Lampadius, the *Praetorian Prefect for Gallia*. He was using Silvanus' uprising as an excuse to cleanse Gallia of his personal rivals.

The door to the cells opened and clanged shut. Boot steps approached out of the fetid enclosures beyond.

'I wondered why the screaming had stopped,' said a rasping voice. 'Meddling, Numidianus, or just anxious to jump the queue?'

Catena stepped into the circle of torchlight. His personal 'pleasures' had taken a toll on his soul since our last meeting. That small mouth, so odd on his brutish, stubbled chin, and that little nose between the mismatched eyes—as ever, these features seemed to have been borrowed from other men and pasted into place.

But something had changed. He frightened me more than ever. Once he had been a human being with expressions I could recognize. Those lopsided eyes had once lit up at the sight of suffering men. Now they looked as vacant as those of his discarded 'clients.'

'I wouldn't dare meddle in your kingdom, Catena. The less time I spend down here, the easier I breathe. But I intrude to bear witness to these procedures against an innocent adjutant, who like yourself, obeys his superiors.'

'Perhaps you'd be willing to take the adjutant's place, slave-boy? I wasn't surprised to hear you were waist deep in the affairs in Agrippina.'

'You can neither charge nor arrest an *agens* for anything he does on duty, Catena. That's the law. And I'm witness to the truth of this man's statement—and more. Your prongs and rack wheels can't claw my testimony off the record there.'

He stared at me through the gloom and then glanced over his shoulder at the cells behind us. Something flickered to life. There was 'the Chain' I knew of old. I detected impatience in his fanatical expression and an unappeased appetite for resistance and surrender.

He'd absented this interrogation because honest, brave Proculus had started to *bore* him. It was as if Catena had so much good food on the banquet table waiting beyond that a simple crust of plain bread like Proculus was a waste of his fine palate. He preferred whinging, cowardice, placations, bargaining, flattery, begging, threats and betrayal—all the futile tricks of desperate souls that entertained his perversion.

'Untie this skeleton,' he told the Worm. 'Write that down,' he said to the scribe. 'Adjutant Proculus is released, according to state procedures regarding interrogation. Bring me that Poemenius instead.'

I unstrapped Proculus and collected his collapsing body into my arms. He might not last another week, but if there was chance he might survive, he deserved it. I carried him like a featherweight child up those horrible stairs and into the light where he belonged. I would find him the capital's best doctor before an hour was up.

'It was like my dream, Numidianus,' he whispered, squinting into the glare of freedom. 'I held fast to the truth, just like in my dream.'

Chapter 23, A Cleansing Fire

—The court of Mediolanum—

The summer's warmth had subsided and left a chilly vacuum filled by fear and death. Constantius' confidence had swelled with his victories over two threats to his authority—earthly challenge from Silvanus and the spiritual challenge from the Bishop of Alexandria, Athanasius.

'Is it finished at last?' I asked Florentius Nigrinianus. Though the religious synod was weeks behind him, the bureaucrat was no less careworn on this cool October day than during the summer mornings he'd sweated to and fro preparing for the avalanche of bishops.

He'd invited me to a quiet, private meal in exchange for an unvarnished account of Silvanus' demise. He didn't trust the other *agentes* as much as myself, he said, because he'd seen me unmask the forgery.

He knew better than to ask me what I thought of a careerist like himself on Constantius' staff. He might have been surprised to learn I respected Florentius Nigrinianus more than many courtiers. Trustworthy or not, the deputy *Magister Officiorum* knew the value of having the facts tucked into his capacious satchel full of documents—just in case.

After I had confided Ursicinus' role in Silvanus' downfall, we found ourselves talking of the theological skullduggery of July and August.

'Constantius ordered me to pack the basilica to the roof with Arians and to refuse *Cursus* travel papers to Athanasius' champion, Eusebius of Vercelli.'

'So the Vercelli man missed the synod?'

'Not quite,' Florentius sighed. 'The passionate Lucifer of Caligari defended Athanasius in violent language. But that provoked the Alexandrian's enemies with resentful outcries and further violence. Then the bishop of Mediolanum, Dionysius, accused the Athanasius' Niceans, not of heresy—not quite—but of disrespect toward the Emperor. That led to a fresh condemnation of the Athanasian clique.'

'Such pacific followers of their Christ.'

'Indeed.' Florentius took a deep gulp of the fine red wine he'd ordered for our quiet meal.

'But the latecomer, Eusebius of Vercelli?'

'Oh, finally poor old Eusebius of Vercelli showed up, bedraggled and disheveled from traveling the common roads. He demanded a vote in favor of Athanasius. Bishop Valens of Mursa picked up Eusebius' draft of a so-called "Act of Faith" and tore it into shreds. Fed up with their wrangling, Constantius proposed a grand tour of the palace during which he introduced the bishops Lucifier, Eusebius, and Dionysius *to Paulus Catena.*'

I choked on my wine. 'They survived?'

'Oh, things didn't get that ugly—here, use my napkin—but after sightseeing below stairs, the three Nicean bishops suddenly volunteered to go into exile. And, surprise upon surprise, the synod ended with a vote supporting Arius' views on the nature of Christ.'

Florentius picked some stubborn bit of nut from his teeth with a fishbone. *'God the Father's Divinity is greater than the Son's, and the Son is under God the Father, and not co-equal or co-eternal with Him.* Subscribe to that, my young Roman pagan, and your career will advance much faster in this city.'

'I'm counting the days until I return to headquarters, thanks.'

Now I understood better why, shortly after our return to see fresh treason trials over Silvanus begin, I observed the Emperor smile at his wife. The Empress stared at him in disbelief as if the gods had stolen his senses. The smile disappeared for good.

Of course such pleasant victories at the expense of justice and truth are often short-lived. If Constantius had spent his childhood reading classics at the knees of a blind old Roman senator, as I had, he might have reined in his soaring arrogance.

What do we think when we read of greedy old King Croesus, who drove the Athenian, Solon, headlong out of his kingdom because the sage ranked noble and selfless men above the king himself?

And do we admire Dionysius, who threatened to kill the poet Philoxenus because when the tyrant was reciting his dreadful verses and all the sycophants applauded, the honest poet sat on his hands?

One doesn't want to go down in men's memories as rivaling Croesus or Dionysius for vanity and cruelty. Honor squeaks through and bides its time, even in our modern minds. I have to believe in that. As Gaudentius and I escorted the accused prisoners south from Agrippina, I even overheard one of Ursicinus' adjutants, that note-taking Ammianus, allow that Claudius Silvanus had been 'a general of no slight merits.'

Roxana overheard him too. She spit in his face.

With Potentius and Verinianus riding on either side, Ursicinus expected public acclaim and imperial reward as he led us into Mediolanum. And indeed, no one was more pleased with events up in Agrippina than Constantius II—not even Ursicinus.

But as the north Italian winter closed in, Constantius would not have the glory of his triumphant theological summer tarnished by the Silvanus scandal. And he did not intend to let General Ursicinus enjoy the credit for putting down the Frankish 'usurper' and accrue yet more popularity in the street.

I often heard it said that Constantius hated brave and energetic men, as Emperor Domitian did in times gone by. He certainly tried to crush successful men by every possible scheme. Far from enjoying greater triumph from his criminal duplicity, General Ursicinus got no credit whatsoever. His conspirators' determination to erase all connections between the murder in the chapel and their hunting expedition many miles away worked far too well.

Constantius acted as if the whole Silvanus affair had resolved itself according to the Fates' intentions for 'Our Eternity's' glorious reign.

The Emperor's last device was to keep Ursicinus dangling under a cloud of suspicion. So far was Constantius from praising Ursicinus' actions in Agrippina, he trumped up a fresh charge—that Ursicinus had embezzled funds from the Gallic treasury while on mission.

None of us *agentes* felt sympathy for Ursicinus but when he heard this accusation, Apodemius shook his head with an odd smile. Our *schola* was in charge of auditing all provincial accounts. Though disrupted times meant inadequate records, we knew—or at least the Castra accountants were fairly sure—that no one had touched those monies, certainly not Ursicinus and his party.

They simply hadn't had time.

Constantius would not be deterred by independent assessments. He launched an investigation through the auditor of the general's office of infantry supplies, one Remigius. It was obvious that Ursicinus was going to be stuck inheriting Gallia's festering problems, but not its top slot.

It was not until weeks later that I wondered how much Apodemius' private briefing with Constantius might have explained these weird embezzling charges that held the proud and resentful General back from supreme military power.

During those weeks in Mediolanum many lives were at stake. Only a few mattered to me.

The morning of Roxana's interrogation, we *agentes* applied for admittance to the *consistorium*. Constantius looked mystified as we filed in. Rufus, Cassius, Gaudentius, myself followed Apodemius' halting steps. Another dozen more junior riders and road inspectors mustered for the occasion strode in behind us.

'*Agentes in Rebus* overflowing our chamber? To what do we owe the presence of your *schola*'s senior officers? We are hearing the testimony of the traitor's adulterous bedmate.'

'We request permission to observe,' Apodemius answered.

'Displaying a surprising prurience for men who hold themselves so above all others in conduct,' Constantius sniffed.

Roxana had to be carried into Our Eternity's presence on a simple litter. She wore a modest veil and a plain beige *palla* over a simple bleached dress, stripped of jeweled belts or silver fertility amulets.

She prostrated herself at the Emperor's feet, though her hands were bound tightly behind her. She still wore Silvanus' garnet ring.

She was helped to her feet. She answered each question in a clear and ringing voice with head held high. She had met and loved Silvanus in the court of Magnentius while attending the wife of Commander Atticus Manlius Gregorius. The tragic battle of Mursa had lost them to each other. She had found work in the court of Gallus, attending the Emperor's sister, *Augusta* Constantia and her invalid daughter.

A smirk crossed the face of the Lord Chamberlain, the eunuch Eusebius. He'd tested Roxana as a double agent pitted against Apodemius and lost her services. But was hardly going to admit to such chicanery now that he was a rising man in Christian circles and Roxana was on trial for complicity in treason.

The *schola* could count on that brocaded slug's silence.

'What did you know of Silvanus' ambitions to claim the purple for himself?' Constantius asked.

'Nothing, *Imperator*, until it was too late. I did everything in my power to persuade him to relinquish his foolhardy claim and return to the bosom of the *Imperator*'s Christian compassion and forgiveness. When your summons was delivered, I begged him three times to place his trust in you. Each time I failed. I place myself in your mercy.'

'You failed us.'

'Yes, *Imperator*. I failed this throne. And I failed a great man.'

'We were briefly persuaded by the discovery of forged letters that Claudius Silvanus was innocent. But his later actions proved him disloyal beyond redemption Do you have any knowledge of the whereabouts of his son, Junius? The boy was the hostage of our court, but fled—no doubt due to prior knowledge of his father's criminal intentions.'

Constantius' voice hardened into iron. 'Where's the boy?'

'I do not know,' Roxana said.

'We believe you do,' said an insinuating voice. Consul Arbetio stood up from the councilors' table and added, 'and the truth is the only thing that will save you from a far more uncomfortable questioning.'

The whole assembly could witness how Arbetio leaned over poor Roxana with a wolfish leer, his eyes flashing with arrogant familiarity. He was eager to meddle in her destiny and to play her savior, if only she would let him.

Roxana glanced at the Consul's hands, rapidly clutching at a sheaf of documents the way he intended to clutch at her. She could have guessed at Junius' hiding place. She could have played for time. Instead, she refused to save herself. She was going to emulate her Silvanus—stubborn and brave until the end.

'We can do nothing for you,' Constantius said, 'if you refuse to cooperate with this tribunal. Do you understand the consequences of withholding information?'

Roxana turned pale. 'Yes, *Imperator*. But I cannot tell you the whereabouts of the boy Junius Silvanus. I do not know.'

The Prefect Lampadius slammed his hand down on the table and twisted toward her with a glare. 'You slept in this traitor's bed, night after night, and yet never once learned where he hid his only son, the last heir and grandson of the Frank Bonitus?'

The rise of the Franco-Romans across Gallia was Lampadius' obsession. The angry resurgence of powerful Franks in the north under young Junius haunted his nights.

'You've heard that an army of united Frankish tribes has crossed the Rhenus and just recaptured Agrippina from Roma?' Constantius asked Roxana. 'The city has been destroyed.'

'No, *Imperator*, I did not know.'

Nor did anyone else in the room until now, I guessed from dozens of startled faces. Apodemius studied his worn goatskin boots. On his mental map, small Frankish pins had jumped the river between that nasty hamlet of Laniogaisus' meeting and the grand gates of the governor's palace already.

There was a hush as the loss of northern Gallia, so hard-won by Silvanus and his intrepid eight thousand marching north, loomed up in the flames of everyone's imagination.

Silvanus' bravery had been all for naught. Gallia was once again being ravished. Who could guess the future of Evochildis and their ladies?

'The fate of Agrippina must remain a secret within this chamber for now,' Constantius sighed, visibly displeased. 'Take the woman to Paulus Catena. We must know where Junius Silvanus is hiding.'

The guards led Roxana toward the doorway to Catena's cells.

Apodemius shuffled forward now, his cadaverous figure blocking the path between Roxana and that dreadful door.

—THE WOLVES OF AMBITION—

'Under Roman law, *Imperator*, no *agens* can be prosecuted for deeds carried out on mission.'

'What in God's name does this have to do with a usurper's mistress?' Constantius looked more than irritated. As puffed up as he was by his synod success, it took little to puncture his demeanor.

'I apologize, Roxana,' the old man said, bowing to her as far as his crooked back allowed. 'This lady is protected by that law, according to her rank as *biarchus* second class, *Schola Agentium in Rebus*. All that she did, she did in the service of yourself and the Empire. This Junius must be found. And we will apply all the means of our department to finding out what this lady failed to discover.'

Arbetio slunk back, step by step, his head lowered, his lower jaw hanging open, and his eyes wary as Apodemius' quavering voice strained to fill the hall.

'But this witness must be allowed to finish whatever testimony is required and then depart under the escort of her superior officers.'

My jaw had dropped as well. Gaudentius scowled. Rufus shrugged at the junior officers who were unable to hide their astonishment. They were too junior to recall the slip of an athletic girl rising to the top of the Castra training classes years ago.

Constantius leaned back into his wide-armed *cathedra*. He was married to Eusebia, so he was no stranger to strong-willed or talented beauties, but even for him, a female spy was an imperial first.

He was utterly confused, but dared not let his bewilderment be perceived by the *consistoriani*.

'Thank you for your service, *Matrona*,' he said. 'The *agentes* are all excused.'

He turned to Aedesius, Master of Admissions, and muttered, 'Bring in Flavius Claudius Julianus. He has made a lonely journey all the way from Achaia and we have delayed his audience for far too long.'

We *agentes* ushered ourselves out of the imperial presence, with Roxana leaning on Rufus' arm. Gaudentius commanded the junior *agentes* back to their duties.

'Why did Roxana have to endure that charade if you meant to declare her immunity as an *agens*?' I asked Apodemius.

'She would have refused,' he said. 'She wants to be remembered as Emperor Silvanus' loyal consort, not the spy in his bed. Given time, she'll thank me for making her safe.'

'Safe? Arbetio will make her life a misery from now on.'

'But Numidianus, that was the best part!' Apodemius laughed. 'Didn't you see Arbetio's face when I publicly announced Roxana still worked for me! No politician of Arbetio's ambition could ever take a member of our *schola* as his lover!'

Apodemius had convinced Constantius and his *consistoriani*. But surely my powers of observation could not have failed me so dismally. Had Roxana never been Apodemius' 'one failure,' but in fact, his most secret agent of all?

'Has she been working for you all along?'

The old man gave a soft chuckle and walked away.

I found myself alone in the grand reception hall outside the *consistorium*. Standing nearby was a round-shouldered, goat-bearded young man wearing a Greek student's scruffy *pallium*. No trousers covered his bronzed, hairy knees.

'I recall you,' he croaked. 'You're that *agens* who signed my road permit, the pagan Numidianus, who knows his letters well?'

'Welcome home, Flavius Claudius Julianus.' I bowed my head.'

'Welcome home? I tremble for my life,' he said, glancing behind him with a nervous twitch. 'Minerva inspires all my actions. Thanks to her, I'm protected by an invisible guard of angels that the goddess has borrowed from the Sun and Moon.'

I cleared my throat and asked, 'So why are you here, *Domine*?'

'The Empress' idea. She embraced me warmly last night when I arrived—she alone is not an assassin. This is the last place I want to be,' he whispered.

'They're about to call you in.'

'If I were in charge I'd empty out the whole place—drive out these thousands of slaves and eunuchs and chefs and toadies and all your fellow spies. I'd cleanse the whole rotten place with holy fire and maybe even restore the rightful gods to their temples.'

—THE WOLVES OF AMBITION—

'Well,' I said, digesting his astonishing admission, 'Christ and Constantius are in charge now—more than ever, in fact.'

'Yes,' he said with an awkward cough, 'and intending to collar me with the thickest imperial rope. You recall that line in the *Iliad*, the one with the pun on πορφύρεος?'

Homer had used 'purpureous' to link dark red blood with the color of kingship.

'*I'm seized by purple death and fate supreme?*'

'That's the line. Can't get that out of my head,' he mumbled.

He was pulling at the wispy hairs on his cheek, mulling this over, when the Master of Admissions beckoned him into the council chamber for the official presentation.

Cousin Julian was back.

※※※

Under strict instructions from the Emperor, Apodemius and I delayed our return to Roma until November 6, the date assigned to celebrate Julian's twenty-fifth birthday. Everyone in Mediolanum was on alert—thousands of officials, scribes, notaries, middlemen and their slaves, thousands more palace servants, and many more thousands of Constantius' palatine forces, all gathered in disciplined formations outside the great city's gates.

A lofty scaffolding surrounded by eagles and standards had gone up over the first week of the new month. On the morning in question, crushed on all sides by jostling palace officials, Florentius Nigrinianus and I guarded Apodemius' fragile bones from injury.

The wait was long. Finally Constantius emerged through the city gates. Before the amassed and curious faces of his soldiers and civilians alike, he led his cousin up the steps. Julian wore a fresh tunic with a stiff, high collar that chafed his raw little chin, shaved clean of its philosopher's beard.

As usual, Constantius betrayed no emotion. His voice was too low for most of the hordes behind our ranks of *viri illustres* to make out a word. But for over a mile behind the clamor at the front, centurions and officials relayed his words back through the waiting ranks.

Apodemius and I were close enough to understand almost every word:

'We stand before you, valiant defenders of our country, to avenge the common cause with a unanimous spirit; and how we shall accomplish this we shall briefly explain to you, our impartial judges. After the death of those rebellious tyrants whom mad fury drove to attempt the designs which they projected, the barbarian savages—as if sacrificing to their wicked Manes with Roman blood—have forced our peaceful frontier and are overrunning Gallia, encouraged by the belief that dire straits beset us throughout our far-flung empire.'

The Senate was spent as a political force. Success today depended on winning over the listening crowd's approval. It was at this point that some soldier way at the back jumped his cue. Soldiers far behind us in the flattened fields started banging their shields in the time-honored sign of military approbation—but sooner than instructed.

Constantius kept going as the premature roar swelled: '. . . remain inviolate. It remains for you to confirm with happy issue the hope of the future that we cherish. This Julian, our cousin, honored for the modesty through which he is as dear to us as through ties of blood, a young man of ability which is already conspicuous, we desire to admit to the rank of Caesar, and—'

Constantius gave up at this point and waited in vain for silence to settle back over the crowd.

'Since, then,' he persevered, 'your joyful acclaim shows that we have your approval also, let this young man of quiet strength, whose temperate behavior is rather to be imitated than proclaimed, rise to receive this honor. His excellent disposition, trained in all good arts, we demonstrate by choosing him. With the favor of the God of Heaven let us invest him with the imperial robes.'

Julian's stiff robe didn't fit. His rounded student's shoulders folded under the weight of it. Encrusted with huge *orbiculi* and *Chi-Rho* letters in gold and purple threads, the garment might well have walked across the stage by itself—it exhibited so much authority and confidence.

—THE WOLVES OF AMBITION—

Constantius took no notice of his cousin's embarrassment.

'... Come, then, to share in pains and perils, and undertake the charge of defending Gallia, ready to relieve those afflicted regions with every bounty. And if it becomes necessary to engage with the enemy, take your place with sure footing amid the standard bearers themselves; be a thoughtful adviser of daring in due season, animate the warriors by taking the lead with utmost caution, strengthen them when in disorder with reinforcements, modestly rebuke the slothful, and be present as a most faithful witness at the side of the strong, as well as of the weak.'

Listening to this torrent of pompous benediction from Constantius, I pitied the poor young man who so loved nothing more than skipping his baths to read. Cowering up on that platform from the thunderous acclaim, Julian looked as miserable as any Constantine I'd ever met—and they were not a happy tribe as a rule, even on their normal birthdays.

'Therefore, urged by the great crisis, go forth, yourself a brave man, ready to lead men equally brave. We shall stand by each other in turn with firm and steadfast affection, we shall campaign at the same time, and together we shall rule over a pacified world, provided only God grants our prayers, with equal moderation and conscientiousness. You will seem to be present with us everywhere, and we shall not fail you in whatever you undertake. Go, hasten, with our united prayers, to defend with unsleeping vigilance the post assigned you, as it were, by your country herself.'

The Emperor then soaked up the deafening cheers with stoic patience before leading the trembling Julian down to a waiting carriage to ride back through the gates to the safety of the palace.

I could swear Julian's lips formed the word, 'purpureous' as his open carriage passed.

'Are you staying for the wedding of the new Caesar to the Emperor's sister Helena?' We three struggled back toward the gates. I knew the *Magister* was only hoping to reach the sanctuary of our little cells behind the Finance Building in one piece.

Florentius steadied Apodemius' halting steps. 'I can set aside four good places in the banqueting hall and a chance to be among the first two hundred guests to congratulate the bride and bridegroom on their future.'

I saw the *Magister* was tired, so I accepted for him. 'That is very good of you. We would be delighted—'

'—but no, I think not.' Apodemius cut me off. 'We must resume our work in Roma without any further delay. Call it the weakness of old age, *Magister* Florentius, but I find my tolerance for watching young people being tortured diminishes with every passing year.'

Chapter 24, What Leo Thought

—ROMA, NOVEMBER 11, 355 AD—

We arrived at dusk at the Porta Aurelia of the old City of Cities. It was probably just about the same hour that up in Mediolanum's frosty marble halls, Julian and Constantius' prune-lipped virgin sister Helena were toasting their awkward union.

Weddings weighed on my mind. I wondered how soon my business at the Castra would be done, freeing me to climb the Esquiline Hill up to the Manlius townhouse to see my son and his mother at long last.

Leo had written that a wedding might take place in the autumn. Was Kahina already the wife of Antonius Drusus? Should I arrive at the old fig tree outside the gate bearing a present for the happy groom and bride? I must not dwell on it.

Normally, at my return from a far-flung mission, I found old Verus waiting for me at a tavern inside the city gates. While I submitted my papers for registration as municipal law required, I'd lubricate the faithful servant with the tavern's plonk-of-the-day into divulging all the juicy developments at home.

Not this evening. Since I was traveling with the *Magister Agentium in Rebus* himself, there was no need to observe the usual protocol of registering an *agens*' presence.

Nevertheless, Apodemius did dismount outside the first and meanest *popina* and instructed me to turn in our horses at the post station. He pulled his hood over his telltale white hair and dodged into the greasy dive. I followed him to a small table in the most obscure corner and we ordered a beaker of *posca*, a dish of milk-fed snails in garlic oil and zucchini slices in cumin sauce.

After about fifteen minutes, a de-mobbed soldier cursed at the other drinkers to make way for him. He elbowed his path through the crushing mob around the wine counter.

I leaned closer to the table to let the troublemaker pass us by, but he pulled up a stool and plunked himself down next to me.

He had no armor, but still sported battle-stained *thoracomacus*. Clumps of wadding stuck out from its leather like muddy clouds sprouting from his shoulders. He probably wore the thing only because he lacked any respectable cloak or other outer garment against the autumn winds.

I would have sworn I'd never seen this miserable veteran before, until he said to me in a perfectly educated Latin, 'Greetings, Numidianus. Glad to see you're still with us.'

Then he leaned over and added, 'We were so worried, *Magister*. The Castra was trying to learn for weeks what happened to you up north. They we heard you were detained in court.'

'What's happening here with Bishop Liberius?' Apodemius asked.

I realized suddenly that under the thick stubble covering the deeply tanned face of this unwashed veteran was none other than my thuggish Pannonian partner from the Castra's Poisons Class of our early training days.

'As soon as the bishop returned from Mediolanum, the privy council here got orders to haul him in and force him to endorse the Emperor's decree against the Alexandrian—'

'Athanasius.'

'But Bishop Liberius said it was unjust to condemn a man unseen and unheard.'

'So he still defies the Emperor's will,' Apodemius said. 'Constantius places extraordinary value on winning over our prelate of the Eternal City.'

'Constantius has said victory over Roma's bishop means more to him than defeat of Silvanus or Magnentius. He has ordered that Liberius be spirited away, but only in the middle of the night, since the people of Roma love their priest so much. Not tonight, but soon, *Magister*, you can count on it.'

'Thanks. Report back to me here a week from today.'

'Watch how you go these nights, *Magister*. The streets are rowdier than ever. Governor Leontius had that rowdy gangster Peter Valomeres flogged in the Forum and banished to Picenum for stoking up the rabble's protest against the arrest of a popular charioteer.'

—THE WOLVES OF AMBITION—

'We'll be careful.'

The Pannonian nodded and gave me a friendly slap on the back. He kicked aside his stool and grabbed a rabbit leg from off a spit with a toss of a coin to the sweating young slave tending the fire. He sauntered off into the night.

Apodemius sighed as he paid for our little supper. 'This religion is so troublesome,' he sighed, 'but we have to live with it.'

'Not if *Flavius Julianus* had his way,' I said. 'If he were emperor, he'd get rid of the entire imperial court to tilt back the sundial to a new pagan age.'

'A schoolboy's fantasy and hardly appropriate policy for a Constantine. Surely that boy was steeped in enough Christian indoctrination to turn him into one of their saints,' Apodemius said as we escaped the crowded streets for a shortcut to the Caelian Hill.

'Perhaps it was just the heat of Athens' debate clubs turning his head, but he did tell me that he would restore the rightful gods to their temples.'

'A fantasy but I'll make a note. Perhaps Constantius murdering all Julian's family set a poor example of Christian charity. He seems to have taken you into his trust, but he's stuck being a Christian and that's that. We now have an untested Caesar in Gallia to keep an eye on. I'll open his new file with those observations of yours, Numidianus. Just when I wonder at how hopeless you are, you produce a nugget of decent intelligence.'

Indeed, as soon as I ushered the old man up to his shabby office, smelling of liniment, mouse droppings, and old wax, he ordered his clerk to tell the Castra archivist to send him all our intelligence to date on Caesar Julian.

'We'll examine what we know of his early Christian training in Caesarea under house arrest and compare it with his philosophical contacts in Greece.' Apodemius rubbed his hands. He couldn't hide his relief at being back behind his desk.

'Also, summon the boy,' he told the departing clerk. 'No, don't go, Numidianus, this concerns you. Your counsel may be needed. Take that box of tacks underneath the map behind me and start moving them as I direct.'

I let the *Magister* rummage through reports piled underneath his desk. Taking guidance from his secret correspondence, I inserted and moved colored pins and tacks. Under my fingers, the Gallic territory pacified the year before shrank down to the contested fields of the coming winter. Here was Agrippina destroyed more thoroughly than ever, territory lost westward all the way to Treverorum and southward to Mogantiacum. Alemannic incursions reached deep into central Gallia—gruesome death, pillage and rapine by Frank and Alemanni tribes inching across the expanse of overused cork on tiny, ominous pinpricks.

Twenty minutes into this depressing task, there was a knock at the door.

'Come in, Junius.'

The boy had shot up by many inches. Given the late hour, he was sleepy but let out an enormous gasp of relief at seeing us both returned.

'We will not dwell on condolences, young man, since we have urgent business in deciding your future. I have a Vesuvius of work overflowing around me, as you can see. But I am indeed sorry.'

Apodemius meant well, but this was too dry for the poor young man. I embraced him in my arms as he fought off tears.

'My mother? Is my mother all right?'

'Wisely kept herself unseen and unheard during this entire disaster. We would have ended this affair differently, but your abused father stood on his proud tradition. Despite what the world says, you have no reason to be ashamed of your name.'

Junius managed a brave smile, giving me a fleeting memory of the gallant, rakish Silvanus in his prime.

Apodemius rose from his chair with a struggle. He came around his desk to Junius and laid a gnarled hand on his shoulder. 'You have obeyed my instructions?'

'Yes, *Magister*.'

'Contacted none of the Franks in Mediolanum? Communicated with no one?'

'No one. Perhaps they think I'm dead.'

'Let's hope they do. Constantius suspects otherwise. We'll have to find a new name and place for you, son.'

'Is it that bad?'

'I'm afraid it is. I wouldn't guarantee your safety any farther than the Subura district down that hill. As soon as Constantius learnt of your presence in Roma, there would be cutthroats on your tail. Gods! He's willing to whisk the Bishop of Roma himself out of this city without a trace! Would he stop at a youngster who could lead the Franco-Romans to march on Mediolanum tonight?'

'I would not do that,' Junius said, 'unless my family asked it of me.'

'Your grandmother would,' I said, 'if she has survived.'

Who knew who was now ruling Agrippina?

'Sit down, Junius.' Apodemius offered him the same stool he always left for *agentes* making their reports—some of them on their last legs after weeks of riding, or worse.

'I propose you choose a new name tonight. I will enroll you for training in our *schola* under your false identity. You impressed me from the first with your courage, your perception, your honesty, and your loyalty. Our service also requires stamina, both physical and mental, flexibility—and a sense of humor doesn't hurt. I want all those virtues and any others hiding behind that pretty face of yours working for me—and me alone. What do you say?'

'I can't,' Junius said. 'I belong with my grandmother, supporting her, mourning my father with the proper rites and taking my place as my grandfather's heir. There is a long tradition of which I'm the last man standing.'

'I would say, the last boy sitting, and only by grace of our discretion. In good time, Junius, perhaps you can reclaim your place, but you'll be no good to your people or to the Empire as a faceless corpse floating down the Tiberis tomorrow morning. We'll give you useful skills, a family, and friendships that will last you far longer than you may choose to serve us. Only, let us protect you for now.'

Junius turned to me, his wide brown eyes pleading for an answer.

'Junius, Constantius tried to torture your friend Roxana to discover your whereabouts,' I said. 'If he was willing to break the spirit and maim the body of a woman your father loved in passing, will he stop at the last vessel of Bonitus' valiant blood?'

'Where's the Toxandrian I freed?'

'He died defending your father against General Ursicinus' Bracchiati hirelings,' I said. 'I was with him at the end.'

Junius turned pale as the reality of so much death sunk in.

'Roxana?'

'She was wounded at your father's side, rather badly. But she's healing now in another city under our protection.'

Apodemius added, 'And under an assumed identity, far from the dangers of the court. Even Numidianus does not know it.'

'I must choose a new name right away?'

'Yes. And we'll start you tomorrow in the cadet classrooms with the sons of eminent governors, powerful merchants, and respected *curiales* from all over the Empire. They've wangled their offspring into our service with letters of reference, fees, and all manner of underhanded inducements,' Apodemius said with a laugh. 'Sometimes I wish they would all send their sons to be priests, but we make use of what little talent comes our way. We already know you have the potential to succeed.'

'I cannot even be called Junius any longer?'

'Not even Junius.'

The boy hung his head, contemplating his isolation from family and tribe. Then he looked up and I heard a distinct ring of northern defiance in his cracking voice. 'Then I choose Childeric, after my grandmother,' and he paused before adding, 'Childeric Merovianus.'

'Excellent. It seems, Numidianus, that although the *schola* has lost a faithful and hard-fighting Toxandrian eunuch, we have gained a Franco-Roman prince.'

Apodemius patted the boy's shoulder. 'Don't worry about hiding your nobility under a cloak for the short term, son. You're hardly the first. Frankly, given the times we live in, I can foresee a day when our entire service might have to join you incognito.'

※※※

It was dawn when I escorted Junius back to the Manlius townhouse to collect his meager belongings. He'd allowed himself a silent weep underneath his hood. I'd pretended not to notice. To lose his mother's companionship, his Frankish mentors at court, and even his identity was not a trifling matter. I'd stifled my personal anxiety about events at home in front of him. But without Verus to warn me of the worst before we reached the gates, there was only this callow stripling to confirm the worst.

'Was there a wedding in the household during my long absence?'

'Not yet,' Junius said. 'They put it off until next week so some high and mighty *rhetor* could return from Sicily—a former teacher that Drusus wants as witness.'

So there it was.

The worst part of it was that it wasn't over. I would have to stand there and watch Kahina join herself in marriage to the handsome and educated teacher. I would have to smile and celebrate as Antonius Drusus became my Leo's stepfather. And what would become of Marcus Gregorianus Numidianus, the true sire of Leo, bastard child of the Commander, and secret grandson of the Senator Manlius?

Like so many unnecessary accretions to a great Roman family tree, the North African Numidianus would stay on as the struggling clan's able and devoted 'freedman.'

I could not even abandon the Manlius household. I was named in the Senator's will to safeguard Leo's estate. I was still needed, I told myself with bitterness, but only to approve a full citizen's decisions and obediently sign away my son's great inheritance—beehive by bloody beehive.

I felt like taking a strong drink. I suddenly wanted many drinks, but Junius wouldn't stop at a tavern. He felt unsafe in the city outside the sanctuary of the Castra Peregrina. He was probably right. In my company, he might be a target of curiosity for anyone spying for Constantius.

So we hastened up the hill, past the familiar public garden and its little shrine and down the old street toward the overgrown fig tree smothering the worn-out Manlius entrance.

Verus was up, as usual, to unbolt the gates, but hustled away, shouting at a young slave to stop spilling bucket water all over the peristyle floor.

Oblivious to the morning routine of his slaves and servants, Leo sprawled on a bench in the atrium with his nose in a book, his little hand grasping a thick stylus. He leapt up when he saw us arrive.

I wrapped him in my arms, but for the first time, he was too heavy to just toss into the air. He was so tall for only seven!

'Why are you so dark?'

'We spent the whole holiday outdoors,' he lisped.

'What's this?' I pulled up his lip to discover a new gap where a front tooth had been.

'I supervised deliveries every day. I visited the warehouses and met all the managers. Lavinia's children taught me how to swim and fish.'

He still missed having the devoted young nurse at his personal beck and call.

'Not too far out in the water, I hope.'

I glanced over his bobbing head, looking out for his teacher or mother.

Verus hobbled back from scolding the minions. 'You need some wine, you two? Fried bread? Fresh oranges? Ham? Nothing like a full larder in September, right Marcus?'

'Anything, anything but that northern butter!'

'Butter, Marcus? When did you ever see that grease in this house? Come on to the kitchens. Been up all night with that *Magister* again? You both look knackered. Junius, lad, have you been crying? What's up with you two? Things is finally getting back to normal around here and you two look like dead-eyed carvings on a sarcophagus.'

There seemed to be more servants underfoot than when I'd left. With a respectful nod or lowered eyes they carried carpets and linens toward the public rooms. One girl was winding autumnal flowers and vines around the columns lining the open space behind.

'Marcus!'

Kahina rushed out of the winter dining room and ran through the atrium toward me. 'We heard terrifying rumors about Gallia,' she said. 'We have been so worried for you! The more Junius told us of the dangers of the Rhenus, the more we prayed for you.'

—THE WOLVES OF AMBITION—

'*Mater* was worried some German wolf would eat you up,' Leo lisped.

Kahina smiled with eyes filled with relief. Verus had told me the truth that night in Mediolanum. Underneath her fashionable goatskin shoes, Kahina's ankles were permanently hobbled with scars. A slave trader's whiplash had furrowed her golden back like wheat field for life. But today her cheeks glowed rosy brown from their holiday in Ostia.

'You should finish your lesson, Leo.' She looked into the boy's upturned face with the stern, loving glance of any mother.

Had her soul cast off its endless mourning? Had her intelligence quickened to the household life around her? After years of patient supervision, had we brought the old Kahina back to us at last—only to see her entrusted to the care of a near stranger?

'Who's paying for this big wedding I hear we're having?' I joked through my confusion.

'Well we're paying a good share, of course. We owe Antonius so much.'

'The boy is doing well?'

'He's *brilliant*,' Kahina gave Leo a loving spank. 'But still so lazy!'

He laughed and ran toward the *triclinium*. 'Antonius Drusus, I'll finish my reading tomorrow. Marcus Numidianus is back!'

'I'll join you in a minute,' I told Junius and Verus.

Kahina led me away toward the atrium.

'What will you wear for the big day?'

'Oh, it doesn't matter what I wear.' She answered in such a disinterested tone, I worried all the more. She seemed hardly aware of the step she was about to take and its implications for all of us.

'Of course it matters. Expense is no problem, you know. It's been many years since you enjoyed shopping like other women, Kahina.'

On her dazed return from the *latifundus* in Hispania, she had been in no condition to even appear in cultivated society. Her mind was cloudy, her body crippled with abuse, and her interest in daily life stunted near to death by suffering.

The nurse Lavinia had burned Kahina's slave rags and bought her mistress an entire new wardrobe with a purse of coins I handed over. Surely these three-year-old clothes were out of style—if Roma's fickle tastes were anything to go by.

She shook her head, 'All eyes will be on Sybilla, won't they? She's the glamorous type.'

'Yes, I heard from Verus that Sybilla is your new friend. She can help you choose your dress.'

'Oh, Marcus, you've missed a lot. Sybilla takes me out to see other ladies for snacks and gossip. I've attended church services with her.'

Her face filled with a wistful, distant expression that made me uneasy again. I drew her to sit next to me on the bench in the garden and kept her small brown hand in mine. I was determined to do my duty to Kahina without betraying my misgivings.

'I see the new teacher has not slackened in his duties to Leo.'

'Antonius is so good with Leo, Marcus, keeping him at his studies or amusing him with interesting games. My worries and sadness fade away when I hear them reading.'

We could overhear Antonius Drusus setting the next day's lesson in the room beyond and Leo's futile protests.

'You do seem happier,' I said. 'Do we owe it to this teacher or to your new friend?'

'I owe it to prayer and the compassion of Christ,' she said in a solemn and deliberate tone. 'I have no interest in new clothes or the vanities of this world.'

Oh, dear, this was an echo of the Kahina of the old days—not the lively girl who had loved me, but the gullible runaway seeking the oblivion of martyrdom. She had always shown a North African's weakness for extreme Christian faith. Her recovery was taking a turn for the devout. I had no interest in thanking the Nazarene for that. Any unscrupulous Roman fanatic could take advantage of her.

I squeezed her hand, 'Kahina, just who is Sybilla?'

Her shoulders dropped back. 'Why Sybilla is *the bride*, Marcus. I thought Leo wrote you. Antonius Drusus was bound to get someone before not too long, but Sybilla Sestia is a true catch. You must know of the Sestia family, Marcus, they—'

'Then Antonius Drusus is not marrying *you*? Leo thought—'

—THE WOLVES OF AMBITION—

'Marrying *me*? Of course not! But he had to marry someone, didn't he? Verus says, from the moment he arrived in Roma, he was fishing hard enough! And what do you think? His hook caught Sybilla!'

What did I think, indeed. I thought I deserved a drink.

The End

Before you continue to the Historical Notes, About the Author, and Glossary, do you want to keep on reading? Here are the other books in this series:

The Veiled Assassin, Embers of Empire, Vol. I
Usurpers, Embers of Empire, Vol. II
A Back Gate to Hell, Embers of Empire, Vol. III
The Deadly Caesar, Embers of Empire, Vol. V
The Burning Stakes, Embers of Empire, Vol. VI

Sign up for a free e-book at eyesandears.editions@gmail.com.

Did you enjoy this book? We'd be grateful if you would introduce Q. V. Hunter to new readers with your comments on Library Thing, Booklikes, Goodreads or the book distribution platform of your preference.

Historical Notes

The story of the incredible failure in imperial communications that led to General Claudius Silvanus' murder in the chapel as handed down to us by Ammianus Marcellinus is a sketchy mess when compared with the historian's meticulous detailing of other episodes. To give one example, Ammianus says that on the day Silvanus donned the purple, a messenger arrived in Mediolanum with the headline news. No historian has managed to explain this telepathic miracle.

No matter how often one scours the chronology, Ammianus' version seems potted with similar contradictions and misunderstandings. A fictional version prompted some necessary invention, e.g. the strongly motivated character of Evochildis, the temporary incapacitation of Apodemius, and the use of Marcus as a conduit for information that was even more muddied in reality.

In fact, the Late Roman historian Michael Kulikowski argues that *the entire Silvanus episode* was a later invention, just an excuse to rid Constantius II of Silvanus before the Franco-Roman soldier became a political threat. Kulikowski's primary evidence is that no coins minted with Silvanus' image have been found to date, when a usurper would mint coins without delay in an attempt to legitimize his authority. Other experts discount such evidence (though not his theory) on the basis that the nearest mint in Treverorum had closed its gates to Silvanus. More confusing, the man who might have authorized the Trier mint to produce such coins, Poemenius, was tortured as part of the purge following Silvanus' death, though no proof of support exists in the form of coinage.

Historian John Drinkwater puts forward other possibilities, including the idea that Ursicinus assassinated Silvanus out of a private feud and cooked up the usurpation tale after the fact.

Meanwhile, author Gavin Kelly suggests that it would be impossible for Ursicinus to pretend ignorance of the elevation on arriving in Cologne and that only by pretending to defect to Silvanus' side could Ursicinus bring off his betrayal.

Other scholars have carefully tracked the days required to move between Mediolanum and Agrippina even in the best of weathers. They cite a number of troubling inconsistencies in Ammianus' version.

As an eyewitness to the betrayal of Silvanus by General Ursicinus, the military officer Ammianus is, at best, a prejudiced observer. His account of the tragedy is unreliable. He veers from painting Silvanus as a threat to the Roman Empire one minute, (perhaps to rationalize his superior officer Ursicinus' deceit,) to depicting Silvanus as an innocent and honorable victim of court intrigue in his final conclusion to the episode.

Above all, the military staffer Ammianus was defending his boss General Ursicinus from accusations of underhandedness and dishonesty toward a fellow military hero. It would not be the only occasion we're left wondering if Ammianus covered up the ambitions in Ursicinus that troubled Constantius II again and again. In our story, Marcus hints as much, recalling Barbatio's confidence that Ursicinus would ascend to the Eastern throne.

The immediate defense in Ursicinus' mouth, quoted by the historian, 'Jealousy, the foe of all good and loyal servants of the Empire...' might also serve as an explanation for Silvanus' comedown.

Ammianus makes no secret of his hatred of Apodemius in this story. As in our version of the Gallus story, *The Back Gate of Hell*, the novelist is caught between the military politics of a historian possibly prejudiced by service under General Ursicinus versus the decisions of a secret agent whose actions seem entirely understandable in hindsight. The rift of distrust and rivalry between the military and civilian establishments that curdled politics under Constantius II can never be discounted.

Ammianus even suggests, without any evidence, that Apodemius was complicit in Dynamius' forgery. What this would have served Apodemius politically is a mystery.

We also wonder at Ammianus' unbelievable report that Apodemius failed to show up in time with the Emperor's recall to Silvanus. Instead, he says that Apodemius wasted valuable days as a troublemaker rooting around Silvanus' regional dependents, as

—THE WOLVES OF AMBITION—

if the General were already a condemned man, and harassing or detaining Silvanus' friends (whom he leaves unnamed) instead of presenting his credentials to Silvanus. Were Apodemius guilty as Ammianus alleges, he would hardly have wasted any time trying to force confessions pertaining to his own forgery.

This begs the underlying question—why would a professional imperial agent at the top of his game and responsible for one of the Roman Empire's most powerful *scholae*, fail his emperor in such a straightforward mission—whatever his loyalties? Ammianus offers no reason why Apodemius would risk his sovereign's trust in stalling. Skulking around the vicinity of Agrippina without 'delivering the mail,' hardly sounds like the same agent who rode a horse to its death in his haste to deliver the executed Caesar Gallus' red shoes to his imperial cousin.

The historians Den Boeft, Drijvers, and Den Hengst don't buy this 'Apodemius AWOL' story, either. They comment wryly that if Apodemius' mission had been to bring down Silvanus with deceit, he would have returned to toss the General's boots at the Emperor's feet as speedily as he produced Gallus' fancy slippers.

'The true fact of Apodemius' mission, presumably gaining intelligence about the moves of Silvanus and his supporters, are obscured from view,' they suggest in *The Last Roman World and Its Historian.*

That obscurity leaves us resorting to our fictional invention—that Apodemius was waylaid, incapacitated, or not fully operational during the crucial days leading to Silvanus' desperate decision. (Herbalists may recognize Guntheuca's medicinal tea as a brew of roots of *elecampane* or *inula conyzae* of the *asteraceae* family, a powerful antibacterial agent that relieves congestion and asthmas, dilates the bronchial passages, and stimulates the expulsion of phlegm.)

As a child introduced to the history of the Roman Empire in the mid-twentieth century, I inevitably received a picture of the 'barbarian invasions' of the Roman Empire like something out of a *Conan* movie—bare-loined men in horned helmets and furs howling unintelligible war cries as they heaved across the Roman border by the thousands in one single tsunami of unwashed humanity.

The true story of the Franks, their gradual integration into the Roman border area over more than a century as an enemy, then ally, buffer community, and finally defender of the Roman Empire, followed by their rise into the highest ranks of military command, was a revelation.

'No story [other than Silvanus'] illustrates better the diverse experience of the Franks in the fourth century,' says Edward James. He cites the identity crisis suggested by an epitaph of the times, *Francus ego civis, Romanus miles in armis*; I am a Frankish citizen and a Roman soldier under arms.'

In the story of Silvanus, we receive a picture of gradations in how Romans lived in proximity but not complete politic unity to barbarian *Germani*. Jonathan Barlow stresses that the 'Romanized' franks were not divorced from their Frankish kinship ties, which by the fourth century reached deep into the highest levels of the military and court networks. But there were deepening cultural divides, e.g. evidence of human sacrifice by the Franks in the barbarian lands extends as late as the sixth century.

Many theories about the speed and nature of the barbarian movement into Roman territory remain disputed. Late twentieth-century historians discarded the outdated theory that 'barbarian invasions' brought the Roman Empire down around their ears in one great raid. They replaced it with the more conciliatory sounding 'Migration Age' theory, but that term turns out to be as elastic as the previous image was drastic.

In some cases, contemporary experts go so far as to argue that only the gold-hungry Huns caused the collapse of an evolving Empire. On the other hand, it is argued that internal weakness in the Roman state and not pillaging nomad troublemakers triggered an irreversible end.

We let the experts continue to haggle over it.

Modern scholars of the Migration Period are in agreement that the Frankish identity emerged in the first half of the third century, possibly out of various earlier and smaller Germanic groups, e.g. the Salii, Sicambri, Chamavi, Bructeri, Chatti, Chattuarii, Ampsivarii, Tencteri, Ubii, Batavi, and Tungri.

It is speculated that these tribes originally spoke a range of related Istvaeonic dialects in the West Germanic branch of Proto-

—THE WOLVES OF AMBITION—

Germanic. The phrase used to free a man, (first uttered in our story by Junius to Meroveus,) is one of the earliest sentences yet found of Old Franconian.

Meanwhile, do we detect a hint of superiority in the Franks of the fourth century over the lesser tribes? They seem to arrive on the historical stage with a more distinctive sense of their own potential.

First, they keep fresh their indignation at the horrific treatment of their two captive kings and their followers by Constantine the Great. Then they negotiate themselves an essential role as preservers of peace and stability along the Lower Rhine defensive line.

Later on, their army officers in the generation serving Constantius II flex their growing competence vis-a-vis a faltering imperial entity, even testing their chances for supreme authority. Of the dozens of fractious and squabbling Germanic tribes that populate Roman history from the time of Tacitus' catalogue *Germania*, the Franks will eventually 'inherit the earth,' so to speak, coalescing into the Merovingian Dynasty that lead to Charlemagne and eventually France, (while the Goths rise to power farther south.)

Meanwhile, the once-cherished 'ethnogenesis' Viennese school of German history contending that these early tribes existed in some proto-national state forming an unbroken line from Tacitus to modern Germany has been debunked as dangerous nationalist nostalgia. So has the wishful thinking of some earlier French historians that the Franks weren't even Germans, but random Celts who had wandered over the Rhine and later returned home to father modern France.

While the Romans tentatively termed these peoples *Germani*, (originally a Celtic word,) the various tribes never thought or spoke of themselves in that sense as one people. Even the Romans used the term sparingly. It is impossible any longer to ascribe to these tribes the psychological progeniture of Wagner, Goethe, or Kaiser Wilhelm—much less Angela Merkel.

So we tread equally cautiously in over-romanticizing or over-anticipating the Franks' eventual dominance over northern Europe.

Still, Claudius Silvanus offers a watershed figure in the barbarians' transition from prisoners-of-war, raiders, and refugees crossing the Lower Rhine a century before his birth to leaders carving out virtual sovereignty from Rome less than two centuries later. With his last-minute defection from the Franco-Breton rebel Magnentius, Silvanus handed a critical victory to his emperor in the Battle of Mursa. Yet via the pen of Ammianus, Silvanus has also left us with his exact words condemning Constantius as variable, overstretched, and dangerously dependent on weakened forces within his ruling circle.

In these two men, we can take a snapshot of the Empire in the mid 350's in microcosm.

As a novelist attempting to portray Constantius from the viewpoint of an Numidian ex-slave, even a classically-educated *agens*, I feel constrained from allowing Marcus to observe in the Emperor Constantius any 'paranoia,' (especially with its modern clinical links to schizophrenia.) I think Marcus would have been familiar with its Greek ancestor, termed παράνοια, which means madness. A modern historian like Barnes can sum Constantius up as a 'cautious, conscientious and not unsuccessful ruler,' while a contemporary like Ammianus says Constantius is guilty of military incompetence, vanity, oppression and weak-mindedness. In his obituary, Ammianus even calls Constantius a tyrant with a cruelty surpassing Caligula, Domitian, and Commodus.

We can also thank Ammianus Marcellinus for Florentius' memorable quip in Chapter Two, 'There are few who even admit that they sleep at all.' The Count of Dreams and his associate, the notorious Paulus Catena, certainly fed the Emperor's insecurities. Even though I have seen Constantius' constant accusations and purges of rivals described as paranoic behavior, perhaps his fears were well founded. During a sustained campaign against the Persians followed by a struggle with Alemannic invasions, he faced three usurpations in one year, then rumors of three more after that.

I try to give him his due.

Constantius was beset again and again by the possibility that talented and popular men could steal his throne while he was busy defending the borders of his world. One imagines that his private moments were taunted by the knowledge that Diocletian

—THE WOLVES OF AMBITION—

had ruled for many years through a tetrarchy of partners while his own father had eliminated rivals and ruled the Empire singled-handedly for many years until his natural death.

These models of successful governance eluded Constantius for a long stretch of his reign. Certain historians would add that our main source for these years, Ammianus Marcellinus, delights in portraying Constantius' court as a nest of vipers and intriguants to the point of possible exaggeration.

Some details in this story may surprise readers. The engineering expertise which with even steep mountain routes were paved may startle readers, but I can assure them that within walking distance of my Jurassien home one finds a two-thousand-year-old paved Roman road two meters wide cutting straight up from the Vaudois plains to the mountain village in which I live.

In my own front yard are yew trees containing docetaxel, which in manufactured form, is used to treat breast, ovarian, and prostate cancers. Fungal from the bark of the Pacific variety of yew produces the other key anti-cancer drug, paclitaxel. Reported cases of surviving ingestion depended on the victim not chewing the deadly berries.

With *The Wolves of Ambition*, we find ourselves only twelve years short of the battle between Emperor Valens and the Tervingi Goths on the Danube and the subsequent eruptions of the Huns attacking the Goths. We are twenty-one years short of the Battle of Adrianople that left the Eastern Army with crippling losses. Some historians mark Adrianople and the Gothic Wars as the true collapse of Rome.

Yet at the close of 355, most of our characters—both fictional creations and those based on historical personages—are busy adjusting to a bookish and untested Caesar in the West. They do not fret about Goths or Huns over breakfast nor do they imagine that these 'marginal' peoples will come so close as the gates of Rome within the passage of a mere century.

Perhaps only the *Magister Agentium in Rebus* Apodemius, with his map full of pins, and flags, foresees this possibility.

Places and Glossary

aeraria—army strongboxes
acetum—disinfecting vinegar
actuarius—a fiscal official charged with the distribution of wages and provisions to the Roman military, (an imperial *actuarius* was in charge of the Emperor's baggage)
ad locutio—formal address to the troops
aerarium—pay chest
Agrippina, (Colonia Claudia Ara Agrippinensium)—Köln, Germany
ala—a cavalry wing
Argentoratum—Strasbourg, France
angon—long spear tipped with a barb favored by German warriors
Antiochia—Antioch, Turkey
aqua mulsa—mead
Augusta Raurica—the oldest Roman colony on the Rhine, now occupied by a museum near Basel, Switzerland
Augustodunum—Autun, France
auxilium palatina, auxilia palatinae—Maximianus (285-310) recruited the earliest palatine *auxilia* from tribes across the Rhine. During the 4th century, they grew to become the largest class of units, amounting to half the field army.
bald—Old Franconian for bold
ballista—a torsion-powered missile projector developed over many centuries. By the Late Roman era the largest *ballista fulminalis* could deliver darts farther than 1,100 meters, e.g. the width of the Danube River.
barritus—rhythmic Germanic war chant of intimidation
Bavacum—Bavay, Belgium
birrus—hooded cloak
Bonna—Bonn, Germany
Brigantium—Bregentz, Austria on Lake Constance
buccinator, buccinatores—player of the *buccina*, precursor to the tuba, a thin, round horn used for signaling

Cambete—near Kembs, France
calceus, calcei—high-cuffed boots originally worn by cavalry riders, later adopted by civilians
candidatus, candidati—the Late Roman emperor's bodyguard, a term first used in 350 AD
Carthago—Carthage, Tunis, Tunisia
Castra Vetera—Xanten-Birten, Germany
caldarium—hot room in baths, heated by a *hypocaust*, or underfloor heating system
cathedra—wide-seated armchair
centena—unit of one hundred men
cerevisia—beer
circitor—rank in both the cavalry and the *agentes*, referring to rider
cisium—light, two-wheeled vehicle
clibius—round shield of Late Roman period, as opposed to the earlier rectangular shield
clinicus, clinici—army medic
codex, codices—bound manuscripts
comes rerum privatarum—imperial officer responsible for the private holdings of the emperor and family.
Comum—Como, Italy
Castellum apud Confluentes—Koblenz, Germany
commendationes—letters of recommendation
comitatus—officers serving Germanic leader in consultation and exchange of loyalties
Concordia et Tribuni—two fortresses near Agentoratum (Strasbourg, Alsace)
conditum—wine flavored with flowers or spices, e.g. coriander, anis, almonds, pepper, cinnamon
Confluentes—Koblentz, Germany
(sacrum) consistorium—secret imperial council of the post-Constantine or 'Dominate' period. There is a difference of opinion as to its membership. It was composed mainly of the heads of the various departments of administration, certainly of those most intimately connected with the imperial household (*dignitates palatinae*): the Minister of Finance (*comes sacrarum largitionum*), the Minister of the Privy Purse (*comes rerum privatarum*), the Quaestor

—THE WOLVES OF AMBITION—

(*quaestor sacri palatii*) or emperor's legal adviser, and the Master of the Offices, (*magister officiorum*.) The prefect whose seat of government was at the capital (*praefectus praetorio praesens*) was probably a member, as well as the Grand Chamberlain (*praepositus sacri cubiculi*), and some officials of the grade *spectabilis*. The members of the council were called *comites consistoriani* or *consistoriani*. It was presided over by the emperor, or in his absence by the quaestor who was obliged to give his decisions in writing; proceedings were taken down by secretaries and stenographers (*notarii*).

contubernalis, contubernales—tentmate, specifically the eight men sharing an army tent.
cornicen, cornicines—army signaler on the *cornu*
Cremona—Cremona, Italy
Curia Rhaetorium—Chur, Switzerland
curiales—members of local government or gentry of a town
Cursus Publicus—Empire-wide state road network
denarius, denarii—A small silver coin issued during the Roman Empire, equal to 10 asses or 4 sesterces, which was replaced in Late Rome by a coin known to modern numismatists as the *Antoninianus*. However Late Roman common parlance continued to refer to payment in *denarii*
discens capsariorum—trainee army medical officer
dispensator—household manager or custodian
Divodurum—Metz, France
domesticus—imperial household servant
dominus—lord (*domine*, vocative tense)
dominula—miss, diminutive of *domina*
Domus Augustae—household of the Augusta, imperial consort
donativum, donativa—bonus pay
draco, dracones—a serpent/dragon shaped tube-like pennant for each cavalry cohort
ducenarius—a cavalry term the *agentes in rebus* borrowed to denote the second highest of six levels, just below *princeps*, followed by *centenarius, biarchus, eques/equites/equitor, circitor*

duplicarius—a pay grade receiving double the basic pay awarded, regardless of rank, for outstanding bravery or service
dux, duces—according to the historian of the Franks, Gregory of Tours, the Franks had *duces*, i.e. military leaders more powerful than their kings
eventiones diplomatae—licenses to use the state *Cursus Publicus*
Fanum Fortunae—Fano, Italy
emporitica—paper too rough for writing, reserved for packaging
fibula, fibulae—shoulder brooch
foederati—confederate units of barbarians subsumed into the Late Roman military
francisca—battle axe of unique shape used in Frankish warfare
fundanum—a strong, intoxicating wine
imperator—emperor
gustatio—starters
imperatrix—empress
leuds, leudes—personal retainers
laetus, laeti—a term used in the late Roman Empire to denote communities of *barbari*, "barbarians" i.e. foreigners or people from outside the Empire permitted to settle on, and granted land in, imperial territory on condition that they provide recruits for the Roman military
latifundium—an agglomeration of small estates into one large one employing many thousands of slaves
latrunculi—Roman strategy game of black and white pieces moved on a gridded board
lictors—bodyguard/escorts assigned to imperial officials
limitanei—troops assigned to border defense
Losanna—Lausanne, Switzerland
lupus—wolf
magister memoriae—master of the rolls, reporting to the *magister officiorum*
manceps—manager/landlord holding franchise for state relay station
mansio, mansiones—state-subsidized way-stations managed by a *cisiarius* under franchise, offering horses, food and accommodation for licensed travelers on the *Cursus Publicus*
manuballista—shoulder-mounted ballista

—THE WOLVES OF AMBITION—

medicus—army medical doctor
Mediolanum—Milan, Italy
mensa prima—'first table' or main course
mensa secunda—'second table' or second course
merum—undiluted wine
meta—the turning point at the far end of a chariot racecourse
milites riparienses—see *riparienses, ripenses*
Moesia Inferior—modern northern Bulgaria
Mogontiacum—Mainz, Germany
moretum—curd cheese pounded with herbs, e.g. mint, rue, coriander, fennel, lovage and mixed with vinegar, honey and garum
Mosella—the Moselle River
mutatio, mutationes—relay station on the *Cursus Publicus*
Mutina—Modena, Italy
Neapolis—Naples, Italy
Niger—very aged, dark red wine
Novaesium—Neuss, Germany
Noviomagus Nemetum—Speyer, Germany, 1st century B.C. home of the Nemeti Germani tribe
nullus—null
orbiculus, orbiculi—large embroidered rondels stitched to a tunic between waist and knees signifying rank
optio, optiones—deputies chosen by centurions, somewhat equivalent to modern lieutenants
ordo Senatorius—ruling class
palla/paenula,(ae)—long, hooded cloak that became associated with praetorians and other guards over the centuries, for woman rectangular shawl or longer cloak
pallium—woolen cloak in style worn by Greek philosophers and teachers
Parcae—the Fate
pedes—ordinary infantryman
petanus—peacetime riding helmet made of leather worn by postal riders
phalarae—decorative metals discs on a horse harness
pileus—a brimless, felt cap worn in ancient Greece and later copied by ancient Rome, associated with the manumission ritual for slaves

plumbata, plumbatae—lead-weighted darts
pocillator—servant who pours wine
Pola, Istria—Pula, Croatia
popina—inn offering food and prostitutes
posca—vinegar concentrate added to fresh water by travelers to make a refreshing drink
praefectus, praefecti—chief officer, prefect
praepositus sacri cubiculi—the most senior Lord Chamberlain of the Empire, managing the Emperor's private chambers and the rest of the staff
princeps officii—secretary general drawn from the *agentes in rebus*, serving during this era as watchdog over important civilian officers in an administrative agency, such as a praetorian or urban prefecture or proconsulate
promoti—soldiers who were given a higher rank on account of good service or favor
pocillator—the slave-child who refilled diners' wine cups, often a favorite
protectores domestici—imperial bodyguards
pugio—Roman dagger
purpureous, (πορφύρεος)—dark, reddish purple
rationibis—military secretary or accountant
regulus, reguli—royals among barbarian leaders, kinglets
Rhenus River—the Rhine, also called the Ripa
rhetor—teacher
riparienses, ripenses—riverbank border *limitanei* troops, from the Latin *ripa* for riverside
Roma—Rome, Italy
sax—single-edged knife used by migration peoples
the Septemzodium—a well-known building built by Emperor Severus at the south-eastern corner of the Palatine, named for the seven planets
schola—a government department reporting to the *magister officiorum*
scutarii—targeteers
signifier—standard bearer
solidus—4.5 gram gold coin issued by Constantine to replace the *aureus*
spatha—long sword used as Roman side-arm

—THE WOLVES OF AMBITION—

Spoletium—Spoleto, Italy
sterculus—shit
stilus, stili—pointed instrument for writing on wax tablets
stola—woman's draped overtunic
subreguli—lesser royals among the barbarians
taberna—restaurant bar, often found near bathhouse, temples, libraries, city gates and other public gathering points
taeneotic—third-grade quality of papyrus-based paper
tepidarium—warm room in the baths that radiated heat from underground flooring
tesserae—mosaic tiles or playing dice from Greek for 'four sides.'
thiufa—unit of one thousand men commanded by a *thiufadus*
thoracomacus—thickly wadded leather garment to protect chafing from armor or to protect armor from humidity.
thunguli—Frankish warriors
tiro, tirones—young soldier, beginner
Toxandria—area of upper Gaul, covering all or most of modern North Brabant, eastern Antwerp, and the north of Belgian Limburg
Traiana—(Colonia Ulpia Traiana) Xanten, Germany
triclinium—dining room
tribunus armaturarum—tribune of the heavy armed cavalry
tribunus stabili—officer in charge of stables
tribunus vacans—tribune acting as staff officer or without specific assignment
tripudium—the three-beat war dance used to the beat of the Germanic *barritus* cry in battle
trustis—Franco-Roman council
tunica—woman's undertunic
tutor legitimus—guardian of an underage child's financial interests i.e. *tutela*
veterinarius—army veterinary surgeon
vicus, vici—hamlet as opposed to *colonia, civitas*, or *municipium*
vir illustris, viri illustres—Late Roman category of distinguished officers of high rank in imperial service
wergild—Germanic compensation for loss of property, injury or death

Acknowledgements

Warmest thanks to Professor Elizabeth Minchin at the Australian National University, Canberra, Australia, who provided the essay by D.C. Nutt published in *Antichthon*.

Deepest thanks to Professor John Drinkwater at the University of Nottingham for his patient and generous response to numerous questions.

I am, however, responsible for any mistakes.

Barlow, Jonathan, 'Kinship, Identity and Fourth-Century Franks,' *Historia: Zeitschrift für Alte Geschichte*, Bd. 45, H. 2 (2nd Qtr., 1996), pp. 223-239 Franz Steiner Verlag

Barnes, Timothy David, *Ammianus Marcellinus and the Representation of Historical Reality*, Cornell University Press, Ithaca, New York

Bowerstock, G.W., *Late Antiquity: A Guide to the Postclassical World*, Harvard University Press Reference Library, Cambridge, Massachusetts, 1999

Brown, Peter, *The World of Late Antiquity*, Thames and Hudson, London, 1971

Bury, J. B., *The Cambridge Medieval History, Volume I*, M. Gwatkin, J. P. Whitney, ed. Cambridge University Press, 1936

Cameron, Averil, *The Later Roman Empire*, Fontana History of the Ancient World, Fontana Press, London, 1993

Den Boeft, J., Jan Willem Drijvers and D. Den Hengst, *Philological and Historical Commentary on Ammianus Marcellinus XXVII*, Brill Academic Publishers 2009

Drijvers, Jan Willem, David Hunt, *The Late Roman World and Its Historian*, Routledge, 2012

Drinkwater, John, 'Silvanus, Ursicinus and Ammianus, Fact or Fiction?' Studies in Carl Deroux, ed., *Studies in Latin Literature and Roman History* 7, Coll. Latomus 227 (1994) 568-76

Faas, Patrick, *Around the Roman Table*, Macmillian, London, 2003

Gibbon, Edward, *The History of the Decline and Fall of the Roman Empire*, in 12 vols, J.B. Bury, ed. with an introduction by W.E.H. Lecky, Fred de Fau and Co., New York 1906, The Online Library of Liberty

Goffar, Walter, *Barbarian Tides: The Migration Age and the Later Roman Empire*, University of Pennsylvania Press, 2006

Goldsworthy, Adrian, *How Rome Fell*, Yale University Press, London, 2009

Heather, Peter, *The Fall of the Roman Empire*, Macmillan, London, 2005

James, Edward, *The Franks*, (The Peoples of Europe Series,) Basil Blackwell, Ltd., Oxford, 1988

Jones, A. H. M. *The Later Roman Empire, 284-602, (Volume 1 and 2)* John Hopkins University Press, Baltimore, Maryland, 1986

Kelly, Gavin, *Ammianus Marcellinus, the Allusive Historian*, Cambridge University Press, Cambridge, 2011

Libanius, *Libanius' Funeral Oration upon the Emperor Julian*

MacDowell, Simon, *Germanic Warrior, AD 236-568*, illustrated by Angus McBride, Osprey Publications, Botley, Oxford, 1996

Mars, Brigitte, *The Desktop Guide to Herbal Medicine*, Basic Health Publications, Boulder, Colorado, 2009

Nutt, D. C., 'Silvanus and the Emperor Constantius II,' Antichthon, The Journal of the Australasian Society of Classical Studies, Vol 7, (1973) pgs. 80-89.

Randers-Pehrson, Justine Davis, *Barbarians and Romans*, Croom Helm, Beckenham, Kent, England, 1983

Speidel, Michael P., *Ancient Germanic Warriors: Warrior Styles from Trajan's Column to Icelandic Sagas* Routledge, 2008

Thompson, E.A. *The Historical Work of Ammianus Marcellinus*, Cambridge University Press, Cambridge, 1947

Todd, Malcolm, *Everyday Life of the Barbarians, Goths, Franks and Vandals*, G. P. Putnam's Sons, New York, 1972

Ward-Perkins, Bryan, *The Fall of Rome and the End of Civilization*, Oxford University Press, Oxford, 2005

—THE WOLVES OF AMBITION—

And thanks again to the patient contributors of Romanarmy.com, especially Associate Webmaster Jasper Oorthuys and Jenny Cline, (Founders,) and especially moderator Nathan Ross

About the Author

Q. V. Hunter's interest in Roman history began with four years of Latin study and university courses in ancient religions. A fascination with Late Antiquity deepened when Hunter moved to a two-hundred-year-old farmhouse near a former Roman colony.

Colonia Equestris Noviodunum was founded around 50 BCE as a retirement community for Julius Caesar's cavalry veterans. It was listed as the civitas Equestrium id est Noviodunus in the Notitia Galliarum, (the fourth-century directory listing all seventeen provinces of Roman Gaul.)

Noviodunum became Rome's most important colony along the Lake Leman—with a forum, baths, basilica and amphitheater. Its potable water came via an aqueduct running from present-day Divonne, France. It belonged to a network of Roman settlements radiating out from Lugdunum (Lyon, France) around the Rhône Valley. Caesar established these settlements to supervise the defeated Celtic Helvetii who were shifted there against their will after the Battle of Bibracte in 58 BC.

As a result of Alemannic invasions in 259-260 AD, much of Roman Noviodunum was razed but it flourishes again today as the Swiss town of Nyon.

Hunter is married to a self-proclaimed 'Ur-Swiss,' a descendant of Alemanni who settled farther north of Nyon in the Alpine lake region that gave birth to the three founding cantons of the Confederation Helvetica, i.e. Switzerland, in the thirteenth century.

They have three adult children who managed to study Latin and Greek in *gymnasium* before the Lausanne education administrators cut back Classics studies throughout the public school system in the Canton of Vaud.

Printed in Poland
by Amazon Fulfillment
Poland Sp. z o.o., Wrocław